Also by R. Cameron Cooke

<u>Sword of the Legion Series</u>
ROME: FURY OF THE LEGION (Gaul, 57 B.C.)
ROME: DEFIANCE OF THE LEGION (Gaul, 54 B.C.)
ROME: TEMPEST OF THE LEGION (Adriatic Sea, 49 B.C.)
ROME: SWORD OF THE LEGION (Egypt, 48 B.C.)

<u>WWII Submarine Novels</u>
PRIDE RUNS DEEP
SINK THE SHIGURE
WOLFPACK 351
DIVE BENEATH THE SUN

<u>Westerns</u>
TRAIL OF THE GUNMAN
SHOWDOWN AT APACHE BUTTE

<u>Other Titles</u>
RISE TO VICTORY
THE CONSTANTINE COVENANT

ROME
HONOR OF THE LEGION

This is a work of fiction. The names, characters, places, and incidents are either products of the author's imagination or are used fictitiously. Any resemblance to persons, living or dead, events, or locations is entirely coincidental.

Copyright © 2021 by R. Cameron Cooke

ISBN- 9798495407756

ROME

HONOR OF THE LEGION

By

R. Cameron Cooke

"We aim at heaven itself in our folly; neither do we suffer, by our wickedness, Jupiter to lay aside his revengeful thunderbolts."

- Horace

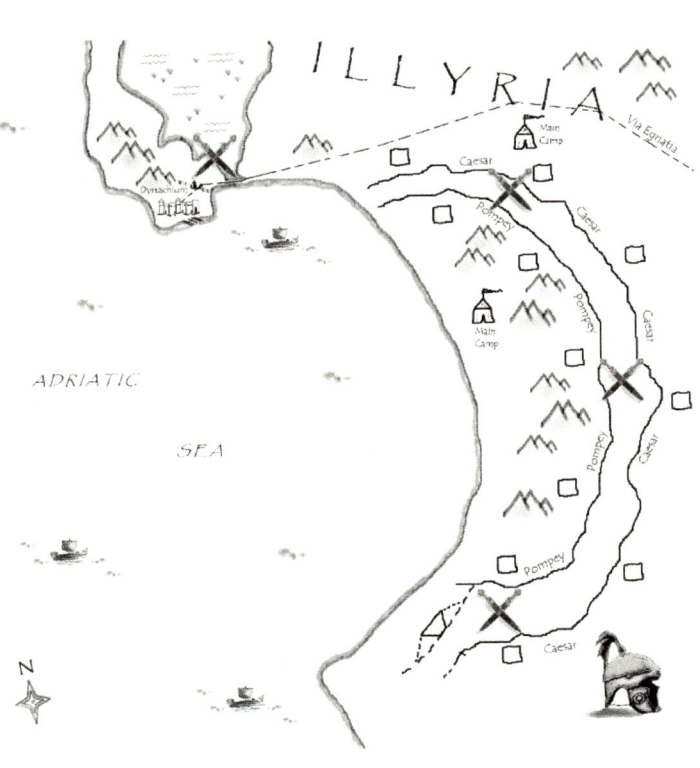

I

The trumpets of war sounded between the opposing lines.

Several hundred soldiers poured over the crests of the hills and charged the works, their faces grim beneath bronze helmets. They knew they were charging to their deaths. Yet still they came, with an ear-splitting war cry to shore up their courage.

A crescendo of loud thumps filled the air as engines recoiled down the line. Straining springs released iron-tipped bolts the length of a man's arm into the oncoming ranks, transfixing two or three men at a time. Giant stones coated in flaming pitch were added to this barrage. They fell from the sky like meteors to bound amid the charging horde, pulverizing entire files and leaving great swaths of crimson earth and burning corpses behind them.

But the attack did not waver. Taking up their blood-spattered standards, the advancing soldiers closed ranks and came on with a renewed fervor. They broke into a sprint a hundred paces from the works, as if salvation lay on the other side of the ditch and embankment beyond it.

It did not.

The rushing troops had not yet reached the ditch when they were met by a thousand javelins taking to the sky. Shields rose across the attacking ranks like the rippling scales of a serpent to meet the deadly storm. A sound like thunder clapped across the field as falling iron met wood. Most of the six-foot-long missiles were blocked, but some found the narrow gaps in the canopy and lanced through exposed thighs, calves, and booted feet beneath. Some impacted the shields with enough force to punch through the layered wood and pierce the arm behind it.

The attackers cast away the shields encumbered by the lodged projectiles and prepared their own javelins, identical to those they had absorbed. The next instant, five hundred arms whipped along the packed ranks sending an equally ominous storm of iron and ash at the defenders. The missiles were still in the air when the attackers drew swords and surged forward again, leaping into the muddy ditch without hesitation.

The defenders met them at the top of the embankment, a wall of shields and swords rising down the line. The opposing ranks pressed together, a winding river of thrusting gladii and jabbing pila.

It was difficult to tell one side from the other. Both sides wielded similar weapons and armor. They spoke the same language, celebrated the same festivals, prayed to the same gods, and bore allegiance to the same great city across the sea. But, today, they slaughtered one another like mortal enemies of old.

It was legion against legion. Roman against Roman. *Pompey against Caesar.*

The attackers fought valiantly. They executed their battle

with spirit and vigor. Still, all their efforts were not enough to dislodge the stalwart defenders who stood shoulder-to-shoulder, an unbreakable barrier of veterans. The defenders were steadfast and brave, the cowards having been weeded out long ago.

As the battle wore on, gaps appeared in the attackers' ranks, which were quickly exploited by the skilled defenders. Officers were singled out, surrounded, and slain, leaving the rest leaderless and confused. A stream of blood formed along the bottom of the trench, a confluence of countless tributaries oozing from the dead. The attackers began to withdraw, first in fragmentary bands, then in droves. The defeated fled across the smoky field of broken shields and corpses, some staggering, some crawling, many clutching horrible wounds. They retreated all the way back to their own lines as the victorious defenders stood atop their works, waving swords and spewing insults after them.

The defenders pilfered the dead and wounded left behind. The walking wounded were taken prisoner. The rest were put to the sword.

*****

In the ditch before the works, a tall centurion stood amongst the mangled corpses. The battle had been won decidedly, but he exhibited no elation. He had the indifference of a soldier doing soldiers' work, immune to the wailing of the wounded, and unmoved by the suffering all around him.

He was a centurion of the Tenth Legion, a veteran killer for Rome, and well accustomed to the horrors of a battlefield.

"Was it a battle they were turned out for today or a

triumph?" a nearby soldier said as he used the ornate breastplate worn by one of the corpses to scrape the mud off his hobnailed boots. "Was this one a bloody general?"

The dead man had not been a general, not even an officer. He had been just a soldier, a simple legionary, and not for very long, judging by his callous-free hands and smooth feet. The lad had hardly been old enough to shave. He was yet another of the newly recruited, newly trained youths filling Pompey's ranks. The decorative armor was too expensive for most common soldiers. It would have been more appropriate on a tribune or a legate.

"It was not for a triumph, Betto," the centurion answered succinctly.

"What's this, then?" the legionary Betto wiped away some mud on the front of the cuirass to reveal a bronze depiction of a she-wolf being suckled by two infants. "What kind of perverted rogue puts babies sucking the teats of a wolf on his armor?"

"It's Romulus and Remus, you idiot," another soldier said.

Betto shrugged perplexedly. "Any bastard who wears that on his armor deserves what he gets, if you ask me."

Several of the nearby soldiers laughed.

The centurion gave a gentle smile. They had marched thousands of miles together across many lands, fighting countless enemies of Rome. Still, only a handful had ever seen the famous city. Few were well-versed in Roman folklore. Even fewer knew the Tiber from the Nile.

The centurion gazed down at the dead boy wearing the breastplate. Ironically, that lad probably could have recited the early history of Rome by heart. Clearly, he had belonged to a landed Latin family. Likely, the armor was a cherished heirloom worn by his ancestors. Now, it would be hacked from his shoulders and sold to some Greek bronzesmith for the foundry.

"Well, I'll be Remulus and Romus!" Betto exclaimed. "Look here!" He tilted up the head of an enemy corpse, holding it by the hair.

"It's Romulus and Remus, you idiot!"

"No, it ain't. This here's Cantus. He's in the Third Cohort. Or, he used to be before he deserted. Now he's dead."

"A lot of these bastards used to be ours," said another, then glanced up at the centurion. "How about that? Old Pompey sent our own against us. He's a clever one, the old cheese stuffer. What do you think of that, *Vitus?...Vitus?*"

But the centurion did not respond. His face was suddenly grim as he knelt beside the corpse of a dead enemy officer and turned over the helmet to examine the face. Not finding what he was looking for, he moved on to the next officer, and the next.

"What are you doing, *Vitus?*" Betto called. But he, too, was ignored.

"Juno's tits, Sextus!" sighed a soldier wearing the wolf's head adornment of a *signifer*. "Can't you see the centurion's busy? Get back to work, you bootlicker, before he does us all a favor and has you flogged!"

If the centurion heard the interchange, he gave no indication of it. Without a word, he began walking along the line, seeking out the dead enemy officers in the ditch, upon the works, upon the embankment, turning over and scanning every placid, contorted, and mangled face. But, clearly, he did not find whom he sought.

The centurion's searching was cut short by the whinny of horses behind him and a cheerful voice almost mocking in nature.

"Still alive, Domitius? *Minerva* be praised!"

Lucius Domitius, fifth centurion of the Eighth Cohort,

Tenth Legion, closed his eyes and cursed inwardly. He immediately recognized that voice, and it grated on him like a dried-up, flaky *tersorium* after three days in the sun. When Lucius turned around and opened his eyes, he saw precisely what he had expected to see, a general officer in his mid-thirties beaming down at him from astride a tall horse. The general wore a fine black cuirass with black greaves and a black-plumed helmet to match. All were of the highest quality, but, at this moment, they were considerably spattered with mud and dried blood. Flanking the general were several mounted attendants similarly outfitted. They cast curious glances at Lucius as if wondering what possible interest their commander could have in this low-ranking centurion.

But Lucius knew. *Saturn's balls*, how he knew!

Lucius crossed his chest with one arm in a salute, as was expected of him, but that was the total limit of the reverence he exhibited. Clearly perceiving this, the general seemed amused.

"Oh, Lucius," the general chuckled. "Trust you to be so gloomy after such a victory."

"Your pardon, sir. I'm always thus after any of my lads have fallen." Lucius said it without a trace of apology in his voice. He let out a sigh and looked up to meet the general's gaze. "Still, I suppose there are those who think it a trivial thing to send men to their deaths."

The statement bordered on insolent, its tone bold and accusatory in nature. One of the attending tribunes instantly nudged his horse forward to reprimand the brazen centurion. A raised hand from the general stopped him. Lucius had not flinched or backed away in the slightest. He regarded the retreating tribune with an indifferent smirk before turning his attention back to the general.

General Marcus Antonius, Rome's Master of Horse and

Caesar's right hand, appeared not at all surprised by Lucius's surly manner, nor did the smile on his face shrink. And why should he feel threatened by the impertinence of a lowly fourth-rank centurion? Once a tribune of the plebs, Antony was now one of the most senior officers in the army and perhaps Caesar's closest confidante. Among Caesar's legions, Antony's authority knew no bounds.

Still, there were few men under the smoke-streaked sky whom Lucius trusted less or despised more.

The feeling was decidedly mutual. Antony hated Lucius every bit as much as Lucius hated him. However, no one would have surmised it from the wide smile the bastard now brandished, scrunched by the constricting cheek pieces of his plumed helmet. The facade was, of course, for the benefit of the legionaries who were gathering around to get a closer look at the flamboyant general. Antony was a celebrity in their eyes and one whom they regarded as a true soldier's general.

With an amused glance, Antony turned away from Lucius to address the men. Soon the general was surrounded by dozens of filthy legionaries clamoring for a mere touch of his hand, his booted feet, his horse's hide. He greeted them warmly, imparted a string of lewd jokes, endeared himself to them as skillfully as a master musician plucking a lyre.

Antony was good at that, Lucius admitted as he watched the pathetic spectacle with arms crossed. As bereft as Antony was of scruples and personal honor, the bastard knew how to inspire men. And he was not a coward. He may have been a lying, scheming, murderous mule's arse, but he was not a coward. Antony's lofty rank would have certainly exempted him from the hazards of the front line. Yet, he was often found where the fighting was thickest.

And he was a capable general, too. This morning, the

bold enemy sortie might have punched through Caesar's thin lines had it not been for Antony's quick thinking. With Caesar several miles away at the northern end of the lines, the Master of Horse had taken the initiative, pulling several cohorts from other places in the line to bolster the defenses here. The additional spears had made the difference.

At one point in the skirmish, Lucius had witnessed Antony hack and slash his way over the works to save an ordinary legionary about to be skewered on the pike of a Macedonian mercenary. And that was why the soldiers adored him. He was a rip-roaring, hard-fighting, hard-drinking, hard-bedding general who was not afraid to stand in the battle line beside them. That was why they were cheering him now.

Lucius gritted his teeth. For he knew there was another, much more sinister, side to Antony.

The crowd of jostling helmets and outstretched arms swarmed the mounted general, much to the visible anxiety of his adjutants. But Antony seemed thrilled by all of it. He drew his blood-stained sword, raised it high over his head, and waited for the soldiers to fall silent.

"Hail Mars, who gave us the victory!" he cried.

"Hail Mars!" came the boisterous reply from the smiling legionaries as they raised their own weapons.

"Hail Caesar!"

"Hail Caesar!" the troops repeated.

"And hail the Tenth!"

"Hail the Tenth!"

The men broke out in cheers, and the uproar commenced again. Grinning and waving, Antony gradually filed his horse through the adoring throng. His attendants brusquely took up positions around him to keep the crowd back as he headed for the next unit down the line.

Antony cast a parting glance over his shoulder at Lucius,

and, in that brief meeting of their eyes, Lucius knew the animosity was still there. And he knew, despite what Antony had said to him, that the general would have much preferred to have found him among the dead.

The insidious bastard, Lucius thought.

After the general and his entourage had moved along, the soldiers settled down. They returned to their work, still wearing smiles. The buffeting breeze carried on it a great commotion of clashing steel, the distant din of combat far to the southwest, perhaps several miles down the line. Whatever fighting raged there was hidden from view by a string of coastal hills. But, here, the battle was over. Now the men of the Tenth Legion set about stacking corpses, shoring up defenses, and repairing shields in the event the enemy had something else in store for them this day.

"Centurion Domitius!" A helmetless, thinly bearded young man in leather armor weaved his way through the toiling soldiers. He was not a legionary, probably an officer's servant. Picking out Lucius's distinctive cross-plumed helmet, the young man approached and saluted.

"Centurion Domitius?" he said.

"Speak, boy! I've not got all day."

The lad shrank at his scowl. The episode with Antony had left Lucius in an ill mood.

"Forgive the disturbance, Centurion," the lad replied in heavily accented Latin. His tone was respectful and polite. Undoubtedly, he had been with the legions long enough to know not to cross ways with an angry centurion. "I am Torbruc, slave to Centurion Sextus Regimus, *primus pilum* of the Second Cohort, Seventh Legion."

"I know who Regimus is! What does he want? If he's looking for bolts or bandages, he can't have them. Our stores are damned near expended."

"My master does not require any of that, sir."

"What then?"

"He bids you come to him, sir." Torbruc paused and pointed down the line to the works occupied by the Seventh Legion, several hundred yards away. "He is over there. He asks that you not tarry, sir."

"What does he want?"

The slave averted his eyes. "I am not at liberty to say, sir. He simply asks that you come quickly."

Lucius raised an eyebrow. With no amplifying information, he had half a mind to ignore the request. He was too busy to go off answering some vague summons from a centurion in another legion. The enemy might try another attack any moment, and his men had not yet recovered from the last one. He had but three score men under arms now, most of them on the verge of starvation.

Still, there was something in this messenger's tight-lipped manner that told Lucius there was a personal element to this request. He sensed Centurion Regimus of the Seventh Legion wished to see him for something other than official business, and that time was of the essence.

Lucius's curiosity was sufficiently piqued. Perhaps he needed a brief diversion, a few moments away. It would give him the chance to contemplate just how he would defend against the next attack with barely half a century to cover his section of the line.

"Tell your master I'll be along directly."

*****

The brunt of the enemy attack had been against the narrow gap between the legions, where the Tenth's left met the Seventh's right. No doubt the enemy had hoped to cause confusion at this critical seam in the line. And now, Lucius crossed that hard-fought ground, a field of death, where slaves stacked corpses and carted them away to the inky funeral pyres.

The dead seemed to stare up at him as he stepped over one corpse after another. Many faces were frozen in that final moment of horror when the blades had ripped out their insides, hewn their necks to the spine, run them clean through, castrated them. There were few good ways to die in a battle.

Most of them were mere boys – eager lads enticed to follow the legendary Pompey the Great and the exiled senators he served, collectively known as the *Optimates*.

Lucius scoffed. *Their fathers should have taught them better.*

The *Optimates* stood against Gaius Julius Caesar, the dubiously-elected consul of Rome, whom they considered a war criminal and self-appointed dictator. The *Optimates* claimed to stand for the old Republic, Rome's traditional laws and values, but Lucius scoffed at such notions. They were no different than Caesar. They were influential men desperately clinging to the power they still held. They talked cleverly, claimed to stand for lofty ideals, made empty promises to keep their legions loyal. But, in the end, they all wanted the same thing – absolute control of the empire and her riches.

The *Optimates* had put their trust in their great commander Pompey to destroy Caesar's army, hoping he might succeed where a dozen other generals, both barbarians and Romans, had failed. If the siege continued going the way it was, Pompey might very well deliver that result.

Still, Caesar had an uncanny knack for pulling victory from defeat. How true that had proven in just the past year. His string of victories in Italy and Spain had been nothing short of extraordinary. In a few short months, he had wrested the entire western half of the empire from the

Optimates' control. And now, Caesar had embarked on yet another offensive, in enemy-held Greece, where he was outnumbered and cut off from Italy. The move had seemed reckless and rife with hubris, if not completely insane. Still, if he managed a victory here – if he managed to defeat Pompey and the largest *Optimates* army ever assembled – the empire would be his.

Many already believed Caesar to be a deity. How many more would subscribe to that belief if he pulled this off?

But Lucius knew better.

Having marched under Caesar for ten years, since the first campaigns in Gaul, Lucius knew well of the great man's many flaws. He had witnessed many blunders and failures that were somehow never included in the official reports read out in forums across the empire.

Caesar was not invincible – far from it. There were times when he was downright fragile and vulnerable. On two occasions during the bloody campaigns in Gaul, Lucius had witnessed Caesar abruptly fall to the ground for no apparent reason. Both times, the so-called deity had been rendered immobile and unresponsive.

Caesar was indeed bold, but, like Alexander, he was just a man, endowed with an incredible run of good fortune. In the end, things always seemed to work out in his favor. He was lucky. And, perhaps, that was the most significant trait a general could possess.

Would that Lucius's own fortune had been as favorable. In his twenty-eight years, he had seen riches and poverty, feast and famine, victory and tragedy, love and loss. As a soldier, he had marched thousands of miles and fought countless battles. He had risen through the lower ranks, albeit reluctantly. He had made comrades and allies.

And he had made enemies – like Antony.

Now, Lucius approached the lines of the Seventh with a

measure of caution. Receiving a summons from a *primus pilum* in another legion was somewhat out of the ordinary. It had been years since Lucius had marched with the Seventh. He knew of the *primus pilum* Regimus but could not recall ever having any personal dealings with him. In those days, Lucius had been a common soldier and Regimus a low-ranking centurion. Their paths had seldom crossed.

Why should Regimus wish to see him now?

The soldiers of the Seventh eyed Lucius with only mild curiosity as they worked to repair the defenses. There were bodies everywhere, piled deep, mangled, with one hardly discernible from the other. Clearly, the Seventh had borne the brunt of the enemy attack. Like the Tenth, the Seventh was a Spanish legion, considered somewhat superior to the others. Like his own men, they were nearly all veterans, the wheat having been separated from the chaff long ago. They had performed well today. Still, Lucius wondered how they would stand up to Pompey's troops in a pitched battle, when they did not have a line of defensive works to aid them. He wondered the same thing about his own men.

In Gaul, the enemy had come from multiple tribes and cultures. They had fought in a variety of ways, but all had been distinctly barbarian. Now, the enemy was Roman. Now, they faced legions drawn from the four corners of the empire. The enemy wore the same armor and marched beneath similar standards. They were trained and disciplined, just like the men under Caesar. Some had, at one time, even marched under Caesar. And they were led by a legendary general whose past achievements made Caesar's look like those of a stable boy.

Soldiers in both armies idolized the great Pompey, whose victories across the world had won him an astounding three triumphs. The fact that the most recent of these had occurred when most of them were mere boys did little to diminish his *auctoritas* in their eyes. If anything, it heightened Pompey's legendary status to a cultish level, as evidenced by the enemy bodies littering the field. So many of these young men had charged into certain death with vigor, all for their general.

Lucius had never laid eyes on Pompey, but he had concluded the enemy commander had to be much like Caesar. He had to be gifted with the same innate ability to draw the best and worst from men, to convince them they could win, no matter how dire the circumstances.

Lucius's path skirted a long line of tarpaulin hurdles. The giant, mobile barriers were used to shield those digging in the trenches from enemy missiles. They now bristled with javelins thrown in the last attack. A cluster of soldiers leaned against one hurdle, eyeing Lucius with casual curiosity as he approached. The soldiers were filthy, their mail armor and tunics gray with mud. Several wore bandages stained with fresh blood.

Just then, Lucius noticed one particularly grimy soldier staring back at him with defiant eyes. A long staff bearing a faded banner rested upon the his mailed shoulder. The soldier was a *signifer*, one of those honored few who bore the standards into battle.

As Lucius passed by, the legionary suddenly snapped to attention, extending the standard as if on parade.

"Good morning, centurion, *sir!*" the soldier belted out in a formal tone. When Lucius kept walking, too preoccupied with his own thoughts to bother with the overly dramatic salute, the man added, "What's the matter, Centurion Domitius? Did those arse lickers in the Tenth not slay enough that you've come to loot those slain by the Seventh?"

The remark was deliberately insolent, and it made Lucius

seethe with anger. He was in no mood for such provocations, good-natured or not. Whirling around, he was a heartbeat away from knocking the upstart legionary into the muck when a smile formed on that mud-spattered face. The smile was both mischievous and familiar – and it instantly melted away Lucius's rage.

"There would be little spoil to gain here," Lucius replied spiritedly. "I've been told Pompey sent his invalids against this part of the line."

The legionary burst out in a fit of laughter, then both men clasped muscled arms and embraced. Lucius knew this soldier well. He knew him from his days in the Seventh, when they were both simple legionaries. They had stood side-by-side through many campaigns, many battles.

"Jovinus!" Lucius said warmly. "The fates have brought us together again, comrade."

"It has been a long time, Lucius. I heard you were with the Tenth. I figured I'd run into you sooner or later. Still wearing the cross-plume, I see."

Lucius grinned. "It hangs over me like a Caunean fig. And what's this?" He pointed at the standard in Jovinus's hands. "No longer a centurion?"

Jovinus shook his head. "I was demoted last spring. You know I can't stay out of trouble, Lucius. Between you and me, I was glad to give up that burden." His smile then lost some of its enthusiasm as he gazed at the field of dead. "But I expect I'll be wearing the plume again before the day is out."

Lucius nodded grimly. "There is much I would like to tell you, comrade, but I have come for another purpose. I've been summoned by Regimus."

"I know." Jovinus pointed to a gathering of men some hundred paces away. "He's over there, seeing to the prisoners."

Amongst the gathering, Lucius perceived several dozen men standing in a single-file line with their hands bound. They were under guard and had been stripped of arms and armor. Nervously, they eyed the snarling, grim-faced men surrounding them, and it was not difficult to discern why. A dozen legionaries of the Seventh stood upon a slight rise holding dripping gladii. A pile of corpses and severed heads lay at the base of the slope before them. As Lucius watched, another batch of terrified prisoners was pulled from the line and forced to their knees. Some pleaded for mercy, others prayed to their gods, while a very few met their fates with silence and dignity. In a flash, the crimson gladii came down once again. The screams were silenced, and a new avalanche of severed heads rolled down the slope to join the others.

Jovinus sighed. "It's no way to deal with fighting men, if you ask me."

"Men?" Lucius replied. "Those are boys in soldier's armor."

"Still, they fought with courage today." Jovinus glanced around, then lowered his voice. "I heard General Antony gave the order."

"What order?"

"To kill the prisoners."

"I heard Caesar himself directed that all prisoners were to be spared."

"You're right, Lucius. Those were Caesar's orders. But Antony has other ideas, especially since old Pompey had our lads strung up and butchered between the lines yesterday. Antony intends to exact death for death. Can't say that I blame him." Jovinus grinned. "But I'd love to see his face when Caesar finds out. I'd give a month's pay to see Antony squirm his way out of that one."

"I wager he'll have no trouble," Lucius said.

"Aye. Caesar loves him like his left *testis*, that's for sure." Jovinus paused to glance over his shoulder. "But between you and me, Lucius, Antony makes me uneasy. I suspect he'd just as soon send the whole army to its death if he thought it would raise him another rung on the ladder."

For a moment, Lucius thought of telling his old comrade just how well-founded those suspicions were. He thought of telling Jovinus all he knew about Antony's sinister dealings, about how the Master of Horse was a lying, traitorous, underhanded bastard. But he refrained. Jovinus was a simple soldier, with simple problems. Why should he be drawn into Lucius's own tangled web?

At that moment, another group of prisoners caught Lucius's eye, a score of men placed apart from the rest. These were a pathetic-looking lot, filthy, their clothing in tatters, their faces marred by mud. They were in various states of health, and a myriad of ages and races, a crude representation of the conquered peoples of the empire.

"Who are they?" Lucius asked.

"Slaves, servants," Jovinus answered. "Antony's ordered them spared. A slave can dig trenches for one army as well as another, I suppose."

There was another chorus of shrieks as the next group of prisoners was beheaded.

"A pathetic end for a soldier," Jovinus repeated.

"Errant youths," Lucius replied coldly.

"At least one ain't."

Lucius looked at him quizzically.

"There's at least one veteran in that lot," Jovinus continued. "A centurion that gave us more trouble than Diana's clenched thighs. Cut down damned near twenty of our lads before we finally brought him to bay. A real Hercules, that one. Reminds me of you, Lucius."

"Known to us?"

Jovinus shrugged. "Not to me. But perhaps you know him."

"Why me?"

"Because he knows you, Lucius. He's been calling for you, more like wailing, for the better part of an hour. He demands to see Centurion Lucius Domitius of the Tenth Legion. Several of my comrades have volunteered to put a sword through the bastard's gullet to shut him up, but Regimus won't have it. Not sure why. Maybe it's courtesy to a fellow centurion. In any event, Regimus summoned you here to oblige the bastard – and here you are." Jovinus paused upon seeing Lucius's face turn grave. "Whatever is the matter, Lucius? Do you know this man?"

Lucius did not answer but simply stared hollowly at the line of prisoners. "Wounded, you say?"

Jovinus nodded. "Severely. He'll likely not live to face his turn under the executioner's blade. Who is he, Lucius?"

Lucius did not hear him. Like a man pulled by an unseen force, he marched on, fixated on the field of execution, leaving the baffled Jovinus behind him.

*****

Another set of freshly severed heads rolled into the ditch as Lucius approached Centurion Sextus Regimus. The *primus pilum* of the Second Cohort, Seventh Legion lounged against the glacis, casually watching the spectacle as he picked from a small loaf of doughy bread that had likely been lifted from one of the enemy corpses. Even amid this field of gore, fresh bread was too irresistible to pass up.

Regimus's plumed helmet sat on the barricade beside him. His lined face and close-cropped gray head were streaked with the familiar red marks left by the constricting helmet and cheekpieces. Upon noticing Lucius, the older centurion assumed a distasteful countenance.

"It's about bloody time!" Regimus spat. "I've more to bother with today than waiting for you, Centurion Domitius. I've got wounded to attend to, soldiers scattered all over this field looking for their units, barricades that need mending." Regimus sighed with annoyance. "And now, thanks to you, I've got a wailing prisoner making demands."

Lucius said nothing. He retained an indifferent expression, deciding not to remind Regimus that it was well within the prerogative of a *primus pilum* to refuse such demands. There was no telling why Regimus had honored the prisoner's wishes. Many soldiers had acquaintances, even kin, on the other side. Perhaps, for some unknown reason, the Regimus felt obligated to this prisoner.

"The bastard's over there," Regimus jerked his thumb toward a mule carcass several paces away, where a soldier reclined against the beast's hide with legs outstretched. The soldier did not move, save for the deep heaves of his massive chest as he struggled for each wheezing breath. He was guarded by three legionaries who nervously held javelins at the ready as if they expected the prostrate man to lunge for them at any moment. "I know not what business he has with you, Domitius, but be swift." Regimus's countenance then changed ever so subtly. When he spoke again, there was the slightest tinge of sorrow in his voice. "He has an appointment with the headsmen."

Lucius nodded. Undoubtedly, Regimus *had* known this prisoner in days past, and this momentary stay of execution had been granted as a personal favor.

As Lucius approached the prisoner, he saw more clearly the extent of his wounds. His mail had been punctured in several places. Blood trickled through the iron links to be instantly absorbed by the cloak beneath him. His head was bare, and his plumed helmet was nowhere to be seen. It seemed he was unaware of Lucius's presence until Lucius was directly beside, looking down at him. Then, there was instant recognition and relief in the prisoner's eyes. For the briefest moment, the pain of his wounds left his face, and he gazed up at Lucius as one might regard a brother. He attempted to raise his head but then abandoned the effort, clearly sapped of all strength.

"Why that face, Lucius?" he grunted weakly. "Did you not expect to see me again?"

Lucius regarded him with reproachful eyes but remained silent.

"Say something, damn you!" the prisoner snapped, a flow of bloody spittle spilling from his lips. "You owe me that at least."

"And much more," Lucius replied grimly. "Though I had hoped to send you to Pluto's Realm myself. Had you met me in battle this day, your death would have been swift."

An odd smile crossed the prisoner's face. "Always the gamester, eh, Lucius? Well, I am through competing with you, my friend. I am through with this world. I gladly leave it. I have but one oath yet to fulfill – one oath before I go to my death happily."

"The oath of a traitor?"

The prisoner struggled to smile. "You despise me, Lucius, I know, the decisions I've made, the pact I broke. But mark me, comrade, you shall be in my debt before the executioner extinguishes my dwindling light. You shall…You shall…" A fit of coughing suddenly consumed him, and it was some time before he could focus his eyes on Lucius again. When he did, Lucius's curious expression seemed to amuse him. The prisoner chuckled painfully between labored breaths, stirring a surge of anger within

Lucius.

"The battle still rages," Lucius returned coldly. "There is yet work to be done. More Pompeiian dogs to slay."

Lucius turned to march away, but a blood-streaked hand feebly reached out to stop him.

"Allow an old comrade one turn of the glass," the prisoner cried desperately. "Please, Lucius. I beseech you. Listen to what I have to say."

"And why should I wish to hear the dying utterances of a traitorous dog?"

The prisoner smiled weakly. "Because I have something to give you."

"What could you possibly —"

"Because I have something to tell you," the prisoner interrupted weakly. His eyes rolled back in his head as if he was struggling to remain conscious. "Because I have something to ask of you."

Lucius thought of leaving, turning his back on this despicable fool and returning to the critical duties he was neglecting. But something niggled at the back of his mind, something that would not let him simply march away. Was it sympathy?

Or was it guilt?

Lucius shot a forceful glance at the guards. "I will have a moment alone with the prisoner!"

Reluctantly, the guards slinked away, if not cowed by Lucius's rank, then by his large proportions. They glanced at his sheathed gladius, apparently amazed that he did not draw it as a precaution. Even now, they feared the wounded prisoner.

Lucius knelt and removed his helmet.

"Tell me now!" he demanded impatiently, staring into the delirious man's jittery eyes. "Do you hear? You *will* tell me now!"

But the prisoner seemed only half there. He slid in and out of consciousness, mumbling the same words over and over.

"*...something to give you, something to tell, something to ask...something to give, something to tell, something to ask...*"

II

Five days earlier...

Caesar's camp near Dyrrachium

"...but the works should extend farther to the south, Mamurra. Do you see, here? They must run past these low hills and on to the sea." Gaius Julius Caesar, Consul of Rome, placed a finger on the papyrus map laid out on the table in the spacious pavilion. Beside him, Mamurra, the master of engineers, struggled to see precisely where the consul was pointing amid the shadows cast by the dim lamplight.

"Forgive me, Caesar," Mamurra said, after making a hurried notation on a wax tablet, then used the stylus to point at the map. "But if your intent is to deny Pompey the grazing fields to the south, he does not need them. His works to the north already encompass a sizable grassland."

Caesar waved a hand dismissively. "I don't want to hear

about the works to the north," Caesar said bitterly. "Your men worked too slowly there."

"Slowly?" Mamurra said surprisedly.

"Yes. It's quite embarrassing, actually. Pompey's green troops out-trenching your veterans. You'd think your men had not spent the last ten years building Juno knows how many miles of works in Gaul."

Mamurra bit his lip and did his best to ignore the insult. Caesar often chose to refer to them as "*your* men" when the outcome was not to his liking.

"The besieged always have less to dig than the besiegers, my lord. It is simple geometry. We must construct two miles of works to every one of theirs. Not to mention, they have –"

"Oh, never mind the north, Mamurra," Caesar said dismissively, clearly wearied by the explanation. "Pompey's hemmed in there sufficiently. We must now turn our attention to the south."

"I would not call a sixteen-mile line manned by seven understrength legions *sufficient*, my lord," the engineer replied, still bridling at the earlier remark. "We're spread thin – too thin. We have a mere 26,000 if we count our convalescents and a few camp dogs. Pompey has nearly twice that number. If he gets reinforced by the sea, he can choose when and where to force a breakout. Worse still, should a relief force come overland from the east, we'll find ourselves caught between two armies with our own strung out along this line. I'm not sure who's under siege, my lord – us or them."

Caesar laughed. "I assure you, *they* are, Mamurra. Didn't the Gauls try the same thing at Alesia? And look where that got them."

"Vercingetorix did not have an ocean to his back, feeding him an endless supply of provisions. Pompey's ships keep him plentifully supplied while we live on *chara* and try to scrape nourishment from a barren land."

Caesar sighed heavily. "How many times have I told you, Mamurra? It is not food that shall decide this battle, but water. If your men have done their jobs properly and have diverted the streams away from the enemy camp, as I have commanded, then this will all be over very soon."

"Of course, the streams have been diverted, my lord. But must we not assume Pompey's galleys are supplying him with water, as well?"

Caesar made no reply. His mind seemed to have moved on to something else, leaving Mamurra to ponder the situation alone.

Did Caesar not grasp how precarious the situation was? Was it not plain enough for the blind to see?

Like pieces on a *latrunculi* board, Pompey and Caesar had spent the winter months maneuvering their great armies across the rocky hills of Epirus and Illyricum. They had continually marched and countermarched, each attempting to lure his opponent into a disadvantageous position and the decisive battle that must inevitably come. But nothing beyond an occasional skirmish had resulted. The great match of all matches had not happened.

More than a year ago, when Caesar crossed the Rubicon in defiance of the Senate, Pompey and the *Optimates* had chosen not to contest Italy. Instead, they had abandoned it, scattering to the far corners of the empire to secure its vital resources and seal off the sea lanes sustaining the homeland. At the same time, Pompey had started training their army, bringing it up to full-strength for an eventual return to Rome.

Prudence would have suggested the outnumbered Caesar fortify Italy against his enemies. But the cunning consul had never been known for prudence. Remarkably, he had gone on the offensive, first defeating the *Optimates* forces in Spain, then redeploying his entire army to Greece to face Pompey.

Aside from the brief blunder of allowing Caesar's army to cross the Adriatic, Pompey's navy was powerful and in firm control of the seas. Pompey had decided to take full benefit of that advantage by keeping his army near the coast, denying Caesar any chance of an escape back across the sea. At the same time, Pompey's cavalry had ranged far inland, slaying livestock and burning farms before Caesar's foraging parties could reach them. For weeks, Caesar's army had seemed doomed to march across the countryside until disease and desertion dwindled it away to nothing.

Then, quite suddenly, Pompey's strategy had changed. The *Optimates* general had gone on the defensive. He had marched his army to the seaport town of Dyrrachium, where there was a vast anchorage that would keep him well supplied from the sea. After fortifying the town with a strong garrison, he had moved the bulk of his 48,000-man army, along with thousands of mounts and pack animals, four miles down the coast. There, he had thrown up earthworks along a range of hills, crowning the heights with a semi-circular line of trenches and redoubts, with the northern end anchored on the sea. The southern end of the line was not yet finished, but it stretched closer to the shore with each passing day. When completed, the entire defensive line would measure some fourteen miles. It would enclose an area large enough to encamp nine full-strength legions with all their auxiliaries and *impedimenta*.

With the line nearing completion, and secure in the knowledge that he held both the high ground and the seaport, Pompey had stayed put. For four weeks, he had not moved, daring Caesar to attack – for it was Caesar who must have a decisive battle now, not Pompey. Pompey could wait as long as he liked. Caesar, on the other hand, had no choice but to attack.

But Caesar, unpredictable as always, had not attacked. Instead, he had done the unthinkable. With an army decidedly inferior in numbers, supplies, and morale, he ordered a contravallation line dug directly opposite Pompey's line. Brazenly, Caesar had decided to lay siege to the larger army, confident he could force Pompey into battle or surrender. This confidence was entirely misplaced in Mamurra's opinion.

But why should Pompey attack? the master of engineers pondered among the thousand other things Caesar had tasked him to do. *Why risk a battle when Caesar's army would almost certainly dissolve within a matter of weeks?*

"Any more news from Thessalonica, Septillius?" Caesar said to one of the legates hovering nearby. "What have your scouts heard?"

"Nothing, Caesar," Septillius replied evenly. "But it is safe to assume they are coming. We do not have much time."

"How long?"

"A week." The legate shrugged. "Perhaps days."

The grim news cast a pall of gloom on the other officers, but it did not appear to faze Caesar in the least. He nonchalantly ran one finger along the map, tracing out a long line the mapmaker had carefully and prominently drawn in dark ink. The line began at Dyrrachium, extended inland for several miles, turned southeast to run down the ten-mile-long valley in which most of Caesar's army was camped, and then angled sharply to the east to wind its way through the mountains, all the way to the map's edge.

Looking over the consul's shoulder, Mamurra bristled with apprehension. That dark line on the map concerned him more than any of his other problems. It was the *Via*

Egnatia, an extremely well-built, twenty-foot-wide, Roman road that connected the Adriatic coast to the distant colonies in the East. A traveler leaving Dyrrachium could follow it for more than seven hundred miles and still not reach its final milestone. Like any Roman road, the *Via Egnatia* could convey legions at lightning speed. And just two hundred miles down that road, beyond the great mountains, lay the city of Thessalonica, home of the Senate-in-Exile, where a second *Optimates* army was rumored to be massing. On a road like the *Via Egnatia*, veteran Roman legions could cover that distance in a mere ten days.

Did Caesar not understand? Did he not see it as plain as the midday sun?

If Pompey's reinforcements suddenly appeared to the east, Caesar's army would be hopelessly trapped between two superior forces – and annihilated.

But before Mamurra could conjecture a diplomatic means of voicing this concern yet again, a group of four men entered the tent, instantly captivating Caesar's attention.

One of the new arrivals, a strong-featured, assertive-looking general in his mid-thirties, approached Caesar without hesitation, while the other three – a tribune and two centurions, each with a plumed helmet tucked under one arm – hung near the entrance.

"Ah, Antony." Caesar smiled as if welcoming the change of subject. "Have you two good men for me, as I requested?"

"I do, Caesar," Antony said, gesturing to the two centurions behind him.

Caesar hardly afforded them a glance, as if he did not care what they looked like. "Can they be trusted?"

"Irrefutably, my lord," Antony replied spiritedly. "You

will not find two stouter fellows in all the army. Both brave to a fault. Centurions Proculus Strabo of the Ninth, and Lucius Domitius of the Tenth."

Caesar looked up with a bit more interest as if he recognized one or both names.

Standing at attention in full armor, Lucius Domitius dared to meet the examining glance of the consul. Lucius saw a hint of recognition, and then the moment passed just as quickly. Caesar's eyes resumed their former indifference as he began to discourse with Antony in hushed tones.

It was, of course, not beyond the realm of possibility that the consul remembered him. Not only had Lucius served in Caesar's army for the past ten years — fighting in the wars in Gaul, Germania, Britannia, and Spain — but he had also saved the consul's life more than once.

At twenty-six years old, Lucius was an old hand, a centurion accountable for the comings and goings of the seventy-three legionaries comprising the fifth century of the Eighth Cohort of the Tenth Legion. He did not especially enjoy the bookkeeping and other mundane responsibilities that went with his position. Marching, fighting, looting, and whoring were always preferable. As a junior centurion, he was seldom invited to the councils of war, and could count on one hand the number of times he had been inside the consul's tent. And that was why this midnight summons puzzled him.

Lucius could not help but wonder if this had something to do with the affair of the Raven Brotherhood, a bizarre episode in which he had become unwittingly entangled a few months back. The Raven Brotherhood, a secret society bent on restoring Rome's ancient monarchy, had come dangerously close to ending Caesar's hold on power. Through an intricate scheme Lucius still did not fully understand, the brotherhood had enticed one of Caesar's most trusted generals into betraying him. Had the plot run its full course, the traitor would have taken half the army over to the *Optimates* side to join Pompey. The brotherhood would have then used that invincible army to take control of the empire and place a man known only as The Raven – an alleged descendent of the first Etruscan kings – on the throne of Rome.

The plot would have succeeded had Lucius not intervened just in time, saving Caesar and the army in the balance. To Lucius's knowledge, Caesar never knew how close he had come to betrayal and ruin, or of Lucius's involvement. Very likely, the consul was still ignorant of the whole affair. At the very least, Caesar still had no idea which one of his generals had planned to double-cross him. That much was clear to Lucius, since the traitor was, in fact, the same man with whom Caesar now conversed in hushed voices – the Master of Horse himself, Marc Antony.

Perhaps Antony had put his treacherous ways behind him. In the months since, Lucius had observed him falling in line, playing the part of the loyal general, at least outwardly, and resuming his place as one of Caesar's most intimate friends.

As for The Raven, the mysterious leader of the secret brotherhood had remained elusive. Lucius had never discovered his identity, only that he was a powerful noble who clandestinely controlled a good number of senators on both sides. And that likely meant he had the *Optimates* on a string, whether Pompey and the rest of the exiled senators realized it or not.

Did The Raven still have Antony on a string?

If Antony knew that Lucius had thwarted the scheme, he had not indicated as such. Still, the animosity between them went back much further than this most recent episode. Lucius knew Antony was cunning and vindictive, and especially dangerous when he was being outwardly friendly. And friendly was exactly how Antony had been since rousing Lucius in the dead of night to come to the consul's pavilion – which was precisely why, beneath his cloak, Lucius now kept one hand firmly gripping the hilt of his dagger.

Antony conversed with Caesar in hushed tones, frequently shooting amused glances over his shoulder at the two centurions. It was evident he was up to something. Lucius did not trust the bastard any further than he could piss.

And who was this other centurion standing beside him? Lucius could not remember ever encountering him before this night.

Like Lucius, the other centurion was broad of chest and muscular of build, but their similarities ended there. Lucius stood a hand's breadth taller and bore the distinct features of his Spanish mother. The other man was clearly Latin, with a complexion like most of the people Lucius had encountered during his brief stay in Rome. And the bastard might very well have just come from Rome, judging by the state of his dress. Lucius's armor was dull from months in the field, his cloak spattered with the gray mud of the trenches, his helmet dented, the wilted centurion's plume missing many feathers. The other centurion, in sharp contrast, looked splendid enough to march in a triumph. His armor and helmet, though modest, gleamed as if polished only yesterday. His tunic and cloak were patched and mended in several places, but both were well cared for and freshly cleaned. The brooch at his neck was simple and bore no inscription or design, but it shined like a candle under the dull light of the lamps. The feathers in his plume were of fine quality, perhaps his only extravagance, and had been arranged with great care into distinct black and white sections.

Were it not for the scars on the man's forearms and the row of medallions on his mail shirt – many of them from the Gallic Wars – Lucius would have pegged him for a ceremonial peacock rather than a fighting soldier.

Perhaps this summons had taken him by surprise just as it had Lucius. Or, maybe, he was one of Antony's henchmen.

"It shall be as you say, Caesar," Antony said with finality, ending his conversation with the consul.

With hardly a nod of acknowledgment, Caesar moved on to the next item of business, the next solicitor awaiting an audience. Such was the way of the great man who juggled campaign strategies, affairs of state, and correspondence with Rome, all at the same time.

"It's all arranged, then," Antony said. He grinned as he looked Lucius and the other centurion up and down and then nodded to the tribune. "Give these two mule pricks their charge, Sextus, and set them on their way."

"Yes, my lord," the tribune replied respectfully. Then, turning to the two centurions, he assumed a decidedly brusquer tone. "This way, then. Don't stand there gawking! I haven't got all bloody night."

If the other centurion found the conceited tribune as annoying as Lucius did, he did not show it. His face remained expressionless, as if set in stone, as he followed the tribune outside.

Lucius followed, too. But before ducking out into the night air, he instinctively cast a final glance over his shoulder at Antony. The general had already returned to Caesar's side, but he was still watching Lucius from the opposite side of the tent. Then, Lucius saw a sly smile form on Antony's lips. There was a devilishly eager look in his eyes, as a sadistic rascal might observe the destruction wreaked by a boulder he had released from a high slope.

A familiar chill ran up Lucius's spine. He had seen that look on Antony's face before, a few short months ago, when the general had dispatched him on another mission – one from which Lucius had not been expected to return.

III

A thousand campfires danced wildly on the brisk wind, a flickering ribbon stretching for miles along the lower coastal hills, marking the course of the trenches and redoubts of Caesar's army. Creak of axle and din of tool emanated from dark spaces where the toil never ceased. Discomfited beasts brayed within pens. Soldiers huddled under cloak and hood, avoiding the fires which were all too often the target of projectiles lobbed from the enemy engines.

Sextus led the two centurions through the narrow maze between the tents, moving briskly and with purpose, turning this way and that, not uttering a word except to scold them.

"Mercury's gold prick!" he exclaimed more than once. "Can you not walk faster?"

Lucius had never met the tribune Sextus before. From the tribune's pale skin and soft hands, Lucius deduced he was one of those foppish young gentlemen recently recruited from Italy. Evidently, his well-placed connections had secured him a position on Antony's staff. The bugger probably didn't know the difference between a prick and a pilum and would run for the rear the first time he found himself facing enemy spears.

Eventually, they reached a clearing away from the bustle of the camp where Sextus finally stopped. As Lucius's eyes adjusted to the darkness, he saw they were not alone. A few paces away stood a pair of heavily laden mules tended by four armed legionaries. The mules appeared healthier than most, and had obviously been hand-picked for the immense burden they carried. Two canvas sacks, stuffed nearly to bursting, were slung across the back of each animal.

The soldiers said nothing as the tribune approached. Clearly, this meeting had been arranged.

"Juno's teeth, it's cold!" Sextus said, impatiently rubbing his hands together. "Let's get this over with, shall we?"

Snatching a lamp from one of the guards, the tribune held it near the mules to reveal the cargo. In addition to the heavy sacks Lucius had noticed before, each animal carried one wineskin and a long, thin bundle wrapped in canvas.

"It's all there," the tribune said with a yawn. "The cargo to be delivered, as we discussed, and the other items you requested, Centurion Strabo." Sextus glanced at Lucius and was clearly entertained by the confused look on his face. "No need to look so befuddled, Centurion Domitius. You will know more very soon. This mission is something of a sensitive nature. General Antony desires all reasonable precautions to be observed, you understand. Centurion Strabo, here, has been fully advised. He will fill you in on the details once you are some distance from the camp – and not before."

Lucius looked at the other centurion for reassurance, a nod of affirmation, a look, anything to give him an inkling of confidence that this was not another of Antony's underhanded tricks. But the centurion did not meet his gaze.

"Well, that's it then," Sextus said with finality. "I believe we are through here. You have your orders."

Lucius watched the men around him as a wayward fawn might observe a pack of lions. He was convinced they intended to murder him here and now, and the rest was just a distraction to put him off guard. But he would not be deceived. He would not be a helpless fawn. Beneath his cloak, his hands were on the hilts of his weapons. He glanced from the centurion to the tribune to the guards, sizing them up and calculating who would make the first move.

The thin-shouldered tribune was of no consequence and would be brushed aside with less effort than it would take to swat a fly. The guards were young and overconfident. Lucius could deal with them quickly enough. Their attacks would be rash and uncoordinated. The centurion, however – the one called Strabo – would be a problem. No doubt, he was an expert fighter, like Lucius, trained in the wars for many years.

With senses attuned to the clink of every mail ring, the movement of every shadow, Lucius watched and waited. He expected them to lurch for him at any moment, to rush him with blades gleaming in the moonlight. He envisioned how he would meet them with his own steel, the natural obstacles he could use to his advantage, the moves and countermoves, all deduced in the space of a few heartbeats, an unconscious assessment born of innumerable battles and skirmishes.

But the attack never came.

Instead, the tribune yawned again and gave Lucius another superior smile. "I suppose you are wondering what's in those packs, eh, Centurion Domitius?" He gestured at the sacks on the mules. "I imagine you'll eventually have a peek, so I might as well save you the trouble. It's silver. Every one of those bags is filled to the brim with silver *denarii*. Enough to make you both rich beyond the fattest merchant of Alexandria." Sextus paused as Lucius stared ravenously at the concealed fortune. "I know I don't need to say this, but I will anyway. General Antony will not stand for any mischief. If a single coin is missing, you will account for it ten-fold. Understand? Deviate from your orders, and you will face the severest punishment, I assure you."

The warning would have sounded more intimidating had it come from the mouth of anyone other than this whelp. It bordered on insulting, but Lucius held his tongue. To his surprise, his new companion did not.

"And suppose the Gauls are not there, as Antony said they would be?" Strabo spoke suddenly. "What then? Will this man and I bear the blame?"

The question had sounded like an accusation.

"Lower your voice, Centurion!" The tribune glanced around as if someone might be eavesdropping. "As I said, this is a sensitive matter!"

"Forgive me, Tribune," Strabo said in a tone that was not in the least bit apologetic. "But I have found it is best to be prepared for the worst. I have been given such assignments by the Master of Horse before."

Sextus's eyes narrowed. "I don't think I like your tone, Centurion Strabo. I would expect such impudence from the rankers or the auxiliaries, not from a decorated centurion. But then, your reputation is somewhat overblown, in my opinion. For the life of me, I don't know why General Antony insisted on you for this task."

"I might have an idea, sir," Strabo replied in a voice

thick with sarcasm. His contempt for the tribune was so blatant, so genuine, that Lucius began to consider this might not be a hatched plot, after all.

The tribune was clearly displeased but not enough to tarry any longer. "Be swift!" he said curtly. "Report directly to General Antony when you return. Speak to no one else. Is that understood?"

Lucius and Strabo both nodded.

"Be off, then. Juno go with you!"

The tribune then stormed off, waving a hand for the guards to accompany him. The torchlight quickly faded, leaving Lucius and Strabo and the pair of mules alone in the darkness.

IV

The two centurions stood for a long moment, staring at each other, each with his cloak drawn around him. Lucius suspected that, like him, his companion was ready to draw his gladius in an instant. Finally, a simple nod was exchanged between them. Strabo took up the reins of the first mule and led the clopping beast into the darkness. Lucius took charge of the second mule and followed.

Silently, they made their way through the camp periphery, weaved through the artillery park strewn with wagons, crossed the half-dug trenches of the outer line, passed the putrid latrines where dark figures stood and squatted. Finally, they were challenged by the outer pickets. Strabo presented a pass bearing the mark of Antony, and they were allowed to proceed.

Strabo guided them inland, through dark gullies, over grassy crests, and along the shorelines of marshes. He followed no clear path that Lucius could discern. Expecting ambush at each thicket, Lucius kept one wary eye on his companion and the other on the way ahead. They kept walking until the flickering campfires sank below the hills behind them and the gray light of dawn began to outline the ridges to their front.

Through mile after silent mile, Lucius's mind began to drift. He dreamt of the golden fields and rolling hills in faraway Spain, where he had played as a boy – where he and his sister had played together, riding the pony they shared.

It was getting harder to remember her face.

He was so far removed now from those innocent days that it seemed his childhood had been lived by another. All that remained were memories – good memories of an innocent boy who had not yet learned to kill, who had looked upon the world as a basket of delectable fruits. Then, there were the memories of that terrible day, indelible memories that blemished any wistful thoughts of his youth. That dreadful day when his family was slain, when his entire world was turned upside down.

Lucius was born into a poor family. His father, a veteran of the Sertorian War, had struggled to scrape a living from a small plot of land bestowed upon him for his army service. Lucius's earliest childhood memory was of lying beside his sister on the cold floor of that cramped hut they called a house, trying to sleep while the pangs of hunger gnawed at their bellies. To two starving children, the crawling insects had looked as appetizing as a platter of figs. But Juno, the protector of children, had been watching over them. They had endured that miserable existence until Lucius's sixth year, when the miracle happened – the miracle that changed everything. Through a stroke of good fortune, their industrious father acquired an abandoned silver mine and quickly turned it into a thriving enterprise, yielding a small fortune. This success made him a prominent member of the local assembly practically overnight, and Lucius and his sister never starved again. In his adolescent years, Lucius enjoyed all the privileges and comforts of a young *eques*, living in a comfortable villa that overlooked the sea. His father saw to it that young Lucius received a formal education from a Greek tutor, paving the way for him to pursue a career in law and politics upon reaching manhood.

But those blessed times were not to last. Lucius had hardly doffed the purple stripe when tragedy struck, and his life changed forever. Less than a fortnight after his fifteenth birthday, Lucius's father, mother, and sister were brutally murdered, the victims of a slave uprising. The family villa was burned to the ground, along with all their possessions. Lucius had been away during the attack, only discovering the morbid scene hours later, just in time to hear his mutilated father's final breaths. Lucius found the bodies of his mother and sister in the house, burned beyond recognition. In one night, everyone and everything he had ever cared for was gone. With no nearby relations, Lucius was cast upon the world a confused and grief-stricken orphan.

Through an obscure legal complication – the source of which Lucius only came to understand many years later – he was stripped of any claims to his father's assets. He had not a single *sesterce* to his name. Reduced from privileged to pauper, young Lucius stumbled through the successive days in a fog, a lost and hollow soul, all his former aspirations suddenly meaningless.

And that was when his father's former patron and chief business rival – the highborn Marcus Aemilius Valens – offered Lucius counsel and assistance. With the concern of an adopted father, Valens suggested Lucius leave what remained of his former life behind and take up his father's first profession, that of a soldier. The Seventh Legion was recruiting in Spain at the time, an ideal opportunity. Indifferent to his own well-being, Lucius enlisted as a legionary recruit and marched off to join Caesar's army in its decade-long conquest of Gaul.

Abandoning his painful past, Lucius embraced the life of a soldier. From the forests of Germania to the shores of Britannia, he fought where he was told to fight and slew who he was told to slay. Through each successive battle, he emerged ever the stronger, like a piece of hammered steel, forged stouter by another turn on the anvil. In time, the memory of his family, of his idyllic youth in that seaside villa, faded to an ambiguous dream.

Only much later did Lucius discover that the slaughter of his family had not been a random tragedy. It had been part of an elaborate plot, arranged by Marcus Valens, Lucius's pretended mentor, to seize his father's mine. Since finding out the truth, Lucius had brimmed with hatred for Valens. He coveted nothing more than to exact revenge on the duplicitous villain. But there was little a lowly soldier could do. Valens was an elite, a member of one of the noblest families of Rome, virtually untouchable. While Lucius was bound to the army, destined to slog away wherever the legions took him.

Over the years, Valens's wealth and power had only increased, even winning him a seat in the Senate. Eventually, he was exposed as a conspirator in a plot to kill Caesar – a plot that was rumored to have been backed by many in the Senate – and was exiled from Rome.

But Lucius knew he would find Valens someday. Perhaps now, with the Republic embroiled in civil war, Valens would crawl out of whatever hole he had been hiding in and try to ingratiate himself with the *Optimates*. If that happened – if Lucius ever got an inkling as to the murderer's whereabouts – he would stop at nothing short of desertion to kill him.

The mule brayed, snapping Lucius back to the present.

"This is far enough," Strabo said suddenly, halting his own mule and turning to face Lucius. The gray sky outlined his frame, largely obscuring his features. Still, Lucius could discern that his cloak was thrown back over one shoulder, exposing the hilt of his sheathed gladius. "I do not know you, Lucius Domitius of the Tenth Legion," Strabo said matter-of-factly. "Nor do I recall your name ever reaching my ears. That is odd, especially since the Ninth and the Tenth have marched side-by-side since landing in Epirus last year. How is it I have never heard of you?"

"I did not cross with the first landing," Lucius offered, realizing his companion was just as in the dark as he was. "I was convalescing in Rome at the time. I came over with Antony's reinforcements only a few months ago."

That explanation did not appear to satisfy Strabo.

"You are a friend of Antony's, then?"

Lucius laughed. "Hardly."

Strabo's eyes narrowed. "That is not the impression I got in the consul's tent. He spoke to you warmly, as one would an old comrade."

Lucius chuckled. "The blessed general and I share a long history. I will not deny that. But it is not a pleasant one." When Strabo's expression indicated he wished to hear more, Lucius added, "I once embarrassed Lord Antony under the eyes of the consul. He has despised me ever since."

"Then," Strabo said, carefully studying Lucius's face. "You are not here as my assassin?"

"I believed you had been sent here with the same purpose," Lucius replied with a grin. "No, I am not here to slay you." He paused before adding. "Of course, it would not have been difficult had I wished to."

Strabo smiled for the first time and visibly relaxed the grip on the hilt of his sword. "Then I must beg your forgiveness, Lucius Domitius. One of my reputation must be cautious, you understand. I do not intend any offense. Whenever I meet someone new, they typically have me at a disadvantage."

"One of your reputation?" Lucius said bewilderedly.

"Yes. You have heard of me, of course."

Lucius shook his head.

Strabo appeared somewhat flustered. "My name, then, at least."

"I was ignorant of your name until this night, and my newfound knowledge has served no other purpose than to associate your face with that name."

Strabo looked back at him in astonishment as if he could not fathom such a possibility. "You mean to tell me you've never heard of Proculus Strabo, descendent of Rufius Strabo, famed soldier of the Punic Wars, who fought against Hannibal's elephants at Zama?"

Lucius shook his head again.

Strabo was beside himself. "There's not a man in all the Ninth who does not know of my distinguished heritage!"

"I'm sure all whom you've told know it well," Lucius said mockingly.

It seemed a long moment before Strabo realized Lucius was making a jest of him. He eyed Lucius coolly. "You do little to gain my confidence with such remarks, Lucius Domitius, but I suppose you are as ignorant of me as you say you are. I will not question the integrity of one who wears the cross plume."

"That is wise."

Strabo let out an awkward laugh. "Always the bold one, eh? Well, I suppose that will be of use where we're going. I suspect we have both been handed a death sentence with this mission. Antony wishes to be quietly rid of us that we may trouble him no more. That being the case, we must both be vigilant from here on."

"And what have you done to warrant the general's wrath?" Lucius asked.

Strabo hesitated before finally answering. "I cheated him at dice."

"You what?"

"I cheated the bloody general at dice! Need I repeat it?" Strabo was clearly growing annoyed at the merriment on Lucius's face.

"And now you think he wants you dead, eh?" Lucius erupted in a fit of side-splitting laughter that reverberated across the rocky slopes. He found Strabo's quarrel with Antony decidedly insignificant compared to his own.

Strabo, however, was not amused. "Damn you to Hades!" he said wrathfully.

Lucius laughed again, so vociferously that the waiting mules began to fidget. A long interval passed before Lucius recovered his wits and dared speak to his fuming companion again.

"Answer me this then, Strabo. If Antony has us marked for death, as you say he does, why does he trust us with this?" Lucius patted the bags of silver on his mule.

"I do not know. It has me more worried than if he'd sent me out alone with that snotty tribune." He eyed Lucius crossly. "At this moment, I wish he had."

"Come now, Strabo. Do not hold a grudge. Surely, you can appreciate a jest between soldiers."

"I am not one to hold grudges. But I am not entirely sure I trust you yet."

"I assure you, my friend," Lucius smiled. "Had I been sent here to kill you, you'd now be with Hector in the underworld."

Now it was Strabo's turn to laugh. "You are sure of yourself, Lucius Domitius. But take care you never try it. I've never met a man from the Tenth I could not best – even on my worst day."

"As you said before, you have never met me," Lucius replied. "But you have my oath, comrade. If there is any treachery here, it will be on your part. Now, suppose you tell me what in Furrina's sacred spring we're doing here. What are we to do with this fortune? Purchase the loyalty of some petty king or despot?"

"We are to deliver it to the Allobroges cavalry."

"Pluto's Realm!" Lucius exclaimed, astonished that such a sum would be entrusted to auxiliary mercenaries. "And what are they going to do with it?"

"Pay their men, apparently. As I understand it, the Allobroges commander claims the last payment never reached them, and he is threatening to take his troop back to Gaul. Caesar needs his cavalry, so we must see that this one makes it through."

"Just the two of us, to protect such a sum?"

"The fewer the tongues, the fewer the rumors," Strabo replied. "Do you think Caesar wants the word to get out that he pays his auxiliaries while his own legions haven't been paid for months? He'd have a bloody mutiny on his hands."

"The devious scoundrel!" Lucius exclaimed.

Strabo nodded grimly. "Aye. We agree on that, Lucius. Were it up to us, the legions would be paid first. But such decisions are above our rank. Orders are orders. We must deliver the silver."

"And where are we to find these Gaul bastards?"

"They've been patrolling the inland hills for the last several days. A rider was dispatched to let them know we're coming. We are to meet them at Naiads Mere. It's a small pond, roughly six miles from here."

"You've been there?"

"No, but I've seen it on a map."

Lucius's eyes fixed on the barren hills ahead. Six miles across open country was a long way, especially with the possibility of enemy cavalry lurking about. Their gladii would be next to useless. Without ranged weapons, they could be easily ridden down and skewered like pigs.

Just then, Lucius realized that Strabo was watching him, apparently amused by the concern on his face. With a slight smile, Strabo reached for the long canvas bundle lashed to the mule and untied the securing bands. The canvas unfurled, and four long javelins plonked onto the ground.

Lucius's eyes blazed with delight as Strabo held out two of the weapons for him to take. Just the feel of the polished wooden shafts in his hands bolstered his spirits. The short sword was good for close-in work, but Lucius preferred the flexibility of the pilum. The four-foot-long wooden shaft tipped with a two-foot iron shank functioned well as both a lethal throwing weapon and a jabbing melee weapon. When wielded properly, the javelin's pyramidal point could pierce most shields and armor.

"I'm surprised Sextus gave you such fine weapons," Lucius said as he examined the shafts.

"I insisted on it. As I did this." Strabo removed one of the wineskins from the mule and tossed it at Lucius, who caught it with one hand. Strabo then removed another identical vessel for himself.

"I knew I would take a liking to you, Strabo." Lucius grinned as he swiftly uncorked the wineskin and turned it upside down like a man who had not drunk in years. The rich liquid ran down his parched throat, filling his body and mind with the familiar warm and calming effect.

As he wiped dribbles of wine from his stubbly chin,

Lucius noticed that Strabo was staring at him, a wry smile on his face. It appeared that he had not yet taken a drink.

"Are you not going to have any?" Lucius asked.

"Aye," Strabo replied.

"Then have some."

"After a moment."

Lucius stared at him perplexedly for a moment before suddenly realizing the reason for Strabo's delay, and Lucius instantly felt like a fool. "Croesus's burning balls! You're craftier than you look, Strabo. I'll not fall for that again."

"You appear to be fine," Strabo chuckled. "I suppose we can rule out poison, then." He then uncorked his own wineskin and held it up in a gesture to Lucius. "To Mars and Jupiter. May they grant us victory. And to your continued health, comrade."

Lucius half-heartedly raised his own wineskin. "To your sister the whore. May her bastards be many and ugly."

Strabo smiled, and they both drank in silence, taking several long draws on the potent liquid, savoring every drop. As they drank, Lucius stared at the mules, eyeing the hefty bags with curiosity. After another gulp, he corked the wineskin and strode over to the nearest animal, where he began unlacing the flap on one of the sacks.

"What do you think you're doing?" Strabo demanded.

"It's not often a soldier sees so much silver," Lucius replied. "If that is indeed what's in these bags. Would you rather know for yourself, or take that bloody tribune's word for it?"

Strabo said nothing, but his face revealed that he, too, was now curious. He came closer that he might see.

When Lucius finally threw back the flap, both men could not help but gasp. Gleaming back at them in the dim light of the dawn were more coins than either of them had ever seen in one place.

It was a fat merchant's fortune – just as the tribune had said.

V

The Greek countryside

Long shadows fell across the mountain valleys as morning broke. Lucius followed his new companion. They led the two mules farther inland, leaving the safety of the lines far behind. Through natural cuts in the mountains, they passed, taking hidden pathways seldom traveled. The chilling silence was broken only by the slow clop of the hooves echoing off the towering rocks around them.

An occasional goatherder hut stood out from the rugged slopes, but all were abandoned, the ashes in the firepits cold to the touch. The inhabitants were not fools. Likely, they had fled at the first sighting of the massive Roman armies, lest they fall victim to pillaging soldiers. When the armies were gone, the folk of these hills would return and pick up their lives where they had left off. Such was the way simple folk outlasted the rise and fall of great empires.

The centurions handled the elevations with little

difficulty. They were accustomed to long marches and much heavier burdens. Lucius often found his eyes straying to the jingling bags. There was enough silver within arm's reach to pay an entire legion for three months – or to set up one man like a king for three lifetimes. With such wealth, he could find that quiet seaside villa of his dreams, where the sun always shined over blue waters. His only concerns would be tending his vineyards, breeding his horses, and bedding the lascivious woman he would find for his wife.

Of course, other things would need to be done first, like hunting down and slaughtering Valens. But once his family was avenged, once he had finally put their tormented souls to rest, he could hang up his shield and live like a proper Roman *eques*. And the means to do all of it was within his grasp. He need only take this silver for himself, slip away, and never go back to the legions.

But then there was Strabo. What would Lucius's new companion say to such a proposition? Would Strabo join him, or try to stop him? But then, Lucius already knew the answer. Strabo was a familiar type – straightlaced, dutiful, by the book, unshakably loyal. If Lucius wanted to make off with the silver, then he knew he would have to do so without Strabo's consent. Quite possibly, over his dead body.

A flash of guilt crossed Lucius's mind, as he thought of the men of his century and what would happen to them if he were to desert. Strangely, he found himself thinking more such thoughts of late – duty, responsibility, things he had often ridiculed as a common legionary. Buried deep within him – so deep that it seldom broached the surface – was an desire to watch over his men, to protect them, and to please those above him. Sometime, Lucius wondered if he was wearing the cross plume, or the cross plume wearing him.

In any event, there were too many hurdles to surmount, both outward and inward. And, so, Lucius put the silver out of his head – at least, for the time being.

At noon, they reached the crest of a low ridge where Strabo stopped to study the valley beyond. The valley was shallow and bowl-shaped, with a large pond at its base. The pond was bordered on the nearer side by a gentle, grassy decline, and on the farther side, by a steep, wooded slope.

"This is the spot," Strabo said after looking around at the prominent landmarks as if to match them up with the map in his head. "*Naiads' Mere.* There can be no doubt. We are to meet the Gauls here."

"Then where are the bastards?" Lucius asked.

"I do not know."

"Juno's tits! I've never known a Gaul to be on time."

"Perhaps they watch us from afar," Strabo suggested. "Perhaps they are waiting to see our intentions. The tribune's instructions were to meet them at the water's edge."

Lucius looked at him skeptically. "Down there?"

Strabo nodded, clearly sharing Lucius's misgivings about the idea. From where they stood, the valley offered no discernible means of escape. If the Gauls had chosen this place for the meeting, then they must have had some reservations about Caesar's intentions. Perhaps, instead of silver, they expected treachery.

But Lucius and Strabo had little choice. With an attentive eye on their surroundings, they descended the gradual slope. The mules stepped livelier at the prospect of a fresh drink, to the point that the centurions were forced to march briskly to keep up with them. The bleached bones of a large animal lay in the tall grass, along with a few rotting axles and splintered wheels, the broken castoffs of travelers of years past. When Lucius and Strabo reached the shoreline, the woods across the water appeared much more ominous than they had from the high ridge. The dark expanse beneath the green canopy was large enough to hide a legion. To the right, a sharp limestone outcropping jutted from the shore, towering a dozen feet or more above the water, its jagged edges reflecting in the mirror-like surface. The natural landmark seemed to denote the spot where the open grass ended and the woods began.

Both centurions were drawn to a scattering of impressions in the mud near the water's edge.

"Cavalry," Strabo concluded after kneeling to examine them. "Several dozen riders, at least."

"Roman cavalry," Lucius added, recognizing the familiar marks left by the leather hoof boots. "But is it Pompey's or ours?"

"Whoever they are, they are long since gone. These tracks are two days old." Strabo's eyes were suddenly fixated on the ground. "Wait. There's something else..." His voice trailed off.

At that moment, from the trees across the pond, a thousand birds noisily took to the sky. The deafening squawks shattered the quiet of the place. The massive flock circled several times over the water then disappeared beyond the next ridge. There was no way of knowing if the birds had taken to the sky of their own accord, or had been startled by something.

"Strabo...," Lucius started to say, but was cut short by an urgent look from his companion.

"We are not alone," Strabo whispered, pointing discreetly to a particular set of prints in the mud.

From a glance, Lucius deduced the reason for his companion's sudden attentiveness. The tracks were fresh, perhaps not even an hour old.

The mules began to bray nervously, but Lucius and Strabo maintained their outward calm, keeping their swords sheathed and their javelins casually resting on their shoulders.

Across the pond, Lucius perceived a momentary glint of steel in the blackness beneath the trees, not once but twice.

"Strabo," he said lowly.

"I saw it," Strabo answered through gritted teeth.

"How many do you reckon?"

"Four to six, if these tracks are any measure. Perhaps it is our friends."

But, at that moment, Lucius sensed an abnormal sound floating on the breeze, a sound that he instantly recognized as the creak of a straining bow.

"Down!" he shouted.

Strabo followed Lucius's lead as two distinct twangs rang out across the water. Both centurions dashed behind the nearest mule only moments before two arrows appeared in the mud where they had been standing. The arrows had come from the woods. Clearly, whoever had shot them had been waiting for the perfect moment to catch the centurions off guard.

As Lucius contemplated this from behind the protection of the mule, a shrill cry filled the air. Lucius peered around the mule's haunch to see six howling figures emerge from behind the limestone outcropping. They were scraggly, bearded men dressed in light mail and wielding swords, axes, and the small round shields commonly used by Gallic horsemen. They were coming on at full charge with murder in their eyes.

Changing the grip on their javelins, Lucius and Strabo prepared to receive their attackers. The onrushing warriors made no effort to maintain good order. The faster, bolder ones far outpaced the slower ones. Their haphazard, disjointed advance bespoke of inept amateurs, rather than skilled assassins.

With little more than a glance exchanged between them, Lucius and Strabo spread out until they were several paces apart, forcing the attackers to split up and take them on individually. Four of the ill-trained oafs ran at Strabo – the instinctive choice, being the shorter of the Romans – while the other two charged at Lucius.

In a moment, Lucius's javelin was beside his ear. He hurled the weapon without thinking, in one fluid motion, putting the precise force behind it, aiming, not at the first attacker, but the second. It was an old trick. Throw at the man least expecting it. And the old trick worked as predicted.

The first attacker, thinking the javelin was intended for him, nearly fell over in the mud ducking behind his shield. At the same time, behind him, the second man continued rushing forward, confident that his comrade was the target. He realized his fatal error a moment too late, just before the lightning-fast projectile lanced through his unprotected side. It tore through leather, tunic, flesh, and hip, leaving a hand's breadth of the gore-covered iron shank protruding from his right buttock. A moment later, the dangling butt end of the wooden shaft drooped and planted itself in the mud, the momentum driving the iron shank even deeper. Pain and disbelief registered on the warrior's face. Dropping sword and shield, he clasped both hands around the shaft. After a vain yet excruciatingly painful attempt to dislodge the six-foot weapon, he toppled over, hopelessly skewered, shrieking as his blood pulsed into the muck.

Upon seeing the fate of his comrade, the first attacker rose in a rage to resume his charge. He was met immediately by the thrust of Lucius's second javelin, wielded like a spear. The warrior only just managed to bat away the jab, clearly dazzled by the blinding speed of a man Lucius's size. Still off-balance, the warrior countered with an uncontrolled backhanded swipe with his sword. Lucius ducked, avoiding the heavy blade by a finger's length, then stepped forward and drove the pilum up under his opponent's shield. The iron point found a small gap in the mail armor, just where the shirt covered the abdomen. Very likely, the mail had been taken off a slain enemy, and the missing links marked the spot where its former owner had received his fatal blow. If that was the case, then the current owner of the armor now suffered the same fate. Lucius's point penetrated the thin tunic and the flesh beneath. He then jerked the weapon back to rip it free, followed by a crimson spray and the man's bulging insides.

With both of his attackers dispatched, Lucius wheeled to assist Strabo. He expected to see the outnumbered centurion struggling for his life, but was surprised to discover that two of Strabo's four assailants were already writhing on the ground in their own blood. A third was stumbling to the rear, clearly senseless, a significant dent in his helmet. Lucius sent him to the afterlife with a quick thrust of the javelin.

The final attacker still grappling with Strabo appeared to be more skilled than his ill-fated comrades. He was the largest of the group and wielded a double-bladed axe with both hands. He swung wildly, shouting in mad frustration as Strabo ducked one swing after another or parried the axe away. The aggravated warrior knew he was being worn down, played with. Still, he continued to try, growling as each successive swing came back weaker than the last.

Finally, the giant warrior's arms were spent. He could no longer lift the heavy weapon and threw it away. Not giving up, he drew out a dagger with one shaky hand, spat at Strabo, cursed him in broken Latin, dared him to come closer. With an icy coolness, Strabo watched his movements, waited for an opening, then struck while the warrior was in the middle of one of his taunts. The gladius moved faster than the eye could follow. Two rapid thrusts. Two perfectly delivered jabs. Then Strabo stepped back beyond his opponent's reach and waited.

Neither of the stabs had penetrated by more than an inch, but they were enough. The warrior looked down at his abdomen with dismay. A fresh stream of blood oozed from the links of his armor, soaking his shirt and trousers. He made no move with the dagger, no last-ditch lunge. He knew he was beaten. He simply met eyes with Strabo then collapsed into the mud.

All six attackers were either dead or dying, but Lucius and Strabo had little time to savor the victory. Bowstrings twanged somewhere behind Lucius. Both centurions ducked low just as two arrows whizzed past them.

Lucius looked up to see two bowmen standing atop the stone outcropping some thirty paces away, notching their next arrows. Grabbing up one of the enemy shields, he dashed for the cover of the mules. Strabo did the same, just as two more arrows zipped by.

The archers made no effort to hide as they loosed arrow after arrow at the crouching centurions who fought to keep the protesting mules from bolting. Clearly, the archers understood their high position on the bluff placed them beyond the range of a thrown javelin.

"We've got to get up there!" Strabo grumbled as an arrow planted itself in one of the coin sacks with a loud clink, provoking a loud protest from the mule. "We'll have to make our way around the back. I'm not sure we can coax these beasts into moving any closer. We'll have to make a run for it."

"Wait," Lucius said.

Strabo looked at him perplexedly. "For what? If these beasts run off, we'll lose our cover."

But Lucius did not reply. He was uncoiling a leather strap he had taken from his belt. As Strabo watched, Lucius took both ends of the strap in one hand and looped the wider, middle portion of the strap around the butt end of his javelin.

"Is that an *amentum*?" Strabo asked.

Lucius nodded.

"Can you hit anything with that?"

A sporting look from Lucius was the only reply.

The bows twanged again. Arrows thudded into the mud at the mules' hooves, and Lucius made his move. Bolting from cover, he bounded toward the bluff with the pilum balanced on his right shoulder. He took three giant steps, then hurled the javelin with his whole body, releasing one end of the strap at mid-throw. The moment arm added by the three feet of straining leather launched the missile with incredible force.

Confident they were safely out of range, the bowmen dismissed Lucius's efforts. They were more concerned with notching their next arrows than watching the flying pilum. When they finally realized the arcing javelin had the elevation and the distance, it was too late. One archer took the pyramidal point of the iron shank squarely in the chest, piercing him through the heart and killing him instantly. Splattered with the blood of his comrade, the other archer panicked and ran, disappearing into the woods behind the bluff.

It appeared there were no more ambushers.

"Athena's arse!" Strabo exclaimed in amazement. "And where did you learn to do that?"

"Gaul," Lucius replied as he coiled the strap and returned it to his belt. "An Aedui skirmisher taught me, and

I have spent the last several years mastering it."

Strabo seemed to find humor in that, then looked around at the dead and dying. "Well, it's certain these fools aren't Pompey's troops." Strabo used his sword to prick the gray checkered cloak worn by the nearest corpse. "I've seen this pattern before. These are Allobroges."

"The bastards we were sent here to meet?" Lucius asked.

"Maybe," Strabo said as his eyes looked past Lucius, then focused on something behind him. "Or maybe we're here to meet *them*."

Lucius turned around to discover that the distant crest of the grassy slope, previously empty and barren, was now lined with horsemen. The long file of silhouettes, perhaps three dozen, all holding upright lances, gazed down upon the two centurions. Even from this distance, it was easy to discern they were Gauls. After a long interval of staring, the horsemen wheeled their mounts and began to move, riding in a snaking column down the slope toward the pond.

Lucius and Strabo made no attempt to flee. If the Gauls meant them harm, there was little they could do about it. They were vastly outnumbered, and there was nowhere to run, save the woods, and that would only delay the inevitable.

As they watched the riders approach, one of the mules brayed as if to get the centurions' attention. Lucius walked to the other side of the nervous beast to examine the feathered shafts protruding from its side. Miraculously, none of the arrows had found the animal's hide. All had lodged in the leather saddlebags. Lucius discovered that one missile had pierced one of the coin bags. He yanked it out without thinking, leaving a small hole through which some of the contents spilled out onto the ground.

Lucius's mouth went dry as he gazed at the clinking

pieces forming a small pile in the mud.

"What are you looking at?" Strabo asked. When he received no reply, he joined Lucius on the other side of the mule.

Neither centurion paid any attention to the thundering hooves rapidly approaching. Both stood mesmerized as they gaped in disbelief at the pieces on the ground.

"Damn Antony!" Lucius uttered when he finally found his tongue. "Damn the bloody blackguard to Pluto's Realm!"

He was not staring at silver coins, but worthless shards of clay.

VI

The clay pieces continued to trickle onto the ground.

"Mars curse me for a fool!" Lucius said with disgust. "To be taken by that old trick!"

Strabo still looked incredulous. "You mean, these bags are full of clay bits?"

"Very likely." Lucius nodded. "No doubt, Antony planned this. He knew we would look in the bags, and so had that whelp of a tribune lay down a layer of silver coins at their tops. The rest is undoubtedly worthless." Lucius peeked over the mule's back at the approaching horsemen. "And now our fates are in the hands of these barbarians. *Damn* Antony!"

Apparently still not convinced, Strabo threw back the flap of one of the sacks, gazed at the shining silver coins, then raised an arm as if preparing to shove his hand deep inside.

"What are you doing, you idiot?" Lucius reached out and grasped Strabo's arm. "Leave it as it is! Those Gauls are expecting bags full of silver. Our only chance now is to fool them as Antony fooled us."

"Antony set us up," Strabo muttered to himself. "He meant to be rid of us."

"They'll be here in moments," Lucius said urgently. He tore off his neckcloth and shoved it into the hand of his stupefied companion. "Plug up that hole! Be quick!"

A firm nudge from Lucius snapped Strabo out of his trance. He did as he was told, shoving the cloth into the hole until it appeared as nothing more than a patch on the inside of the bag. Lucius kicked the clay shards, doing his best to scatter them in the mud and grass. He was not entirely satisfied with his progress when the riders drew near, but stopped lest he draw attention to the objects.

Lucius and Strabo stepped out from behind the mule as the Gauls descended upon the scene in a cacophony of hooves and clanging shields. The centurions were quickly surrounded. Whinnying mounts stomped in the mud and splashed through the frigid waters. Lance points and helmets gleamed in the sun. There were not just three dozen mounted warriors, but nearer one hundred, the others having approached from different directions. Far from their home beyond the Alps, they wore a mishmash of clothes and armor in various states of repair, but their cloaks were all the same distinctive gray checkered weave of the Allobroges.

Lucius recalled the many times he had seen similar cloaks on the battlefields of Gaul streaming behind barbarian horsemen as they charged Roman lines. Lucius had often been on the receiving end of those attacks, which is why now it was all he could do not to draw his sword and prepare to defend himself. But the fact that the riders had not yet trodden them under hoof was encouraging – that, and the white armbands identifying them as Caesar's auxiliaries.

Amongst the shuffling chargers, a mud-covered figure emerged on foot with a rope around his waist. He was thrust into the middle of the circle. His clothes were torn to ribbons. His body was a bloody mess of scrapes and cuts. Clearly, he had just been dragged for some distance behind the horsemen. Half delirious, the captive stumbled, then collapsed in the mud. It took a moment for Lucius to realize this was the same archer who had fled into the woods. Evidently, the horsemen had captured him before he had gotten too far. Clearly, he was one of their own countrymen.

"And who has Caesar sent to us?" A deep voice said in heavily accented Latin. The speaker nudged his horse out from the others. He was no more than thirty years of age, of medium build, with scraggly locks of black hair that fell beneath his helmet. His pink face was unaccustomed to the Greek sun and was marked with blisters that disrupted the evenness of his patchy beard. He was one of the few not carrying a lance. His cloak and mail armor were of a finer quality than those of his companions. He sat on a black steed that stood a hand's breadth higher than the other mounts. Clearly, this man was a warlord, a noble among the Allobroges.

Despite the aura of authority the warlord exuded over the others, he wore an appeasing expression and seemed amused by the sight of the two centurions.

"Do they not have tongues?" the warlord said finally. He had obviously been formally tutored in the Latin language.

"They are mere common soldiers, cousin," a shrill voice said in a less refined dialect.

A second man moved his horse forward to join the other. Judging from his attire, this man, too, was evidently a noble. He was tall and gangly and seemed awkward on the back of his horse. He looked snide and sinister, with a long, drooping face and beady eyes that stared back at the centurions derisively.

"Caesar dishonors us with this pathetic embassy," the long-faced man said, almost spitting the words. "It is an insult, cousin!"

"Do they wish to speak for themselves?" the pink-faced warlord asked, looking down at the Romans.

"Centurions Strabo and Domitius, at your service," Strabo replied firmly. "We have indeed been sent by Caesar. We seek Lord Roucill of the Allobroges."

"You are addressing him, vermin," the long-faced man sneered, gesturing to the other noble. "You stand before Roucill, son of Recel, *prince* of the Allobroges."

The pink-faced warlord identified as Roucill seemed momentarily perturbed when neither Roman appeared impressed.

"And this is my cousin, Egu," Roucill said, introducing the long-faced man. He then gestured to the surrounding horsemen, who watched with indifference. "And these are my warriors, every one of them an expert horseman and lancer. Every one sworn to serve me unto death."

"Hail Lord Roucill!" the long-faced Egu shouted, raising a fist to the assembled troop as if on cue.

"*Hail Roucill!*" The horsemen answered in unison. But Lucius detected something lackluster in their response, something forced. A soldier could tell when other soldiers were just going through the motions, when their allegiance was out of obligation rather than respect.

"And what of these?" Lucius asked wryly, kicking one of the corpses at his feet and pointing at the bound archer. "Did they swear to serve you as well?"

"Mind your tone, Roman!" Egu snapped. "Or you'll be dancing on the end of my lance! You are speaking to a prince of the Allobroges."

Roucill calmed him with a raised hand. "Be at ease, cousin. These are our friends. Yes, Caesar's soldiers are our friends. They must be treated with the utmost courtesy."

Lucius could not tell if there was a trace of mockery in the Gallic prince's tone, or if it was just the accent.

"These are your men, are they not?" Lucius pressed him. "Why did they attack us?"

"There are bad apples in every lot," Roucill said dismissively. "Caesar's own legionaries have been known to desert from time to time. From what I hear, they are deserting him in droves lately. Our own ranks are not immune to such problems."

All geniality vanished from the warlord's face as he turned his gaze on the captive archer. The severely injured man still lay on his back in the mud, breathing heavily from his ordeal. Roucill took a lance from one of the nearby warriors.

The archer's eyes grew wide with terror. He cried out in the Gallic tongue for mercy, but his pleas were cut short. Raising himself in the saddle, Roucill brought the lance down in a forceful thrust, driving the point through the archer's chest, pinning him to the ground. Roucill left the shaft swaying in the air, still lodged in the gargling, kicking man.

The warlord then turned to a hooded, frail-looking rider whom Lucius had not noticed before. Aside from a cadaverous chin and jawline, the man's features were veiled within the shadow of his cowl. He wore a tattered black robe that hung on his bony frame like a man's garment might fit a child. Unlike the others, he wore no armor. A sinister-looking dagger hung from a belt of frayed rope around his waist and appeared to be his only weapon.

"Remember his name, Catugna," Roucill addressed the

hooded man while jerking a thumb at the dying archer. The Allobroges prince was now speaking in a dialect of the Gallic tongue, which Lucius understood from his many years in Gaul. "Remember the names of these other scum, as well. Their families will be sacrificed to Toutatis upon our return home. Such is the fate of traitors and thieves."

"As you say, my lord," the hooded man, the one called Catugna, answered in a raspy voice.

Lucius could not recall ever seeing this corpselike figure before. Still, he instantly recognized the garb and the sect to which it belonged. Catugna was a druid, one of those mysterious wizards, witches, and chroniclers of the Gallic peoples. The mere sight of the ancient mystic sent a chill up Lucius's spine, though he did not know why. He was not one to believe in magic or evil spirits. While Lucius did believe some great unseen power found mild amusement in the daily toils of men, sometimes even stooping to intervene in their affairs, he did not believe these unwashed druids were possessed with any more supernatural abilities than the next man.

Still, he had witnessed them do remarkable things in Gaul and Britannia – things he could not explain. He had seen them heal illnesses and seal up wounds. He had seen them curse bodies of water such that any who drank from them were afflicted with violent maladies. He had seen them curse bountiful fields such that nothing ever grew there again. And he had heard them foretell events that came to pass, everything from changes in the weather to the deaths of kings – even incidents in his own life.

Of course, there had to be some kind of trickery behind it. No man could tell the future, not even the priests of Rome with their ridiculous omens and superstitions. That's what Lucius kept telling himself.

But it was not important what he thought, or any other

Roman thought. It was what the Gauls believed that mattered. And the druids had an astonishing degree of influence over them, often surpassing that of the Gallic kings and nobles.

How many battles had been fought because druids like Catugna had stirred revolt in the souls of the Gauls? How much death and destruction might have been avoided had Caesar simply done away with that troublesome sect?

Now, as Lucius watched, a trembling, bony hand emerged from the dark sleeve. The druid began to mumble something unintelligible and otherworldly. Whatever the meaning of the sinister chant, the Gallic horsemen were instantly cowed by it. They were struck with fear, many staring with wide-eyed terror at the droning wizard. Many struggled to control their skittish mounts. Those closest to the corpses backed away as if every mortal soul within reach of that claw-like hand would fall victim to the foul utterance. The incantation was spoken in a tone barely above a whisper. Yet, Catugna's voice reverberated inside Lucius's head as if they were his very own thoughts.

When the curse was finished and the withered hand withdrew back inside the sleeve, horses and riders calmed again. Lucius glanced at Strabo to see if the druid's words had had the same effect on him. But the frequent cut of Strabo's eyes at the mules indicated he was more concerned about the Gauls discovering the true contents of the bags.

Lucius looked back at Catugna among the horsemen more than a dozen paces away. Surprisingly, the druid appeared to be looking back at him. The wizard's eyes were hidden within the shadow of the deep cowl, but somehow Lucius knew they were staring directly at him. No, they were staring *through him,* as if to penetrate his soul.

Again, Lucius felt the icy shiver that he could not explain. His lungs seemed stuck between breaths, and he had to force himself to look away before he could breathe again. When he turned back to look at Catugna, the druid had vanished. Where the hooded figure had stood an instant before, there were now only horsemen.

Surely, there was a reason for it, Lucius bolstered himself inwardly. A man could not simply vanish into thin air. The frail Catugna had merely filed back to the rear ranks. That had to be it. And that was what Lucius kept telling himself as Roucill steered his horse over to the Romans.

"I commend you, brave centurions, for finding your way here without incident." The Allobroges prince smiled down at them. "I'm sure you know this country is crawling with enemy spies."

"We saw no one other than these idiots," Lucius said, kicking one of the bodies on the ground.

"You can be sure Pompey's men saw you," Roucill replied. "They watch us even now. The great Pompey has eyes everywhere. Every farmer, every shepherd, every fisherman, even the beggars and lepers. They are all agents of Pompey. If I have learned anything from my time in this dismal, rock-infested country, it is that Caesar is not as revered by the Romans as he claimed to be in Gaul. Here in Greece, he is met with disdain by everyone. I wonder if Caesar himself is aware of it. I wonder if his own troops are." Roucill's eyes examined their faces as if searching for some affirmation.

"We are officers of the legions, my lord," Strabo answered robustly. "We do not concern ourselves with politics nor the whims of peasants. War is our calling."

"Perhaps, the two of you marched with Caesar in Gaul?"

"If you are asking whether we have fought against your kind before, then the answer is yes. I've slain more of your countrymen than I can count. I'm sure Centurion

Domitius, here, can say the same."

Roucill was clearly angered by Strabo's bluntness, but quickly regained his composure. His cousin, however, bristled openly at the remark.

"Roman dogs!" Egu scowled. "Roman scum!"

Strabo ignored the outburst and continued. "We did not come here to discuss our past campaigns, my lord. We came to deliver this." He gestured at the sacks on the mules. Very businesslike, he then produced a papyrus document and stylus from his pouch and handed it to the mounted prince. "Thirty thousand silver *denarii*. The consul sends his compliments and expects this will satisfy your needs, and those of your men. You need only make your mark here, and we will be on our way."

There was a measure of impatience in Strabo's manner. Obviously, he was attempting to hurry the transaction along, hoping the mules might be accepted without a close inspection of the bags. Still, Lucius wondered if he was pushing the act a bit too far.

As Roucill scanned the bill of receipt shoved into his hands, Lucius saw the fires of suspicion growing in his eyes. He got the impression the Gallic noble was not pondering the document, but how the centurions might be deceiving him.

After a long interval, Roucill folded the papyrus, tucked it away, and grinned widely at the two Romans. "But it is not our custom to conduct business in so abrupt a fashion. You have had a long journey, eh? Let us feast together before you return to your consul. The two of you will come to our camp."

"That is courteous of you, my lord, but I am afraid we –"

"You needn't walk," Roucill interrupted as if he had not heard Strabo. "We have spare mounts for both of you."

He pointed at several riderless steeds, apparently the mounts of those killed in the ambush.

"Tonight, we shall foul the air and talk of old campaigns," Roucill said. "Then, tomorrow, we shall discuss this business."

Strabo bit his lip in frustration before stammering. "As I said before, my lord, we must decline your generous hospitality."

"But I insist." Roucill smiled politely, but his eyes were cold.

"Centurion Domitius and I are expected back at camp within hours."

Roucill shook his head. "Night comes quickly, and the countryside is a dangerous place for two lone men. The enemy spies undoubtedly saw you this morning. They will be ready for you on your return. If you head back now, you are sure to be snatched up by the enemy."

"Any delay and Caesar will send patrols looking for us," Strabo countered.

"Then I will send one of my fastest riders to the consul to inform him you will remain with us overnight. Tomorrow, I will send you back under the protection of my own *oathsworn*. Surely, Caesar will agree to that."

Strabo seemed flustered at having his bluff called. He should have backed down. He should have acquiesced, but he did not.

"If you doubt us, my lord," Strabo challenged, "you are at liberty to count the money here and now while we wait."

Lucius cursed inwardly but did his best to remain calm. He wished he had thought quickly enough to head off Strabo's brashness, to stop him from overplaying their hand, but now it was too late. The fool had blundered into a corner, and now their deceit would surely be discovered.

Fully expecting Roucill to do precisely as Strabo had

suggested, order the bags emptied onto the ground, and the silver counted, Lucius was surprised when he did not. Instead, a long moment of silence ensued in which the Allobroges warlord appeared oddly discomfited. Lucius saw a surreptitious glance stolen between Roucill and Egu.

It was not until that moment that Lucius realized the horsemen were divided into two distinct groups – or rather, two castes. One caste consisted of the two princes and about a dozen other knights and bodyguards, conspicuous in their superior armor and horses. The other was comprised of ordinary soldiers. Though the two groups rode as one, it was clear their ranks did not mingle. They kept to their own kind, as if an invisible barrier separated them. This was certainly not unusual, but Lucius sensed a measure of friction between the two castes. Or was it animosity?

And there was a marked difference in their deportment. The common horsemen seemed fixated on the sacks of silver. Like a band of pirates, they eyed the supposed fortune as if on the verge of seizing it for themselves. Conversely, the knights watched the commoners with guarded apprehension. They held their lances at the ready, as if they might have to use them to protect the treasure at any moment.

Finally, Roucill nudged his horse over to one of the mules and lightly tapped the flat of his sword against the bags. A satisfied smile crossed his face at the expected tinkle of the contents within. He then turned to address his men.

"My warriors, Caesar has been true to his word!"

"Let's divide it up now!" said one of the horsemen, triggering a resounding cheer from the others.

As one, the horsemen began moving toward the mules. They stopped when a hand signal from the glowering Egu prompted the knights to form a protective circle around the pack animals.

"Wait, my brothers!" Roucill entreated with raised hands. His manner and tone were much less threatening than the drawn swords and lowered lances of his entourage. "Has the smell of silver made you mad in the head? Have you already forgotten our brothers back at camp who are due an equal share? Would you rob your own countrymen?"

After some grumblings, the horsemen seemed to accept their leader's argument and backed away. The tension between the groups abated, but Lucius got the sense it was only a temporary reprieve.

At Roucill's orders, the troop dismounted, and the horses were allowed to graze and water. The riders busied themselves with cinching up harnesses and repairing leather sandals for their horses' hooves. Still, the fever for the silver never left their eyes. They frequently glanced at the mules and spoke lowly amongst themselves.

At one point, Roucill took Lucius and Strabo aside.

"Do you see now, my Roman friends, why I insist you accompany us?" he said in a hushed voice. "It is not the enemy I fear will waylay you, but my own men. It is difficult to control them when they are in such a state. You will camp with us tonight. Anything else would be unwise."

VII

The camp was a two-hour ride away. Lucius and Strabo spent those hours in the center of the column, praying to Juno the makeshift plug in the sack would not jostle loose. At every rest, they contrived how they might escape. But Roucill's bodyguard was never more than a lance-length away, and they knew that no Roman foot soldier could outride a Gaul.

The camp of the Allobroges was situated within a secluded canyon large enough for three hundred horsemen and their mounts to bivouac and remain generally hidden. A gurgling creek nearby provided water for the horses, while a grove of cypress trees provided firewood and concealment.

Like most of Caesar's auxiliary cavalry, the Allobroges cohort had been deployed far inland, away from the siege, to harass and report on any reinforcements coming to Pompey over land. Typically, an auxiliary cohort was assigned at least one Roman officer to act as an overseer, but the Allobroges were an exception. Either Caesar had a great deal of trust in Roucill and Egu, or he simply did not have enough officers to spare.

The column arrived at the camp just as the sun was setting, as cooking fires were being lit, and horses groomed. They arrived to the cheers of their waiting comrades. The adoration was once again initiated by Egu, who seemed to be Roucill's herald, as well as his cousin.

"*Hail, Roucill!*" shouted the hundreds of horsemen looking up from various states of upkeep or lounging. They exalted their leader with mechanical enthusiasm while their eyes followed the pack animals. Evidently, the entire cohort understood what the mules carried.

Lucius wondered how loyal these men truly were to Caesar. From all appearances, their chief motivation was money – not all that different from the legions. Every army Lucius had ever belonged to had been augmented by a considerable number of auxiliaries. Most had proven invaluable in battle. But he was not sure he wanted these particular auxiliaries covering his flank.

How the tables had turned! he thought. It was the Roman way to divide and conquer, pit one enemy tribe against another, inflame age-old grievances, ally with one, and defeat the other. It was how Rome had conquered again and again. It was how Caesar had subdued Gaul. But now, the Romans were divided, and the barbarians, like these Allobroges, were helping one faction against the other.

By the time the column came to a halt, hundreds of Allobroges warriors had dropped what they were doing and crowded around the procession. But the pack animals were immediately escorted away by the knights to a separate grouping of large tents – obviously, the tents of the nobles. This drew a general murmur from the gathering that quickly blossomed into an uproar.

Roucill raised his hands to silence them.

"Wait, my brothers!" he pleaded. "Yes, our friend Caesar has been true to his word. He has finally sent us this long-overdue payment. But we cannot distribute the silver fairly without first counting it."

The crowd settled down somewhat, but Lucius was surprised to see how many still brazenly voiced their disappointment. In his experience, the Gallic nobility held immense authority over the commoners, with the power to order entire families killed for the slightest infraction. But that did not appear to be the case here. Despite Roucill's confident and composed manner, the assembled soldiers were a hair's breadth away from becoming a riotous mob.

"We must account for every denarius, my brothers," Roucill continued. "We must make certain it is all there. In the morning, under the light of dawn, and under the scrutiny of your own eyes, we shall tally the fortune. Each man shall be given his due." Upon receiving more glares than smiles, he assumed a more amiable tone. "Months ago, when we left our homeland to join Caesar in his war, I told you every man would come back with more silver than he could earn in a lifetime. You have made good on your promise, my sword brethren, and so have I. You have been my loyal companions across many thousands of leagues. You have followed me to foreign lands. You have fought for Caesar and the Romans. Now, your reward awaits you! Just one night more, and you shall have it! Every one of you will be rich, just as I vowed!"

The crowd was clearly not pleased with the delay. Still, the cooler heads among them prevailed. The assemblage grudgingly dispersed, resigned to wait another day.

The Allobroges settled around the whipping campfires for a long night of feasting on roasted pheasant and rabbit stew. They imbibed copiously, spoke loudly, laughed heartily, and exhausted bodily gasses freely from both ends. Fresh casks of wine continued to appear, as if out of nowhere, and soon the whole lot was too drunk to care about anything. A few of the warriors cast dubious stares at Lucius and Strabo. But, otherwise, the common horsemen seemed uninterested in the Romans.

Lucius and Strabo were directed to take their supper with the nobles who sat around a fire apart from the others. Roucill was overly accommodating, speaking in Latin as he told jests, recounted old campaigns, and refilled their cups time and time again. Egu, on the other hand, was not so hospitable. He sat dark and brooding, never smiling and seldom speaking.

The other knights, whom Roucill referred to as his *oathsworn* – the warrior sons of prominent Allobroges families – clearly disliked dining with the Romans but seemed to grudgingly accept the situation. They exhibited great obeisance for their leaders, though it appeared more out of obligation than admiration. It was clear that, while they followed Roucill, they feared Egu. The prince was the intelligent one, his cousin the enforcer.

The other nobles spoke only in Gallic. Still, Lucius deciphered enough to understand that the sacks had been placed in Egu's tent with a heavily armed guard of *oathsworn* to watch over it. From all indications, the false coins had not yet been discovered.

This was confirmed later when Roucill leaned in toward Strabo and Lucius. He spoke in a hushed voice that the others might not hear.

"I suppose you know how much silver you brought me?"

Strabo nodded. "The agreed-upon amount, my lord."

The Allobroges prince smiled at this answer. "Well, then, tomorrow, when you go back to Caesar, you may tell him that Roucill of the Allobroges keeps his word as well. My horsemen will continue our patrols and punish his enemies wherever we find them. Tell him that. Caesar will like that, eh?"

"He will indeed, my lord," Strabo replied, glancing uncertainly at Lucius after Roucill had turned away.

At one point in the evening, Strabo nudged Lucius to direct his attention toward a particularly boisterous group of horsemen. The intoxicated warriors were amusing themselves by throwing scraps of food and discarded bones at three large objects hanging in the trees above them. Lucius had not noticed the objects before. In the flickering light of the fires, he had to stare long and hard before he shockingly realized they were men – or had once been men. The three unfortunates no longer bore any resemblance to humankind. They had been transformed into gruesome monsters, likenesses that dwelt only within the darkest nightmares. Stripped naked, they had been suspended several feet in the air, tied by hand and foot, as one might string up the carcass of a deer to drain it. Their faces were bruised and swollen, their eyes gouged out, their teeth and tongues missing, their battered bodies streaked with countless lacerations. There was no telling over how many days they had suffered, yet, remarkably, they lived. One even cried out feebly for merciful death to come.

Lucius was hardened to the gore of battle, he had seen many horrendous things, many brutal killings, but even he had to pause at the sight of these wretches.

"Ah, I see you are admiring our prisoners," Roucill said with delight. "Egu's handiwork."

"It is the way we deal with all enemies of Caesar, eh?" Egu said, unable to hold back a yellow-toothed grin, as if proud of the grisly trophies.

"Who are they?" Lucius asked tepidly, suspecting that

these pathetic creatures might be Pompey's men – in other words, fellow Romans.

"Who are they?" Roucill said with a contemplative smile, evidently detecting the centurions' disapproval. "They are dirty Parthenians, those vagrants Caesar crushed before the siege. Some are still roaming about the country, looking for food. Bah! The pathetic imps! They should have the courtesy to crawl off into a hole and die. These fools were caught trying to steal my grain."

Egu frowned at his cousin's answer but said nothing more. It had clearly been a lie, quickly contrived to not run afoul of his guests. Lucius decided it was best not to challenge Roucill on the claim. If the false coins were discovered before he and Strabo could slip away, it would very likely be them hanging from the trees tomorrow.

Later in the evening, when all the Allobroges were wildly drunk, Roucill called in the watchmen that they might participate in the merriment, too – a reckless thing to do in enemy country. But then, Lucius concluded, the watchmen were of little value considering the raucous celebration that could be heard for miles around.

Roucill then gave another order, and a dozen captive women were brought out and given to the inebriated warriors. The women were Greeks by the look of them. They screamed as their clothes were ripped from their bodies, revealing pale curves in the moonlight. They were lifted bodily and passed around the throng before each was enveloped by a gang of barbarians.

Through the cries and the screams, Egu laughed out loud, the awkward, deviant laugh of a degenerate mind. Roucill simply smiled, as a parent might find amusement in the folly of children. But there was something else in the face of the Allobroges prince, something behind the smile Lucius had not noticed before. He seemed deep in thought, his mind burdened as if on the brink of some weighty decision.

It was at that moment that Lucius suddenly understood.

He understood now why the watchmen had been called in, and he knew the true reason the silver had been kept apart from the ordinary warriors.

And he knew what Roucill and Egu were up to.

VIII

The young Allobroges warrior Cudi yawned as he struggled to keep his eyes open. His head bobbed again, but he quickly shook himself awake. Looking up, he was reassured by the sight of the two sleeping figures in the darkness twenty paces away. The Romans were still there, prostrate and bundled under their cloaks. They had not stirred. They had not even turned over. They slept as soundly as if they were within the perimeter of their own camp.

The overconfident pricks.

Cudi sat on the ground with his back against a tree. His sword was stuck in the ground within easy reach should he need to use it. A few paces away, his watch companion Samo also sat propped against a tree. Samo looked back at him, embarrassment on his moonlit face. Cudi had caught him napping.

They were both tired. How many hours before dawn? Two, maybe three?

It was their job to ensure the Roman guests did not try to slip away in the night, a job they had been given since they were the youngest of the *oathsworn*. Back at the tents, the other *oathsworn* made quiet but hasty preparations while the rest of the cohort slept.

This foray into Greece was Cudi's first campaign, his first time riding with Lord Roucill. And now, after many disappointing months attached to Caesar's army, raiding scrapheap villages up and down the coast for little plunder, it looked like this campaign was finally going to be profitable, after all.

All was going according to Lord Roucill's plan. There would be no interference from the three hundred common horsemen, who now lay passed out in pools of their own urine and vomit, having drunk themselves insensible. Aside from a loud chorus of snoring that rose above the buzz of the night insects, their section of the camp was silent.

Cudi looked at the Romans again. Still there. Still rolled up in their cloaks. Still sound asleep.

The two centurions had been directed to bed down apart from the rest of the camp. Roucill had explained that their presence offended some of the other warriors. The Latin fools had bought it, of course. They were too stupid to guess the real reason. They had no idea the fate that awaited them.

And they deserved it, Cudi concluded. All Latins deserved death for the thousands of crimes their kind had committed in Gaul.

Tomorrow morning, the horsemen would have their fun with these Romans. The two Latins would feel the outrage of the Allobroges. It would not be over quickly.

Cudi chuckled to himself as he gazed at the sleeping figures. *Have a pleasant rest, fools. You will never have another.*

Then, Cudi noticed something odd about the

slumbering figures. They appeared to have shifted. Obviously, they had rolled over in their sleep. But what was strange was the size of the lumps beneath the cloaks. They looked smaller.

Was his drowsiness playing tricks with his head?

Cudi sighed. *Best to be sure.*

Tugging his sword from the ground, he got to his feet. But before he took one step toward the sleeping figures, a commotion stirred in the distance. A hundred yards away, among the tents of the *oathsworn*, something was happening. Shadows argued in hushed voices. It was impossible to discern what was being said. Still, Cudi picked out the distinct voices of Roucill and Egu above the others. Heated words were being exchanged between them. Something was clearly wrong.

Cudi had lost count of how many times the two princes had argued in the past months. They had come to blows more than once before Roucill could rein in Egu's short temper. But it appeared there was more to this ruckus than the usual squabbling between the two kinsmen.

As Cudi watched, two dozen figures emerged from the cluster of tents bearing torches. Firelight glinted off drawn steel. The *oathsworn* were marching swiftly and with a purpose. And they were headed this way.

"Looks like the plan has changed, Samo," Cudi whispered to his fellow watchman. "Looks like Lord Roucill intends to deal with these Romans here and now."

Receiving no answer from his companion, Cudi glanced over to discover Samo with a bowed head, chin on chest, apparently sound asleep.

"Wake up, Samo!" Cudi knelt and shook him urgently. "You don't want Lord Egu to find you like this!"

But Samo did not stir. Cudi's fingers touched something warm and slick on the man's mail shirt. He gasped when

Samo's head rolled to one side with no resistance. The moonlight revealed a large, glistening wound across his neck.

Samo was dead.

Another glance at the Romans sleeping beneath their cloaks, and Cudi quickly put it all together. He realized at that moment that there were no Romans beneath those cloaks. The Latins had somehow managed to slip out unseen, leaving behind mounds of grass, fallen branches, or some other mediocre replacement for their broad-shouldered forms. Cudi understood, too, that the Romans had silently cut Samo's throat while Cudi had been distracted by the disturbance at the tents.

And Cudi understood that he would die next.

This comprehension came to him a moment before he could shout the alarm, a moment before the two feet of shimmering steel came out of the night. The point of the gladius drove through Cudi's neck, severing arteries, throat, windpipe, and nearly decapitating him.

His lifeless body fell beside that of his dead comrade.

IX

Lucius wiped his blade onto his victim's tunic. The body of the young guard still spasmed on the ground, his mail armor clinking like a bell as if to beckon the torch-bearing figures coming from the nobles' tents.

Roucill and his *oathsworn* would be here in moments.

"Do you think they inspected the sacks?" Strabo whispered nearby, his own blade still dripping from dispatching the other watchman.

"They are not coming with swords drawn to wish us goodnight," Lucius replied wryly. He pointed to the corral near the tents of the common horsemen. "To the horses! Move quickly! It's our only chance!"

The pair made a mad dash into the darkness, leaving their helmets and cloaks behind in hopes of throwing off the Gallic knights. They scrambled low to the ground, sprinting from one dark depression to another until they reached the corral.

The Gauls were expert horsemen and trainers. They

relied on this exceptional training rather than extensive restraints to keep their mounts in line. Thus, their corrals consisted of nothing more than a series of rope barriers drawn taut between trees.

There were upwards of three hundred war steeds hemmed into this corral, and as many harnesses draped over the lines.

"Grab a bridle!" Lucius said. "Can you ride?"

Strabo nodded skeptically. "Not well enough to outride men born in the saddle."

"You won't have to. Let's move!"

The mass of horses protested little as the centurions ducked under the ropes and filed in among them. Once in the center of the herd, and sufficiently hidden from anyone outside the corral, they set about picking two mounts. This proved more of a challenge than Lucius had anticipated. The Gallic animals were obstinate with the strange men whose scents and manners were unlike that of their masters. Though somewhat skilled at riding and caring for horses, Lucius still struggled to find one cooperative enough to yoke. Strabo fared no better.

Through the gaps in the herd, Lucius saw two dozen torches approaching the corral. The Gauls spoke in hushed voices as they fanned out in pairs to envelop the perimeter. Apparently, they had discovered the dead guards and had correctly deduced the Romans' next move. The mail shirts of the *oathsworn* glittered dully in the firelight.

"They're onto us," Strabo said with urgency as he struggled to keep his bridled mount from moving. "But why haven't they sounded the alarm? They could summon a hundred warriors here at the snap of their fingers."

Lucius suspected he knew the reason, but before he could share his conclusion with Strabo, the voice of Roucill intoned out of the night.

"We know you are in there, Romans," the Gallic prince called. "You cannot escape."

Lucius and Strabo said nothing. The beasts bumping into them on all sides were becoming agitated from the ring of torches. The two centurions did their best to remain out of sight.

"Come out," Roucill said. "There is nowhere to go."

"Come out or we flay you alive!" It was Egu's voice this time, in his much more rudimentary Latin .

A hushed reprimand from Roucill silenced him.

After a long pause, Roucill spoke again. "You have been very ill-mannered guests, my Roman friends. We took you in, protected you, fed you from our own table. And how do you repay our generosity? You try to deceive us with bits of clay." He paused as if waiting for a response before continuing. "And then you killed poor Cudi and Samo. I expect more from Caesar's soldiers. I expect more from those I have embraced as friends."

The Allobroges prince was clearly attempting to maintain a calm and confident air. Still, Lucius detected a tinge of anxiety in his voice. It was highly likely the false coins had only just been discovered. That would explain the earlier commotion in the nobles' tents.

"Why do they wait?" Strabo said in a hushed whisper. "There are more than twenty of them. Why do they not rush us?"

Lucius grinned. "Because they fear what we are about to do."

"And what are we about to do?"

"When I give the word, mount up and follow me. Stay close and ride like bloody Neptune with his arse on fire."

Before Strabo could inquire any further, Roucill's voice called out again.

"I do not wish any harm upon you, Romans. "Nor do I

wish to lose any of my warriors flushing you out. Come, give yourselves up, and I swear before the gods you shall not be —"

"Now!" Lucius exclaimed, while the Gaul was still speaking.

Using the nearby horses for leverage, Lucius and Strabo quickly vaulted onto the bare backs of their resisting mounts. The *oathsworn* spied them and sang out, but Lucius did not hesitate. He urged his mount forward through the multitude of animals. Strabo steered his own horse to follow. The other beasts whinnied in protest, some rearing, some kicking. Lucius drove through the frenzied mass toward one side of the corral, reins in one hand, gladius in the other.

Seeing what was about to happen, Roucill shouted desperately at his men to stop the Romans by any means, but none of them had bows or throwing weapons.

A few scooping swipes of Lucius's gladius made short work of the rope barrier. He cut away the mainstays on one side of the corral, opening an escape for the aggravated herd. He then used his *amentum* like a whip to further provoke the animals. Strabo tried to do the same with his open hand, and nearly slipped off his horse into the stamping hooves. He settled on shouting with his stentorian voice.

The horses began to dash from the corral, first in small groups, then as one, a mighty stampede, like the release from a flood gate. The two centurions held on as their mounts moved with the throng. Lucius hearkened back to the extensive riding of his youth. Strabo struggled to simply remain on the horse's back.

A horn sounded somewhere. The warriors awoke across the camp in a confused panic. Freed horses ran in all directions, ripping out tent pegs, trampling sleeping men, kicking hot coals from the smoldering campfires to set the tall grass ablaze. Soon, the camp was overtaken by mayhem. Men cried out in terror. Some climbed into the trees to escape the stomping hooves. Others fled. A few brave ones attempted to capture the maddened animals.

Once free from the throng, Lucius and Strabo got their mounts under control and steered them toward the black countryside. Lucius could not resist the urge to laugh as they left the burning camp behind them. The shrill voices of Roucill and Egu were distinct above the din, shouting at their warriors to get after the scattering horses. It would be hours, perhaps days, before they could track them all down.

Lucius and Strabo rode hard through the darkness for several miles before finally reining in their tuckered mounts. The noise from the camp had faded to a few muffled cries in the distance.

Lucius grinned. "Those mule turds will be hard-pressed to follow us without horses. I wish I could see the look on Egu's face right now."

Strabo allowed a smile then furrowed his brow. "But, what now?"

Lucius shrugged. "Simple. We go back to Antony and report the mission accomplished. Tell him we delivered the payment, as ordered. *And* we watch our backs."

"How long do you think it will be before the Allobroges report the false coins to Caesar?" Strabo said, clearly not keen on Lucius's idea. "Antony will be sure to point the finger at us. He'll say we stole the silver."

"You're assuming Caesar wasn't complicit in the whole thing from the beginning," Lucius countered. "For all we know, it was *his* idea to trick the Gauls. And I can't say that I blame him. That bastard Roucill and his imp of a cousin are two devious rogues if ever I've seen one." He shook his head. "No, Strabo, my friend. We have two choices, as I see it. Either we return to the army and act like nothing happened, or we desert. And I, for one, have marched too many Juno-forsaken miles to leave the legions empty-handed. When I leave someday, it will be with a pension or a fortune, whichever comes first."

Strabo eyed him with mild disgust. "You are indeed a mercenary. Have you no honor? What about your duty to Rome?"

"We fight for our comrades, my friend – and for ourselves. I'm surprised you haven't learned that after all these years."

"*You* may fight for your friends, but I certainly don't!" Strabo said adamantly. "I fight for Rome and for the sacred honor of my family. And I say we go directly to Caesar with this. We report what happened, just as it happened, and trust in the consul to strip Antony of his rank and shame him."

Lucius shook his head hopelessly. He was about to say something witty, something to further inflame his comrade's temper, when the thunder of hooves suddenly came out of the darkness ahead.

Dark shapes moved faster than he could comprehend. A shaft of moonlight revealed the bowed heads of charging war steeds next to leveled gray poles. The next moment, Lucius felt as though the immortal finger of Jupiter had struck him in the chest. As if shot from a catapult, he was suddenly in the air, tumbling head over heels.

The next thing he knew, he was face down on the ground, struggling to breathe and unable to move.

X

More horses emerged from the night and reined in. The impacts of their hooves vibrated the soft earth against Lucius's face. When his senses returned to him, he saw that he was encircled by several mounted riders bearing lances. No doubt, one of these had unhorsed him. The blow had been delivered with pinpoint accuracy at full gallop. The blunt end of the lance had struck him squarely in the center of the chest. Had it been the business end of the weapon, he would have been skewered like a piece of raw meat. Strabo lay nearby, also gasping for air, having suffered a similar blow.

Lucius then realized that the riders were, in fact, the Allobroges *oathsworn* – all two dozen of them, save the two he and Strabo had slain. As he lay there coughing and wondering just how in the Seven Hills the bastards had managed to capture so many horses and catch up with them so quickly, several dismounted and approached. Four of the *oathsworn* disarmed the stunned centurions, then drew them up onto their knees. Two others held daggers to their throats.

With the cold steel pressed against his skin, Lucius saw Roucill and Egu step forward, the latter sneering, the former looking grave. They were fully dressed in mail and helmets.

"That was no way for guests to behave," Roucill said with a small smile. "You made quite a mess back there. It will be some time before all the horses can be rounded up."

"Horses?" Lucius said defiantly between coughs, his frustration getting the better of him. "That's what you call those mangy Gallic beasts?"

Instantly, the smile left Roucill's face. His sword came up in a flash, the gleaming point a fingernail's breadth away from Lucius's right eye. But after a few deep breaths, the Gallic prince smiled again and lowered the weapon.

"You are right, Roman. Those horses back there are indeed mangy beasts. Whereas these...," he used his sword to point at the surrounding steeds. "These are not."

Through glazed eyes, Lucius realized these were not the poor-looking specimens they had set loose. These were the *oathsworns'* own mounts. Obviously, they had been corralled separate from the others, something Lucius had not anticipated.

The horses were all saddled, harnessed, and weighed down with baggage, preparations that could not have been done in such a short time, which meant they had been done beforehand, which meant Roucill and his *oathsworn* had planned to steal away this very night – just as Lucius had surmised.

Roucill and Egu and the knights had never planned to share the silver with the rest of the cohort. They had intended to make off with it while the common horsemen slept off their drunkenness. Roucill had likely invited Lucius and Strabo to stay the night to serve as a distraction when the horsemen woke up and found their nobles and the money gone. What better way to delay their pursuit than to place two hapless Romans at their mercy on which to vent their anger? By the time the horsemen had tortured Lucius and Strabo to death, Roucill and his *oathsworn* would be far away.

They had probably only discovered the false coins while making their final preparations to leave.

"Now," Roucill said, bringing the sword back up. "Tell me where you have hidden the silver."

"We were ordered to deliver the sacks," Strabo replied. "That is all. If they did not contain what you expected, the treachery was by someone else."

"Someone else? You mean Caesar."

"I have told you all we know."

"Then am I to conclude that my dear friend Caesar has deceived me? I am beyond words." Roucill placed a hand on his chest in a mocking gesture, drawing snickers from the onlooking *oathsworn*. "To think the great consul of Rome would lie to an ally. Who would ever conceive of such a thing? And how foolish of him to do so when he is trapped and outnumbered in a foreign land."

Strabo pursed his lips, clearly frustrated by the ridicule. "I never said Caesar deceived you. As I said before, we do not know where it is. We are simple soldiers. We have done nothing more than carry out our orders."

"I have known many Roman centurions," Roucill said, kneeling before Strabo and studying his face. "Am I looking into the eyes of a simple soldier, or those of a liar? Let me tell you what I think, my Latin friend. I think you and your comrade here have taken the silver. I think you hid it somewhere in these hills before we met you at the pond."

"If you doubt us, then simply take us to Caesar," Strabo challenged. "Let him sort this out. If we are guilty, then he will decide our fates and surely compensate you for your loss."

Lucius grimaced. Clearly, Strabo had not deduced the Gauls' true intentions as he had. Lucius knew Roucill had no intention of ever seeing Caesar again. Telling the truth was the surest way to get their throats cut, and so he must head off Strabo's error.

"It's no use, Strabo," Lucius grunted between coughs. "We must tell them. We must strike a bargain with this Gallic scum."

This drew a confused look from Strabo. "What in Pluto's Realm are you talking –"

"You were saying, Roman?" Roucill interrupted, turning his attention to Lucius.

"You're right, my lord. We hid the silver just as you said."

"That was a very shameful thing to do." Roucill shook his head in mock disappointment. "Very selfish, too. That silver was promised to my men. They are no different from you Latins. They have families to feed."

"Which men?" Lucius asked audaciously.

"What did you say?" The Allobroges prince was clearly surprised by his brazen manner.

"I was wondering which of your men that silver was for – the ones back at the camp, or just these whores' whelps?"

In Lucius's half-dazed state, he did not see the flat of the sword that struck him across the side of the head, knocking him down and making him see stars again. When he was forced back to his knees, he saw that it was Egu who had struck him. Roucill was holding his enraged cousin back, calming him. And Lucius smiled inwardly. He had accomplished what he had intended.

Roucill smiled amicably when he turned back to face them. "If you were to tell me where the silver is, not only would I let you live, I would be willing to give each of you a fair share."

"Let us live?" Lucius said. "You mean like those scarecrows you let that depraved bastard hang up in the trees?"

Egu grunted something animalistic and stepped forward but was stopped by Roucill's outstretched hand.

The smile left Roucill's face. "I am an impatient man, by nature, and my offer has just changed. You will tell me where the silver is. If I believe you, I will let you live. That is all you can hope for at this point."

"We do not –" Strabo began to speak, but Lucius interrupted him.

"We'll take a third for our share, and you'll give us back our weapons and our mounts. Only then will we tell you where to find it."

Roucill gave a mirthless laugh, then continued in a low, ominous voice. "You think yourselves blessed by the gods? Do you think sharpened steel will not flay the flesh from your bones? That you cannot bleed? Oh, you will, my friends. You will bleed. You will know unimaginable pain. You will be deprived of your faces, your manhood, of anything that made you who you were. You will beg for death for what will seem like an eternity, but it will not come. It will not come."

At that moment, one of the *oathsworn* stepped forward.

"Riders approaching, my lord."

Roucill turned his attention away from the Romans and exchanged glances with Egu as three horsemen emerged from the night.

"Lord Roucill!" one of them exclaimed joyfully with a wide grin. "My lord, we thought that was you!"

The three men walked their horses into the circle and saluted their prince. They were common horsemen. They rode bareback and controlled their mounts using crude loops of rope for bridles. All three were shirtless, sweating, and out of breath.

"The whole cohort is scattered about the countryside, sire. These here mares nearly ran us into the ground." The horseman's gaze settled on Lucius and Strabo. "Ah, I see you've caught the scum, sire. The lads will be pleased to hear it."

"You have done well, Lasci," Roucill said with a welcoming smile. "Are there any others with you?"

"Others? Oh, no, my lord. We are certainly the farthest out. The rest of the lads are way behind – " Lasci did not finish. A lance had been thrust between his shoulder blades by the *oathsworn* that had slipped behind him. Before his shocked companions had time to react, they, too, had been run through. The bodies of the three horsemen crashed to the ground just a few feet from Lucius, the gushing black blood shimmering in the moonlight. When the bodies had finished twitching, Lucius met eyes with Roucill.

"So, it is as I had suspected," Lucius said.

At that moment, voices sounded in the distance, the voices of many other horsemen hunting down stray mounts. They were drawing closer.

Roucill and Egu exchanged concerned whispers too low for Lucius to make out. Obviously, they were deciding what they should do. They could not remain here. If they wanted the silver all to themselves, they had to keep the Roman prisoners all to themselves. They still needed Lucius and Strabo alive, and that was encouraging.

When the brief conference was over, Roucill made a quick gesture to the men restraining Lucius and Strabo. The cold steel was removed from Lucius's throat, and that was a welcome relief. But the relief did not last long. The next moment, Lucius felt a sharp blow across the back of his head, something solid, like the hilt of a dagger.

He faded in and out of consciousness as several men cursing in the Gallic tongue lugged his large frame over the back of a horse like a pair of saddlebags. Then they were riding hard and fast, thundering hooves all around him in the darkness, his flailing body absorbing every bounding stride of the horse.

XI

"Wake up, Roman dog!" the voice of Egu snarled. "Talk, or, by Odin, I'll flay you alive!"

A whip cracked, and the biting sting of the lash roused Lucius from his stupor. He was bound to a tree, his arms and legs extended around the trunk in a tight embrace. He had been stripped naked. His tunic and armor were nowhere to be seen. As the pain of the new stripe on his back began to diminish, he realized his face was throbbing from some earlier beating, and one eye was nearly swollen shut.

How long had he been there? Hours? Days?

Somewhere behind him, men conversed in Gallic. He turned his head to the left, straining to look on his captors, but could see only a few. Most were beyond his field of vision. The few he saw he recognized as Roucill's *oathsworn*. They lounged on the ground, chewing on strips of dried goat meat and studying his suffering with enjoyment.

Turning his head to the right, Lucius saw that Strabo

was bound to the tree adjacent to his. Like Lucius, he was stripped bare, his face marred by many bruises.

"Your obstinacy will not serve you." Roucill's voice sounded behind them, his tone laced with poisonous sympathy. "It would be a pity for warriors like you to meet such an ignoble end. Egu will whip you until nothing remains but strips of flesh clinging to bare bones. I have seen him do it. He takes great pleasure in watching his enemies die slowly. It is a deplorable sight, believe me. No way for a warrior to die. It must be humiliating for you. Will you not tell us now where it is? Tell us now, and your suffering will end."

Another dozen lashes were issued, another set of stinging stripes to add to the scars of years past, another interval of unbearable pain which both men endured without uttering a sound. Again, Roucill stayed Egu's hand, and both Gauls retired to a spot several paces away to converse with their warriors in secret. They spoke too rapidly for Lucius's dazed mind to follow, but it was clear there was something of a disagreement as to what to do with the obdurate prisoners.

"Do you still live, Lucius?" Strabo murmured through blood-coated lips. "I feared they had beaten the life out of you."

Lucius turned his throbbing head to look at his companion, and, slowly, his mind began to clear, fragments coming together to form coherent memories. He was able to piece together the agonizing events of that morning.

He remembered a jostling night ride of many miles over hills and fields, then the black waters of a putrid marsh. Dancing hooves had splashed the tainted murk onto his face, constantly reviving him. He remembered traversing deep spots, where his head had been submerged nearly to the point of drowning, much to his captors' amusement.

Finally, they had reached this place, a small patch of dry land, a small island in the vast swamp. And here, the Gauls had interrogated them, from the gray light of dawn to the noonday sun, delving out so many lashes that Lucius had lost count.

"Have you told them anything?" Lucius mumbled.

"What is there to tell?" Strabo replied. "You led us down this path, not I."

"We have to think of something. Lie to them. Lead them on an empty chase to buy ourselves more time. Anything."

Strabo shook his head weakly. "I doubt they will believe anything we tell them at this point."

Lucius strained to look behind him, but it was no use. "Do you know how many there are?"

Strabo shook his head. "As far as I can tell, no more than a score. That bastard Roucill and his cousin, and a handful of knights and household warriors. They have deserted their cohort. That much is clear."

"The buggers planned to keep the money for themselves all along." Lucius sighed. "Well, at least we don't have the others to contend with."

Strabo raised an eyebrow. "It doesn't matter how many there are, comrade. Unless you and I come up with thirty thousand *denarii* while strapped to these trees, they will butcher us. This is the payment we get for so many years of service." Strabo spat out a mixture of blood and saliva, then gazed meditatively into the misty swamp . *"Over the iron shield the spiders weave their threads,"* he quoted. *"Rust bites the pointed spear and double-edged sword. No more is heard the trumpet's brazen roar. Sweet sleep is banished from our eyes no more."*

"I did not count you a poet." Lucius forced his swollen lips into a smile.

"Did you ever ponder, Lucius, what you should do, were

you not a soldier?"

Lucius shook his head, though he thought of it quite often.

"I have ever strived to be worthy of my family's legacy," Strabo continued. "I once dreamed my name would be spoken in the same breath as that of my famous ancestor Rufius. Now I find myself asking what he would do were he in this army, under these generals." Strabo gritted his teeth as if reluctant to continue. "I *know* what he would do. And I know what I must do. You are my witness, Lucius. Here and now, I curse Antony for the rogue and lying scoundrel he is. I curse Caesar, too, for a traitor. And I vow never to march in their service again."

Lucius stared at Strabo for a long moment. The oath had taken him by surprise. Lucius had assessed Strabo as one possessed with an unassailable sense of duty and a steadfast devotion to his legion. But now, like the cracks in a city wall when seen up close, Lucius saw holes in Strabo's exterior, long-simmering doubts that were beginning to boil over.

"Do you not believe that a bit excessive?" Lucius said. "I'll wager Caesar had no hand in this. Antony is to blame, and that snot-nosed tribune of his. Let us save our wrath for them."

"I have said it, comrade. I tell you plainly, should I somehow survive this, I shall never serve Caesar again. By Mars – and before you – I swear it."

"Turning your back on Caesar means turning your back on your legion," Lucius reminded him.

Strabo appeared to consider the significance of that for a moment before finally responding. "Aye."

None of it mattered, anyway. Lucius thought. The Gauls would surely kill them. Their bodies would be left to rot in this swamp and would never be found. Rumors and speculation would abound back at camp about the mystery of the missing centurions Strabo and Domitius, who marched off into the wilderness, never to be heard from again.

The conversation among the Gauls turned into a heated debate now. Many curses were uttered by Egu. From what Lucius could gather, Egu wished to cut up the prisoners right now and flee Epirus before the other horsemen came looking for them. Roucill, on the other hand, was more interested in finding the missing silver. The *oathsworn* offered little input, aside from grunts of assent or dissent. This back and forth continued for some time.

"Strabo," Lucius said wearily. "There's something I've meant to ask you."

"What is it, comrade?"

"Just how in Pluto's Realm did you manage to cheat Antony at dice?"

Strabo looked back at him incredulously. "You wish to know that, at a time like this?"

Lucius forced a smile. "It would give me great pleasure. Have you anything more pressing to do?"

Strabo shrugged then adjusted his arms as best he could to a less painful position. "It was nearly three years ago, in Gaul, just after the victory over Commius. The Ninth had just been paid – a farthing of what was owed us - but paid, nonetheless. With the men's spirits running high, and much drinking and caroling about, Antony showed up with fresh casks of wine and a challenge for any man who could best him at dice. He came under the guise of raising morale, but he was only there to deprive a few inebriated soldiers of their newly acquired *denarii*.

"The game started out innocently enough. Many a soldier came, and many lost every last *sesterce* to Antony's rolls. This went on throughout the evening, with Antony always coming out on top. After each round, his winnings were quickly collected by his personal slave and promptly locked away in a small chest. Over the hours, he amassed a small fortune.

"I was, perhaps, the only man there that night who remained sober enough to be suspicious of Antony's incredible luck. I began to watch his every move, and soon discovered his run of good fortune was of his own making. On the occasion he began to lose, one of his adjutants would raise a cup and propose a good-natured salute to the general's opponent. This salute was resoundingly answered by the onlooking mob. In every match, that moment marked a turn in fortune for Antony. He would start to win again. I realized the boisterous salute was intended to distract the inebriated mob while Antony's slave slipped something to him in the shadows. From that point on, Antony would win roll after roll until his stupefied victim was cleaned out. Antony was nothing more than a swindler, plain and simple.

"As I watched Antony continue to steal money from my mates, the whole thing began to grate on me. I thought of all the brave lads that had died assaulting one particular oppidum of the Treveri, where the works were insurmountable, and Antony had been well advised of it. A burning rage overtook me, and I decided to act.

"Spying a pair of unused dice on an upturned cask, along with a half-drained flagon of wine, a plan formulated in my mind, as if Mars himself had placed it there. I pocketed the dice, grabbed up the sloshing flagon, and made my way through the crowd pretending to be wobbly of knee and hopelessly drunk. Upon passing by Antony's slave, I purposely tripped and stumbled into him, knocking him on his arse. I fell on top of him, emptying the contents of the flagon into his eyes as I fell. In the few moments we were tangled on the ground, my hand rummaged inside his cloak, found the pocket with the loaded dice, and exchanged my dice for his.

"This done, I rolled off the disoriented slave, him none the wiser. I apologized profusely to Antony for the disruption. He graciously accepted my apology, offering me a fresh cup and a seat in the next game. This I had expected, for Antony no doubt believed me drunk beyond my wits, an easy victim. I went along, playing the part of the naïve fool, accepting the drink and the challenge much to the crowd's merriment.

"The first rolls favored us equally. We exchanged the same set of coins between us four or five times, neither of us making any appreciable gains. Finally, the moment came when Antony planned to turn the tables on me. As before, the tribune raised his cup and issued a good-natured salute to my health. Like everyone else, I tipped back my cup, but watched out of the corner of my eye as the slave leaned in toward Antony and made the exchange. Expecting the odds to now turn in his favor, Antony's wagers increased in value and brashness. But the odds did not change this time. The dice were well-balanced, leaving it to the gods to decide the winner, and they chose me. Fortune favored me in the subsequent rolls. I won more often than he, and my winnings began to grow considerably. He was forced to dig into his reserves. Finally, after I had taken back nearly a third of what he had stolen, Antony conceded defeat to the resounding cheers of my comrades. He abruptly resigned from the game, congratulating me and calling me a clever gamester. Outwardly, he accepted his losses in good sport, but there was a brief instant when our eyes met that I saw a flash of utter hatred there. He knew I had been up to something and that I had purposefully spoiled his game.

"I retired to my tent that night with a certain degree of

satisfaction that I had done justice for my fallen comrades, but the victory was short-lived. In the next days, it became apparent that I was a marked man, that Antony had it out for me. My century was placed at the forefront of every battle and given every dangerous task. If there was a hazardous ravine to scout or a suspected enemy ambush that needed flushing out, I was invariably called upon. Since then, I have counted no less than eleven suspicious circumstances in which I might have been killed by accident. This mission makes an even dozen." Strabo paused, then smiled reminiscently. "Still, I would do it all over again. To see the look on Antony's face that night, to see him break out in a cold sweat as his winnings dwindled away,...well, I'd trade every medallion on my chest to live that moment again."

After Strabo's tale, Lucius could not help but throw back his head in laughter. He laughed a deep, hysterical belly laugh that sent shooting pains through his outstretched limbs but felt good at the same time. The laughter became contagious, and Strabo joined in. Their combined maniacal furor stirred a flock of birds from the boughs above.

But their merriment was swiftly cut short. Egu's leather cord sang through the air, snapping twice and adding yet another pair of crimson stripes to their muscled backs and buttocks.

"Quiet, Roman curs!" he snarled. He was suddenly just behind them again. "Laugh again, and I'll carve out your lungs!"

XII

"**M**y patience grows thin, Romans," Roucill said. He moved to a spot where he could squat and face them both. "I have a mind to let Egu do what he wishes with you. Did you know he hates all Romans? His wife and daughters were raped and murdered by a tribe Caesar chose to ally with, a tribe that also happened to be our ancient enemy. Like fools, you Romans bumble into age-old conflicts you do not understand. You try to force your ways onto cultures that existed when Rome was but a dung heap."

The whip cracked twice more, and both centurions did their best not to wince from the pain.

Roucill shook his head in disappointment. "If you persist in this obstinacy, I will have no choice but to bend to my cousin's wishes, and you do not want that, I assure you. Egu is not like other men. Ever since we were boys, he has been obsessed with pain and torture. He hungers only for the torment of his enemies. Your blood will placate him more than you know — certainly, more than the silver you stole."

A blade slipped from its scabbard somewhere behind Lucius, not just one, but many blades. He imagined the wild-eyed Egu and several of the *oathsworn* standing just a few paces behind him, preparing to inflict the aforementioned torment. But then, Lucius saw alarm on Roucill's face and noticed that he, too, had moved one hand to the hilt of his sword. The Gallic prince turned his attention away from the prisoners to look intently at a bank of dense brush lining one edge of the small island. Beyond the foliage arose the sound of churning water and the slow clomp of hooves in the mud.

An animal was stepping out of the swamp onto the dry land.

Moments later, a hooded figure emerged on foot leading a mule. The cloak and the slight frame it lay upon were familiar to Lucius, though he had only seen them once before, and then only briefly.

It was Catugna the druid.

"Odin's prick!" Roucill cursed as he visibly let his guard down. "Why did the lookouts not alert us to your coming?"

"I choose when to be seen," Catugna replied petulantly, his voice no more than a whisper but somehow as clear as the cocking of a distant rooster. "And when not to be seen,"

"And just where in the Eight Spokes of Taranis have you been? We've been waiting here for hours!"

Catugna did not appear to have heard the prince. Instead, he stopped and studied the bound Romans. Once again, Lucius felt the glittering eyes deep within the dark hood staring directly at him. The familiar shiver passed up his spine, and time seemed to stop briefly. Perhaps it was the effects of the lash, or the many hits he had taken to the head. Yet again, Lucius could have sworn the druid regarded him with some kind of recognition.

"I asked you a question, druid!" Roucill demanded impatiently.

"And I told you not to harm the Romans!" Catugna hissed bitterly, whirling around in a rustle of tattered robes.

"You forget yourself, wizard," Egu snarled. He stepped forward, extending his blade in a threatening manner. "You forget whom you serve!"

Catugna seemed unfazed by the three feet of sharpened steel leveled at his abdomen. In one swift motion, he threw back his hood, revealing a pair of pale blue eyes that stared up at the warrior as if to bore a hole through his chin. The gaunt, pale face of the wizard was like parchment stretched over a hollow frame. It seemed the face of death itself, as if he had stepped out of the crypt. His head was covered in a frizzed tousle of whitish-gray hair that hung down to his bony shoulders. He appeared to be on the point of emaciation, yet there was something hardy about him. Lucius got the sense that his gaunt frame had once been brawnier than the bare essential muscle it was now. And those eyes – those liquid blue eyes – seemed to hold a power all their own. With them, Catugna appeared to have subdued Egu's mirth. The warrior who had been threatening the druid mere moments before now lowered his blade and took one step back as if in a trance.

Was there something supernatural about it, or was Egu merely hesitant to harm the druid lest a curse be placed on his kinfolk for a thousand generations? Lucius could not accept the former explanation, but the visible change in the normally blood-thirsty warrior could not be denied.

"I serve the spirits of river and earth and wood," Catugna said boldly as if to remind his prince of something he had explained many times before.

Anger flashed across Roucill's face, but he quickly

controlled it. He seemed to consider carefully before speaking again. "We are in a dire position, Catugna. We welcome your counsel, as always. The Romans have not told us where the silver is. Egu is simply encouraging them to –"

"The silver no longer matters," Catugna said succinctly.

"What?" Roucill seemed dumbfounded. "I do not understand. You are the one who said I would need it to buy the loyalty of the chieftains back home. You said it was the only way I could succeed my ailing father as king. You said the prophecies were all favorable. Are you now saying you were wrong?"

"The prophecies always come true, O prince."

"Then how do you explain what has happened?"

A thin smile formed on the druid's dark lips. "Where mortals see a single rope running from end to end, the spirits see the intricacies of the weave, the interlacing fibers, the infinite twists and turns that must work together to reach a necessary end."

Roucill screwed up his face. "Your words baffle me."

"The spirits have ordained a new path for you, lord prince." Catugna pointed to the west, where a cluster of coastal hills rose above the mist as gray shapes. "The riches you desire are to be found there."

"In Dyrrachium?" Roucill said in disbelief.

"We must go there."

"Are you mad? The city is fortified by Pompey's legions."

Catugna smiled patiently. "Do not fear Pompey. He will pay you handsomely for bringing the prisoners to him. You must take them there at once."

"Bah!" Egu interjected, his temporary daze having worn off. "Do you expect us to just ride up to the gates and crave an audience? Surely, they will cut us down before we are close enough to hail them."

"You will be allowed to enter," Catugna affirmed. "You will be taken before Pompey, and you will be rewarded."

"Do not listen to this skeleton!" Egu pleaded, grabbing hold of his cousin. "There are other ways to secure your kingship. Let us carve up these Latins as we used to in the old days. Let them beg their false gods for mercy. Odin will be pleased. He will bless us with a swift journey home."

Roucill removed Egu's hand from his arm. "Catugna has advised my father for many years, cousin. He has never led us astray."

"And I've been by your side since we were boys," Egu retorted. "This druid is a charlatan. When have his prophecies ever truly come to pass? Do you not see how he veils them in words he can twist to his own purpose? He will get us killed, cousin. Pompey is just another deceitful Latin. He is no different from Caesar or any other. If he allows us to enter the city, it will only be to have us garroted for his entertainment."

"Last night, the spirits spoke to me clearer than they have in many moons," Catugna assured the prince. "They revealed to me many things. Your destiny lies with Pompey. He is not your enemy. If you take these Romans to him, he will greet you with open arms. You will help him against Caesar, and he will help you become king of the Allobroges."

Egu laughed heartily. "This wizard can no more foretell the future than he can predict how many turds he's going to make tomorrow."

"Wait!" Catugna hissed, casting a sinister glance at Egu before turning back to Roucill. "There is more you must hear, O prince."

"Go on," Roucill said, waving off the exasperated Egu and gazing at the druid as if entranced.

"This is the defining moment in your journey, Roucill, son of Talos," the druid said, captivating the prince with his intense eyes. "To stand among the great kings of the Allobroges, you must first prove your worthiness. The spirits have decreed it. A crossroad has been placed before you. Choose wisely, and success and power will be yours. Choose poorly, and the precise opposite awaits."

"Meaning?"

"Misery and death."

Roucill seemed to turn white at the words, but Egu only laughed again. "Absurd! Are you going to let this wraith scare you again into doing his will, cousin? Let me give you a true prophecy." Egu then strode over to Lucius and placed the point of his sword against Lucius's genitals. "I predict this one will die a eunuch. Do you wish to see my prophecy fulfilled? Give me the word, my prince, and my blade will make him squirm!"

Lucius felt the cold steel press firmly against his crotch, felt the putrid breath of the snarling Gaul against his neck. The pressure of the blade increased almost to the point of drawing blood. He did not wish to give the bastard the satisfaction of seeing him flinch, but the pain was too intense. Egu let out a wicked laugh.

The indecisive Roucill looked back and forth between Catugna, who seemed serenely indifferent, and Egu, who was practically salivating at the prospect of slaughtering the prisoners. But, before the prince could make up his mind, one of the *oathsworn* galloped out of the swamp onto the dry land and reined in his mount. It was one of the lookouts.

"My prince!" he said, agitatedly pointing behind him. "The cohort!"

"What of them, Dedrick?" Roucill demanded.

"They are coming, sire!"

"How many?"

"All of them, my lord."

"All?" Roucill said incredulously. "You mean the entire cohort has pursued us here?"

"It appears so, my lord. We saw them crest the hills to the east and enter the marsh. They are heading this way, riding hard."

As if to confirm the report, splashing hooves were suddenly audible above the buzz of the insects. The whinny of horses being pushed to their limits sounded in the distance. There were hundreds of them.

Shock and fear were visible on Roucill's face as confusion overcame him.

"But how could they have followed us so quickly?" Egu voiced what his cousin was probably thinking. "They are simple artisans and farmers. They have no smarts among them, no leaders."

Roucill's face was suddenly fixed in a scowl. He glanced suspiciously around the assembled warriors. "One of you has betrayed me!" he snarled. "One of you, or several of you." He pointed a trembling finger at the suddenly nervous *oathsworn*. "I will find you out if Egu must torture every last one of you! Wherever the treachery lies, I will uncover it! Do you hear? I will find you and feed your entrails to the dogs!"

Lucius let out a sigh of relief as the distracted Egu withdrew the cold steel and turned his attention to the warriors. Roucill and Egu strode from one to the next, staring each one down with an accusing glare. It was at that moment that Lucius noticed Catugna had withdrawn back inside his hood. He watched in silence as panic and paranoia overcame the prince. Oddly, Lucius sensed that the druid was smiling inside that dark cowl, that he found a sinister delight in seeing his lord so terrified.

"I suggest you address this some other time, my lord,"

Catugna said finally. "The cohort is fast approaching. We must ride for Dyrrachium. We have no choice now. If you wish to live, we must go."

Roucill shot a wild glance at the druid as if he might order his head lopped off in the next moment. But, after a few deep breaths, he seemed to digest the wisdom of the advice.

"Of course. You are right, Catugna. We must leave at once." Shaking himself back to lucidity, Roucill gestured at Lucius and Strabo. "Egu, cut them down. Get them ready to ride."

XIII

Dyrrachium

The afternoon sun blazed over the battlements of Dyrrachium. The brick embrasures were as hot as ovens. The weapons of the idling watchmen were like branding irons to the touch. The breeze wafting in off the bay offered little comfort. At this time of day, the only relief was afforded by a narrow angle of shade cast by the gate tower. But the watchmen did not dare venture near it today. The shade was occupied by a grim-looking, middle-aged Roman general who tapped his foot impatiently as he squinted beyond the wall.

The general wore a flowing black cape over a gleaming bronze cuirass that matched the tinsel of gray in his thinning brown hair. His face was clean-shaven, tanned, weathered, with a severe jawline that gave him something of a permanent scowl.

Every soldier on the wall, whether Roman or auxiliary,

knew to keep clear of this senior officer who had a reputation for venting his anger on the nearest accessible victim. They were wise to do so. Because, on this particular day, General Titus Labienus, chief deputy and master advisor to Pompey, was in a foul mood. He was, in fact, seething with resentment.

When Labienus had taken the boat across from the camp earlier that morning, he had not expected to spend his day standing on the wall. He had come to Dyrrachium for another purpose entirely, to attend an important meeting of a very private nature – a meeting that was not official army business. Labienus had hoped to keep his brief excursion a secret and be back at camp by midday, before Pompey ever got wind of it. But, somehow, the bloody army commander had found out beforehand. No sooner had Labienus stepped onto the wharf that morning than he was met by a messenger with a note written by Pompey himself.

My Dear Titus, the message had started. *Since you are going into town today, there is something of great importance I would like you to do...,*

It had been Pompey's not so subtle way of informing Labienus that he was being watched, *always*. And so, Labienus had put his other affairs aside for the moment and followed Pompey's instructions. And that was why, for the last several hours, he had been on the wall like a common soldier on guard duty, fuming over his missed appointment.

He had a right to be offended. He was, after all, the most senior general in the *Optimates* army, second only to the self-proclaimed great man himself. Though most of the time, his position was titular in nature. Pompeius *Bloody* Magnus, the exalted conqueror of Asia and the bloody commander of all the *Optimates* forces in bloody Greece, did not take advice from bloody anyone, not even his chief deputy. And that irritated Labienus to no end.

He sighed as he stared out at the camp across the bay. He would not have to put up with Pompey for much longer. That assurance, at least, made the current arrangements somewhat more palatable.

From the shade of the tower, Labienus scanned his surroundings. The wall upon which he stood ran along the east side of Dyrrachium, facing the mainland. It was the only wall needed since the town's other sides were protected by natural barriers.

Dyrrachium stood on the southwestern tip of a small island, shaped like an elongated triangle. It measured a mere five miles in length from the narrow apex at the north to the broader base at the south. A spine of hills ran up the west side of the triangle, eroded into chalky, impassable cliffs by the incessant surges of the Adriatic. The wide beach on the southern coast – the base of the triangle, which formed a natural bay with the mainland – presented a danger only from an enemy that controlled the sea, which Caesar did not. Thus, the only viable direction from which Caesar could attack, should he be so foolish, was from the east. There, a generally barren plain stretched out beyond the wall for nearly a mile until it met a marsh that separated the island from the mainland. The marsh was extensive and deep, making it impassable by wheeled vehicles and infantry. The only traversable connection between the island and the mainland was a single, narrow isthmus at the southeastern tip of the triangle. Over this causeway ran the final leg of the *Via Egnatia*, the thousand-mile-long road connecting the great cities of Asia to the trading port at Dyrrachium.

Labienus gazed out to the east, his eyes following the angled legs of the *Via Egnatia*. The road ran across the land bridge, then inland for several miles before turning abruptly southeast and disappearing behind a small chain of coastal hills. The hills were shrouded in a thin veil of smoke continually nourished by a thousand cooking fires. The opposing armies were encamped there. From this distance, Pompey's outer works were just visible as a series of jointed stripes snaking along the tops of the hills. Another set of stripes, nearly parallel to Pompey's but several hundred yards farther inland, marked the lines of Caesar's army. Caesar's lines ran all the way to the shore, effectively cutting off the land route between Pompey's camp and Dyrrachium.

The fact that all communication between the camp and the town had to be done by boat was only a minor inconvenience, but it greatly annoyed Labienus. It annoyed him because it did not have to be so. The notion that Caesar, with inferior numbers, had managed to squeeze Pompey's army into a semi-circle only a few miles wide, with its back against the sea, infuriated Labienus. His anger was not directed at the enemy but at Pompey, who was apparently complacent about leaving things as they were.

Labienus had argued for an all-out attack, had encouraged Pompey to trust in their superior numbers to carry the day, had begged that they act at once before Caesar managed to pull another miracle out of his arse and slip away. But Pompey had rejected his proposals outright. The so-called great general intended to wait until Caesar's army was so depleted by hunger, disease, and desertion that victory would be assured. It was all part of Pompey's master plan.

Caesar must be lured into believing he was meeting with a measure of success, Pompey had explained. Give Caesar just enough rope to hang himself. The longer his army remained here, the more it would wither away. He would find little sustenance from the countryside. And Pompey's army would continue to be supplied by the sea, firmly controlled by the *Optimates* fleet.

And so, Pompey would not attack. He would wait, and his army would continue to dig in. And Labienus had no choice but to go along with the foolery.

Pompey had chosen to place his camp a few miles down the coast from Dyrrachium, on an elevated spot well-suited to accommodate his 48,000 troops. This position he had fortified to near impregnability. The line of earthworks and redoubts started on the shore some three miles south of the causeway. From there, it cut a fourteen-mile-long semi-circular path inland, along the hilltops, before curling back toward the sea. Its unfinished end would, very soon, anchor at a spot six miles down the coast from the northern anchor.

Not wishing to yield Dyrrachium and its valued trading port to the enemy, Pompey had taken care to garrison the town with several cohorts. But this attempt at maintaining some semblance of trade normalcy had failed.

Labienus glanced over his shoulder at the tiled roofs of the sprawling seaport town, its apartments and houses, forum and magistrate offices, merchant stalls, and extensive docks. An unnatural silence hung over the place.

Typically, the wharf would be bustling with trade ships filling and emptying their holds. Creeping squares of white canvas would speckle the bay, stretching off to the horizon. Caravans would crawl along the *Via Egnatia* as far as the eye could see, like tiny beads on a string. The bazaar would be alive with trade, a commotion of braying animals, swirling dust, and bartering traders. The exasperated tinkers running the stalls would struggle to restock the wares on their shelves to keep up with the demand.

Now, aside from a handful of anchored ships and a few

small boats pulling between the city and the camp, the harbor was empty. With two giant armies encamped nearby, the wiser merchant captains had chosen to avoid the port entirely.

Likewise, no traffic flowed along the *Via Egnatia*. The traders were absent from the streets. Dyrrachium's many merchants, the guilds of jewelers, goldsmiths, and silversmiths, struggled to sell their wares at unprofitable prices to a transient soldiery more interested in whoring and drinking. The formerly affluent trading hub had fallen into a base existence, where only the vile harlot master and seedy fortune teller thrived.

But the dearth of trade was not the main problem plaguing Dyrrachium at the moment.

"No more for you!" a voice barked farther down the battlement, breaking Labienus from his contemplation.

An irate centurion was jerking a sloshing waterskin away from one of the archers. The bowman was a Thessalonian auxiliary. He proclaimed his innocence in Greek, but the excessive dribble on his beard and tunic clearly displayed that he had been drinking copiously.

"You know the rules, you Greek cocksucker!" the centurion snarled. "A quarter cup each! No more!"

The centurion then used his baton to administer several hard blows to the archer's shoulders and back while the others watched in silence. At the same time, a nearby scribe took down the offender's name. The dripping water vessel then continued on its journey, carefully passed down the line from one bowman to the next.

That is one thing you failed to consider, isn't it, my illustrious Lord Pompey? Labienus thought with equal measures of aggravation and gratification. *What good does it do to keep your men well-fed and well-supplied when they're dying of thirst?*

The water shortage was an unanticipated consequence

of Pompey's ridiculous *wait-and-hope* strategy. Caesar controlled the rivers and streams flowing from the inland mountains to the sea, and these he had dammed up or diverted such that Pompey's lines did not receive a single drop.

With an army numbering in the tens of thousands, along with an inordinate number of horses and pack animals, a disaster was in the making. Of course, Pompey did not deserve all the blame. In their infinite wisdom, the senate-in-exile had failed to commission ships to bring water to the army, likely assuming Pompey could dig his own wells. But Pompey's confined camp was so close to the shore that any wells dropped had yielded only saltwater.

And so, instead of using his powerful fleet to bombard Caesar's camp with balls of flaming pitch, Pompey was forced to use the ships to fetch water for the army. The massive *quinqueremes* and *septiremes*, with their hull-crushing rams and boulder-throwing engines, had been reduced to mere water scows. They cruised up and down the coast, continuously seeking out tributaries and streams from which to quench the army's thirst. The temporary remedy was just keeping up with consumption, but it could not go on much longer. The fleet was perpetually at sea, pushing the overtaxed oarsmen to the point of exhaustion and depriving the ships of much-needed dockyard time.

Pompey blamed the dismal situation on the Senate. The Senate blamed Pompey. Privately, Labienus blamed them both. The exiled senate sat in plush accommodations in Thessalonica, enacting laws that would go into effect upon Caesar's defeat. They acted as if the war were already won, and their victorious return to Rome a foregone conclusion. Meanwhile, the army went thirsty.

The shortage of water was affecting morale, both in the camp and in Dyrrachium. A foreboding of doom hung over the town.

The solution was obvious to Labienus. They must attack Caesar at once. But, alas, old Pompey was obstinate. His plan was to wait, and no deviation from that plan would be brooked. Having been told of his own greatness nearly every day of his life, Pompey believed every one of his ideas worthy of inscription. True, the old bastard did have three triumphs to his name, but the last of those had been awarded over twelve years ago. Judging from the present situation, Labienus was beginning to wonder if they had been truly deserved.

Perhaps the slave in Pompey's triumphal chariot had not whispered loud enough. Or maybe those ridiculous elephants had just been too bloody loud for Pompey to hear anything.

Labienus checked the position of the sun.

"What hour is it?" he demanded of the nearby centurion.

"Just past the seventh, sir."

"Mars curse him!" Labienus murmured. "This is a bloody waste of time!"

Wiping the sweat from his brow, Labienus ignored the curious glances from the archers. The Thessalonians idly fingered the strings of their bows like lutes as they waited. They were probably wondering the same thing he was. *Why had they been summoned here upon the wall to stare at an empty expanse of sand for hours on end?*

The longer Labienus waited, the more he was convinced Pompey had diverted him here to ensure he missed his previous appointment. Pompey must have been wise to it. That was the only thing that made sense. It certainly made more sense than the orders in Pompey's message.

The message had instructed Labienus to draw a half-cohort of archers from the city garrison and wait on the wall. For…*what?*…an event that seemed far-fetched, to say the least. Now, after waiting nearly four hours, Labienus felt like a fool.

Taking orders from Pompey was almost as painful as taking orders from the inept Senate-in-exile. But, thank the gods, he would not have to endure it much longer. Another was coming – one whose *auctoritas* eclipsed that of Pompey, one blessed by the gods, who was destined to restore Rome to her former greatness.

The Raven.

Labienus smiled, drawing comfort from that name. That name. That secret name. A vague myth to the masses. A beacon of hope to the few nobles privileged enough to belong to the brotherhood. Rome had lost its way. The Raven would put it back on course. Soon – very soon – the great man would be revealed. Rome would unite under his banner, and the empire would be ruled properly, efficiently. This latest spate of would-be dictators would be forgotten, their lives insignificant in the grand scheme of things.

But until The Raven revealed himself to the world, Labienus had to play the part of the loyal general. He must keep up all appearances. He must do Pompey's bidding, which is why he now stood on the wall, twiddling his thumbs.

Just then, several archers began to point at something off in the distance.

"There, General!" the centurion reported. "Riders coming out of the swamp!"

Labienus looked up and could hardly believe his eyes.

Yes, there were horsemen – a handful, perhaps a score – about a mile to the east. They had just emerged from the swamp and were riding at full gallop toward the city. From their unique manner of riding, Labienus deduced they were Gauls – Caesar's Gauls, most likely. They were pushing their mounts to the limit as if their lives depended on it.

The coastal breeze shifted suddenly, revealing a banner attached to the end of a lance held by one of the lead riders.

Labienus could not help but be astonished. Not at the sight of the approaching Gauls, but because everything he was seeing was precisely as Pompey had predicted. Pompey had told him to be on the lookout for a band of riders approaching under a speckled banner. And, indeed, at the head of those Gauls, fluttered a standard showing white spots on a black field.

But how in Jupiter's name could Pompey have known?

Suddenly, a maelstrom of mist and spray rose from the edge of the swamp. Another group of horsemen emerged onto the dry ground, this one much larger than the first. Some two or three hundred mounted Gauls wielding iron-tipped lances and small, round shields spilled out onto the plain and immediately pushed their horses hard after the first group, apparently in pursuit.

"Stand to," Labienus commanded.

"Archers, stand ready!" the centurion bellowed down the line. "Ready artillery!"

Within moments, every archer was at the battlement, nocking arrow to bowstring. They anxiously awaited the next word from the general as the high-speed chase played out on the field before them.

The first group of riders was well ahead of the slower-moving horde. Even from this distance, Labienus could see that they were mounted on better-bred, better-nourished steeds. These powerful beasts opened the gap between them and their pursuers. But their flight came to an abrupt halt when they reached the outer defenses some hundred yards from the wall. An unmanned abatis of sharpened stakes had been planted on the near bank of a freshly excavated ditch. The barrier ran unbroken in a long arc from the southern shoreline to the low hills north of the town. It was a recent construction, intended to discourage any attempt by Caesar's legions to rush the city walls, and it now retarded the progress of the horsemen. The first group of Gauls, though fazed by this hindrance, did not lose heart. Leaping from their saddles, they immediately produced axes and began hacking away at the obstruction as the thundering hooves of their assailants closed behind them.

Labienus watched with amazement as the Gauls worked feverishly to uproot the abatis. He wondered just who in Typhon's Tartarus they were and how Pompey had known they were coming. Though old and set in his ways, Pompey was certainly not an amateur at the game of intrigue. He undoubtedly had trusted agents embedded within Caesar's army, and perhaps these Gauls were among them. Perhaps there was more to Pompey than met the eye.

Within moments, the Gauls had cut a hole just wide enough to permit the passage of two horses abreast. Then they were in the saddle again, filing through the breach and riding at breakneck speed for the city gate.

Meanwhile, the pursuing riders had gained much ground on their quarry. They reached the hole in the abatis mere moments after the first group had passed through it. But here, their pursuit stalled. Where a score of horsemen could traverse so small an aperture in an orderly fashion, the horde found it not so easy. Those first to arrive at the break reined in as if uncertain whether to follow their prey through it. This pause forced the hundreds behind to rein in as well. The whole mass then quickly fell into a disordered jumble of skittish horses riding in circles and kicking up dust and sand. It was clear that no one was in charge. A few warriors shouted at their comrades to form an orderly line. Few listened, and soon the tiny gap in the barricade was a bottleneck through which squeezed a sporadic discharge of only two or three horsemen at a time.

"Fools," Labienus mumbled, shaking his head. He turned to address the line of Thessalonian bowmen. "Aim for the second group! The second group only! Is that understood? If any man in the first group falls, I'll have ten of you hung from the wall before day's end!"

The order was translated into Greek by the centurion. The archers nodded their nervous comprehension all down the line. They knew it was not an idle threat. The name of General Titus Labienus was whispered in fear around the campfires of both armies. He was known to be meticulous in planning, cold and calculating in battle, merciless with prisoners, and downright cruel to shirkers within his own ranks.

The abatis stood at the maximum range of the bowmen, something the Gallic horsemen would have realized had they been endowed with any sense at all.

There was treachery afoot down there, Labienus mused, and Pompey was somehow involved in it. In any event, he had his orders, odd as they were, explicitly stated in Pompey's message.

Labienus nodded to the centurion.

"Aim!" the centurion shouted, raising his baton. Two hundred Thessalonian bows were pulled to maximum draw and pointed at the sky. The staves creaked from the strain. "Let fly!" The baton came down, and the bows twanged as one.

A swarm of missiles took flight from the wall, hung in the air for several seconds, then came down like hailstones upon the stalled masses. At the same time, half a dozen scorpions recoiled on their platforms, each giant bolt clearly visible as it floated over the field and descended into the crowd.

Distant cries of horror were carried on the buffeting

wind as men and beasts felt the sting of the deadly iron tips. The archers released another wave, and another, turning the disorganized cavalry into a panicked mob. Horses kicked and jumped in confusion, many impaling themselves on the sharp spikes. Riders were thrown from their mounts and were instantly trampled to death by the stomping hooves. One Gaul, his right arm ripped off by a scorpion bolt, clung desperately to his bridle with his other hand. But his terrified horse had gone berserk, whirling round and round until the mangled rider lost his grip and was flung onto a sinister spike that spitted him like a speared fish. One dismounted horseman ambled to his feet as if in a daze, a dripping, feathered shaft protruding from one eye socket. The next instant, two jostling horses came together, smashing him between them.

As more riders fell, the ground beneath was pounded into a mush of blood, gore, and sand. Soon, the breach was entirely blocked by a grisly stack of writhing horses and crushed men. Those few horsemen trapped on the inner side of the barricade were quickly brought down by arrows. Many dismounted and tried to climb back over the barrier but did not make it. They died with arms outstretched, their backs bristling with quivering shafts like so many targets on a practice field.

The Gauls outside the abatis faced the choice of attempting to open a new breach under the deadly barrage or fleeing. Those still in control of their horses quickly chose the latter. Wheeling their protesting mounts, they rode back to the swamp at full gallop, abandoning any of their horseless brethren who could not be scooped up along the way. Few of those who fled on foot made it beyond the archers' reach. The routed survivors limped away, leaving a field of dead and dying behind them.

"Hold your arrows!" The centurion commanded.

The archers relaxed their bows and began stretching sore arms and shoulders. Many chortled at the sight of the slaughtered Gauls. The abatis now displayed a macabre assortment of lifeless, perforated bodies, as if it had been built for that purpose alone. The first group of riders, the ones who had been pursued by the others, remained untouched as they arrived at the gate.

"Have your men stand down," Labienus ordered the centurion.

As the murmuring Thessalonians filed past Labienus to climb down from the battlement, he took a moment to examine the approaching riders. Their weapons, armor, and horses were of high quality, placing them among the Gallic nobility – or *knights*, as Caesar had often referred to them in his official reports. By their dress, Labienus guessed them to be Allobroges. After nearly a decade in Gaul, he had little trouble making that distinction, and it brought to mind the many times he had fought against their kind. He had been second-in-command to Caesar in those days, a position he had only grudgingly accepted on the insistence of the opportunistic, glory-seeking proconsul himself.

The great tactician! Labienus sneered inwardly. *The great general! Hah! I won those battles for him. I fought the hard campaigns while he took the glory. Caesar could no more lead an army than he could grow hair on top of his head.*

Labienus hated Caesar with every pulse of his heart, and those years in Gaul had only made him more resentful. Shortly after assuming the role as Caesar's deputy, he had been propositioned by members of the senate to be their covert agent within Caesar's inner circle. He was to keep a watchful eye on the unpredictable, dangerous man they all feared. And he had done as they had bid. He had played the part of the good deputy, biting back his loathing for the man he served, all the while sending clandestine reports back to the Senate. Time and again, they had promised to summon Caesar back to Rome to answer for a plethora of corruption charges, but the summons never came.

As always, the senators had been all talk, no action. They had let Caesar march into lands where Romans had no interest being and wage war on peoples whose lands and cultures added little value to the empire. They had let Caesar gain unimaginable popularity among the masses, allowing him to sponsor festivals from the spoils of his victories. They had allowed his letters to be read to a fawning public who awaited each embellished battle description as they might the next verse in a pornographic poem.

And now, the empire was in turmoil because the lazy, do-nothing senators had let it get to this point. Had they only acted, Labienus would not currently be serving under a self-absorbed, over-the-hill commander who was on the verge of surrendering yet another province to the tyrant.

The Raven was the only remedy to this calamity.

A thousand agents in every corner of the empire did his bidding, whispered his will to the rulers of Rome's client kingdoms. Officers planted in both armies waited for his signal to declare their allegiance to him. And it would not be long now. The day was fast approaching when The Raven would overthrow the useless senate and assume the long-vacant throne of Rome.

There were few who knew The Raven's true identity, only those in the secret brotherhood. Those in the brotherhood had sworn fealty to him, clandestinely renouncing all other vows and allegiances. On the day The Raven revealed himself, they would publicly throw their full support behind their new king. That included their fortunes, their swords, and their lives.

Some said The Raven was descended from the royal line

of the Tarquins, but Labienus cared little for such absurdity. All that mattered to him was that the new king would do away with the unwieldy republic Rome had long outgrown, and restore her to her true greatness.

The Republic. Labienus scoffed at the notion. The nobles and the plebs held it up as sacrosanct, an institution that could not be dissolved or even reconsidered – as if the absurdly weighted voting assemblies somehow represented the will of the people. The *corsus honorum* was no more than a pathway to corruption, a means for radicals like the Gracchi brothers to rewrite the laws of the republic to suit them and their cronies. Rome was too grand to be ruled by the whims of an illiterate, fickle mob or a power-hungry Senate. It needed consistency. It needed honor. It needed a king.

It needed The Raven.

Patience! Labienus told himself. *The cloth would soon be dropped.*

He watched with mild curiosity as the Gallic riders filed through the open gate below. Upon reaching the inner courtyard, they were quickly disarmed by a contingent of legionaries. Two of the horsemen – one with a patchy beard and pink face, the other gangly and awkward – were evidently the leaders of the motley band. They began expostulating to the arresting soldiers in broken Latin, claiming to be friends and allies of Pompey. Labienus recognized one of the leaders as a prince of the Allobroges tribe whom he had seen at one peace council or another during his time in Gaul. And again, he was perplexed by the fact that Pompey somehow had dealings with these people.

Labienus's eyes were then drawn to two men who stood out from the rest due to the fact that they were stark naked. He had noticed them before, when they were still some ways off, and had attributed their nakedness to the Gallic custom of going into battle wearing nothing, literally, but a sword. Upon closer inspection, it was apparent that these two were stripped bare because they were prisoners. Their hands were bound, and their horses were drawn by the other riders. It was a marvel they had managed to remain in the saddle for the duration of that wild flight. But then, Gauls would know best how to properly secure an immobilized man to the back of a horse.

The shade of the prisoners' skin bespoke of an upbringing in sunny, temperate climates. Their hair was cut short, and, unlike their captors, they did not wear beards.

Romans. Labienus concluded.

Both were sturdily built, and one looked tall enough to be a German, but they were most certainly Romans. The tattoos on their upper arms were irrefutable evidence they belonged to Caesar's legions. But what in Pluto's Realm were they doing with these Gauls? Pompey's message had not mentioned anything about Roman prisoners.

"What shall we do with these Gauls, my lord?" the centurion of archers was suddenly standing before him. "They claim they're here to see Lord Pompey, that they have important information for him. And they've got two Roman prisoners with them, too – Centurions Domitius and Strabo from Caesar's army."

The names sounded familiar, but Labienus could not place them. He had served with so many like them in Gaul. But, no matter. They were traitors and destined for the chopping block – that is, if Pompey did not grant them clemency first, as he was apt to do of late.

At that moment, beyond the centurion's shoulder, Labienus noticed a man slinking about on the other side of the yard. A few bystanders had gathered to view the new arrivals, and this man moved among them. He was a pudgy, beady-eyed man of a far eastern ethnicity. He wore a fine tunic, but the brass ring around his neck identified him as a house slave. While the attention of the other curious onlookers was fixated on the Gauls, the slave's eyes were looking directly back at Labienus.

When the slave realized he had been spotted, he disappeared into the crowd. Labienus quickly deduced his purpose.

My absence from the gathering has been noticed. No doubt, that fool was sent here to check on me.

Staring across the water at the army camp, Labienus felt the frustration of a man who served two masters. Pompey would be keenly awaiting his return with the Gauls in tow. The longer he tarried, the more Pompey would grow suspicious as to the reason.

"What shall we do with them, sir?" the centurion said again.

"Take the Gauls to the wharf!" Labienus snapped crossly. "I shall join them there directly."

The cowed centurion saluted, then fidgeted before asking, "What about the Romans, sir? Shall they be taken to the wharf, too?"

Labienus thought for a moment before answering. "No. Take them to the prison here in town."

Pompey's message had said nothing about Roman prisoners, so Labienus would do with them as he wished. And he wished to keep them here, far removed from Pompey's all-too-generous offers of mercy. It was yet another point of contention between them.

Leaving the protesting Gauls and the adamant centurion arguing in the courtyard behind him, Labienus marched into the town with a purpose. He had an appointment to keep, even if he was deplorably late.

Pompey would just have to wait.

XIV

Hidden beneath the largest and most extravagant *domus* in all Dyrrachium was a dark sanctum that few knew about, and even fewer had ever entered. It was seldom used, preserved only for rituals of the utmost significance, like the one today.

Faceless servants moved in the shadows preparing the animals for the ceremony. A cow, a pig, and a sheep had been scrubbed clean by a dozen slaves, carefully combed and perfumed. Gilded strands draped their four-legged bodies like the regalia of kings. And well they could have been the kings of the animal world for their flawless hides, stout muscles, perfect teeth, and manicured hooves. The beasts were led quietly into the chamber, calmed by herbal blends and lured by choice carrots and cabbage – the finest one could find in the besieged city.

A circular aperture in the high domed ceiling cast a solitary beam of sunlight onto the center of the vast room. There, upon a pedestal, stood a statue of polished marble twice the height of a man. The figure was that of a bearded warrior in full battle regalia. The chiseled face was authoritative, assured, and daunting. The painted eyes seemed to stare at the blank wall opposite, but the placement was intentional. Had the marble eyes been capable of seeing through the concrete, across the Adriatic, and through the mountains beyond, they would have gazed upon the great city of Rome, three hundred miles away.

Fixed within the massive, outstretched hands of the statue was a perfect spear of gleaming bronze.

Before the statue knelt a figure in a hooded purple robe. The hands clasped together were those of an older man, though the nails were perfectly cut, and the skin wore a healthy tan. A bronze mask with emotionless features hid the entire face from view, but curls of white-gray hair escaped from one side of the hood.

Eleven other masked and hooded figures stood in the outer recesses, just beyond the light. They chanted a repetitive verse in an ancient Latin spoken by the old ones.

We are the Twelve.
He is the One.

Mars be with him.
Mars save him.
Mars protect him.

We are the Twelve.
He is the One...

The chant grew louder though the voices were still little more than a whisper. As if of one mind, the eleven robed ones glided forward to converge on the platform, each holding a gleaming dagger away from his body as if the mere touch of it meant death. They approached the beasts slowly, steadily, while the slaves made every effort to keep the animals calm.

At a signal from one of the robed figures, the blades struck in unison. The sacrificial animals were slain. Their throats were cut, the lifeless carcasses dropping to the floor in heavy thumps. Streams of blood ran down the angled floor, channeled into a circular pool around the base of the statue, where the man in the purple cloak knelt. Warm blood curled around his knees, soaking the slack of his robe, but he did not move.

The chanting then increased, no longer whispers, more like wailing from the underworld. The voices reverberated from one wall to the next until it seemed they came from every direction at once, an uncannily loud pulse that pressed on the ears like the depths of the sea.

Then, it happened.

The bronze spear moved. Just a tiny vibration at first. But the tremble rapidly intensified with the crescendo of the incantation until the shaft began to rattle against the marble fingers that held it. Robed priests and slaves alike gaped in awe at the phenomenon and were induced into chanting louder. The spear nearly danced within the statue's loose grip, dumbfounding the observers.

The only exception was the kneeling, purple-robed figure in the center. He remained silent with head bowed, hood and shadows concealing his face such that the others did not see the sinister smile that formed there.

XV

Two more figures emerged into the sunlight from the shadowy lane between the houses. Both figures were wrapped in cloaks with hoods drawn. They had obviously left from one of the servant's entrances. They descended to the cobbled street and immediately dispersed down different alleyways, conspicuous in their attempt to remain inconspicuous.

One hundred paces down the sloping street, Labienus was marching toward the same house with an urgency equal to that of those scurrying away from it. The two cloaked men were the fourth pair to exit the opulent *domus* since Labienus had turned the corner and the house had come into view.

Clearly, the assembly had adjourned. And, clearly, he had missed it.

One of the last pair to depart had failed to secure the lower clasps of his cloak before stepping outside. A gust from the bay had unfurled the cloak long enough for

Labienus to spy a gleaming pair of bronze greaves and a skirt of ornamented *pteruges*.

A legate? Or, perhaps, a member of my own staff?

There really was no way to know. The identities of The Twelve were as closely guarded as the existence of the brotherhood itself. They were, no doubt, high-ranking officials – army officers, senators, legates, priests, governors – men in positions of power who could influence their own spheres of the empire. They were not even permitted to know one another's identities. On the rare occasion they all came together in one place, they met within dark chambers with faces hidden behind masks. Numbers were used in place of names, assigned in order of seniority, and reassigned whenever death or incapacitation necessitated a new induction. Their true identities were known only to The Raven. The Twelve knew one another only by number.

And Labienus, who now pulled the cloak and hood tighter around him as he walked briskly toward the house, was Number Twelve.

As gatherings of The Twelve were so infrequent, it went without saying that to miss one was unacceptable. For the newest member, it was inexcusable.

Now, thanks to Pompey's little errand, Labienus would have to make amends for his absence.

The house was perhaps one of the wealthiest in the empire. It was certainly the most luxuriant in Dyrrachium. With most of the town transformed into a locked-down, manure-strewn fortress overrun by cursing soldiers, shifty-eyed slaves, and braying mules, this quarter had remained relatively untouched. And that was because it contained the plush estates of the magistrates, guild masters, and other gentry who had grown enormously wealthy off the goods passing through the busy seaport. Two dozen or more extravagant properties lined the well-maintained street. To garner the support of these elites, Pompey had designated the district off-limits to all troops. While the rest of the citizenry hunkered down, praying that the roving bands of drunken soldiers would bypass their homes, the elites lived much as they had before. At least, those who remained did. Most of the wealthy families had fled at the first sign of a siege, taking their valuables with them aboard their own private yachts.

Typically, this street would have been teeming with rich men in white togas conducting business from overly elaborate litters while well-dressed servants ran to and fro. Now, it was deserted. Most of the houses were empty, except for the few slaves left behind to maintain them.

But the owner of the magnificent *domus* had not flown as the others had. *He* was not like the others.

He was not like any other.

Intending to remain at least as discreet as those who had come before him, Labienus walked around the side of the house to the *posticum*. There, he was greeted by a well-dressed servant, the same bald man whom he had seen snooping around the city gate earlier.

"Welcome, my lord. The master is expecting you." The servant's lips were curled into a fake smile. "There is no need to conceal your face, my lord. The others have already left."

There was something conniving and deceitful in the man's beady eyes, but none of the intelligence that would have made such qualities dangerous. At the snap of his fingers, two slaves appeared and took Labienus's cloak. Other slaves padded about in the shadows, busily tidying up the place. The aroma of smoked fish and fresh blood filled the air.

"The master invites you to join him for refreshment, my lord. Please follow me." The servant guided him across an inner courtyard ringed by marble columns to another doorway where long curtains turned over in the breeze. Through the curtains, they were let out onto a wide veranda that afforded an unobstructed view of the town and shimmering bay beyond. A large wooden lattice was held up by a series of fluted columns. Carefully pruned vines snaked up the columns to meet overhead, the entangled canopy shading the entire terrace from the afternoon sun. A cluster of cushioned divans sat in the center of the veranda, and it was from one of these that Labienus's host rose to welcome him.

The stately, intelligent-looking man who now extended a hand in greeting exuded complete authority even in such a simple gesture. He was more than a decade older than Labienus – sixty-years-old, at least – but the loose-fitting Tyrian purple tunic revealed the trim form of a man half that age. The radiant, suntanned skin glistened with traces of oil. Damp, white-gray hair was plastered back on his head. He had obviously just been bathed and scraped. But even in his half-put-together state, he was unlike anyone Labienus had ever met. He was the embodiment of strength, wisdom, assertiveness – everything Rome needed.

"Apologies for my absence, my lord," Labienus stammered under the other's scrutinizing eyes. The smile on the lined face was more cordial than pleasant. A long moment of silence passed before a hand was finally extended in greeting.

"The sun is hot, and the day is long, General," his host said, gesturing to the opposite couch. "Please, join me. Please, sit."

Labienus did as directed. As his host returned to his own seat, Labienus could not help but notice that the cushions were made of the finest silk. Spanish napkins and Bithynian painted ware adorned a small table nearby.

Pewter bowls arranged in neat rows overflowed with almonds, fresh dates, and figs, all nearly impossible to come by in the besieged city. Two glimmering goblets filled with wine could have been the prized possessions of an Asian prince. The wealth on casual display left Labienus speechless, just as it had on the other occasions he had visited this house.

"Drink, my friend," his host said. "This day proves to be longer still." There was a hint of derision in the statement, but Labienus was careful not to react to it. He knew full well he was being tested.

Turning up the goblet, he let the wine course down his parched throat. He was pleased to discover it had been diluted with a plentiful portion of water, far more than was allowed by the rationing. But then, such restrictions did not apply to his host – nor should they.

And that was because Senator Marcus Aemilius Valens, oligarch of Spain, hero of the Sertorian and Servile Wars, was no ordinary man. He was a sly politician, a brilliant strategist, a mercantile genius. Some believed him blessed by the gods. Some believed him a traitor. Still, others believed he was not a man at all, but a divinity in the form of a man.

At such absurdities, Labienus scoffed. Valens was a man, a mortal like himself. There was no doubting that. But if it were possible for a mortal to brush with the deities, Valens would be the one. Few men were more admired, both secretly and openly.

Stories abounded of the enigmatic senator's extravagant tastes, his travels to exotic lands, his lucrative business ventures. Tales of his exploits were the subjects of conversations at dinner parties throughout the empire. The affluent whispered about his vast wealth with envy. It was said he could buy and sell entire kingdoms, and that he had done so more than once in the far east. The Parthian King of kings purportedly counted him a dear friend.

For the last decade, Valens had been publicly deemed *persona non grata* in Rome, consigned to a life of exile for crimes against the state. But there were many, Labienus included, who secretly believed the senator should have been commended for those so-called ill deeds. Still, the exile had done little to diminish his fame. Valens was said to have villas in every major city of the empire, some even grander than this one. A thousand slaves and servants did his bidding. If anything, his lengthy exile had served only to increase his wealth and heighten the mystery surrounding him. He was not an exile in the eyes of most, more like a legend.

And that would serve well in the coming days.

The patricians and plebs would sooner swear fealty to a legend. And when that glorious day came, when Valens was finally crowned King of Rome, they would swear allegiance to him. They would bend the knee as their long-dead ancestors had to the Tarquins, Numa, and Romulus. They would serve Valens, or they would die.

Because Marcus Aemilius Valens was, in fact, The Raven.

"Many traveled a considerable distance to be here," Valens commented dryly, gesturing at the harbor where four unflagged yachts lay at anchor apart from the other vessels. They had not been there the day before. "Indeed, it is rare that assemblies of the brotherhood are missed."

Labienus did his best to appear comfortable under his host's dissecting gaze. Clearly, his infraction was not going to be quickly overlooked.

"It was most discourteous of me, my lord. Again, I offer my humblest apologies." The contrite words came unnaturally. Labienus was not accustomed to apologizing.

"I had every intention of being there, but circumstances beyond my control necessitated my absence."

"Of course, General. You have our greatest confidence."

The words were friendly, but Valens's face displayed no sympathy. His eyes examined Labienus as if to peer into his soul and seek out any mistruths there.

It was at that moment that Labienus noticed the four bodyguards standing statue-like in each corner of the patio. They were giant, dark-skinned warriors, mercenaries from Arabia, each one head and shoulders above the tallest man in Pompey's army. Veils hung from bronze helmets to hide their features. Sleeveless, black leather cuirasses revealed massive arms the size of an ordinary man's legs. Large, clasped hands rested upon long-handled axes with curved double blades polished to a shine.

This was not the first time Labienus had seen the menacing Arabians, but never before had he been as discomforted by their presence as he was now. On a previous visit, he had learned they were gifts from the *satrapes* of Edessa, another of Valens's high-placed acquaintances. Though the Arabians appeared indifferent to the conversation, Labienus suspected that they were watching him behind those veils for the slightest hint of treachery.

"You see, my lord," Labienus explained, "I was given a message when I stepped off the boat this morning. It was from Pompey. It was quite unexpected. It contained orders he wished me to carry out at once. Had I ignored it, Pompey's suspicions would have surely been aroused."

"And what were these orders?"

Valens had asked it like he already knew the answer. And, of course, he did. That bastard of a chief servant had probably been snooping around all day, paying off anyone and everyone for information.

And, so, Labienus recounted the morning's events in their entirety while Valens listened, showing neither pleasure nor displeasure. Labienus's dry throat forced him to return to his cup often through the telling, until, halfway through his story, he drained it.

No sooner had he taken the last mouthful of wine than a female slave materialized from the shadows bearing a decorative ceramic decanter in both hands. At the sight of her, Labienus stopped talking and stared involuntarily. He was a battle-hardened, duty-bound, professional general. Still, even he could not help but gasp at the woman's striking beauty. She was quite possibly the most perfect woman he had ever seen. She had the olive skin of an easterner, smooth, flawless, and temptingly accented by the white, transparent dress that threatened to fall off her shoulders at any moment. Her face was a perfect oval, her crimson lips full and pouty. Her hairline started high on her forehead, the shimmering black locks combed back to light on her shoulders like ribbons of silk. And her eyes... long-forgotten arousal surged deep within his core at the briefest glimpse of their dark, opalescence. Her bare feet tread noiselessly on the tile floor, her rounded hips just peeking from the open sides of the wispy garment with every step.

Labienus had entirely forgotten what he was saying. And, for the moment, he did not care. The fragrance of Syrian perfume filled the air as the slave leaned over to fill his goblet, her silken hair brushing his bare knee like the flitting wings of a butterfly.

The girl could not have been more than twenty years of age. No doubt, she was yet another of the many exotic treasures Valens had acquired on his journeys. It was said that the great man's one weakness, if he had one, was his penchant for young, delectable maidens. As utterly breathtaking as this one was, there must have been a hundred like her across his various estates. Playthings for every season, every mood, every whim. Trophies to gaze upon or hold whenever he pleased. Once again, Labienus found himself in sheer admiration of this man who would one day be king of Rome.

As the woman was tipping the pitcher over Labienus's goblet, the strap of her dress fell off one shoulder, exposing a perfect, joggling breast. Labienus could not help but ogle. Upon realizing the state of her garment, the woman made a sudden movement to fix it and, in so doing, overfilled the cup, spilling wine onto Labienus's legs, greaves, and boots.

"Curse you, whore!" he snapped, rising red-faced and holding the goblet out away from him. Instinctively, he drew back his hand to strike her, but then abruptly stopped, suddenly remembering where he was and to whom she belonged.

The woman quickly knelt to clean the spilled contents with her dress, glancing with apologetic and fearful eyes up at the general and then at her master.

"A thousand pardons, my lord," the chief servant was suddenly there bowing low to Labienus.

"Just remove her, Cimon," Valens said with evident annoyance.

"Yes, my lord," the servant replied, then grabbed the sobbing woman by the hair and roughly dragged her along on all fours as one might lead a leashed dog. "Come, girl! You will pay for that!"

Her pleas for mercy could be heard long after they disappeared inside the house.

Labienus looked expectantly at his host, waiting for the customary apology, but then realized none would be forthcoming. It was, of course, beneath the imminent King of Rome to apologize for spilled wine. If Valens wished a dozen pitchers of wine poured over Labienus, then, by Juno, the general would bloody well sit there and take it.

"As I was saying, my lord," Labienus continued. "It was just as Pompey had said in his message. A score of riders came out of the swamp – Gallic knights fleeing their own kind to come over to our side. I don't know how Pompey could have known, unless he has agents among the Gauls. That must be it! Nevertheless, we made short work of those pursuing them."

"And those you admitted were all knights of the Allobroges tribe, you say?"

"That's right, my lord. A couple princes and their bodyguards and *oathsworn*. I ordered the bastards taken into custody. Pompey's friends or not, I won't have a bunch of unsavory Gauls roaming about behind our lines unattended." Labienus raised the cup to his lips to take a drink. Over the brim, he saw Valens looking back at him with eyes that indicated he knew the statement was not entirely truthful. Labienus cursed the bald servant under his breath. Removing the cup from his face, Labienus acted as if he had just remembered something. "In truth, they were not all knights. There was a druid among them – one of those creatures they believe can talk to the spirits – and two prisoners."

"And who were these prisoners?" Valens asked with keen interest.

"Romans. Centurions from Caesar's legions. I cannot remember their names."

"Was one of them called Domitius, perhaps?"

"Yes, indeed!" Labienus replied in amazement. "A tall, broad-shouldered fellow. How did you know?"

"From what legion?" Valens asked, ignoring the question.

"I do not know, sire. I did not ask. One traitor's as

useless as another."

"Could it be...after all these years?" Valens said, putting a hand to his chin. He gazed at a spot on the floor for a long moment as if deep in thought.

"Do you wish me to summon him here, my lord?"

"No," Valens replied distantly. He appeared ruffled, but the moment passed quickly, and he moved on to the next item. "What business does Pompey have with the Gauls?"

"Unknown, my lord. I know only that I am to take them to him straightaway. My launch is waiting at the wharf as we speak. If I tarry much longer, suspicions will surely be raised."

"And the Romans? Are you taking them, too?"

Labienus shook his head. "My orders said nothing about Romans. Those Gaul bastards wanted to present them to Pompey as gifts, but I put a stop to that. Not that I give a damn about those traitors. I'd have killed them on the spot if Pompey hadn't standing orders to the contrary regarding enemy prisoners. But I won't have Romans paraded around as trophies of dirty Gauls. I ordered them taken to the jail here in town." He paused, sighing heavily. "But, I suppose Pompey will send for them when the Gauls tell him about them. He'll send for them and then offer them a chance to come over to our side, as he does for all prisoners. The misguided fool!"

"You disagree with that policy?" Valens asked, his face displaying the first hint of amusement.

"Indeed, I do, my lord. There's little good that can come from coddling the enemy. How can we strike terror in their hearts on the battlefield if they don't fear us, if they don't fear what we'll do to them? I say kill them all. Let them die the slow deaths of traitors. Let Caesar's men know they're better off running away than fighting under him. So much of warfare is in the mind, you know. Pompey does not seem to grasp this. But, alas, I must follow the orders of that overvalued buffoon." He paused and glanced hesitantly at his host. "I'm sure things will be different when you are in charge, my lord."

"I will enact the same policy," Valens replied succinctly. "We must be merciful if we are to bring the empire together."

"That is utter foolishness!" Labienus blurted out, voicing his feelings a bit too passionately. At the raised eyebrows of his host, he quickly added, "What I mean to say, sire, is that some might think that unwise. Caesar's men are hardy soldiers. I should know. I trained them. But they are scoundrels to a man. I wouldn't trust a single one."

"I understand Caesar's army is in a poor state."

Labienus nodded. "They are deserting in droves over there. Morale is low, which is why I've been petitioning Pompey to let me strike now, while Caesar is weak. I know his ways. I know how to beat him. And we need to beat him before our own men start dropping from thirst."

"And how would you regard the state of Pompey's troops?" Valens said with a smile.

Labienus clenched his teeth. Again, Valens was probing his soul, reading his very thoughts. And he had just hit a sore spot.

"Deplorable, my lord. I will not hesitate to admit it, nor to lay the blame squarely where it belongs. It's Pompey's doing. He has taken charge of the training personally, and he is doing it all wrong. He insists on teaching antiquated tactics that might have worked long ago in his campaigns in the east but won't work against Caesar's veterans. The men gaze at him in awe, hanging on every word. In truth, I think he enjoys it. It's more about satisfying his ego than teaching them what they need to know to stand in the battle line."

"And the officers? Do you have the same opinion of

them?"

"I suppose the legates are promising, if you overlook that they bend over backward to kiss Pompey's arse. They're skilled generals, for the most part. I have a few reservations, but nothing serious. The tribunes, on the other hand…are another story entirely. A more worthless collection of pampered, utterly incapable fops I have never seen. Coddled too much as children, I expect. They mock the drills, mock the centurions, mock their duties, mock any hint of discipline. They strut about the camp like Alexanders incarnate, finding humor in anything and everything, as if this is all a game put on for their personal amusement. Meanwhile, not one of them knows his prick from a pilum. Their nights are spent hosting wild parties in their over-furnished tents as if they were back in Rome." Labienus cursed under his breath. "And what does our blessed general do about it? Absolutely nothing! And why? Because the misguided youths are the sons of senators in Thessalonica, and he fears losing their support. The old fool!" He paused to glance at Valens. "Were I in command, sire, I'd see things put right. I'd have those dandies decimated – twice! And if their fathers defied me, I'd have them beheaded as traitors. Senator or no!"

"I have every confidence that you could, my friend," Valens said neutrally.

Labienus forced himself to pause and take a long drink, not wishing to speak too quickly or overstep his bounds. "In any event, sire, I can handle the army. If Pompey would just give me the word, I'd rout the enemy before the next sunset." He looked at Valens. "Perhaps the time has come for you to make yourself known to the world. Assume the throne, and let me deal with Caesar."

Valens shook his head. "Not yet, my friend. I am more concerned about the senators in Thessalonica than I am

Caesar. There are still one or two that must be brought into our circle before we can make our move."

"And, meanwhile, Caesar has a chance to escape us again."

"He is a fly, General, to be brushed off when we see fit. When my kingship is announced, and men on both sides see a true descendent of Numa Pompilius on the throne, they will forget about these petty, would-be dictators. I know what the people want, what they need, have always needed – a king with the valor of Hercules and the wisdom of Pythagoras. They will welcome my rule. They will swear fealty to me. And I will set Rome back on the path to greatness. Soon, the so-called Republic will be but a bad memory, a barbaric time before the noble enlightenment. The people will build monuments to me. Indeed, they will deify my name."

As Valens spoke, his eyes were filled with a wild excitement that seemed somewhat out of place for his normally austere nature. Evidently, visualizing these aspirations for the thousandth time produced no less euphoria than the first.

"Surely, a good many will, sire," Labienus mumbled into his cup.

Valens looked suddenly annoyed. "Many?"

"Of course, sire."

"But not all will, you mean to say."

"No ruler has the support of all his people, sire." Labienus chuckled awkwardly as if to lighten the sudden tension between them. "There are always those who question a king's lineage."

"I am a direct descendant of Mamercus, son of Numa Pompilius," Valens said boldly. "I am The Raven, of whom the ancient oracles have prophesied for centuries. I dare any man to deny it."

"None of us in the brotherhood will ever doubt that, sire."

"You are implying that some outside the brotherhood will?"

Labienus cleared his throat. "Well – never let it be said that *I* subscribe to such theories, sire – but there are those who claim Numa had only a daughter."

"They are wrong."

"And then there are those who say Mamercus was but one son of Numa, that there were four sons in all."

"Indeed." Valens was growing visibly perturbed.

"But, why even mention Numa at all, sire? Say you are a descendant of Romulus and leave it at that. Your *auctoritas* will speak for itself."

"Numa was the first king of the Romans," Valens said. "There is no higher lineage in all of Rome."

"Truly, he was *king* of the Romans, sire."

"Why do you say it thus?"

Labienus hesitated, but Valens prodded him with a fierce glance. "You know what people say, sire, about old Numa – those who care about such things, anyway. They say he was a Sabine, and not a Roman at all."

"That is an unqualified falsehood," Valens seethed. "Numa was Roman, just as I am."

"Of course, sire. But it makes no difference. Roman or Sabine, I will serve you as my king, regardless."

"General Labienus, I insist that you forthwith clear your mind of such nonsense and that you cease to recount such rumors. Is that understood? Such scandalous lies spawn doubt in the simple-minded. Rebellions blossom from such lies. Any man who claims such things when I am king will be thrown from the Tarpeian rock." Valens took a deep breath and continued in a milder tone. "Besides, I have the scrolls of Numa in my possession."

Labienus forced his eyes wide, trying his best to appear awestruck. Such relics never really inspired him. Any fool could say he found the records of Numa. Still, as a loyal member of the brotherhood, Labienus did his best to act thrilled by the news.

"The ancient scrolls, sire! That is quite incredible!"

"Recovered from the tomb if the ancient king himself," Valens added, his eyes revealing that he saw right through Labienus's woeful acting. "Had you attended the ritual this morning, you would have seen the scrolls for yourself. The others saw them. When the time is right, I shall put the sacred texts on display in the forum for all to see."

"Yes, my lord. And I'll be the first to quash any rumors that might pop up regarding those books. You have my oath on that!" Labienus made a discomfited noise, then retreated to his goblet, realizing he had, once again, said too much.

"Rumors?" Valens raised an eyebrow. "What rumors, General?"

"Nothing, sire. A mere triviality. An old grumble among the *populares*. Nothing to be concerned about."

"Tell me, gods curse you!"

"Well, surely you have heard that some question the authenticity of the ancient registers."

"I have not."

"It's quite absurd, really," Labienus said with an uneasy laugh. "Some claim the true records were destroyed when the Gauls sacked Rome centuries ago. They say the current registers were written some time afterward to favor a few particular families – *yours*, for example. People will believe anything these days, as you well know, sire. I suppose there might be one or two cynics who might question your ties to Numa on that account. But we can deal with them easily enough."

Valens said nothing, though he was clearly displeased by this continual naysaying. And Labienus, who knew well of his own tendency to provoke anger in his superiors by pointing out things they had overlooked, took that as a sign that he had overstayed his welcome. Quickly draining the rest of the cup, he rose and bowed.

"Forgive me, sire. I've lost track of the time. Pompey will certainly inquire as to my tardiness should I delay any longer. I must go."

"Of course." Valens sounded more relieved than anything else.

"Thank you for your most generous hospitality, sire. I shall not miss any future gatherings. You have my oath on that."

"Before you go, General...the Roman prisoners."

"What about them, sire?"

"I have some unfinished business with the one called Domitius. I do not wish to involve you in my personal affairs, General. It is necessary that I deal with this matter myself."

Labienus nodded. "Say no more, sire. You know how I feel about Caesar's scum. But whatever you plan to do, I recommend you do it quickly. Pompey is desperate for veteran soldiers. When those Gaul bastards tell him two of Caesar's centurions are in the jail here, he won't waste any time. He'll have them marching in our ranks before the day is out."

Valens gave an appreciative smile. "Then go, my friend. Return to our lord Pompey. Play the good lieutenant, advise him as best you can, and keep me informed. I shall take care of the prisoners."

As he was leaving, Labienus caught a glimmer of the same apprehensiveness Valens had exhibited upon the first mention of the centurion's name. It passed just as quickly.

Still, Labienus left wondering what business someone like Valens could have with the centurion Domitius.

XVI

Valens watched from the veranda as Labienus hurried away on the street below bundled in cloak and hood. The general was such a single-minded brute, taxing to endure at times. Too rash to be trusted with an entire army. Too skilled to be dismissed out of hand.

Still, this news of his had been most welcome.

"The gods favor me today, Cimon," Valens said.

"Have they not always, my lord?" the chief servant replied amicably.

"The son of Domitius is under my power at last. That little legal matter in Spain, that has been a thorn in my side for so long, can finally be put to rest."

"Yes, sire."

"You know what must be done."

"Whatever you bid, sire."

"Select the strongest of my Macedonian oarsmen. See that they pay Domitius a visit tonight. Twenty *sesterces* to every man. Fifty, to the one who strikes the killing blow."

"It shall be as you say, sire."

"And no weapons, Cimon. It must look like a prison brawl. I don't need Pompey sticking his nose into my business."

"Yes, sire."

Valens smiled. The gods had indeed blessed him. After all the years of uncertainty, the plans, the careful playing of one side of the senate against the other, he was finally on the cusp of achieving his destiny. He felt as invigorated as a young tribune.

Scanning the western horizon, he saw an empty azure field beneath a scattering of clouds. No sail in sight. The vessel from Italy was late.

Cause for concern? Surely not. Held up by the port officials in Brundisium, no doubt. Surely, that was it.

A throat cleared behind him, breaking his thoughts.

"Still there, Cimon?"

"Y-Yes, sire."

"Were my instructions not clear?"

"Abundantly clear, sire. It shall all be done as you command."

"Then why do you tarry?"

"Forgive me, sire, but I cannot help but think of the embarrassment Baseirta caused for your distinguished guest, the general. She is not fit to be a house slave."

Valens sighed. He knew where this was going.

"Let her be sent to the fields, sire, that you be spared any further embarrassment." Cimon paused, then added keenly. "Even better, sire. Let her be sold on the market that you may be rid of her once and for all. I am sure I can fetch a paltry sum for her. Say the word, and it will be done this very day."

A small laugh escaped Valens' lips. "You would do anything to have her for yourself, wouldn't you, Cimon?"

"I-I do not know what you mean, sire. She is a dirty Parthian slave."

"A dirty slave whose beauty is unmatched by any other for a thousand leagues."

Cimon blushed but did not respond. The fool's desires were obvious. He salivated for the soft young slave that he could not have, just as a dog eyed a piece of raw meat beyond its reach.

Valens could not fault Cimon. The beautiful Baseirta was a delectable treat. Of the many dozens of concubines he kept in his thirteen villas across the empire, she was, by far, his favorite. Her flawless figure was second to none, but that was not the primary reason he delighted in her wares. His stable of courtesans was unlike the harems of other powerful men. They were more than mere possessions, more than objects to satisfy his carnal desires. Every one of them represented a conquest, a victory over some opponent, a trophy to add to his growing collection.

The beautiful slave never came to his bed willingly. None of them did, and that was the way he preferred it. Knowing they detested him, knowing they despised him for what he was doing to them, was far more arousing than the curves of their bodies. The moment a whore appeared to be enjoying it, he either sold her or consigned her to the fields.

He particularly enjoyed delving into the treasures Baseirta had to offer. She was the perfect combination of defiance and beauty. And she had many reasons to hate him, aside from being a slave whom he bedded at will. Once, in her former life, she had dared spurn his advances. Now, she was paying the price for that insolence, and she would continue to pay for many years to come. Mistress or slave, it made no difference. She was his now.

In the end, he always got what he wanted.

Maybe someday, when he finally tired of her, he would let the fool Cimon have his way with her. But not today.

"Where is she, Cimon?"

"She is down in the sanctum, my lord. I have put her to work with the other slaves cleaning up the blood." Cimon gave a forced laugh. "I thought it fitting, sire, since she was so clumsy to spill wine on your guest. She can spend the rest of the day mopping up —"

"Before you go, Cimon," Valens interrupted him, "have the girl cleaned up. Have her prepared properly and taken to my bedchamber. I will be there directly."

Cimon seemed to dither a moment before responding. "Y-Yes, my lord."

The servant tramped off into the house, his visible frustration drawing a measure of amusement from Valens. Valens was now alone on the veranda, aside from the stone-like bodyguards and a single raven clucking atop the capstone of the nearest column. He crossed to the edge to get a better look at the blue expanse of the bay.

Small boats glided across the water, their oars rising and falling soundlessly in the distance. Most of the boats pulled between the city and Pompey's camp on the far shore, but a few drove out to the ships at anchor. Some of these carried members of The Twelve back to the vessels that would convey them home. Cornelius to Athens. Venturius to Carthage. Sempronius to Alexandria. And many others to their own corners of the empire, where they would return to their official offices and await his signal. And that signal would not be long in coming.

Everything was arranged.

Let the armies of Pompey and Caesar whittle away at each other. Let them suffer a bit longer. Let the soldiers in both camps grow frustrated to the point of mutiny. Then, at the right moment, Valens would give the signal, and the machine would be set in motion. In a single night, embedded assassins would eliminate Pompey, Caesar, and their loyal lieutenants. At the same time, carefully planned uprisings would break out in provinces across the empire, the local garrisons routed, farms burned, and the various proconsuls seized.

In the chaos and famines that followed, a small group of well-placed, well-compensated senators would propose a radical measure to restore the peace – do away with the Republic and reestablish the kingship. A theater of sorts would ensue, mainly for public benefit, in which a pair of censors would be appointed to examine the sacred records and determine who should sit on the throne. At an opportune moment, the books of Numa would be found, establishing the line of Mamercus as the only legitimate pedigree to the kingship. It would be determined that Valens was the only living, direct descendant of Mamercus and, therefore, the only legitimate heir to the throne. In the forum, before all the people, Valens would be offered the crown, which he would refuse at first. Some meticulously choreographed bargaining would then ensue, which would conclude with the senate agreeing to dissolve and hand ultimate power of the state over to him. Before the crowd, Valens would recite some carefully scripted oration purporting that this responsibility had been forced upon him, and he only accepted it in the interest of restoring peace. And, just like that, Valens would have absolute authority.

One day, Rome would regard him as Great Father, Lawgiver...Emperor. Yes, he would not simply be a king. He would be the highest king of all, the endeared patriarch of a noble dynasty that would rule Rome for a thousand years – an eternal empire.

Of course, there would be some resistance from those

who still believed in the misguided notions of a republic. But even the most patriotic senators had a price. Whatever that price was, Valens had the means to pay it.

The mob, however, was another story. They were unpredictable, prone to exalting a hero one day, crucifying him the next. They were driven by passion and easily stirred to violence. But they were also categorically superstitious, which was why Valens had gone to great lengths to obtain the legendary books of Numa. Lost for centuries, the scrolls now sat enshrined at the foot of Mars in the private sanctum beneath the marbled floor at his feet.

The sacred books were said to have been written by Numa himself. They consisted of twelve volumes of holy script, twelve of philosophy, and one establishing the bloodline of kings. The scrolls had been entombed with the ancient king upon his death. But many generations later, a great flood had dislodged them, and they had been recovered intact. According to legend, the Senate had ordered the scrolls' immediate destruction, lest their wisdom put monarchical notions in the minds of the people. But a patriotic senator had intervened and had the scrolls spirited away to a hidden cave far from Rome.

Now, hundreds of years later, Valens had found the sacred texts – or rather, those he had paid had found them. Whether these scrolls truly were the genuine books, or exceptionally good forgeries, really did not matter. What mattered was what people believed.

A few hours ago, the conclave of the brethren had sanctified the scrolls as legitimate. Soon, the Senate and people of Rome would accept them, too.

Valens noticed a boat shove off from the wharf loaded down with passengers. It pointed its prow southward, then rapidly picked up speed. The oars rose and fell at a breakneck pace as the launch headed for the army camp across the bay. Undoubtedly, Labienus was aboard.

Number Twelve. Valens sneered inwardly.

Labienus was a firebrand. His aversion for Pompey could hardly be contained. He would have to be watched, lest he expose the whole scheme in a moment of careless rage. Valens still wondered if inducting him into the brotherhood had been wise. Still, some fruits had come of it – the unexpected capture of Lucius Domitius, for one.

Valens managed a smile. He had chosen not to tell Labienus of his connections with Lucius Domitius, that Domitius's father had been a soldier in Valens's legion during the Sertorian War. Or how the older Domitius, a base and simple farmer and a client of Valens's after the war, had, through some blind twist of fate, stumbled upon a profitable mining venture that had raised the low-born bastard to the equestrian order practically overnight. Or how the uppity Domitius had let his good fortune go to his head, thought himself above his station, and dared challenge Valens's stranglehold on the trade of southern Spain.

To restore things to their proper order, Valens had been forced to take extreme measures. He had arranged the murder of Domitius and his family, as well as the confiscation of the dead man's assets, including the prosperous mine that, after more than ten years, still pulled twenty million sesterces of silver from the ground annually. The immense profits from the mine had sustained Valens's affluent lifestyle all these years. Indeed, they had been instrumental in putting him within a hair's breadth of the throne, allowing him to bribe senators and other prominent officials to do his will.

All friends and business associates of the older Domitius were long dead, having met with tragic accidents over the years. Domitius the younger, the one called Lucius, was the only survivor. He was the only one left who could contest Valens's ownership of the mine, though the dimwitted fool probably did not even realize it. Moreover, should the scandalous tale of the mine and the murders ever reach the ears of the Senate…well, that would undoubtedly muddle Valens's plans for the kingship. At the very least, the bribe price for their loyalty would go up.

And so, the final loose end must be tied. The line of Domitius must be silenced forever. Domitius the Younger must die.

Of course, Valens had tried it before. He had tried to have young Domitius killed several times. Through an unfortunate twist of fate, one of those bungled attempts had resulted in Valens's own exile from Rome. But that would not happen this time. This time, by the grace of Fortuna, Domitius had been placed at his mercy. What better proof was there that Providence was guiding him inevitably to the throne?

Valens took in a full breath. The sea breeze buffeted his whitish-gray locks. The warmth of the balmy sun tingled his lined face. The raven tattoo on his chest warmed beneath his tunic. And he felt as vivacious as a twenty-year-old.

It would all be his, everything he now beheld – every city, every port, every tribal village beyond a thousand horizons.

He looked to the west again. Still no sails, not even a mast, on the great blue expanse.

No matter. The packet would come soon enough, no doubt bearing propitious news from Rome.

While he waited, he had other, more pleasant business to attend to. He would give the girl an exceptional ravaging this afternoon. Cimon better have prepared her just as he liked.

Valens had not missed the defiant look in the fair

Baseirta's eyes earlier, as she had been dragged away by the chief servant. As always, they had conveyed an implicit declaration that, no matter what he did to her physically, she would never be his. Her mind was free to curse him as she wished.

He laughed inwardly.

She hated him far more than the others did. Who could blame her? Still, she would let him do with her as he pleased.

She had no choice.

XVII

The obscene frescoes adorning the walls of the master's bedchamber sent a surge of revulsion through Baseirta.

They always did.

Demoniac smiles. Lust-filled faces wild with unnatural ecstasy. Embellished bodies locked in every manner of carnal embrace. It was as if those frozen figures on the wall were taunting her, laughing at what she must endure.

On a signal from Cimon, more slaves entered the room to dress her hair, nails, and eyes. At the same time, those who had just bathed her and covered her quivering body in fragrant oils retired with her filthy garments.

Baseirta held back her tears. She had cried too often in the past months not to have control over them. She had withstood far too much to be fazed by what awaited her. As he often did, the master would use her as an object, a thing with which to expunge his passion. In the world she used to inhabit, the loathsome Roman would have been unworthy to look upon her face, much less fondle her every curve. She, Baseirta of Gugark, once chaste as the pure snows of Ararat, once attended by her own slaves, once desired by every noble suitor in the Seven Great Houses, was now the personal whore of the vile and twisted Valens.

He would not be gentle. He was never gentle.

She stared mindlessly at the wall as the older slave women transformed her from the filthy slave girl into a Persian princess of western men's fantasies, scented like the petals of the lotus. It was not a difficult transformation. For that was what she was. That was what she had been, not even a year ago.

Before her, the colorful art portrayed a tanned and well-muscled man with a gray head and oversized phallus bedding a dozen women at once. Clearly, the man was intended to be Valens. But who were the women? Certainly, not her. The women in the fresco smiled as though they enjoyed his attentions.

Baseirta emphatically did not.

"You'd like to kill yourself, wouldn't you, my blossom?" Cimon the overseer said, grinning. He had been watching impishly from the corner as the slaves prepared her, sniggering whenever one of the attendants inadvertently bumped one of her loose breasts. He was a salivating fiend, his eyes clearly communicating every one of his deviant desires. And now he laughed. "You'd like to kill yourself, but you won't. Isn't that right, girl? You know what will happen if you do. You know who'll pay the price for such impudence."

Kill myself? No. Stab Valens through the heart as he sleeps? Yes. But one would be as harmful as the other. All my suffering to this point would be for nothing. I can do neither. Nor can I escape this torment. Anahit, preserve me!

A slight nod was the only reply she conveyed outwardly.

"And don't you ever forget it, my blossom. You will do

your job right. You will do it the way the master likes it, and he'll go easy on you. Maybe he'll go easy on me. Then, someday, when the master is through with you and casts you off, maybe I'll take you for my own."

She felt bile in her throat. If it was possible to despise a man more than she did Valens, it was this loathsome cockroach who scurried from one exploitation to the next.

Cimon continued. "If you promise to be nice to me, as you have been to the master, perhaps I will arrange it sooner." He looked at her intently, his face dead serious now. "I can ease your torment. I will not demand your treasures as often as the master does. But, when I do, you will have to serve me with equal vigor. Do you believe you could do that, my flower?"

She felt like spitting on him, but she did not. In her former life, had a servant dared address her in such a manner, her father would have had the fool dragged by horses until the rocks and barbs had removed every shred of flesh from his bones. Now, herself a slave, she could do no more than avert her eyes from her antagonist.

Another laugh from Cimon. "Still shy, eh, my flower? Do not worry. I know his weakness. I know what I can get away with." He crossed the room, took her chin between oily fingers, and tilted her head so that she would be forced to look him in the eyes. "You don't think I have that power, do you? You think me just another slave? Ha, see, my flower. The master is smart, but only as smart as the information I give him. Cimon is the real master here. Mark me. I'll have you out of his bed and into mine within a fortnight. Then you'll be singing your night song to Cimon, not Valens."

If any fate could be crueler than the one I now endure...

She could not help the tears that now flowed down her cheeks. Cimon was a devious little man, a snake among the fruit baskets. He presented a loyal countenance to his master but took great pleasure being above the rest of the house slaves. He watched those he desired with devilish eyes. Aside from Valens's concubines, there was not a single slave Cimon had not raped. The concubines were the forbidden fruit, the master's prized possessions, and he was very particular about them. He would never loan one to a colleague, much less to a low-born slave like Cimon. Still, the snake-of-a-chief-servant knew Valens eventually tired of all his concubines. When she was ultimately expelled from the harem, Cimon would make his move to acquire her. Then, he would have complete power over her.

And that was something Baseirta dreaded even more than her present state.

The servants had finished working on her and drew back for Cimon's approval.

"Much better!" he said. "Now, you two, prepare the master's bed. And, you, go tell the master the girl is ready. Quickly, now, or I'll flog your miserable hides!"

As the slaves hurried off, Baseirta stood before Cimon with hair coiffed, eyes and nails painted, thin ribbons of gold accentuating her naked hips and breasts. The overseer's ravenous eyes studied her supple curves. "Ah, yes. Much better indeed, my blossom. The master will be pleased. Perhaps almost as pleased as when I have that soldier murdered."

Baseirta did not know what the uneducated degenerate was talking about. But any curiosity left her thoughts when Cimon suddenly drew close and took in a lungful of air less than a finger's length from her quivering bosom. He then stepped back, eyes shut, as if envisioning some perverse fantasy. When he opened them again, they were looking squarely into hers, and a chill ran up her spine.

"Perhaps the master will reward me after I kill the

soldier. It is important to him. Perhaps he'll give me anything I want."

He smiled, showing a mouthful of yellow teeth. Another shudder passed through her.

"Yes, it will not be long now, my flower, my blossom, my Asian lotus..." His voice faded as he followed the remaining servants out of the room.

Baseirta stood there alone, naked, awaiting the master.

Oh, father. She fought back the tears again. *If I did not love you so, I could not bear any more of this...*

XVIII

The air was heavy and dank in the subterranean prison. The dungeon reeked of human filth, the collective mildew of a thousand years. Slimy rocks jutted from unevenly cut walls and glimmered under scanty lamplight. The rocks were cold to the touch, transferring a foul residue to anything that brushed against them. Hollow sounds echoed through the narrow passages – maddening shrieks, incoherent mumblings, human suffering. An incessant dripping seemed to emanate from every dark corner, penetrating the mind, accentuating the agonizingly slow passage of time.

The haggard, long-bearded man seemed impervious to the bleak surroundings as he slept on the opposite side of the chamber. Lucius concluded he was old, though it was impossible to tell from the filthy, matted hair and grimy face. It seemed the old man had not moved from that spot since Lucius and Strabo had been admitted to the cell the day before.

The cell they shared was a square cavern carved out of the rock, measuring no more than five yards on a side. Three walls of the cell were solid rock, while the fourth consisted of an iron grating that ran from floor to ceiling. The grating contained a single hinged door so low that one needed to stoop significantly to pass through it. Far down the passage, a flickering oil lamp hung from the wall. It was the only source of light, and it was meager at best.

The old man had been sleeping when they had arrived and had continued to sleep as if unaware of their presence. Aside from an occasional moaning, snoring, or some other involuntary bodily utterance, there had been little indication he was even alive. Unsure of the fate that awaited them, Lucius and Strabo had decided to follow standard army routine and sleep in shifts. They had been given threadbare tunics. Lucius chose to wear his like a loincloth to avoid the stinging pain of the frayed fabric on his back which still smarted from the flogging in the swamp.

A dull bell sounded far down the passage, presumably proclaiming the changing of the guard. Lucius had heard the bell four times now.

Sixteen hours.

Had it been sixteen hours? It seemed much longer.

It seemed like days had passed since that mad, jostling ride under the storm of whistling arrows, when Roucill and Egu and their knights had escaped from their enraged countrymen and gained asylum at the gates of Dyrrachium. The Roman garrison had taken custody of Lucius and Strabo, under the vociferous protests of Roucill who did not wish to be separated from his prizes.

But they were separated. The two groups were then marched in different directions – the Gauls toward the docks, and Lucius and Strabo toward the town. Though still in a daze, Lucius had the presence of mind to look back at the Gallic princes, intending to part ways with an obscene gesture. But Lucius's attention was instantly drawn to one of those following in the princes' entourage who, surprisingly, was looking back at him. It was the druid Catugna. His eyes were fixed in that same piercing, contemplative stare that Lucius had seen before. It was as if the pale-faced wizard knew something about him, some dark secret, something shameful in his past – or, perhaps, in his future. Again, Lucius felt a tinge of familiarity. He had seen those eyes before, been under their scrutinizing gaze. Of that, there could be no doubt. Though not here, not in this manner. The nudge of a spearpoint broke Lucius's concentration as the soldiers prodded him along. When he looked again, his view of the druid was obstructed.

Under their new captors, Lucius and Strabo were directed into the heart of the town, where the stench of the fishmonger stands permeated everything. The soldiers turned them onto a side lane, toward a neglected quarter where an earthquake had reduced many buildings to piles of bricks. Starving beggars and cripples clawed at their legs as they were led past. Soon, the wide, cobbled streets gave way to narrow footpaths that climbed into the hills to the north of town. Finally, they stopped in a hollow where a wooden platform and winch assembly stood over a wide hole in the earth. The winch was like those used for hoisting heavy cargoes onto ships. This one was used for lowering the condemned into Dyrrachium's vast subterranean prison.

The squeaking of the winch faded with the light as Lucius and Strabo rode the platform down into pitch blackness. Down, down, and down, until the hole was no more than a pinpoint of light above them. The platform came to rest on a hard, rocky floor where another exchange of custody took place under torchlight. The callous jailers had directed them through low, twisting passages, past dark cells where ghoulish eyes stared back from the shadows. Finally, they had arrived at the cell with the sleeping old man, where they had been unshackled and shoved inside without a word of explanation, and the door locked behind them.

Now, their scruffy cellmate continued to sleep soundly, seemingly oblivious to their presence. Lucius found it almost humorous and managed a small laugh before dismissing the old man and turning his attention back down the passage beyond the grating. It had been hours since the last guard had passed by. It was possible there were none around, or one might be just beyond his view, for all he knew. Lucius wondered how the sound might carry were he to try his hand at wrenching the iron bars free of their foundation. How much time would he have?

The dancing flame within the distant lamp cast fluttering shadows on the wall. It set Lucius thinking about his men, the century he had left behind.

What would those idling vagabonds be doing right about now? Nothing good, for sure. The bloody mule turds were probably celebrating his absence.

Amid his musings, Lucius suddenly sensed a presence in the darkness, something close by. Turning his head, he was shocked to discover a pair of glittering eyes less than an arm's length away, staring intensely into his. Lucius dashed to the side instinctively, expecting to be attacked, then realized the eyes belonged to the old man, their hitherto sleeping cellmate. The haggard figure now squatted sprightly with knees drawn up under his chin. Somehow, he had snuck up on Lucius without making a sound.

The lamplight finally afforded a good look at the man. Deep creases of age lined an olive face. Thick streaks of gray ran through a mane of matted hair. His beard extended to his chest and was completely gray, save for the stains left by whatever gruel he had subsisted on down here. Clearly, the old one was of eastern origins, from beyond the Greek Isles. His dark, wild eyes stared back at Lucius with the intensity of near madness.

Not knowing if the old man intended harm, nor whether he carried some hidden weapon under the rags he wore as clothes, Lucius proceeded with caution. He nudged Strabo awake, who, upon noticing the nearness of their cellmate, bolted upright.

The old man glared back at them, his intense eyes darting from one to the other. He muttered something in a language Lucius did not know. Whatever it was, it did not sound friendly.

"I did not understand that, old one," Lucius said.

The easterner stared at him a long moment, then spat on the floor. "I said, your stench offends me, Roman!" This time, the old man spoke in perfect Latin.

Lucius and Strabo exchanged amused glances.

"*Mithra* curse me!" the easterner continued with nostrils flaring, his teeth bared in a grin that exuded more disgust than delight. "Will I never be released from this suffering? Must I now share this miserable hole with Latin vermin?"

"Careful, old one," Strabo said. "We are soldiers, and we are in no mood to be insulted, even by a raving fool."

The easterner reared his head back in a fit of laughter. His cackling resounded off the stone walls, prompting a reproach from an unseen jailer down the passage.

"Soldiers, you say?" the old man said with a suppressed grin after regaining his composure. "That much is obvious. Roman legionaries, no doubt. Am I to quiver before your excellencies? Should I bow down? *Mithra*, save me!"

His manner was utterly disingenuous.

"Where are you from, old one?" Lucius asked, ignoring

the challenge. Clearly, to have any hopes of escaping this dungeon, it was in their best interest to befriend this man — even if he was mad in the head.

"*Mithra* curse you, boy!" the easterner snapped. "I'll not casually converse with Latin vermin like this is some Syrian bathhouse!"

"Watch yourself, old man," Strabo said. "If you wish me to dash that gray head of yours against the wall, I will oblige."

Again, the old easterner laughed heartily. "You talk boldly, youngling, but you know not to whom you speak. I was spitting heads on pikes long before you were born, and I would have no trouble adding two more to my tally."

Strabo cursed, advancing at him with clenched fists, but Lucius reached out a hand to stop him. The old easterner had not even flinched. He crouched there smiling, buoyant eyes and jagged teeth amid the frazzled hair as if welcoming Strabo's attack.

"Don't waste your strength on the mad," Lucius said to calm his comrade. "No doubt, this old fool is locked away down here because his mind left him long ago, and no one had the heart to put him out of his misery."

The easterner looked amused as if seeing right through Lucius's change in tactics. "I am here, young man, because this is where the Romans put those whom they fear, those whom they could not break."

"You are Syrian then?" Lucius asked. "Or, perhaps Egyptian?"

"Syrian? Egyptian?" The old man spat on the floor again. "Bah! That's what an uneducated Latin would think. All those with skin darker than yours are from Syria or Egypt. Is that as far as unlearned minds can reach? I am neither."

"Then where are you from?"

"Where am I from?" he replied mockingly. "One does not ask Varaz Vizur, *Marzban* of Gugark, where he is from like he is some traveling street performer!"

"*Marzban* of …" Strabo made an attempt to repeat the title then gave up. "I've never heard of such a place."

"Nor shall you ever hear of me," the old man snarled. "Your kind saw fit to remove my existence from the written records most thoroughly."

"Then you belong to a conquered people, eh?" Strabo concluded.

"Conquered?" Varaz Vizur exclaimed aghast. "There are not ten thousand legions that could conquer Parthia, young man. Your fool-of-a-general Crassus tried it, did he not? And met his doom. A most glorious day, was that!"

"You were there, old one, at Carrhae?" Lucius asked with some fascination.

"Indeed, I was. My thousand cataphracts slaughtered many hundreds of Latins that day!" He shot a glance at Strabo. "I myself rode down more than three dozen."

"I had many comrades in that army, Parthian," Strabo said with gritted teeth.

"Then perhaps some of your friends were crushed under the hooves of my steed. Regrettably, I cannot tell you what their faces looked like since they were all fleeing."

Again, Lucius's hand stayed Strabo's advance.

"Parthian filth," Strabo muttered.

"Mind your tongue, vermin!" This time, Varaz moved toward Strabo, shuffling across the floor like a scurrying animal. When he was within an arm's length of Strabo, he began moving from side to side in an invisible half-circle. The strange moves looked like a tribal dance, but Lucius assumed it to be some kind of eastern fighting technique.

Strabo was clearly unimpressed by the maneuvers, standing with fists clenched, ready to land a blow on the old man at the first opportunity.

"Wait!" Lucius stepped in between them. "To fight each other is futile. We are all prisoners here. Reserve your ire for our common enemy."

Strabo stepped back. The easterner ceased his odd dance then slowly retreated to his corner of the cell. The three sat there for some time in silence. The stillness was finally broken by a muffled human shriek that came from far down the passage. The scream then diminished, as if rapidly moving away, until it was no longer audible.

"I can see you are new to the dungeon," Varaz said at the perplexed looks on the Romans' faces. For the first time, he spoke in a civil tone. "It is the Pit of the Damned. If you become ill or maimed down here, or if they just decide they need your cell for a more valuable prisoner, they dispose of you rather cleverly. You are thrown into a bottomless pit called the Pit of the Damned. It is in one of these *Mithra-forsaken* caverns."

"Then you haven't seen it?" Strabo asked.

Varaz smiled at his skepticism. "Oh, it is real, Roman. I have been in this dungeon for nigh on ten months. In that time, I have not seen the light of day. I have not heard the song of birds, nor the crash of the ocean, nor the voice of women, nor that of children. But I have heard that. More times than I could count. Men have come, and men have died. Yet I remain. I do not know why. Perhaps as an amusement to the gods."

"Why do you not end it, old man?" Lucius asked lightly. "Have the last laugh on the gods."

"The Roman way, eh? No, young man. This world is not yet done with me, and I am not done with it. Every day, I pray to *Mithra* for justice. The fact that I am still alive gives me hope that my prayers might yet be answered."

The old man leaned back against the wall and sighed, all

traces of his former aggression gone. For the first time, his movements matched the gray hair on his head. He closed his eyes and slowly drew his legs up under his arms as if the movement caused him great pain. His earlier vigor had come at a cost.

The change in the old man's demeanor was welcome, but Lucius wanted some answers.

"If you are this Parthian noble you claim to be, how is it you came to be here?"

Varaz opened his eyes and looked back at him suspiciously. "First, you will answer me, Latin. I have overheard enough of the guards' conversations to deduce that the Romans are engaged in civil war. That Pompey commands one army and Caesar the other. And that Pompey controls the town above us to which Caesar now lays siege. It has been a small comfort to me in this wretched hole to hear of Romans killing other Romans. It pleases me to no end. So, I deduce that you are either deserters, or soldiers of Caesar, or both. Which is it?"

"We are not deserters," Lucius replied. "We belong to Caesar."

Strabo sneered at that. Clearly, he had not forgotten his vow in the swamp.

Varaz, however, clapped his hands together and burst out in another bout of giddy laughter. "Vile Romans putting one another to the sword! *Mithra* be praised!"

The laughter continued, echoing hollowly off the rock walls as Lucius and Strabo watched with mounting frustration.

"Now, old man." Lucius finally interrupted his merriment. "Tell us how came you here."

It took a long moment for the Parthian to compose himself. "I am here because I made the foolish decision to swear allegiance to the Parthian prince Mithridates when he murdered his father, the Parthian king Phraates, and assumed the Parthian throne."

"Then you chose to serve the man who became king?" Lucius asked, prompting a nod from Varaz. "It seems like the right choice to me."

The old man allowed a smile. "It was, until the brother of Mithridates, a reprobate called Orodes, murdered Mithridates and took the throne for himself."

"Did you not have the sense to simply swear fealty to the new king?" Lucius asked.

Varaz's smile faded. "Of course, I did! But Orodes never forgot my service to his brother. Even my valorous deeds at Carrhae were not enough to cleanse me of that offense. I remained at my estate in Gugark, a loyal vassal, managing my corner of the empire and sending Orodes twice the required tribute every year. I never traveled to Seleucia and never received a visit from the king. Years passed, and I began to believe the king had forgiven me. How wrong I was.

"One day, I received a visitor, a Roman senator bearing an introduction from Orodes himself. The king counted the Roman his friend, and so I welcomed him into my house. Having been banished from Rome, the man was to stay as my guest for some time, and I was expected to afford him all the courtesies and privileges of royalty. He was a despicable Latin like yourselves, but much more arrogant. I loathed him from the start. In no time at all, my uninvited guest began to take advantage of my hospitality, ordering my servants around as if they were his own, demanding his choice of my concubines each night. What could I do but acquiesce? The king had ordered me to cater to the Roman's every wish." Varaz's face twisted into a snarl. "But there was one wish I would never entertain. The villain became infatuated with my daughter and demanded I give her to him as his wife. I nearly had him decapitated on the spot. There is a limit to a man's hospitality, after all. Pssssh!" Varaz spat on the floor.

"Did this Roman senator have a name?" Lucius asked reluctantly.

"His name? I will not speak his name. I will not utter that abominable name unless it is to curse the villain before I cut his throat!" Varaz paused, allowing his rage to cool. "In any event, it soon became evident to me that this Roman was assessing my estate and all that I owned, like a buyer on the market. I grew ever more convinced that some arrangement existed between him and Orodes regarding my fate.

"Then, one day, my fears were manifested in the arrival of a delegation from the king, bearing a warrant for my arrest. My guest had accused me of treason, claiming he had evidence that I was conspiring with Orodes's son Phraates to overthrow him. The charge was blatantly false. I saw it for what it was – a means to have me removed without inciting a revolt from my cataphracts. They had ever been loyal to me, but Orodes succeeded in branding me a traitor, and that was enough to sway them.

"In the end, I was imprisoned, and the Roman was given all my possessions. My kin were made his slaves, including my poor daughter. Some committed suicide, but most were sold to traders from foreign lands. My family was scattered to the four winds, never to return. The Roman kept my daughter, and he kept me. Now, I am his captive, and my daughter is his…" Varaz's voice wavered. He was overcome with emotion. "When word of the war between Caesar and Pompey reached Parthia, the Roman came here to Dyrrachium and brought us with him. I was placed down here and, by my reckoning, have not left this chamber for ten months. As for my daughter, I do not know what has become of her. I am told that she lives, but I do not know what to believe. I try not to think of what she must be suffering at the hands of that beast. If I thought on it too long, I would certainly bash my head against these rocks. My only prayer is that blessed *Mithra* will put the neck of that demon within reach of these two hands before I die."

"Why have they not killed you, old one?" Strabo said bluntly. "If you've been down here all this time, it seems your master would be better off sending you into that pit with the others than keeping you alive."

"He is not my master, Latin! Varaz Vizur serves no Roman dog!" The Parthian's ire did not last but a moment. A sudden thought had clearly come to him. "A more intriguing question is, why are the two of you here? Someone up there wants you alive."

It was indeed a good question and one that Lucius had been pondering. Why had they not been executed? Why bother holding them here? Lucius could not come up with a logical answer.

"What were those odd moves before, old one?" Strabo asked, now affording the easterner a measure of sympathy. "Were you wishing to dance or fight?"

"Count yourself fortunate I stopped, Roman, and pray that you never again face the Parthian form of Pankration."

"You mean Greek wrestling?" Strabo chuckled. "Is that all?"

Varaz smiled, showing yellow teeth amid his gray beard. "Laugh if you wish. Our techniques are far superior to that of the Greek – or the Latin. Should it ever be administered on you, you will understand. Thank whatever false Roman gods you pray to that your friend here stayed my hand."

Strabo laughed again.

XIX

Over the next several hours, Lucius tried several times to get Varaz Vizur to reveal the identity of his captor. A possibility niggled at the back of Lucius's mind, a thought too fantastic to be true, but one that he had to confirm for his own sanity. But the old Parthian remained true to his vow and would say nothing.

At one point, an uncharacteristic stillness fell upon the dungeon. No voices, no screams, nothing. The silence was deafening.

"Something is happening," Varaz commented. "It is never this quiet."

Then, voices were heard in the passage, the shuffle of many feet. A procession filed into the dull light beyond the grating – six men, presumably prisoners, led by a single guard. The prisoners wore plain, sleeveless tunics, revealing broad shoulders and powerful arms. Their gait was not that of soldiers but of seafaring men. From his brief interlude as a rower in a war galley, Lucius identified their lopsided proportions as those of oarsmen.

Strangely, the new prisoners were not shackled. They offered no resistance as the guard unbolted the door to the cell. There was a casual yet orderly manner to their movements as they filed inside, each one glancing at Lucius and Strabo with churlish, almost self-assured smiles before taking a seat along the opposite wall. For newly consigned inmates, they seemed remarkably light-hearted. Lucius did not miss the sidelong glance from the guard who bolted the door then retired down the passage without uttering a word.

Something was indeed happening, something carefully choreographed.

The largest of the new arrivals was a tanned brute with bushy eyebrows that met as one above his nose. He snuck frequent glances at Lucius and Strabo while the others seemed to watch only him.

Strabo presented an outwardly calm demeanor, but a cut of his eyes conveyed that he, too, had noticed the odd behavior. Varaz Vizur was not as subtle. He leaned in close to the centurions.

"These men are assassins, as clearly as the sun shines on a cloudless day," Varaz whispered cheerfully as if welcoming the excitement after so many months of boredom.

"But are they here for you or us?" Asked Lucius lowly, never taking his eyes off the men across the chamber.

Varaz chuckled. "Since I have been here for a long time, and you have only just arrived, I'll wager they are here for you. Be wary, young ones. They are Macedonians, by the looks of them. Trust them only to stab you in the back. The one with the heavy brows is the leader. You must kill him first."

"We know, old one," Strabo said lowly. "And just why

the devil do you care, anyway?"

The Parthian looked at him as if the answer were obvious. "If there's anything more despicable than the dirty Latin, it's the foul Macedonian."

Lucius waved the old man away, wishing no further distraction while he kept his eyes on the six across the room. They pretended to be lounging but yawned incessantly and shifted nervously, the tell-tale signs of men preparing for violence.

Lucius scanned the cell for anything that might be used as a weapon, but there was nothing. Aside from a single waste bucket, the cell was utterly barren. Abandoning that hope, he shifted his study to the six brutes, mentally sorting them into three groups – the hesitant, the unpredictable, and the thoughtful.

If the contest came down to raw strength alone, the oarsmen would surely win. They appeared to be well-nourished, which meant they probably did not come from the fleet. More likely, they belonged to the crew of a private galley and were hired out by their employer as thugs from time to time. They were probably amateurs, not trained fighters.

If we could only throw them off somehow,...a distraction, or...

Suddenly, Varaz stood up and stretched with a loud yawn. Stepping forward to face the newcomers, he addressed them. "Do you all know what my comrades here and I were just discussing?"

Lucius cursed under his breath, before realizing what the old man was doing. They needed a distraction, and this was it. The thugs were clearly surprised by the direct question and now looked to their equally confused leader for guidance.

"We were wondering," Varaz continued. "Do the men in Macedon still bugger the goats, or do the goats bugger the men?"

The insult had the desired effect. It was the thick-browed leader that made the first move. He did not rush at the old Parthian, but at Lucius, low and fast. Lucius was ready for him. He brought a knee up to meet his attacker's face. The nose crunched, and a torrent of blood ensued. The stunned leader fell to the side, clutching a ruined face. But Lucius had no time to savor the victory. Another brute came right behind the first. He slowed upon seeing the fate of his leader, and Lucius took full advantage of that hesitancy. Side-stepping the advance, Lucius used one hand to force the brute's head down, then let the charging man's own momentum carry him into the wall. Skull succumbed to rock with a sickening crack, and the brute fell to the floor twitching.

Meanwhile, a few paces away, Strabo was fending off the three men who had gone after him. Strabo had not fared as well. Though two of his attackers were bleeding from split lips, they had managed to brace his arms between them and were using their rowers' strength to keep him in one place. A third attempted to land punches between Strabo's wild kicks. Blow after blow struck Strabo's face and midsection. He thrashed around violently, but the oarsmen's grip would not be broken.

Lucius saw all this in the space of a heartbeat, but it distracted him long enough for the last brute to catch him at a disadvantage. With a giant muscled arm, the attacker seized Lucius around the neck from behind. The arm instantly closed like a vice, squeezing without mercy while the other hand pushed against the back of Lucius's head. Lucius's neck threatened to snap within seconds if he did not find a way out of the hold. With his powerful legs, he pushed off the floor, trying to force his attacker into the wall, but his bare feet could not gain traction on the slick surface. Desperately, he pried at the massive bicep, but his strength was failing fast. The exertion of the last few days had taken its toll. His sight began to dim. His legs began to wobble.

Then, from the corner of his blurred vision, Lucius spied a flurry of flapping gray hair and rags dash across the floor toward the struggling Strabo. It was Varaz Vizur! The old Parthian moved in the same strange manner that he had before. Strabo's attackers dismissed the wiry old man, clearly not considering him a threat.

That was a mistake.

In the blink of an eye, Varaz was crouching under the wide stance of the brute that was punching Strabo. With lightning speed, the Parthian punched upward with both fists into the man's groin. The brute shrieked in pain and dropped to his knees, clutching his genitals. The next moment, Varaz formed his fingers into pointed cones and jabbed them into the dazed man's eyes. He struck over and over, in rapid succession, until both eyes had been reduced to oozing pools of jelly.

Those holding Strabo looked at their blind and screaming comrade in dumbstruck horror, confused as to whether they should turn to meet this new threat or keep their grip on the Roman. While they dithered, Varaz acted.

Like a spider, the old Parthian scampered across the floor to the brute on Strabo's right, then proceeded to drive rapid punches up into the man's crotch. Not daring to let go of the powerful centurion, the brute could do nothing but absorb the repeated blows. His face turned beet red with pain under the pummeling, until, finally, he released his hold on Strabo and crumpled to the floor. Now facing even odds, Strabo used his newly freed hand to grasp the other brute by the hair and wrestle him to the floor, where both rolled and flailed in an effort to kill each other.

Lucius saw all this happen in the span of a few moments, as the immovable arm around his neck slowly squeezed the life out of him.

Then, he felt something rustle past his legs, felt the grip on his neck suddenly slacken, heard his opponent let out a cry of pain, then release him entirely. Lucius collapsed face down on the cold floor, close to unconsciousness as the blood flowed again, and his senses slowly returned. He heard men scuffling nearby, rolled onto his side, saw Varaz struggling with the same thug who had been choking him. But now, it was the thug's turn to struggle. As before, Varaz had employed his unorthodox yet devilishly effective method to disable the man. But, this time, the old Parthian had not let go of the target organ. He had the man by the genitals, which he squeezed and twisted without mercy. The thug screamed in anguish, slammed his fists down onto the old man's head and shoulders, one feeble blow after another, in a desperate attempt to remove him. He implored Varaz to stop, begged him to the point of tears, but the old Parthian only grinned and tightened his grip further.

Still prostrate but rapidly regaining his strength, Lucius felt something clawing at his feet. Looking down, he saw the delirious eyes of the heavy-browed leader, his smashed nose a blossom of red. Lucius cocked one leg and delivered a solid kick to the man's face, planting his heel firmly into the remnants of the shattered nose. Blinded by his own blood, the leader crawled away to the far corner of the room holding his dripping face in one hand.

Three of the six thugs moaned on the floor. The one with the shattered skull lay unmoving. The remaining two were losing in their struggles against Strabo and the Parthian.

Then, Lucius saw a glimmer of steel on the floor. It was

a small dagger. One of the brutes must have slipped the weapon past the guard. Or, perhaps, the guard knew all about it. Regardless, the blade was now just within reach of the brute squirming under Varaz's grip. The distressed man noticed the weapon at the same time as Lucius, and Lucius was but an arm-length too far away to stop what was about to happen.

"Look out!" Lucius shouted to Varaz, but the warning came too late.

The brute snatched up the weapon and plunged it into Varaz's shoulders. He stabbed again and again in desperation. The old man did not cry out as the red splotches on his tunic expanded. He tried to maintain the grip on his opponent's genitals, but he faltered under the sixth thrust of the dagger. Before the blade came down a seventh time, Lucius was there to stop it.

Taking hold of the thug's forearm, Lucius did not bother trying to pry the weapon loose. He forced the wrist to pivot, directed the point of the blade straight into the man's neck, drove it to the hilt with full force until the red tip emerged from the opposite side. The wide-eyed brute choked and gargled, his open neck spraying blood onto the wall as he tried in vain to yank the blade free. Finally, he collapsed, dead.

Lucius rushed to Varaz's side and was quickly joined by Strabo who had just finished breaking the neck of his own opponent. Lucius gently rolled the wheezing man over, then cradled the shaggy gray head in his hands. Varaz looked up at him. Blood trickled from the Parthian's mouth, but his expression was oddly complacent.

"Why did you help us, old one?" Strabo said. "You should have minded your own business."

"It was wonderful." Varaz managed a smile. "Even if to help filthy Romans. I will finally leave this wretched place. I will walk the shores of the Tigris with my ancestors."

"You go to them with honor," Lucius said. He would not give false hope to a dying man.

The Parthian then motioned for Lucius to lean closer. Lucius complied.

"Remember, youngling. These assassins were not put here by happenstance. Someone wants you dead – you and your friend there. They want you dead, quietly and secretly. Be wary."

Varaz then reached up and grabbed Lucius's hand with surprising strength. After prying open Lucius's fingers, he placed a small metallic object in his palm.

It was an amulet of some kind, hardly the size of a fingernail, with etchings on one side that Lucius could not make out in the dim light.

"What is this, old one?" Lucius asked.

But no answer came, nor would the old Parthian ever speak again. Varaz Vizur was dead.

"The cantankerous, old bastard," Strabo said regretfully. "Never gave me the chance to take back my earlier words."

"Pluto take his soul," Lucius said. "And he'd be taking ours, too, had the old man not intervened."

"What did he give you?" Strabo asked.

Lucius shrugged, turning the amulet over in his hands. "Perhaps the only item of value he still possessed."

"Juno's crotch! What the devil is going on here?" a voice boomed from the passage.

Lucius and Strabo looked up to see several armed guards standing on the other side of the grating, peering into the cell. The jailer nervously fumbled with the bolt before the door was thrown open, and the guards burst inside. They quickly separated Lucius and Strabo from the dead Parthian. The six brutes, some dead, some groaning, were dragged to the opposite side of the cell. An army tribune in bronze cuirass entered and surveyed the room, a frown of disgust on his face.

"What were these men doing in here?" the officer demanded, pointing at the thugs.

"I-I do not know, excellency," the jailer fidgeted nervously. "I do not understand. I did not authorize – "

"Remove them, at once!" the tribune snapped.

"Y-Yes, excellency."

"You are incompetent and stupid!"

"Y-Yes, excellency."

One of the guards discovered the dagger, yanked it out of the dead man's neck, and presented it to the tribune.

"And I suppose you also don't know how this got in here?" the tribune said to the jailer.

"I-I do not know, excellency. I always have new prisoners searched thoroughly. I cannot explain it."

"Consider yourself fortunate these two are alive. Otherwise, Pompey might have had that dense head of yours removed from your shoulders. As it stands, I have a mind to tell him of this."

"Please, no, your excellency!" the jailer pleaded, hands clasped before his face. "I swear by Athena, I do not know how these men got in here. One of my guards must have admitted them by mistake."

"Then I suggest you get control of your guards, jailer. Have them all flogged for good measure."

"An excellent suggestion, excellency. I-I will see to it, at once. Perhaps you would be so kind as to tell the general – "

"You, there." The tribune had already redirected his attention to the Roman prisoners. "Centurions Domitius and Strabo, I believe?"

Lucius and Strabo stood, instinctively coming to attention before the senior officer.

"Are you injured?" the tribune asked.

"No, sir," Lucius replied.

"Then answer me promptly when I ask you a question, damn you!"

"Yes, sir."

"This is your lucky day. The general wishes to see you."

"The general, sir?" Lucius inquired.

The tribune looked annoyed. "Lord Pompey – the general of the army, or does Caesar not tell his troops who they are fighting? I wouldn't be surprised if that bloody traitor kept it from you. Otherwise, the whole lot of you might desert, eh?" The tribune chuckled mechanically at his own jest.

"Sir?" Lucius was perplexed. "I'm not sure I understand."

"Lucretia's chaste arse! Do I have to spell it out for you? His Excellency, General Pompeius Magnus, has sent me to fetch you. Juno knows why you weren't taken to him before." He gestured at the jailer. "I've ordered this fool to bring a washbasin and fresh tunics. You are to clean yourselves up and join me topside. There's a boat waiting to take us back to the camp. Do not tarry." The tribune twisted his nose in discomfort. "Now, you will excuse me. The stink of this place makes me want to vomit. I'll be waiting outside. Remember, do not tarry!"

XX

Hours had passed since Lucius left that dark, dismal prison. And yet, his eyes were still unaccustomed to the glare of the late morning sun.

He yawned under the watchful eyes of two legionaries while he waited outside the pavilion. The daily life of an army camp went on around him. Nearby, Roucill and Egu also waited. The Gallic princes eyed him grudgingly, clearly unsatisfied with the current situation. Lucius returned their stares defiantly, taking great pleasure in their frustration.

Lucius and Strabo had arrived in Pompey's camp less than an hour ago, escorted by the tribune and a small detachment of legionaries. Riding in the boat across the bay, it had seemed strange to approach the enemy camp from the other side of the lines. Until now, he had only seen the tops of the enemy works winding along the crests of the hills. Now, standing on the other side of those hills, he was amazed at how many tens of thousands of troops were packed inside the besieged camp. It was one of the largest concentrations of men he had ever seen – and quite possibly the sloppiest.

The orderly rectangular structure of the standard marching camp had been abandoned here, whether from laziness or the impracticability of maintaining symmetrical dimensions on such hilly terrain. Thousands of white canvas tents dotted the landscape. Uneven pathways wound between them, forming natural lanes where streams of bobbing helmets and bare heads moved. Soldiers and slaves did camp work in various states of dress and armor. Others seemed content to lounge. The inescapable aroma of dung hung in the air, seemingly unaffected by the stiff ocean breeze.

The camp was not regimented to Lucius's satisfaction – or the satisfaction of any centurion with a shred of pride. And yet, the troops seemed eager and in good spirits. Quite remarkable, considering the obvious water shortage. The constant protests of ten thousand horses and pack animals corralled on the adjacent slope served as a reminder of that morbid fact.

Lucius and Strabo were directed up a hill to a collection of larger pavilions overlooking most of the camp. Clusters of senior officers in polished armor paused in their conversations long enough to glance inquisitively at the prisoners as they passed by. Finally, Lucius and Strabo were admitted to the largest of the tents. It was carpeted inside, and lushly furnished with all the comforts of a country villa. Roucill and Egu were there, taking sips from shiny goblets across from a glowering legate whom Lucius recognized as General Labienus. The general had once been Caesar's deputy in Gaul, and he looked as peevish and discontented now as he had back then. Having witnessed his cruelty toward prisoners on several occasions, Lucius concluded their future looked grim.

And there was another, too, a gray-haired, somewhat

portly man with high eyebrows and bold features. He wore a simple yet finely woven tunic. Lucius did not need to be told who he was. Somehow, Pompeius Magnus, the exalted general and hero of countless tales of glory, was everything Lucius had expected, and, at the same time, nothing he had expected. There was certainly nothing awe-inspiring about Pompey's appearance, though Lucius got the feeling Pompey himself thought otherwise.

The aging general examined the new arrivals with tired, thoughtful eyes as if he could somehow measure their worth from a single glance.

"Ah!" Roucill had said excitedly. "Our prisoners! You see, my lord Pompey. Just as we told you. Two of Caesar's centurions. They are our gift to you."

"Our thanks, friends," Pompey had said with a dismissive gesture. "But, as I said before, I am more interested in your knowledge of Caesar's works."

"But Great Pompey! As you can see –"

"My dear Roucill," Pompey had interrupted. "You and I will walk the lines together, and you will show me where Caesar is weakest. Indeed, I have many questions for you. But first, I will speak with these centurions. You may wait outside."

"There is no need to speak to them!" Roucill had objected. "What is there to discuss? They are your enemies. Execute them and be done with it. If you wish, Egu will gladly do it for you. And if you see fit to reward us, we will –"

"Tribune, escort these men out," Pompey had interjected, clearly annoyed by the Gallic prince's nagging. "I wish to see the prisoners one at a time. Have one wait outside while I talk to the other."

And Strabo had been the first to discourse with Pompey. That had been nearly an hour ago, and Lucius still awaited his turn outside the pavilion, staring back at the fidgeting Allobroges princes. It was unusual for the general of the army to spend so much of his valuable time with a lowly centurion. Nevertheless, Lucius suspected he knew what the meeting was about. From the deplorable state of the enemy camp, it was clear Pompey lacked enough qualified centurions, the backbone of any Roman army. He was surely offering Strabo a commission. And, judging from Strabo's earlier sentiments about Antony and Caesar, vowing never to serve either one again, Pompey might have found a willing recruit.

The flap was suddenly drawn aside, and Strabo emerged. He gave Lucius a single, grim nod, but said nothing before being led away by the guards. Lucius detected something different in his demeanor, an internal struggle that had not been there before.

"Centurion Domitius!" the tribune called from the open flap. "The general will see you now."

Moments later, Lucius was standing at attention in Pompey's chamber while the great general poured himself another cup of wine at a nearby table.

"Lucius Domitius, eh?" Pompey studied him across the several paces separating them. "The name is familiar to me, yet I cannot quite place it. Have you ever served under me, young man?"

"My father served with you in Spain, my lord."

Pompey closed his eyes as if to search his memories. "Domitius...yes. I vaguely remember a centurion of that name. That was so long ago. Yes, I believe there is a resemblance. How is your father?"

"I regret to report he died long ago, sir."

"Well, that is unfortunate," Pompey said with seemingly genuine sympathy.

A deep, contemptuous sigh came from Labienus, who

lounged on a couch in the corner, observing the interview in perturbed silence. He clearly disagreed with the friendly exchange.

Pompey stepped closer to Lucius and examined the bruises on his face. "You do seem a bit worse for the wear. You and your comrade, both. I understand there was a scuffle in the prison?"

"Begging your pardon, General, but this happened before we ever reached the prison. This was the doing of those Allobroges bastards out there." Lucius paused, then could not help but add, "I never thought I'd see the day when one Roman would sanction the flogging of another by barbarian scum. I think my old *pater* must be rolling over in his tomb."

"Mind your tongue, traitor!" Labienus snapped, but Pompey silenced him with a glance.

"I quite agree, young Domitius," Pompey said with a cheerless smile. "They overstepped their bounds. And under different circumstances, they would surely not see the next sunset." He sighed heavily. "But, in war, as in politics, it is sometimes necessary to crawl into bed with those we despise. Surely, you understand that better than most. I understand you served in Gaul?"

Lucius did not reply. His eyes remained accusatory.

"Do not look at me that way, young man!" Pompey said, the first inkling of irritation in his tone. "The blood spilled in this war is on Caesar's head, not mine! He is the one who marched on Rome! He is the one who brought war to Greece!" Pompey's face had turned red, and a vein pulsed near one eye. He took several deep breaths before returning to his formerly calm demeanor. When he spoke again, it was with forced coolness. "However, you are quite right in bringing this injustice to my attention. I will indeed see to it that the Allobroges are punished – when all this is over."

He allowed a friendly smile. "Few of us wish to be here. Fewer still wish to fight our brothers on the other side. I, for one, would much rather spend my older years gardening at my country villa than in the field under arms. I'm sure that feeling is shared by many of your comrades serving under Caesar. It saddens me to think of the fates they will suffer. So many promising young men dishonored and exiled, if not killed outright on the battlefield, or under the executioner's blade."

Lucius stared straight ahead, unfazed, and this seemed to amuse Pompey.

"You don't believe me, do you?" Pompey said tiredly. "You have marched under Caesar for so long, you believe him infallible. But I assure you, my young friend, for all his bluster and fanfare, Caesar is still quite the novice. The northern frontier is not like these coastal lands. Gaul is not Greece. Caesar is accustomed to facing a disorganized rabble thrown together by half-mad Gallic chieftains. Smash their first attack, and the rest go running, eh?" He looked sternly into Lucius's eyes. "I assure you, it will not be so when Caesar faces me in battle. He will learn a hard lesson. My legions have been personally trained by me. They are the best in the world, far superior to his so-called *veterans*." Pompey smiled. "I do not mean to offend you, young man. You are, no doubt, very brave. You would not be a centurion otherwise. But you serve a man who is glorified well beyond his true abilities."

"He's managed to subdue all of Gaul," Lucius spoke up, almost involuntarily.

Pompey chuckled. "Yes, over the span of eight years. Do you know how long it took me to conquer Armenia, Syria, and Judea?"

Lucius shook his head, slightly embarrassed. He had only a slight notion of where those places were.

"Three years, my young centurion! Three years and as many kingdoms conquered. Your Caesar could not have done it in a lifetime."

"And yet, he is enclosing you against the sea as we speak," Lucius said proudly. He did not know why he felt the need to speak up for Caesar. Perhaps, it was that day at Alesia when he had been promoted to centurion after saving Caesar's life. The promotion probably had less to do with Caesar's gratitude than filling vacancies in the Tenth. Still, it had imbued Lucius with a strange loyalty that sometimes prompted him to do foolish things – like speak defiantly to a living legend who could order his execution at the wave of a finger.

But Pompey seemed more entertained than insulted, as one might find humor in the ignorance of a child.

The great general crossed the room to a table and beckoned for Lucius to join him. Upon the table lay a large chart with curled edges held down by ornate weights molded into the shapes of legionary emblems – a howling wolf's head, the grimacing face of an eagle, a horse with flaring nostrils, a majestic lion in the midst of a roar. Pompey moved each weight with a dull thud, placing them farther apart such that the entirety of the chart could be seen free of obstruction.

Labienus rose from his seat in protest, but Pompey waved him off.

"Come here, young man," he said calmly to Lucius. "Come here and see the certain destruction of your famed Caesar."

Lucius obeyed. Standing next to the general, he immediately identified the chart as a map of the area around Dyrrachium. Pompey's defensive lines were represented there, along with Caesar's opposing lines of circumvallation running nearly parallel. From their northern ends anchored on the sea, the lines stretched inland, curved southerly for several miles, and then westerly back toward the coast. Both lines were perhaps only a few days from reaching the beach. It was a massive excavation, on the scale of the works at Alesia. By Lucius's reckoning, Caesar would soon have Pompey completely hemmed in by land. Yet Pompey appeared quite smug, as if he were the besieger, not the besieged, and everything was proceeding according to his will.

"I show you this, young man, as a lesson. You will never return to Caesar's lines unless it is with a sword in your hand marching in my own ranks." It seemed Pompey said this to allay the heightened concern on Labienus's face. "I could have you killed, Centurion Domitius – you and your comrade – but what purpose would that serve? What a waste of fine soldiers who have served Rome so well. Much better if you live and continue to serve her long after the tyrant is crushed and forgotten." Pompey paused as if to allow Lucius to ponder that, then pointed at the map and continued. "You see here the lines as they are today. Every day, we extend our lines closer to the sea, and Caesar, believing I am trying to avoid encirclement, extends his lines to counter mine. It somewhat resembles an arch, don't you think? Like the great arch supporting an aqueduct. But, as you must know, Centurion, it takes many more bricks to span the crown of an arch than the base. Here, see. Caesar is the crown. I am the base. And I have many more bricks to spare. Every day, Caesar loses more men to desertion. Soon he will not have enough bricks to do the job. He will continue to match my works with his own, and his lines will be drawn thinner and thinner, until they are but strands of hair. In one week, he will have single centuries covering stretches of the line that require full cohorts. This will no longer be a siege, young Domitius. It will be a massacre in the making. And that is when I will break him." At that moment, Pompey's calm demeanor changed. He was suddenly vibrant, planting his right fist firmly into his left palm, nearly salivating at the prospect of Caesar's defeat. He quickly moved several figurines representing individual cohorts to one side of the map, like an eager adolescent playing a game of shells. "Here is where I will hit him! On his extreme left, where his lines are thinnest." He then dispersed the markers onto the other side of Caesar's lines to demonstrate how swiftly his troops would break through. "I will strike him hard, with overwhelming numbers. Caesar, in his panic, will see the disaster developing and will pull troops from the right to stop it, but this will only aid me." To illustrate, Pompey moved several unpainted and cracked pieces representing Caesar's forces – many of them phallic idols, some merely broken bits of clay. "Then, I will strike on his right with my reserves. With his lines broken in two places, my superior cavalry will dash through and roll up his flanks. Those who stand and fight will be crushed in the vice. Those who flee will be ridden down."

As he might crush a cockroach scurrying across the chart, Pompey slammed down a heavy, elaborately decorated piece firmly on Caesar's main encampment. It took Lucius a second glance to realize the piece had been crafted in Pompey's likeness, with the same stern features but appreciably less girth.

"Total victory," Pompey said with finality, letting out a sigh.

He studied Lucius's face for a moment as a playwright might await an audience's ovation after the opening night's performance. But Lucius remained stoic. Pompey smiled tiredly and returned to his chair, collapsing into it as if he had just fought the very battle he had portrayed.

"What say you, Centurion Domitius? Surely, you now see the futility of Caesar's position. Join me, and all will be forgiven and forgotten. You will be given arms and armor and your own century before the day is out. And you will be paid."

Still, Lucius did not respond.

"How can you remain loyal to such a man?" Pompey said with growing annoyance. "A man who has betrayed his nation, his people, the very people who elevated him."

"It is not Caesar who holds my loyalty, General. I am sworn to the Tenth."

"Then you place your legion above your country?"

Lucius nodded.

"Well, I suppose that suits the simple-minded. It may interest you to know that your companion was not so narrow of vision. He was much more open to reason. Does this change your mind?"

Lucius did his best to appear unfazed by the revelation. *Could it be true? Had Strabo carried through with his vow?* Whatever course Strabo had chosen, Lucius knew that his own was already chosen for him. Perhaps it was his father's steady hand reaching out from Elysium.

"Well?" Pompey demanded.

Lucius gave a slight shake of his head. "No, my lord."

"Legion above Rome, eh? Above everything. That is expected, I suppose. Pity. You remind me of the stalwart soldiers I led in Asia so very long ago."

Pompey averted his gaze to his cup. He stared into the red liquid while absently drawing one finger around the rim. In that pause, Lucius saw a transformation take place. The façade of the great and powerful man fell away, replaced by what Pompey really was – old, tired, worn out, wishing away the burden he carried. He seemed adrift in thought.

But before long, his face hardened again. His brows

drew together in an air of authority. When he spoke again, his voice was cold, indifferent.

"Unfortunately for you, Centurion, all efforts to bring the Tenth, and the other wayward legions, over to our side have failed. Caesar's legates remain loyal to him. And since you insist on remaining loyal to your legion, you are my enemy. I have little use for enemies within my camp, especially when every drop of water must be tallied. You will have a day to think it over. Such is the offer extended to all our Roman prisoners. Valiant soldiers deserve that much. Tomorrow, I will have your final answer. After that, my leniency will have reached its end."

The tribune and guards were called, and Lucius was led out of the tent.

Labienus watched the prisoner go with disgust. He loathed this ridiculous exercise, these attempts to lure the treasonous soldiers with promises of reward when they deserved only death.

This Lucius Domitius was the one Valens had spoken of. Presumably, the scuffle in the prison had been his doing. For some reason, Valens wanted the bastard dead.

"What is it, Labienus?" Pompey said after they were alone again. "Something troubles you. You do not approve of my offers to these men."

You trouble me, you fat oaf! If you spent as much time fighting the enemy as you do coddling him, Caesar's head would be on a damned pike by now.

"There are sixty-five prisoners in the stockade, Great Pompey," Labienus replied, his tone conveying none of the aggravation he felt within. "Sixty-seven, counting these two centurions."

"Yes."

"Sixty-seven traitors who cannot be trusted, who will only infest our ranks with seditious ideas should they accept your offer."

"Sixty-seven men who once fought for Rome," Pompey countered.

"With respect, my lord, they forsook their allegiance to Rome when they chose to follow Caesar. They put a sword in the tyrant's hand to take all of Italy. Let me put them to death immediately, Great Pompey!"

Pompey shook his head. "It will sour in the bellies of their families back home, my friend. Remember, these are our brothers and neighbors, our fellow Romans. Everything we do here will be visited upon us tenfold if we are not prudent."

"And I say every breath they draw is an offense to the gods, an offense to every man here who remains true to Rome."

"They will die when and if they refuse to join us." Pompey eyed him. "That is final. And I wish no more gruesome executions by those Germans of yours. The prisoners' deaths must be clean and swift. Is that understood?"

"Hermanus and his men are skilled at what they do, my lord. It is for our own men to see, as well as Caesar's. I have arranged for the prisoners to be divided up and distributed to various points along our lines. The soldiers on *both* sides will see the fate that awaits traitors."

Pompey sighed heavily. "This is a solemn occasion, my friend. I fear you make a sport of it. It is shameful, the auxiliaries watching with amusement while we brutalize our fellow countrymen."

"It is effective, my lord."

"I forbid you from any further such executions. Is that clear, General? Those who agree to join me will be greeted with open arms. Those who do not will be put to the sword. Clean and swift!"

"Yes, my lord."

"Men want to be inspired. They respond to gold and glory far better than they do to threats."

"Then perhaps it would be best to take them into battle, that they might achieve gold and glory." Labienus had tried to keep his tone respectful, but it had come out accusingly. He fully expected Pompey to be offended, to admonish him, and give him some lengthy diatribe on the folly of bringing the enemy to battle too soon. But, surprisingly, he did not.

"I quite agree, General," Pompey said with an uncharacteristically scheming look that took Labienus entirely by surprise.

"My lord? Do you mean...?"

"Come back to my pavilion this evening for supper, and bring the legates of the First, Third, Fifteenth, and Sixteenth Legions. I will have orders for you."

Could it be the old oaf finally intended to act?

Labienus bolted to his feet and gave a slight bow. "Yes, my lord. I shall return this evening with the legates, as you command."

"And, General..."

"Yes, my lord?"

"Send in those Allobroges fools, will you?" Pompey sighed, touching his temples as if he had a headache. "I must walk the lines with them."

XXI

The Allobroges *oathsworn* had been separated from Roucill and Egu. With their weapons confiscated, they had been placed under constant guard and ordered to wait in a spot close to the shore, away from the tents of the legions, and a bit too close to the latrines.

The wind from the sea whisked Catugna's matted gray tresses as he watched the pavilion on the distant hilltop where the two princes conferred with Pompey. Catugna sat somewhat apart from the *oathsworn*. They never spoke to him, dared not look upon him, avoided the mere glance of his scourge-casting eyes. As fierce as the sword warriors were in battle, willing to throw their lives away on a whim to defend their lieges, their courage wavered when it came to *him*.

They were afraid of him. He knew it, even took pleasure from it, sometimes.

Out of the corner of his eye, Catugna saw one of the Roman guards watching him with fascination. The young legionary could not have been more than sixteen years of age. He had probably never seen a druid before, had most likely never been north of the Alps, and was perhaps mesmerized by this woad-painted creature of myth and nightmare.

Catugna wheeled abruptly on the lad, glared with his wild eyes, gritted his teeth, growled like a rabid wolf. The startled soldier practically tripped over himself backing away, stirring a fit of laughter from the other guards. The embarrassed youth quickly regained his footing but came no closer and kept a firm grip on his spear.

The soft underbelly of the empire on full display, mused the druid. *They know not the imminency of their demise.*

The evil that had blighted the northern lands for so long would soon come to an end. Rome would fall. It had already been decreed.

The spirits had spoken to him, even before he had crossed the Alps with Roucill and Egu. On the sixth day of the moon, he had climbed the sacred oak. He had retrieved the blessed mistletoe, and he had sacrificed three virgins – one for Toutatis, one for Aesus, and one for Taranis. And, as his dagger had twisted within those virgin breasts, the sacred three had awoken. They had spoken to him. The others of his kind swore they had heard only gurgling gibberish, but *he* had heard them. The sacred three had spoken through the dying virgins.

They had spoken in the voice of his mother.

Catugna was pulled from his daydream by the sight of the tall centurion being led to the prisoner stockade. He followed the centurion's every movement with more than a casual interest. Long-buried memories stirred. If ever he had doubts before, there could be no questioning now. Even from this distance, he recognized the broad shoulders and confident gait.

Of all the Romans he should encounter after all these years...

Clearly, their paths had been woven together at the tree of creation. The spirits had placed them both here, at this precise time, to fulfill the prophecy. There could be no other explanation.

At that moment, another group emerged from the tent, led by a file of *fasces*-bearing *lictors*. It was Pompey walking beside Roucill and Egu. The three men conversed as they wound their way through the camp, with Roucill doing most of the talking.

At the sight of the two loutish idiots trying to weasel their way around the stately general, Catugna could not help but let out a mad, cackling laugh. The outburst startled the nearby *oathsworn*, as well as the Roman guards.

Catugna was still laughing when the procession walked past the spot where he and the *oathsworn* idled. Roucill was clearly embarrassed by the disturbance. He shot a quick, scathing frown at Catugna without deviating from his discussion with Pompey. Egu's glare lingered a bit longer. Catugna ignored them both and continued chuckling.

Eventually, he did fall silent, but not out of any fear of the princes. Catugna stopped because Pompey himself had turned to look at him. It was a casual glance. Their eyes met only briefly across the crowd, long enough for Catugna to give a barely perceptible nod. Pompey did not return the gesture, and just as quickly turned his attention back to the princes.

As the group moved on, heading toward the distant line of works, Catugna smiled within his cowl. He had not expected Pompey to acknowledge him, but the general had seen him, all the same.

Ah, my lords Roucill and Egu, you poor, misguided fools. If only you knew of your own insignificance. If only you realized that you are but small parts of a much grander scheme.

But sometimes, the spirits chose to use fools. Even the gods enjoyed a good laugh.

XXII

It was midday, the time when direct sunlight shined down into the interior courtyard. The green shrubs and vibrant flowers were their most vivid at this time of day. A few bees and other flying insects flitted from one blossom to another, zipping in and out of the sun's rays. Flawless marble statuettes of Jupiter and Juno glistened beside the tiled pond where lilies floated on a shimmering surface. An assortment of exotic fish cast brilliant hues from beneath.

Cimon had hardly noticed it all before, except to scold the house slaves when any aspect of it was out of place. He had never stopped to appreciate it. And now he wondered if these would be the last pleasant things he would see in this lifetime.

He had been the bearer of bad news before. One could not be the chief servant of a man like Valens without stoking his anger from time to time. But Cimon, the conniver that he was, had always managed to temper that anger or redirect it, often onto one of the other slaves. But, this time, he knew it would take more than obeisance and deflection to avoid the master's wrath. If he did not think of something fast, his next steps might be his last.

But the garden, and any thoughts of his potential doom, momentarily evaporated when he entered the master's expansive bedroom and was met by a sight that took his breath away. Upon the bed lay Baseirta, curled on her side, facing away from him, her perfect curves accentuated by the sunlight filtering through the high windows. She was nude but for a silken blanket drawn halfway up her flawless hip.

Cimon's loins burned with desire. He wanted her. He wanted her more than anything in this world.

Was she whimpering? Oh, no matter. She was a sight from heaven, a gift from the gods, the perfect woman, made for a man's pleasure. And, one day, Cimon intended to be that man. One day, when the master was done with her, she would be his – assuming he outlived *this* day.

"Well, don't just stand there gawking," Valens's voice jostled Cimon from his musings. "Report."

The senator was standing on the other side of the room, his arms outstretched while two female house slaves rubbed him down with oil – his custom after a spirited romp. The giant Arabian axemen were there, too, one in each corner, their faces hidden by veils, their thick hands resting atop the double-blades of their axes, the butt ends of the long handles resting on the floor.

Cimon swallowed hard at the sight of those polished, razor-sharp blades. He had seen more than one man quartered and decapitated by those hideous weapons. And he knew of their horrid deeds before they had come to serve Valens.

While in the service of the detested Potentate of Hatra,

the Arabians had prevented no less than sixteen attempts on their master's life. It was rumored that the potentate had felt so secure under their protection that he had continued eating his supper during one attempt while the big men slew twice their number of assassins. It was said the potentate often cursed at the Arabians and beat them, claiming it was good for them to remember whom they served. The silent giants accepted this treatment and continued to protect their master until one day when they were bluntly informed their pay would be reduced by half. The following morning, the potentate was found in pieces around his estate, no two limbs or digits unsevered, no two found in the same place. The axemen had carried out the dismemberments at the site of each insult, applying tourniquets to keep their former master alive as they dragged him from one spot to the next. It was said he did not die until the final and most painful digit was removed.

Fully aware of their history, Valens had made it a point to pay the Arabians handsomely and punctually. He also allowed them to commune with their eastern divinities whenever they wished, a liberty they seemed to prefer over the pleasures of wine and women. They were perfect warriors, devoted only to their gods, their craft, and their master. Their axes slew at Valens's whim.

"The offerings to the *Penates* have been made, my lord," Cimon said cheerily. "They portend a most auspicious day." He was stalling. The presence of those axes had sapped his courage.

"What else?" Valens demanded impatiently. "Surely, you have not come here just to tell me that."

"Forgive me, sire," Cimon said modestly. "But would it be possible to send the slaves away? The news I have is for your ears alone."

Valens grabbed a towel from one of the body servants

and gestured for the slaves to leave. "Take Baseirta with you."

The two women helped Baseirta to her feet, draped her in the silken blanket, and escorted her out of the room. Cimon could not help but watch the shapely form beneath the wrapping saunter away, her oscillating hips stirring lurid fantasies within him.

Once again, Valens's irritated voice tore him away from his daydream.

"I assume you bring me news of young Domitius?"

Cimon stammered. His eyes instinctively flashed from one guard to the next. The presence of those sinister blades was making it difficult to remember the words he had rehearsed.

"I-I think it would be wise to send the guards away, too, sire. They do not need to hear what I have to —"

A single glance from Valens told him that was not going to happen. There was no way out. His only hope was to twist the facts such that the master would not put all the blame on him.

"I-I regret to report that Domitius lives, sire."

"He lives?"

"Yes, sire. I-I am sorry. I do not know what went wrong. I did as you commanded. I chose six of your strongest bargemen. Paid off the jailer. Told him to put our men in with the two soldiers. Told him to leave them unwatched. The men did as they were told. They tried to kill Domitius, but…"

"But…what?" Valens demanded, his eyes blazing with fury.

"Before they finished, a tribune arrived to fetch the prisoners to see Lord Pompey. And, just like that, Domitius was gone, sire, carried away across the bay and beyond our reach."

"You moved too slowly, then," Valens said accusingly.

"Y-Yes, sire. But it appears no suspicions have been raised, other than that nosey tribune. Just give the word, sire, and I'll see that he's dealt with."

"No, you incompetent fool! You will only muddle things further." Valens took in a deep breath. "I assume Domitius did not escape without injury?"

Cimon looked at the ceiling as if having difficulty recalling. "I do not know, sire. I do not believe so."

"Summon my oarsmen. I want to hear what happened from their own mouths."

"Ah, yes. Well, about that, sire...I regret that there were some casualties..."

"How many?"

"Two, sire."

"Two wounded?"

"Two dead, sire. Four wounded." Cimon said it with a casual air, hoping to move on quickly from this subject. He forced a chuckle before adding, "The dimwitted bastards won't stroke an oar for a good while, sire, but I've already selected a batch of replacements. A handsome lot, too, sire. Would you like me to summon them?"

"How is it six of my oarsmen could not overcome two soldiers?" Valens demanded.

Cimon could see his attempt at humor had been sorely misplaced. "They had weapons, sire. Well, one weapon. A dagger. I don't know how it got in there. Domitius must have slipped it past that fool of a jailer."

"More likely, one of *your* fools brought it in!"

"If he did, it was against my express orders, sire. Androtimos is a dull-headed brute, but I made it clear to him there were to be no weapons. I'd bring him here to answer for it, sire, but his jaw is broken, and his face is all wrapped up in bandages."

"So, Androtimos is responsible, eh?"

Cimon nodded modestly.

"Remove his bandages and have him lashed to the prow of my barge as an example to the others."

"Yes, sire. At once." Cimon hesitated. "How long should he remain there, sire?"

Valens looked at him as if the answer were obvious. "Until there's nothing left of him."

"Yes, sire."

Cimon was reluctant to share the rest. For there was more bad news to tell. Every time he glanced at the Arabians, his courage faltered. But he knew, at some point, the truth would come out, and then it would only be worse for him. Better the master found out by his own silver-tongue.

"I-I'm afraid the old Parthian was also killed in the brawl, sire."

Valens looked incredulous. "In the name of Juno, how?"

"It seems the centurions were put in the same cell with Varaz Vizur, sire."

"How could anyone be so idiotic as to do that?"

"It was a misunderstanding, sire. A happenstance mistake. Almost a comedy of errors, one might say." Cimon started to chuckle but quickly suppressed it when Valens scowled. "You see, sire, when I overheard the names of those prisoners at the gate yesterday, and overheard they were to be taken to the prison, I made a brief stop on my way back here. I knew you'd want Domitius and his mate set aside until you decided what was to be done with them. So, I stopped by the prison and told the jailer to do just that. I paid him ten good *sesterces* and told him he should consider the new prisoners as belonging to you, sire. I suppose the fool reasoned, since the old Parthian was being held there on your orders, he would just keep all your prisoners together. Finding adequate space is always a problem down there. Still, it was a foolish supposition on his part, sire."

"A foolish supposition indeed." Valens's accusing stare indicated his statement did not apply to the jailer alone.

"Of course, I chastised him, sir," Cimon said quickly, trying his best not to be dissuaded by the look of disgust on his master's face. "I told him not to ever expect another job from you, sire."

"Does *she* know?" Valens asked directly.

"No, sire. How could she? And not to worry, sire. She won't. I'll make sure of that. I've several of the old man's letters to her, which I saved for just such an occasion. I'll give her one from time to time to keep her convinced he's still alive, and she'll continue to be your obedient slave, just as before, sire. Nothing will change. I assure you!"

"You will see to it that is the case," Valens seethed. "If she runs away or mars her beauty in any way, you will answer for it."

"Y-yes, sire. Not to worry."

"Where is Domitius now?"

"I've had a man watching him, sire," Cimon said proudly. "I thought you'd want to know. Domitius and his comrade were taken to Pompey's tent. Then from there, they were taken to the stockade where the other prisoners from Caesar's army are kept."

"Pompey will have offered Domitius a position in his army," Valens postulated.

"You are right, sire. My man reported the same. But word has it, Domitius refused. That means he'll be put to death with the others in the morning. So, you see, sire? All is well!" Cimon said it with confidence. He had been keeping this, his only good news, for last.

Valens sighed heavily. "Caesar's soldiers are boastful and

bold. But when they see the executioner's blade dripping red before their eyes, they will turn into sniveling cowards. They will swear allegiance to Pompey faster than they would to their own mothers. Domitius will be no different."

"Y-Yes, sire."

"I do not have time to deal with this now. The packet from Brundisium has finally arrived. It will anchor within the hour. I must go aboard at once. I will be gone for several hours, quite possibly late into the night." Valens's eyes settled squarely on Cimon. "I am placing this Domitius business in your care. Domitius must not leave the stockade alive."

"Yes, sire. It shall be arranged."

After being dismissed, Cimon returned to the courtyard and breathed out a great sigh of relief. He ignored the swaying flowers, the buzzing bees, the warm sunlight, all the things he had thought he would never see again. He was consumed with self-gratification, pleased with his own cunning, his ability to divert the master's anger. And now, he must get rid of this soldier to fully restore the master's confidence in him.

And he would, by Zeus!

Strolling through the garden, he pondered his many options. He had killed for Valens before. There was the *magus* of Asaak who had spoken ill of Valens to the wrong people. There was the rival senator's wife who had threatened to go public with the affair. There was the rug peddler in Alexandria selling forgeries he claimed to have been woven by the famed Timasion of Dardania. And the list went on…

There were many ways to do away with a prisoner, given enough time for planning. But Cimon did not have the luxury of time. How was he to go about killing a man who was locked in a stockade with dozens of other prisoners, a stockade guarded by legionaries who may or may not be open to bribes? And Cimon made it a rule never to try to bribe a soldier. One never knew if he was driven by money or patriotism.

At that moment, Cimon heard the sound of water being poured into a basin. It came from beyond the hallways leading to the front of the house. He instantly knew what it was. Racing across the courtyard, he dashed into a side chamber that served as a storeroom, where a small window afforded an excellent view of the atrium. The little port was often used to size up guests as they were greeted by the house slaves, but today Cimon used it for other reasons.

As expected, the sound proved to be the beautiful Baseirta, washing at the small pool in the atrium. She was completely unaware of his presence. He watched her as he had countless times before, delighting in her perfect breasts, her sensuous legs, and every rivulet curling down her flawless bronze skin. She was irresistible, the essence of perfection.

As Cimon continued to gaze open-mouthed, his devious mind began to churn. An idea brewed as to how he could deal with the soldier and obtain his one desire simultaneously.

An Armenian prince once had the misfortune of outbidding Valens for a prized bull. Cimon had dealt with that young fool easily enough. First, he had convinced a Byzantine alchemist to teach him how to make an exceptionally lethal poison. Then, he had simply bribed a high-priced whore to seduce the prince and administer the concoction. A few drops in the prince's wine had done the job quite effectively. The young fool had not died peacefully.

Now, Cimon would do away with Domitius in the same

fashion. And the seductive whore that would snare the trap would be none other than Baseirta.

And how to get her inside the stockade? Well, that was simple, too. It was a custom of Pompey's to give each new batch of condemned prisoners an ample portion of wine and whores for a *Saturnalia*-like debauch on their final night – one last effort to persuade them to join his army. The prisoners in the stockade were set to be executed on the morrow. That meant the orgy would happen this very night.

Cimon would bribe the local brothel-keeper who was on contract to provide the women for tonight's entertainment. Baseirta would accompany them into the stockade. She would carry the lethal concoction in a hidden vial, seduce Domitius, then poison the soldier's wine when he wasn't looking. Come morning, Domitius would not wake up, and anyone who cared would assume he drank himself to death.

Cimon would be sure to instruct Baseirta not to administer the potion until after Domitius had bedded her. Perhaps a good plundering from a full-blooded soldier was just what she needed. She might even enjoy it. But, whether she did or not, she would have to go along with it. She would have to follow Cimon's instructions to the letter. As far as she knew, her father was still alive and facing torture if she displayed the slightest disobedience.

Acquiring the ingredients for the poison would not be difficult. However, someone the size of Domitius would require a few more drops than the feeble Armenian prince had. Cimon had noted the impressive proportions of Domitius at the gate. The muscled centurion was massive, scarred, savage, a solid warrior in his prime – certainly, far more vibrant and robust than the aging Valens.

It was very likely Baseirta *would* enjoy it.

But, no matter. When Cimon reported to the master the

next day, he would explain that Domitius was dead but that the girl had been forced to sleep with him to see it done. Valens would be enraged that his prized concubine had been defiled by another man – *that* man. But, once Valens had time to calm, once he realized the silver mine was now undisputedly his, his temper would subside. He would consider the girl an acceptable loss and order her taken to the slave market to be sold to the highest bidder. Then, Cimon would go on his knees and implore his master to let him buy the girl with the money he had saved over his many years of service. The master would probably see right through his scheme at that moment. Still, the death of Domitius would surely assuage his anger. Valens would forgive Cimon and allow the purchase to go through.

Cimon salivated as he watched Baseirta clothe herself. Again, an almost imperceptible sobbing reached his ears.

Do not cry, my blossom. Before the sun sets on the morrow, you will no longer have to endure him. You shall have a new master.

XXIII

"Are you not tired of it, Lucius?" Strabo asked. He stared out at the glittering sea. The setting sun painted his face a golden hue.

"I have never seen anything quite like it," Lucius said as he casually examined the tiny amulet given him by the old Parthian. He held the metallic disk close to his face to make out the intricate etchings. They portrayed a meticulously detailed mounted archer. The horse and rider were frozen in a moment of high-speed action, the archer turned in the saddle, aiming at something behind him. The more Lucius studied it, the more it fascinated him. "How could a man carve such a thing? I sometimes wonder if it was crafted by fairies."

"I was not referring to that trinket," Strabo said tiredly. He had been attempting to engage Lucius in conversation for some time.

The two centurions sat apart from the rest of the prisoners. The stockade holding them was situated upon the seaward slope of a small hill located some distance from the tents of the legions. The enclosure was nothing more than a square of tightly bound palisade posts measuring some fifty paces to a side. Still, it adequately contained the three score men within. As the most senior captives, Lucius and Strabo occupied the higher ground, giving them an unobstructed view of the bay beyond the far wall.

Lucius recognized some of the other prisoners, but none were from his legion. A scant few of the prisoners were frontline infantry. Most were teamsters or engineers, captured when their diggings took them too close to Pompey's lines. And there were a handful of younger men, recruits that had deserted Caesar's army only to be captured by Pompey's. The mood was somber throughout the confined space as they contemplated the fates that awaited them.

The aroma of smoked fish mixed with the foul camp smell filled the air. Pompey's soldiers congregated around freshly lit campfires just beyond the wall, casually conversing as they prepared the evening meal. The familiar sounds made Lucius think of the men of his own century who would be doing the same, at this very moment, just beyond those hills to the east.

Strabo stared off at the horizon, brooding over the chain of events that had brought him here, and those who were responsible for it. Yet, he seemed more perturbed than melancholy. Lucius, too, was deep in thought, contemplating death and the afterlife. He was torn between a desire to live and a longing to join his family in the fields of Elysium, to see them again, to drink from the river of forgetfulness.

He had, of course, faced death a thousand times, had spent the long, sleepless hours on the eve of battle knowing the next day he might fall under the enemy's blades. But the possibility of survival had been ever-present at the back of his mind, that naïve, selfish notion that many others would die, but he would live. This time, however, he faced certain death. Thoughts of the gods and the afterlife carried a different meaning and preoccupied him as they never had before.

The figure on the amulet fascinated him. Perhaps, on any other night, under any other circumstances, he would have cast the little charm aside. But this night, here and now, it left him pondering the old Parthian. What gods had he prayed to? How was it that his gods had created men that walked, breathed, and died the same as those made by the Roman gods? Or the Greek gods? Or those of the far-off Celts? Was there not a single thread tying them all together? If Lucius had learned anything from his numerous campaigns in as many lands, it was that men were the same wherever they dwelled. They looked different, spoke in different tongues, practiced different customs, but, at their core, they were the same. There was a master scale that balanced it all, that kept a man from becoming too formidable yet saved him from total destruction – hubris tempered with humility. It allowed men like Caesar to succeed where others failed. And so, there must be some great hand dropping weights on that scale, guiding the course of the world, a god more significant than all the others – a god of gods. Did that great omnipotence view the evils of man with amusement, repugnance, or indifference?

Lucius could not tell.

Undoubtedly, the spirits of his father, mother, and sister knew the truth of it, wherever they were. Perhaps, tomorrow, he would know, as well.

"Will you stop staring at that thing and listen to me?" Strabo interrupted his thoughts.

After a final glance, Lucius finally tucked the amulet away and turned to his comrade.

"What is on your mind?"

Strabo nodded appreciatively. "We have marched similar paths, you and I, Lucius. I've killed more men than I can remember. We both have. For years, we've followed our leaders, done their bidding, burned every village and town they told us to. And only now do I see them for what they are." Strabo paused, swallowing hard. "And I feel ashamed."

"You did what you were told, like any good soldier. There's no shame in that."

"There is shame in serving men you do not respect. I don't respect them, Lucius. Do you not tire of serving men you don't respect? Do you not tire of serving Caesar and Antony?"

Lucius shrugged. "I've never placed my hopes in generals. They desire only promotion and glory and will happily step over your bloody corpse to achieve them. No, comrade. Trust the lads you march with, the coins in your purse, the steel in your hand. That's all you can count on in this world."

Strabo shook his head. "You're not hearing what I'm saying, Lucius. I could never trust Antony again. I could never tell my men to throw away their lives for such a man."

"In a few hours, we will no longer have to worry about such things, comrade. Yonder is the last sunset we shall ever see. Let us savor it and not speak of Antony."

Returning to his malaise, Strabo was clearly dissatisfied with Lucius's reply. Lucius, for his part, was being purposefully obtuse. He knew to what Strabo was alluding, but he did not wish to entertain the thought or be tempted to for a single moment.

It was not until the sun had sunk into the yellow sea and shadow enveloped the world around them that Strabo spoke again.

"I told you my grandfather marched under Publius Cornelius Scipio."

Lucius nodded.

"My grandfather was a centurion of the *triarii*," Strabo said distantly. "Where I am from, in Beneventum, everyone knows the story of Rufius Strabo. He marched in the great war against Carthage. He crossed the sea with the valiant Scipio and defeated Hannibal and his elephants at Zama."

"I've heard of the campaign."

"It is said my grandfather struck down two elephants with his spear that day, a feat that earned him a place in Scipio's triumph." Strabo smiled as if comforted by the tale. "They saved Rome, Lucius. They were heroes, my grandfather and his comrades. I always envisioned following in his footsteps. I swore I'd be a soldier as valiant and as mighty as Rufius Strabo."

"Then you have fulfilled your oath, comrade."

Strabo frowned. "What will the stories say about us, Lucius? That we enriched ourselves marching in the mercenary army of a tyrant? And that's what we are. If Caesar had not promised an enormous payment of gold to every man – a promise he has not yet made good on, by the by – do you think they would have sworn allegiance to him? They might very well be fighting for Pompey."

"They followed him across Gaul."

"Yes. And we both know what Caesar did in Gaul – what *we* did for him. You think, when all this is over, people will look back on those campaigns favorably?"

Lucius said nothing, partly because there was much truth in what Strabo said. There had been much mischief in Gaul, sinister acts that never made it into the reports to

Rome, despicable acts against the women and children of the conquered. Lucius was disgusted by it as much as Strabo was. Whenever possible, he had used every means to stop such cruelties. The men of his century knew his mindset and dared not cross him. Every soldier was entitled to a portion of the spoils. He could sell his prisoners in the slave markets or keep them as his own. But Lucius would not stand for the rape or murder of innocents. Still, such mercies were seldom reciprocated by the enemy. War was a terrible business, the organized and sanctioned savagery of man. The only way it would end was if all men served under the same banner, worshipped the same gods, strove for a common purpose.

One might as well wish that mules had wings.

"Best to leave such thinking to the legates," Lucius said finally. "One man cannot set the world aright. He can see that justice is done within his own domain, look after his mates, and pray the fates will smile upon him. The rest is in the hands of the gods."

The conversation had ended, neither wishing to discuss it further. Strabo was clearly frustrated by Lucius's deflection. Lucius had no desire to go back over decisions he had already come to terms with.

Lucius knew what Strabo was suggesting, but that option was out of the question. Lucius could betray Antony. He could betray Caesar. But he could never raise a sword against the men who had followed him into battle, who had taken his lashes, who had fought beside him.

Come morning, he would die a loyal centurion of the Tenth, his honor intact.

XXIV

Night fell. The stockade was shrouded in darkness. Campfires flickered through the narrow gaps between the palisade posts. The prisoners were subdued, sullen, reflective, as the stars coursed above them for the last time.

Then, a sudden raucous broke out in the camp beyond the palisade. It was not the sound of war but of joy. Those prisoners standing on the high ground, who could see over the wall, saw the reason for the cheering.

Far across the bay, barges had shoved off from Dyrrachium's docks. There were half a dozen of them, each mounting a lantern on bow and stern. They floated across the dark waters in a single column, their dipping oars leaving frothy patches on the water behind them. The fervor in the camp grew in intensity as the flotilla drew closer. By the time the wet bows skidded to a stop on the sand, cheering soldiers were crowding the shore by the thousand.

The passengers disembarked. Dozens of lithe figures in

hooded cloaks leaped over the bulwarks, showing only delicate bare feet beneath the hems of their gowns. Brawny slaves came ashore, too, bearing weighty casks and crates. The procession then resumed on the land. The torchlit column of hooded figures and slaves weaved through the applauding troops to the stockade gates, where they were met by grinning guards who allowed them to proceed inside.

Knowing what to expect, Pompey's soldiers watched from beyond the walls atop makeshift ladders and upended carts. But the baffled prisoners, who now backed away to make room for the new arrivals, could only gaze in wonderment.

When the parade came to a halt, a rotund man of indistinct age wearing an extravagant sapphire toga stepped forward. He waved a torch over his head, and the crowd fell instantly silent.

"Compliments of the Great Pompey!" he proclaimed. "The general extends his respects to you, the condemned, on your final night. He thanks you for your service to Rome and magnanimously extends his offer to you once again in hopes that you will join him. To that end, he sends you these gifts. Something to enrich this night, whether it be your last in this life, or the last as a soldier of Caesar."

At one sweep of his arm, the three dozen cloaked figures stepped forward. One by one, they doffed their hoods to reveal painted faces more enchanting than many of the prisoners had ever seen. Every woman had been selected for her exquisite beauty. Gold, dark, and amber tresses were arranged in extravagant braids framing equally diverse complexions. A maddening roar of approval came from those outside the wall.

The casks of wine were brought forth. The crates were opened to reveal an abundant feast of fruits, vegetables, and cooked meats. And the women were set upon by the ravenous prisoners – all except for one woman.

She had not dropped her hood. The rotund brothelkeeper, who had doubled as master of ceremonies, quickly whisked her away before any prisoner could harbor ideas about her.

As she was being shuffled through the crowd, Baseirta saw the shadows of wild, desperate faces. Sweaty, salivating men jostled her from every side, but the brothel-keeper kept a firm grasp on her arm. He pulled her along with an armed guard following just behind. The brothel-keeper kept smiling and apologizing, explaining that she was reserved for another. One prisoner stepped in his path to challenge this reservation and instantly received the spiny hilt of the guard's sword to his face. The prisoner's crushed nose and dislodged teeth effectively dissuaded the others.

It was not difficult to find the prisoner in question. Baseirta had overheard Cimon giving the brothel-keeper an extensive description of the man. Tall of height. Broad of shoulder. Thewed arms and legs. Square face. Few of the inmates possessed all of those attributes. The brothel-keeper found him – an incredible hulk of a man, standing in one corner of the stockade. Another prisoner, equally imposing, and fitting all the descriptions, aside from the height, brooded a few paces away. The pair were the only ones who appeared indifferent to the revelry around them.

"Do I have the honor of addressing Centurion Lucius Domitius?" The brothel-keeper wore an artificial grin as he addressed the tall one.

A grunt was the only reply.

Baseirta had averted her eyes for most of the lively jaunt across the lust-filled crowd. Only now did she dare to look up at the man to whom she must give her body – and whom she must kill. And she was not prepared for what she saw. The broad, muscular chest before her thoroughly filled out the plain tunic covering it. Her eyes moved up the towering figure, past the daunting shoulders, to the rugged face and the scar adorning one chiseled cheek. And when she met those steadfast eyes looking down at her – eyes that somehow conveyed savagery, intelligence, and compassion, all at once – she involuntarily skipped a breath. A chill ran through her, and her knees went weak with fright.

Or was it something else?

The longer those captivating eyes gazed into hers, the more her fear turned into fascination and curiosity. There was something fierce yet unthreatening about them, something that told her this man was not like Valens or Cimon.

But before Baseirta could collect herself, the brothel-keeper reached over and untied the knot at the nape of her neck. Her cloak collapsed into a heap at her feet. Instantly, she was naked, her breasts quivering and bristling from the light brushing of the falling garment. She had been forcibly disrobed by that licentious scoundrel Valens too many times not to have become anesthetized by it. Yet, she felt suddenly embarrassed to be under the gaze of the magnificent man standing before her.

The obsequious brothel-keeper smiled gleefully. "The Great Pompey sends you this gift, Centurion Domitius, to fulfill a man's deepest desires, no? He hopes you will reconsider his offer."

That was a lie, Baseirta knew. The blackguard brothel-keeper had been paid by Cimon to bring her here. Pompey knew nothing about it. It was all the work of Valens. For some reason, he wanted this Domitius dead. For her part, she only knew that she must kill Domitius tonight or her poor father would suffer horrendous torture tomorrow.

It pained her to think of her father, a nameless prisoner locked away in some unknown dungeon. At one time, he had been a proud magistrate with lands, titles, and the favor of the royal court. He still would have been, had the vile King Orodes of Parthia not betrayed him. Orodes had stripped her father of all wealth and titles. Everything had been handed over to Valens. The fact that it had been given to an accursed Latin had been the ultimate insult. The thought of it infuriated Baseirta. Now, her father was a hostage, she was a slave, and both were far away from home.

And she must murder a man she did not know.

Father, help me. I must kill this man for your sake, no matter how innocent he might be.

She sensed more than felt the tiny vial hidden in the elaborate weaves of her hair. According to Cimon, the vial contained more than enough of the noxious mixture. A few drops would do the job. Once the poison got past his lips, there would be no reversing it. It acted quickly – or so she had been told.

Oddly, the second and most puzzling part of her instructions gave her more trepidation than killing Domitius. She was to lie with him before poisoning him. Cimon had been explicit about that. It was what the master desired.

Baseirta shuddered whenever she tried to understand Valens's depraved mind. Being a party to his sadistic ways repulsed her to her core, but she could not refuse. Cimon assured her she was being watched. He would know if she deviated from her instructions in any way.

But, perhaps there is a way I could…

"Well," said the brothel-keeper, nudging her forward. "I shall leave you two alone. My guard will remain to ensure you are not bothered."

Of course. The guard was Cimon's eyes.

"Your man is not needed. Take him with you." Domitius suddenly spoke in a deep, commanding voice, surprising Baseirta.

"Really, I must insist, Centurion –" the brothel-keeper expostulated but was cut short by a glare that could have melted iron.

"Take him with you, or I'll throw him over the wall after you, and you can tell Pompey to go bugger himself!"

The rotund man was speechless for a moment. "Oh, well, as you wish. Fare you well. We shall return for her in the morning."

He gestured for the guard to follow, and both men disappeared in the mingling shadows, leaving Baseirta standing there alone, naked before the massive prisoner.

She expected Domitius to sweep her up in his arms, to carry her off to a dark corner and aggressively have his way with her, but he did not. Instead, he simply stared at her for several long moments, clearly admiring what he saw.

"What is your name, girl?" he said finally, his tone demanding but not harsh.

"I am Julia."

Domitius laughed out loud. "No, girl. Your real name. If I had a *sesterce* for every whore I've met named Julia, I'd be retired and living in a seaside villa in Spain."

She looked at him with surprise. What did it matter what her name was? She had been told that all Roman soldiers liked the name Julia. Apparently, not this man.

"My name is Baseirta," she replied.

Domitius nodded with satisfaction. "Enchanting, and much more suitable."

She flinched as he took one step toward her, but then realized he was not reaching for her but for the cloak on the ground. He picked it up, brushed it off, enclosed her in it once again. Baseirta was stupefied. She did not know how to react.

The next moment Domitius was ushering her over to a spot against the palisade wall, not far from the other soldier, who seemed lost in a mood. Domitius sat down beside her. She thought for sure this would be the moment when he took her, but he merely held one arm around her in a protective manner.

"Do you not desire me?" she said after they had sat like that for some time.

"I would not be a man if I didn't, lass," he grinned widely. "But it is not my way to take a woman against her will."

"But I wish to," she said as believably as she could, her father at the forefront of her thoughts. "I want to."

He smiled again but shook his head. Silently, she panicked, her thoughts racing. This was going to be a lot harder than she initially thought. How would she get the centurion to lie with her when he was like this? And more importantly, how would she get him to swallow the poison? She had planned on simply pouring it into his drink, but he was not drinking like the others. Perhaps if she managed to seduce him, he would desire a drink after he had expended himself. But her thoughts were suddenly interrupted by three shadows standing before them.

"You, there!" a slurring voice said. "If you're not going to use the girl, then give her to us!"

The three men stood there threateningly as if they would use force should their request be refused, but Domitius just yawned unperturbed.

"You have drunk yourself more courage than you possess," he said. "Move along before you are sorry you didn't."

"Saturn's tits! Who do you think you are keeping her to

yourself?"

"I am Centurion Lucius Domitius of the Tenth Legion," he snarled.

This had an immediate effect on the three, whose bravado suddenly dissolved, despite their inebriated state.

"Do not worry, lass," Domitus ensured her after they had left. "No one will touch you tonight."

And he had not lied. The prisoners seemed to be in a state of mindless oblivion, most having made up their minds about tomorrow's decision. That resolution seemed to have freed them of any inhibition. Those who would remain loyal to Caesar were aware that this was their last night in this life. Those who had decided to go over to Pompey knew they would live the rest of their lives in shame for betraying their legions.

But as the hours passed, and every other female was violently handed off from one group of drunken prisoners to another, Baseirta remained safely wrapped in Domitius's massive arm. Amid the wine-driven chaos transpiring all around them, his immovable hand held her firmly but gently. It was a manner in which no man had ever touched her before, not even during her privileged life as the pure and unattainable daughter of the *Marzban* of Gugark.

For the first time in a very long time, she felt protected. She felt unafraid. The deadly task she had come here to perform faded from her thoughts, replaced by the dreams of what her life could have been like had the gods chosen a happier path for her.

In her young life, she had never known love, she had never been genuinely held by a man, and she concluded this must be what it felt like to be loved, not simply desired. She found herself drawn to him, burrowing into his side, putting her cheek against his chest, and resting her hand on his firm abdomen.

At that moment, she noticed the small metallic object on his chest peeking from the fold of his tunic. It was attached to a small chain around his neck. Almost by instinct, she reached out and grabbed it, holding it before her eyes in disbelief. Even in the scant light, she knew the etchings over which her fingers ran. She knew them like she knew her own reflection.

"What is this?" she demanded, unconsciously tugging on the chain around his neck.

"You can have it if you like," he said indifferently. "I've no use for it where I'm going."

She could not speak. A flood of thoughts consumed her. Why would this Roman possess this talisman, the object she had made for her father when she was but a girl. Her father would have never parted with it as long as he drew breath. Could that mean…?

"It is beautiful," she said with forced pleasantness. "Where did you get it?"

"Off an old man. He was a prisoner in Dyrrachium."

Her heart skipped a beat. She tried to control the emotion in her voice when she asked the question she did not want to ask. "You say he *was* a prisoner. Is he no longer?"

He shook his head. "He's dead."

The words struck her like lightning. Her eyes welled up with tears.

Dead, in some cesspit of a prison!

Her father, her one hope, the last thing she loved in this world, was gone, and with him, whatever vestiges had remained of her spirit. All her suffering of the past months, the depravity, the carnal whims of that scoundrel Valens…

I have endured it all for nothing!

"What is wrong, lass?" Domitius said, evidently sensing the sudden change in her demeanor.

She did not answer. It was all she could do to remain calm, to keep up the façade. And as she lay there, contemplating her father's terrible fate, wondering how he met his death, the sorrow in her heart transformed into a burning hatred for Valens, for Cimon, for the Latins, for Orodes – for any who had a part in his demise.

Was this soldier his murderer? How else could he have come by the amulet? It was all she could do not to tremble with rage at this brute who had pretended to be so noble but was just as wicked as the others.

Almost instinctively, her hand moved up to free her hair, letting the tresses fall. In so doing, it found the hidden vial. She kept the tiny ampule out of sight. Then, blindly, she used two fingers to remove the cork, her eyes never leaving the soldier's face. He seemed unaware that she was scrutinizing him as he turned his attention back to the goings-on in the stockade. She watched his mouth, counted the intervals between breaths. She would have to move quickly, strike at the right moment, just as he was inhaling. She would not get a second chance. And she would use the entire contents.

Yes, this killer of old men will surely die!

And she would watch him die. She would watch his eyes turn cold with fear as the poison coursed through him, watch him convulse hopelessly, as he had watched her father's final moments. She was a heartbeat away from making her move when Domitius suddenly spoke again.

"The old fool saved my life," he said, staring off in the distance, still seemingly oblivious to what she intended.

Her hand froze where it was as she registered what he had said.

"He saved your life?"

He nodded. "The crazy old fool jumped into a prison brawl when he shouldn't have." He smiled and looked at her. "It's a long story, lass. But he gave me that bauble before he died. As I said, take it with you. If you do not, one of those bastards out there will only loot it from my corpse tomorrow."

"Then you were a prisoner with him?" she asked uncertainly, her fingers groping out of sight to replace the cork in the tiny vessel.

He nodded.

She dropped the vial and took the amulet in her palm, kissing it, squeezing it, running her fingers across the rough face as the tears streamed freely down her cheeks. Upon seeing this passion toward the object, the soldier removed the chain and handed it to her. She sat upright, took it in both hands, kissed it again, and pressed it to her breast as if she might feel the essence of her father from the touch of the cool bronze.

Domitius seemed slightly amused but said nothing.

When Baseirta had collected herself and was leaning on the soldier again, she felt a sudden calmness wash over her, a sense of contentment. For her father had not died miserably under torture, after all, but in a final act of bravery. He had undoubtedly given the amulet to this soldier as a token of respect. And now, her father's spirit was at peace, and she was finally free of the bonds that had kept her subservient to Valens for so long. Her mind was free from worry, refreshed by a clarity of purpose.

And she understood what she must do – what she wanted to do.

She raised her face to the soldier's and, with one delicate finger on his scarred cheek, turned his stubbly face toward her to gaze deeply into his eyes. The next instant, she was kissing him, warmly, passionately, brazenly. Her fingers moved of their own accord beneath the drawn cloak, caressing his rugged features, touching his sturdy shoulders.

Her soft breasts pressed against his solid chest. This time, her seductions overcame his resolve, and his giant hands moved to pull her closer. In those powerful arms, she was his, not out of submission, but desire – *her desire*.

Her hand released the muscled arm long enough to find the vial on the ground and tuck it away under her cloak, where she could later retrieve it. Then, she was pulling him to her again, pressing her lips to his with a vitality that clearly surprised him. It surprised even her.

Tonight, she could dream. She could forget. She could love. She could be content.

And, tomorrow, she would have her vengeance.

XXV

The stockade was dark and silent. Men in various states of consciousness lay everywhere among puddles of spilled wine and urine. The women had left hours before, pulled from the arms of the inebriated prisoners and carried off with much less flourish than their arrival. Most had left in a dazed state, bruised and forever traumatized.

Lucius sat against the palisade, looking up at the fading stars, awaiting the glow in the east that would portend the dawning of his final day. He had managed to get a few hours of sleep in the sensual embrace of the young woman who had acted so strangely throughout the night. When they had come to collect her – too soon, it had seemed – her only parting gesture had been an affectionate smile. Her kind eyes had exuded a sense of inevitability, more accepting than sorrowful, presumably for his impending fate. Then, without a word, she had drawn her cloak around her and allowed the guards to lead her away.

What a strange lass, Lucius thought, to have appeared so

frightened at first, and then to have given up her delights with such vigor.

He had expended his robust and ample passion on many a willing maiden, but he could never force himself on a woman. The horrifying final moments his mother and sister had endured at the hands of a crazed mob of rioting slaves were always at the back of his mind. This young lass had been hardly more than a girl, not more than a year or two beyond womanhood. She was very likely under the threat of violence from that fat brothel-keeper. Thus, Lucius had intended not to lie with her, to protect her only, to make his last act in this life one of which the spirits of his mother and sister would approve. But the lass had assailed him with an unadulterated yearning that had shattered all his defenses.

He was, after all, only mortal.

It seemed odd that Pompey would have sent her to him, for those of her beauty were often reserved for the legates. But Pompey was in dire need of centurions and was perhaps hoping an exceptional gift would change his mind. It had not. If anything, it had made Lucius more at peace with his impending fate. And now he sat waiting for the gray dawn and praying to the god of gods that he would die well.

A few paces away, Strabo sat brooding, as he had all night. He sipped from a wineskin, staring out at the black sea beyond the stockade. He seemed just as oblivious to his surroundings now as he had all through the revelry. Clearly, his decision was weighing heavily on him.

Lucius had made no attempt to converse with him. What was there to say? They had chosen different paths.

"The spirits protect you, good centurions," a voice broke the silence.

Lucius looked up and was startled to see a black figure

standing not five paces from him. A thousand night watches had honed Lucius's senses to the minutest disturbance. Yet, this figure had somehow managed to creep up on him undetected. Disconcerted and suddenly alert, Lucius scrutinized the figure as it stepped into the shards of light filtering through the palisade. The drab, black cloak was instantly familiar to him, as was the icy chill that crept under his skin when the hood was finally thrown back. The fierce eyes and pale countenance were unforgettable.

"You seem to have kept your wits about you," the druid said in a hushed, gravelly tone.

It was the druid – the one called Catugna. Lucius did not exactly fear this shadowy enchanter of the Gauls. Still, to suddenly encounter him here, within the stockade, this close, was unsettling.

"Enough to snap the neck of one who creeps up on us in the night," Lucius responded, rising to his feet.

"Be at ease, Roman!" Catugna raised his hands to show he held no weapons. "I come in peace. I come as a friend."

Lucius glanced at the seated Strabo and then back at the druid. "We both felt your peace on our backs, wizard!"

"Keep your voice low, Roman, or you will have the guards on us! I have managed to distract them only momentarily. Remember, it was I who intervened for you in the swamp. Had I not stayed Egu's hand, you and your friend would now be rotting corpses still tied to those trees." Catugna paused, his lips curling into a small smile. "Besides, if I were your enemy, why would I have come here? Why would I now place myself at your mercy?"

For the first time, Lucius detected something else in the druid's accent, something that was not quite Gallic. The remnants of another tongue were there, perhaps several. Nevertheless, the druid appeared to be alone, just as he claimed. And his only visible weapon was a dagger sheathed at his waist.

Again, Lucius looked at Strabo, but the other did not return his gaze. He remained silent and introspective, seemingly indifferent to the druid's presence.

"Say what you have to say and be gone, wizard," Lucius said. "I prefer not to spend my little time remaining attending to your drivel."

Yellow teeth grinned in the darkness. "Yes, indeed, we have little time! At dawn, the executioners will come for you."

"Did you come here to tell us what we already know?"

"I said speak softly!" Catugna hissed urgently. "Do you wish the guards to hear?"

"Happily, if it means being rid of you." At that moment, Lucius caught a strange scent in the air, a scent that made him twist his face into a scowl. "Juno's arse! What is that foul stench?"

Catugna looked confused for a moment, then produced a small sack from his cloak, the odor of which was overpowering. "A concoction for lightning and thunder," the druid explained. "Onions, pilchards, and, of course, the hair of a virgin."

"I understand why she's a virgin," Lucius said sardonically, then looked up at the starry sky. "And I see no clouds, you crazed fool. I'm surprised that noxious blend hasn't brought the guards down on us by now. Or maybe you killed them outright with one whiff of it."

"Enough!" Catugna pursed his lips at the mockery. "Caesar is doomed! Pompey has the high ground and the greater numbers. The outcome is certain if we do not act quickly!"

"Perhaps you remember, druid, you, and those whore's whelps you call princes, threw in your lot with Pompey.

Why should you care what happens to Caesar now?"

"Roucill and Egu have joined Pompey. I have not. I am Caesar's loyal servant. I have been his covert agent within the Allobroges camp for many months."

"Anyone could claim that."

"It is true, Latin! Years ago, when all other Romans wanted to punish the druids for the uprising of the Carnutes, Caesar intervened on our behalf. He showed mercy to my kind. I am forever in his debt."

"Maybe Caesar was wrong to show you mercy," Lucius retorted. "As I recall, your kind always likes to stir the coals. *Never trust a bloody druid.* That's what we say in the legions. Isn't that right, Strabo?"

Strabo was not paying attention.

"We have little time for this nonsense!" Catugna whispered fervently. "Your comrades out there are heading for certain doom unless you listen to me! I have information that will tip the balance decidedly in Caesar's favor. You must take me to him."

Lucius chuckled. "And how do you suggest we do that? Those guards aren't going to just let us walk out of here."

"We will leave the way I came."

"How's that?" Lucius asked skeptically.

"Over there." A bony hand pointed to the north side of the stockade. "I have burrowed beneath the wall."

"And no one saw you do it?"

"Some fool parked a cart too close to the palisade. It hid me while I worked, just as it now conceals the armor and swords I have brought you."

"And what about the pickets?" Lucius asked. "If we make it through the camp, we still have to get through the lines. I don't suppose that foul concoction of yours can spirit us past the works."

A small smile formed on Catugna's lips. "Leave that to

me. I will get us through Pompey's lines. You get us through Caesar's."

Lucius eyed the druid suspiciously. "This reeks of Roucill and Egu. I'm guessing Pompey didn't pay them enough, and now they want to go back to Caesar."

The druid's eyes stared intensely into his. "Know this, Roman. Roucill and Egu have no hand in this. They have no influence over me, nor shall they ever. I come at the bidding of one who wishes victory for Caesar, one who despises the hypocrisy of the *Optimates* and the weakness of Pompey." Catugna seemed to hesitate. He then drew back his cloak to produce a folded piece of papyrus which he held out to Lucius. "I have sworn to give this only to Caesar, but if it can prove to you that I am truthful... Here! Read it if you can!"

Lucius knew how to read in Greek and Latin, another skill to thank his Greek tutor for. It had served him well in his rise up the ranks.

Taking the document, he unfolded it and held it up to a sliver of light from the campfires. The letter was written in Latin. Upon initial examination, it appeared to have been written in haste. There were several spots where mistakes had been lined out. Moving the papyrus across the light, he read it, then reread it. And he was amazed by what it contained.

The letter had been written by a Latin hand and signed by one Gaius Aquilius. It was a name Lucius had never heard before. Presumably, this Aquilius was some disgruntled legate of Pompey's. The letter appeared authentic enough. At least, it could not have been written by any Allobroges. No Gaul could write their characters like that. But there were still many things that did not seem to add up.

"Why would this Aquilius trust you to deliver this?"

Lucius asked.

"Because Caesar knows me," Catugna replied curtly. "Better still, he trusts me. If this message is delivered by my hand, Caesar will believe its legitimacy."

"And why do you need us?"

Catugna smiled. "You know the lay of the trenches and the watchwords of the pickets. You can see me safely through the lines. You *must* help me! This letter means victory for Caesar."

"Enough, wizard!" Lucius said brusquely. He was leery of the whole thing. Still, with the prospect of escape dangling before him, the possibility of living to fight another day, he was prepared to take the chance. He folded the document and handed it back to the druid.

Catugna held out a hand to shake, which Lucius met with a scowl.

"Know this, wizard. We are not friends. Any treachery on your part, any move to unsheathe that dagger, and I will snap your neck like a twig."

The druid simply smiled and nodded.

"Let's go." Lucius nudged Strabo to break him out of his musing. "Let's see if this jackanapes is telling the truth."

But Strabo made no move to rise.

"Did you hear me? We're leaving!"

"Not I, Lucius," Strabo finally answered.

Lucius looked at him in disbelief. "The means of escape lies before us. You mean to go over to Pompey, even now?"

"I do," Strabo said expressionlessly. "And I will give you until the changing of the guard before I alert them to your escape."

"Bloody bastard!" Lucius snarled.

"It is only my respect for you, Lucius, that keeps me from raising the alarm right now." Strabo paused, then added, "Or forcibly taking that letter from you."

A sudden rage brewed within Lucius as he stared contemptuously at his former comrade. He could not believe what he had heard. It was all he could do not to kick Strabo. Had he a weapon, he might have done worse.

Then Catugna was whispering in Lucius's ear like a serpent. "He presents a great risk, Centurion. Take my dagger and slay him quickly, that we may go!"

"No," Lucius seethed. "I will not kill him. Not like this. Let the bastard live with his treachery. The time he has given us will have to suffice. I suppose we must thank him for that."

"Mars protect you, Lucius," Strabo offered forlornly, clearly tormented within. "I will pray that you make it."

"Hear this now," Lucius said evenly. "If one day we should meet in battle, you will die on my sword. I will show no mercy."

Strabo nodded gravely. "And I will ask for none. Fare you well, comrade."

XXVI

General Quartius Quintinus, commander of the Tenth Legion, had misgivings about this impromptu visit. He was still unsure what to think about the two men who followed close on his heels as he made his way to the consul's tent.

This morning, as on every morning, he had risen long before sunup to review the quartermaster's reports under lamplight while nibbling on a few scraps of hard bread dipped in honey. The reports were getting more dismal with each passing day, a never-ending list of shortages, items needed to maintain the mile-long stretch of the line assigned to the Tenth. And he needed more of everything – pila, arrows, timber, flintstones, trenching tools, boots, and, most of all, legionaries. He needed another thousand men, at least. He would settle for a hundred. But the deficiencies in men and material were not the reason he was on his way to see the consul this morning.

A pair of unexpected visitors had interrupted his morning routine, the same motley pair who followed him now. One was a Gallic druid who looked as though he had just woken from the crypt. The other was a tall centurion who wore a coat of ill-fitting leather armor and a shoddy helmet dented in several places. These two were why Quintinus had dropped everything to huff nearly three miles from the Tenth's lines to Caesar's headquarters in the main camp.

A runner would not satisfy this time. Caesar had to hear this from his own lips.

Upon reaching the consul's tent, Quintinus and his two companions were admitted into the main chamber. They found Caesar sitting at a meager breakfast with his senior officers. Antony was there, much to Quintinus's dismay. Publius Sylla, commander of the Sixth Legion and the senior legate on this end of the line, sat there, too. Mamurra, the master of engineers, was speaking to Caesar, while a handful of adjutants ate in attentive silence. All were fully dressed in bronze and leather cuirasses, except Caesar, who wore only a purple tunic. The consul slowly chewed on a morsel of food while half-listening to Mamurra.

"Lots of barge activity on the bay this morning," Mamurra said, shifting in his chair to avoid an irritating circle of sunlight shining through a tear in one of the canvas walls. "It appears Pompey is moving some of his cavalry out of the city and back to the camp. The purpose for this is not immediately clear."

"It's clear enough," Antony chuckled. "He's moving the beasts because there's no water for them in Dyrrachium. And he'll find none in the camp, either, eh?"

Caesar smiled at the remark but said nothing as he continued eating. Only after an orderly leaned over and whispered something into Caesar's ear did he appear to notice Quintinus and his two followers.

"Ah, Quintinus! Won't you join us?"

"Thank you, Caesar, but I cannot," Quintinus replied uncomfortably. "I beg your pardon for this disturbance."

"Nonsense. This is an unexpected pleasure. I was planning to ride down to your end of the line later this morning." Caesar's tone was friendly and welcoming, but his expression somewhat soured when he noticed the scruffy pair standing next to Quintinus. Caesar waved a finger at them. "What is the meaning of this, Quintinus?"

"To be honest, my lord, I'm not quite sure."

"Get on with it, General," Caesar sighed impatiently. "I've no time for trivialities today."

"Forgive me, Caesar. I will be succinct. I do not believe you will find this to be trivial. These two came through my lines this morning." He gestured to the druid. "This one claims to know you, Caesar. And he claims to have an important message for you. He says the message is from one of Pompey's generals. I would have dismissed it out of hand, but –"

"Yes, I know him," Caesar interrupted. "And who is this fellow with him, Quintinus? He looks familiar."

"This is Lucius Domitius, my lord, one of my centurions. He's the one who –"

"– the one who you commissioned to deliver the special shipment to the Allobroges, Caesar!" Antony interrupted with unmasked malevolence. "He's been missing for four days, as has the cargo that was entrusted to him. He's a bloody deserter and should be taken outside and executed, at once, Caesar. We commend you, Quintinus, for bringing him to justice, but why is this traitor not in irons?"

Domitius cleared his throat as if he wished to speak, but Quintinus waved him silent. Quintinus would have preferred Domitius not be here at all. He had only brought the centurion along to corroborate the druid's story. And now Quintinus must defend the centurion or lose yet another man he so desperately needed on the battle line.

"Begging your pardon, Caesar, but Domitius did not desert. He was captured and escaped. He is the one who brought this other to me. They slipped through the lines not two hours hence."

"Don't be so easily fooled by this rascal, Quintinus," Antony said derisively. "I know him well. He's a bloody shirker if ever there was one."

Quintinus forced a cordial tone. "If Centurion Domitius is a deserter, my lord, then why would he return to our lines of his own volition?"

Antony was about to reply when Caesar suddenly addressed the waiting druid.

"I did not expect we would ever see you again, Catugna."

The consul was clearly more interested in the druid's story than Domitius's unauthorized absence. Antony seemed to sense this and did not press the issue further.

Catugna stepped forward and gave a reverential bow. "It is only through great difficulty and the grace of the sacred ones that I have managed to return, Great Caesar. I regret to inform you that Lord Roucill and Lord Egu have betrayed you. They have gone over to Pompey."

Caesar nodded, clearly already aware of this. "I must admit, I was surprised a few days ago when word reached me that my auxiliary cavalry was attacking the walls of the city. Especially since I had not ordered such an attack. But we apprehended a good many of the survivors, and they told us what truly happened. Even now, I can scarcely believe it. Roucill and Egu swore to serve me. I was their patron. I was their friend."

"Not to mention, you paid them a bloody fortune," Antony murmured under his breath.

"It is unfortunate but true, my lord," Catugna said

apologetically. "Roucill and Egu and their knights have joined your enemies, and Pompey has welcomed them with open arms. I, of course, had no choice but to feign obedience."

Antony sneered at that, but the druid maintained his composure.

"But fortune has smiled on you, yet again, Great Caesar," Catugna said. "This turn of events has proven most fortuitous. A message has been entrusted to me by one in Pompey's camp who still bears allegiance to you. But I must respectfully ask, Caesar, that I give it to you in private. Such was the charge given me."

"I wouldn't trust this unkempt waif as far as I could piss," Antony jeered. "I say toss the fool out on his ass that we might return to our victuals."

Caesar smiled. "Catugna is an old friend. His people owe their lands and fortunes to me. If any of our Gallic allies can be trusted, they can."

"My lord Caesar is too kind," Catugna said, shooting a venomous glance at Antony, who received it with amusement. "And your words are true, Great Caesar. I am forever in your debt and forever loyal to you above all else. It is in the spirit of that loyalty that I have come now. It would have been easy for me to accept the hospitality of Pompey, as Roucill and Egu have done."

"Perhaps we should award you the Grass Crown for such gallantry," Antony said mockingly.

"I do not seek glory for myself as others do, my lord," the druid replied coldly to Antony, then turned back to Caesar. "The message I carry is of great importance. Time is of the essence. I humbly ask again, Caesar, if I might give it to you in private?"

Quintinus, who had only been half paying attention, heard the centurion beside him clear his throat as if he wanted to speak.

"Damn it, Domitius! Stand still, man!" Quintinus whispered harshly, embarrassed by the disturbance. Did this fool Domitius not know his place? A low-level officer should not speak unless spoken to, and this one was already marching on thin ice.

But the others did not seem to have noticed the disruption.

"Oh, very well," Caesar said finally. "Quintinus, have your man leave us, along with the guards. Let us hear what our friend Catugna has to say."

"Yes, my lord," Quintinus nodded and directed those of lower rank to the door. "Go on! Out, all of you! You, too, Centurion Domitius."

"But, sir," the centurion said in a low voice. "I must speak to the consul. There is something I wish to clarify, for the record."

Does this fool not know when to give up?

"I said *out*, Domitius!" Quintinus retorted. "You've made enough of a nuisance of yourself already. Return to the legion and resume command of your century. Juno knows what they've been doing without an officer for the past few days."

The centurion appeared displeased with the dismissal but eventually nodded and followed the guards out of the tent.

"Forgive me, Caesar," Catugna said. "But I must ask that Lord Antony and the others leave as well. This message is for you alone. The sender made that very explicit."

"No," Caesar said, for the first time using an imperious tone rather than a friendly one. "One does not stroll into my tent unannounced and make demands, Catugna. My generals will remain. I have nothing to hide from them, especially an irregular communication from the enemy's camp."

A long moment of silence passed in which Catugna appeared to consider the ramifications of delivering the message with all the legates present. Finally, he reached into his cloak and produced the document.

"Let me see it first!" Antony waved a hand briskly.

Catugna hesitated at first but then, after a nod from Caesar, handed the message to Antony, who pompously snatched it away and perused the contents. After a few moments of reading with a furrowed brow, he looked up at the druid.

"Have you read this?"

Catugna nodded. "I was told to commit it to memory in the event it was lost or destroyed."

Antony handed the letter to Caesar. Caesar's face brightened as he read it first silently, then out loud.

To Gaius Julius Caesar, Consul of Rome, encamped near Dyrrachium

Remember my service to you in Gaul and the love my family has for you. Remember the pledge I made to you on the eve of the Ludi Romani last year. I stand by that pledge. I am eternally your man. These past months, I have pretended loyalty to Pompey with the hope that I might be placed in a position to help you. Great Caesar, that moment has come. Fortuna has placed me in command of the garrison in Dyrrachium. The town is yours. The citizens are loyal to you. I will assure the loyalty of the soldiers.

Come to the gates on the morrow. A purple banner draped from the embrasure will mean all is well. Once Dyrrachium is yours, Pompey will be forced to sue for terms. The war will be over, and you the victor.

Remember this deed when you return to Rome in triumph. The blessings of Juno be upon you!

*I am forever your devoted servant,
Gaius Aquilius*

"Can this be true?" Caesar said with astonishment. "It is indeed the hand of Aquilius."

"But can you trust him, Caesar?" Antony said. "He has been with Pompey all this time. Surely, this is a trap."

"And yet, it might not be," Caesar said optimistically.

Antony gestured at the druid, who was still standing there. "We don't need this one listening to our every word while we debate it."

Caesar nodded and smiled at the druid. "Our thanks, Catugna. You may leave us now. Go to the mess tent and get something to eat. I will summon you when I need you."

The druid bowed, cast a sidelong glance at Antony, and then departed.

"I can't believe you're actually entertaining this fairy tale," Antony commented after the druid was gone. "Come now, Caesar. Tell me all that was for the druid's benefit."

Caesar appeared not to have heard him. Instead, he stared at the document, reading it over and over, his eyes fixating on the signature, studying it closely as calculations seemed to turn over in this head. When he finally looked up, he had obviously come to a decision, and there was a new zest in his tone.

"I want one cohort each from the Sixth and the Thirteenth turned out near the isthmus in one hour. I will lead them personally."

"Is this wise, Caesar?" Antony protested, his tone absent of its former jollity. "You know Aquilius is a tricky bastard."

Caesar gave a small smile. "It bears merit. He owes me."

"So do half the legates on the other side. This is madness, Caesar. You can't go through with it."

"Antony, I want you to return to the left end of the line. Take charge there in the event this is a trick to turn our attention to the right. General Sylla, you will remain here, in command of the main camp, while I am gone."

Antony and Sylla nodded reluctantly. Mamurra looked concerned. Quintinus pondered the unreviewed ledgers back in his tent and how he might manage a moment alone with the master of engineers to discuss how in Hades he was supposed to maintain his works with half a bloody legion.

"I am aware of the risks," Caesar said, looking from one general to the other. He gave a wry smile. "One hundred *sesterces* says Aquilius hands the town over to me."

"I'll take that wager," Antony said. "And ten more says that druid bastard is nowhere to be found by sunset."

"Done," Caesar said spiritedly. "And I intend to hedge my bet by having you keep an eye on Catugna. I do not want him with me when I go before the town, but make sure he is kept nearby and under guard in the event of treachery."

"I thought you said you trusted him," Antony said with mild amusement.

"I do,...but be wary of him."

"Of that scarecrow?" Antony laughed. "I've seen more meat on a chicken leg. My mother could knock him senseless with her tits."

"His kind are not to be underestimated."

"Have no fear, my lord. I shall see that he is watched." Antony then drew an uncharacteristically sincere expression. "But please reconsider, Caesar. This whole thing reeks of treachery."

Caesar's smile faded, his face turning suddenly grim. He

looked around at each of his generals. "We are losing this siege. You all know it. Our soldiers are losing heart. More are deserting each day. Another week and Pompey won't need to win on the battlefield to achieve victory. Something must be done."

The mood in the tent was suddenly melancholy and fatalistic. Without another word, Caesar returned to the table, took his seat, and resumed his breakfast, signaling for the others to do the same.

Wishing he could return to his legion, Quintinus sighed imperceptibly and sat down to join them. The bloody ledgers would just have to wait now. But then, maybe the morning would not be a complete loss. Perhaps he could get a word in with Mamurra after breakfast was over…

XXVII

The sandy isthmus connecting Dyrrachium's island to the mainland was a quarter of a mile long and less than one hundred paces wide at its narrowest point. It was an imposing bottleneck for any advancing army and the main reason Caesar had made no attempt on the town. Moreover, the confined earthen bridge let out onto an empty plain, every square yard of which was within reach of the city's engines. And that was why, on this late morning, the two battle-ready cohorts from the Sixth and Thirteenth Legions remained ready on the east side of the isthmus while Caesar proceeded across it with a small group.

The advance party consisted of sixteen men, most of whom were Germans of Caesar's personal bodyguard. They rode in two columns with Caesar in between. The long swords of the German warriors were drawn and resting on their shoulders. Four well-dressed tribunes rounded out the party. They rode in line abreast out in front of the consul, helmets glimmering in the sun, tall plumes and gray capes whipping in the wind.

The land bridge let them out onto the plain, and the group spread out. Caesar had his first unobstructed view of the city walls. The battlements stood empty, their rough-cut stone faces gleaming white. Everything was quiet; even the scattering of huts and animal pens outside the wall looked abandoned.

The lack of activity gave Caesar pause. But, then, what else would he expect? If Aquilius was indeed in control of Dyrrachium, the defecting garrison was likely formed just inside the gates, preparing to receive their new leader with honors.

To Caesar's left, out on the bay, a dozen fishing boats cut minor disturbances in the glassy water. They tacked their way toward the wharf, sails luffing lazily as they prepared to put in after a long night of fishing. There were no warships in the harbor, aside from a dismasted galley moored at the docks and covered in scaffolding. A scattering of yachts and other small vessels rode quietly at anchor.

By all appearances, nothing looked suspicious. All was serene. Yet, an uneasy feeling lingered.

Again, Caesar had to remind himself that all of this had been ordained. Was that not obvious by now? He had met with one success after another in Gaul, Italy, and Spain. Even when the odds were against him, even when his generals vehemently opposed his plans, everything he touched turned to gold. And so, it followed that the message delivered by Catugna was yet another gift from the gods. Aquilius would turn Dyrrachium over to him, and Pompey would be forced to pull his army out by sea, or surrender.

Caesar kept telling himself to remain confident in his chosen course. What other choice did he have? Time was on Pompey's side.

A mass of birds suddenly rose from the dense marsh on the right. They squawked noisily as they took to the sky. A ribbon of a thousand flapping wings curled out over the water toward the fishing boats.

Was it an augury for good or evil? Caesar would have given ten thousand *sesterces* to glimpse through the eyes of one of those birds and see beyond the walls.

"We are just beyond the range of their bows here, Caesar," one of the tribunes turned in the saddle to report.

The party was approaching the abatis. Caesar could make out the spot where the Allobroges had cut their way through the barrier, and he could see that the breach had already been repaired. A fresh row of wooden spikes had been planted to replace the old ones.

Directly ahead, the road appeared to be barricaded where it crossed the abatis. But, as the party drew closer, it became apparent that the barricades had been shifted to form a zig-zagging passage just wide enough for two horses to ride abreast.

A door opened in welcome, or the jaws of a trap. Caesar ruminated.

Many of the mounts began to fidget at the sight of the narrow corridor. Caesar reached out a hand to calm his.

"A purple banner flies from the battlement, Caesar!" the same tribune reported. "Shall we proceed?"

Caesar squinted to make out the distant banner. Indeed, it was there. The long band of purple streamed from one of the towers near the gate. It had not been there a moment ago. The expected signal had been sighted. Presumably, all was well. Still, every man and beast was on edge.

At that moment, the figure of a man appeared on the wall, staring back at them from an embrasure.

Is it Aquilius? Am I a fool for even being here?

"Something is not right, Caesar," the tribune voiced the thoughts of the group. "We cannot risk you. Let us proceed while you remain here."

A noise resounded across the field, the sound of squeaking hinges. Caesar and the others looked up to see that the gate was slowly swinging inward. It continued until it was wide open. A solitary figure emerged wearing the accouterments of a senior officer. He was too far away to identify. The officer stood there for a long moment staring back at them across the plain before removing his helmet and beckoning with one arm for them to approach.

It is Aquilius! It has to be.

"We will proceed together," Caesar said determinedly.

With evident reluctance, the tribune motioned for the others to follow him. The procession collapsed into a column to navigate the passage through the obstacles, the four tribunes in the lead.

The last file of Germans entered the passage at the same time the lead tribunes were emerging on the other side. Caesar's view was again blocked by the barricades on either side. As he approached the exit, a giant hand suddenly grabbed the neck of his cuirass and yanked him off his horse, pulling him roughly to the ground.

A cry of alarm erupted from the front of the column. The next instant, the air was filled with a sound like hail falling from the sky. The confined horses shrieked and bucked as arrows sliced down into hide and flesh. Those riders still in the saddle when the storm hit were instantly riddled with feathered shafts. Men crawled frantically to escape the stomping hooves. Caesar was nearly bludgeoned several times as a German bodily dragged him to the rear while three others drove their longswords into the hearts of the kicking beasts that were blocking the way. Other warriors held shields to protect the consul.

Upon reaching the relative safety of the abatis, the earth shook with a series of dull thuds. The next moment, a great stone burst through the barrier and took off the head of a German not three steps away from Caesar, showering him with droplets of blood.

Many Germans were down, transfixed by half a dozen arrows each. Two of the tribunes lay crushed under a carpet of flailing horses. Peeking over the abatis, Caesar saw that the walls of the city were now lined with hundreds of archers. The bowmen discharged an incessant storm of arrows at the beleaguered party. At the gate, spear-wielding infantry spilled through the open portal, howling with a frenzy as they ran toward the hunkering survivors. Stones hurled from the enemy engines continued to bound over the abatis and through it, blasting deadly splinters everywhere.

"Damn Aquilius!" Caesar shouted. "Damn that blackguard!"

"My lord!" A sand-streaked, helmetless tribune got his attention and pointed toward the water. "The fishing boats!"

The hitherto innocent fishing craft were, in fact, nothing of the kind. Lolling sails had been cut away. The vessels now moved swiftly, propelled by dozens of sweeping oars. Tarps had been thrown back to reveal scores of armed men packed behind the bulwarks. The overloaded boats were headed at full speed toward the beach at the isthmus. Clearly, they intended to cut off Caesar's retreat.

"We must go, consul!" the tribune said, wincing from a broken arrow shaft protruding from his shoulder. "We must go before you are taken!"

Without waiting for confirmation, the tribune nodded to one of the bodyguards. The German left the cover of the abatis and sprinted across the sand to one of the fallen horses. With arrows pattering into the dead beast, the German unstrapped a long pole from the saddle and began running with it back toward the abatis. Halfway there, he was struck down by a torrent of arrows. Instantly, the tribune pointed to another German, who broke from cover without hesitation and picked up the pole dropped by his comrade. As the archers attempted to bring him down, the German climbed up onto the abatis, unfurled a giant yellow banner attached to the pole, and began waving it from side to side. Moments later, a two-foot-long scorpion bolt pierced him between the shoulders, emerging from his chest in a fountain of blood.

The dead German crumpled. The banner fell, already torn to ribbons. But the signal had been given. The cohorts waiting on the other side of the isthmus would now be on the move.

"Form *testudo*!" The tribune commanded the surviving Germans.

Caesar waited while the bodyguard formed a crude variation of the Roman formation.

So, the auguries had lied. Aquilius had lied!

And, now, perhaps everything he had worked to achieve would die here on this field with him. He would die a fool – a fool who had allowed himself to be lured into a trap, a fool who had believed himself invincible.

He did not know what would happen now, only that he would never let them take him alive.

"Come, my lord!" the tribune shouted.

Caesar nodded and joined the officer at the center of the upturned shields. Then, with arrows clattering on the canopy, and thudding stones threatening to shatter the tight formation at any moment, the *testudo* began to crawl back toward the isthmus where the cohorts were marching to the rescue.

XXVIII

From a rocky knoll two miles east of the isthmus, the tribune Sextus watched Caesar's beleaguered party in the distance.

"What is happening?" he demanded in a panic. "*In Juno's name*, can someone tell me what is happening down there?"

The four legionaries he had brought with him appeared just as confused. They, too, gazed mesmerized at the disaster unfolding on the distant land bridge.

Things were not going according to plan. Antony had given Sextus simple instructions. He was to take the druid to a place where Caesar's approach to the city could be observed. Then, upon seeing a green banner from the distant party – which meant all was well – he was to follow Caesar into the city, bringing the druid with him.

But the banner had not been green. It had been yellow – the danger signal. *Caesar was in trouble!*

"What is happening?" Sextus said again to no one in particular.

"Caesar is under attack," a raspy voice replied, laced more with amusement than alarm.

"I can see that!" Sextus snapped at the druid.

The hooded enchanter was perched on a nearby rock, watching the distant battle. A sudden gust fluffed the hood, allowing Sextus to catch a glimpse of his face.

Were his lips curled up in a smile?

The four legionaries that had accompanied Sextus moved higher on the knoll to better view the causeway. Sextus started to follow them but then stopped halfway, remembering that he was supposed to be watching the druid, and so contented himself to observe the action from where he was.

Catugna watched the feckless young fool from behind. He counted the distance separating them – no more than ten steps – close enough. The four legionaries had moved well up the hill, much farther away – far enough.

Smiling, Catugna turned his attention back to the action on the isthmus.

That's it, Roman dogs. Watch as your illustrious Caesar is butchered.

The overly confident Caesar had fallen victim to his own vanity. It was likely that the consul was already dead, struck down in the first fusillade of arrows. It was too swift an end for the tyrant who had visited such destruction on the Gallic tribes – a poor recompense for the hundreds of thousands he murdered. Still, Caesar would be dead, and the world would be rid of a despot. The prophecy would be fulfilled.

Everything was proceeding as the sacred spirits had foretold.

The survivors of Caesar's party had formed into a tight formation of shields and had begun to move back toward the causeway. Giant stones thrown from the walls looked like pebbles in the distance, kicking up clouds of sand all around the compact formation. The extreme range and the small target size were proving difficult odds for the artillerymen to overcome. In a few more moments, Caesar and his men would be out of range. But they would find their situation hardly improved.

A dozen craft had already beached themselves near the land bridge. Two hundred men were pouring out onto the shore to cut off the retreat. Simultaneously, a mass of infantry stormed out of the city gate in pursuit of the fleeing party.

The tight formation quickened its pace, then came apart entirely. Shields were cast away as every man in Caesar's group sprinted for the causeway. At the same time, the two cohorts from the Sixth and Thirteenth marched from the opposite end of the causeway to aid them. The cohorts numbered some six hundred men, tightly packed into a column of centuries. Seeing this threat to their flank, the amphibious troops turned to meet the oncoming cohorts at the narrowest point on the isthmus.

Sextus and the four legionaries raised their fists in a cheer at this favorable turn of fortune. But then, a dull horn resounded in the distance. All five Romans fell abruptly silent as they watched a mass of infantry burst from the marsh on the north side of the isthmus.

"Are they ours?" Sextus called up to the legionaries on the higher ground, but they returned only shrugs.

Catugna, on the other hand, brandished a grin that went unseen by the others.

No, you idiot. They are not yours.

The troops coming from the swamp belonged to Pompey. Like the fake fishing boats, they were part of the elaborate plan to capture or kill Caesar. They had been hiding in the thick brush and waist-deep, mosquito-infested water all morning. And now, Caesar's rescuing cohorts were beset from two sides. Steel clashed against steel. The serried ranks combined into a general melee. Soon, the entire isthmus was shrouded in a dusty haze.

"What's happening?" Sextus whined like a child. "What is bloody happening down there?"

Catugna knew what was happening, and he knew how it would end. Even if Caesar managed to reach the rescuing cohorts, he was outnumbered and caught on a spit of land too narrow for maneuver. It was only a matter of time before his men were surrounded and massacred. No legions would be pulled from the siege lines to help. Pompey had seen to that, yet another cog in the general's elaborate scheme.

Out of the corner of his eye, Catugna saw Sextus approaching him. It had finally dawned on the dense fool that treachery was afoot. Stopping just in front of Catugna, Sextus rested one hand tentatively on the hilt of his sword, as if unsure whether to draw it. He had made the fatal mistake of not summoning the four legionaries to back him up. They were still up the slope watching the battle.

"General Antony will wish to see you after –," Sextus was cut short by a sudden blur of movement. Before he could draw his sword an inch, the point of Catugna's dagger drove with incredible speed through the opening in his armor under his right armpit. The blade was inserted and extracted before Sextus even knew what was happening. Icicles of pain instantly coursed through his chest and extremities.

Like so many others, the young tribune had underestimated Catugna. He had misinterpreted the druid's pale, gaunt build for sluggishness and frailty.

The poison worked quickly. Sextus's limbs seized up as if frozen in ice. He fell to the ground stiff as a log, his eyes rolled back, his mouth foaming, hardly a sound escaping his lips. The four soldiers up the hill were still fixated on the distant battle, unaware of the fate of their officer.

Sextus's horse stood close by, tied to the gnarled stump of a tree. Catugna placed a boney hand on the beast's neck and whispered an incantation to keep it still as he mounted. Then, with the battle still raging on the distant causeway, he silently rode away.

XXIX

In the main camp, General Publius Sylla mulled heavily over what he should do as the battle raged on the isthmus. He had been left in command in Caesar's absence. His first inclination was to pull a cohort out of the thinly manned siege lines and rush it to Caesar's aid. But that idea was put on hold when alarm horns sounded to his front and frantic reports began arriving of enemy movement near the works. The reports had been panicked, inconsistent, absurdly succinct, and infuriatingly sparse of detail. Piecing them all together, it seemed that thousands of men had sprung out of the earth less than an arrow's shot from the lines.

But how could that be?

Now, after an interminable wait, the adjutant he had dispatched to confirm the reports sat on a horse before him just outside the headquarters tent, white-faced and out of breath, his eyes wild with horror. The horse was skittish and lathering after being pushed to its limits.

"I beg to report, it is true, General! The enemy is

attacking!"

"I know that, you fool," Sylla said petulantly. "I sent you to find out how many and where."

"At least ten thousand, sir," the red-faced officer replied. "All infantry by the looks of them. Advancing on the lines of the Sixth."

Sylla grimaced.

So, the message from Aquilius had been a ruse. It had sounded too good to be true, and it was. And now, the enemy had launched a major attack while Caesar was away. And Sylla silently wished he could pass the burden of command onto someone else.

"What are you doing?" Sylla snapped when the officer began to dismount. "Stay on that bloody horse and get along to Antony! Tell him what we are facing here and to send whatever help he can!"

The tribune saluted and rode off, seemingly thankful to have something to do away from the critical eyes of his general.

Sylla donned his helmet, mentally fortifying himself for the task ahead. Caesar would have to manage for himself on the isthmus. There was a battle to fight right here. A battle that may very well decide the outcome of the war.

XXX

The letter from Aquilius had indeed been a ruse. Pompey had orchestrated it all, from the crafting of the message, to the escape of Lucius Domitius, to the ambush on the isthmus. The plan's final and most significant element was the attack on Caesar's main camp, an audacious roll of the dice to end the entire war in one decisive moment.

Pompey was engaging his enemy in two places at once, and he expected to win on both fronts. Caesar would be captured or killed on the isthmus, while the main attack would punch through the siege lines and take the enemy camp. Pompey's horse would then storm through the gap and roll up Caesar's thinly spread army like an Egyptian carpet. Pompey was counting on panic and confusion to spread like wildfire.

For the main attack, he had assembled nearly half his army, four full legions, sixteen thousand men. Overall command had been given to Labienus, an honor which the firebrand general had accepted with joyful enthusiasm.

Pompey had presented the bold plan to the legates during supper on the previous night. They had welcomed it, applauded it, and drunk many toasts to Pompey's health and the plan's assured success.

Caesar's main camp was located to the northeast of the great line of circumvallation, just beyond the reach of Pompey's engines. Opposite the camp, in the neutral ground between the lines of the opposing armies, stood a series of sharp hillocks and shallow ravines that, in some places, approached within two hundred yards of Caesar's works. Through some oversight, Caesar had neglected to seize the hazardous positions, and Pompey intended to fully exploit that blunder.

"Strike hard and fast!" Labienus had imparted to his columns as they had passed through their own lines under the dull glow of the moon. The troops had been instructed to keep their weapons sheathed, helmets tucked away, shields within leather covers. "No prisoners shall be taken today. Remember, they are traitors to the Republic. Kill their officers! Spear them in the eyes! Drive your swords into their groins! Make them pay for serving the tyrant."

Stirred to a quiet but vengeful fury, the four legions had crept under cover of darkness into the natural defiles. They had hunkered there through the night undetected by the enemy pickets. As the first golden rays spilled over the crests of the distant mountains, they had waited, listening to the conversations of the oblivious enemy, smelling the stomach-churning aroma of the *chara* breakfast.

Sweltering in their armor, some passed out from the heat. Officers and men alike grumbled at the interminable wait. But no man dared rise from his hiding place. Each legion was under threat of decimation should a single man alert the enemy prematurely. Timing was critical to success. Their attack must coincide with the ambush on the causeway.

Finally, the moment came.

At a signal from Labienus, the concealed troops went into action. Centurions stood and began barking orders. *Signiferi* rushed across the uneven topography to plant their standards. Sixteen thousand men emerged from the ravines and gullies like the dead rising from the underworld, quickly falling into ranks as the thunderstruck enemy pickets looked on. The four legions established a loose oxhead formation. Two legions formed a column in the center flanked by a legion on both wings.

The oxhead was moving forward before the defenders sounded the horns of alarm. But the horns were hardly necessary. The collective roar of sixteen thousand men was sufficient to send the startled defenders into a frenzied rush to man the works. The four attacking legions advanced on a stretch of the line defended by a single, half-strength legion – the Sixth.

Severely depleted from its years in Gaul, the Sixth Legion consisted almost entirely of redoubtable men, the hardiest of those recruited in Spain all those years ago. They had faced their share of ambuscades and were immune to the terrors such overwhelming numbers would have struck in the hearts of greener men.

The left wing of the attack struck first. It came against a section of the line commanded by a seasoned tribune, one Volcatious Tullus. If the absent Caesar could have chosen the man to face the enemy first, it would have been Tullus. Tullus's fastidiousness made him unpopular with his men but perfect for commanding a defensive line. Unlike most, Tullus had not been surprised when the enemy had suddenly appeared to his front. Upon learning of the fight on the distant isthmus, he had ordered his three cohorts to stand to. He often did the same upon sighting a flight of birds, a wild animal dashing from the hills, or any other sign that might foretell enemy movement. His men despised these all-too-often needless calls to arms. But they were thankful for them on this day.

When the attack hit, Tullus's men were ready with javelins in hand. They greeted the advancing ranks with a devastating storm of the six-foot-long projectiles, felling many and spiking many more shields with the heavy encumbrances. The stunned attackers crossed the trench and began climbing the works. An avalanche of heavy stones was released by the defenders, tearing gaping holes in the leading ranks. Shields splintered. Bones shattered. Dislodged helmets spun through the air as skulls were smashed by the bounding objects. Those who avoided the stones were met at the crest by a line of shields and thrusting pila. The deadly iron points plunged into eye sockets, open mouths, and exposed necks. Severed arteries sprayed into the air. Men cried out in pain and terror.

Having abandoned their own shields, many attackers tried to block the javelins with bare hands or arms and ended up speared like fish. Those who managed to grope their way past the pila were immediately beset by gladii jabbing from underneath the shields, mutilating booted feet and unprotected legs.

The attacking legion had more significant numbers by far. Still, Tullus's cohorts had the high ground, and they stood upon that ground as they had on a hundred battlefields, stalwart and unwavering. Time and again, the attacking legion fell back, reformed, advanced up the slope. Time and again, it was beaten back with appalling losses.

No breach would be possible here. Tullus and his men could not be dislodged. The left side of the attack had failed.

On the other side of the oxhead, the legion on the right

wing had the misfortune of going up against something they had not anticipated – two cohorts of German auxiliaries. The Germans had been attached to the Sixth to augment the legion's numbers. After weeks of tedious digging, interspersed with horrific barrages from Pompey's artillery, the long-haired, bearded warriors were eager to finally bloody their broadswords. They welcomed the attack with a sadistic delight particular to their kind. Cowering behind fortifications was not their way. It was repulsive, cowardly, and far too Latin. And so, ignoring the rebukes of their Roman officers, the Germans rose from cover and charged down the works headlong to meet the enemy.

The sight of the oncoming barbarian wave sent a ripple of hesitancy through the attacking ranks. Many of the new recruits stopped entirely. The young soldiers had been told to expect a stunned, disorganized enemy. Instead, they found themselves face-to-face with the stuff of nightmares. These were not like any auxiliaries in Pompey's army – foreigners to whom they had grown accustomed. These were howling, wild-eyed savages, some armored, some naked, some covered in tattoos, some gigantic beyond belief, all berserk with the battle lust.

Before the cursing centurions could form the legion into a defensive line, the Germans were among them. Hacking their way into the stunted ranks, the crazed warriors crushed skulls, lopped off heads, hacked away limbs. A bloody mist filled the air, magnifying the terror and chaos. As reckless as the Germans' attack was, there was a method to it. They went after the centurions and tribunes first. They singled out and surrounded every Roman of authority, chopped them to pieces, threw their severed heads into the rear ranks to provoke even more panic. When all the officers had been slain, the Germans went for the standard-bearers, then anyone else shouting orders, until the legion finally devolved into a muddled, leaderless mob scampering back to its own lines.

The right wing had also failed.

But the failures on the wings, disappointing as they were, did not dismay Labienus. He had planned them as parries, mere feints, meant to draw defenders away from the center where the head of the ox would strike after a set delay. The head was the main assault. It was aimed at a square-shaped fortification that sat on a height just behind the enemy works and commanded the siege lines in both directions. Once the fort was taken, Caesar's men would be forced to abandon the adjacent works. Then, Labienus would have a protected funnel through which he could send his reserves and the waiting cavalry.

The eight thousand men forming the head pressed their attack with a verve not possessed by the legions on the wings. The soldiers of the two center legions were made of stouter mettle. They were veterans from Syria, survivors of the disaster at Carrhae, men who knew well the horrors of battle and were not easily shaken by them. And, most significantly, they were possessed with a fanatical desire to regain their sacred honor.

The Syrian legions swelled against the outer works, a wave of iron helmets and spear points. They sent as many javelins back as they received, keeping the defenders' heads down. At the same time, a contingent of slaves planted ladders and hooks. With these, the Syrians quickly surmounted the works, overcame and slaughtered the outnumbered defenders, reformed, and advanced up the steep slope to the fort's palisade wall.

To deal with the palisade, a ram had been fashioned out of a mast taken from a war galley. The twenty-foot section of hardened oak was borne by two score slaves, one score relieving the other every two hundred steps. When the ram reached the slope, both groups pitched in for the final uphill leg. Muscles tightened, veins bulged, men grunted as the massive object was hauled toward the wall atop forty shoulders.

The fort was defended by a single cohort of the Sixth, commanded by the legion's *primus pilum*, a centurion named Minucius. Minucius, a hardened leader of many campaigns, had a mere three hundred spears to repulse thousands, but he was determined to hold the fort to the last man.

Upon sighting the ram amid the swarm below, Minucius ordered the scorpions in the towers to strike down any man who dared touch it. And this they did to significant effect, transfixing one unfortunate slave after another. When a third of the slaves had fallen to the deadly bolts, the rest could no longer bear the massive weight. The ram slipped from their clutches, dropped, and rolled back down the slope, crushing many beneath it.

But the Syrians continued to claw their way toward the palisade. Iron-tipped arrows found the gaps between the shields. Javelins sliced into exposed necks and shoulders. Stones clattered off shields, clanged off helmets, thudded into skulls, dropped men where they stood. The fallen became yet another obstacle for the attackers. The earthen slope ran slick with gore, wreaked of exhausted bowels. Cries for help emanated from the nightmarish crush, yet the Syrians kept climbing. Many tumbled wounded down the blood-streaked incline, only to crawl back upon regaining their senses. Despite the fierce fire, the ranks finally reached the wall, where they compressed and melded into one. One legion merged with the other and zealously set about forcing a breach.

Inside the fort, a thin line of legionaries stood along the foot of the palisade. They used swords and daggers to lop off hands and digits attempting to dislodge the posts from the other side. Pila were thrust at the gnarled faces between the gaps. Minucius had another thin line deployed on the fire step atop the wall. The legionaries there were armed with eighteen-foot *sarissas* borrowed from the Greek auxiliaries. They plunged the lengthy weapons down into the dark spaces between the upturned shields, again and again. The sharpened points were extracted each time dripping with fresh blood. The attackers attempted to use scaling ladders, but these were swiftly shorn of climbers by fifty-pound stones dropped down their lengths.

The Syrians rolled their dead to the rear, a steady avalanche of corpses that piled up at the base of the slope. Losses were mounting, but they were gouging holes in the wall at a dozen places. Surely, one of these would break through.

Centurion Miniscus knew that any breach would mean the instant loss of the fort and the slaughter of his men. He also knew that he did not have enough legionaries to cover the entire perimeter. Thus, he kept two flying platoons in reserve – one consisting of twenty of his best fighters, the other comprised of his best engineers. And these he dispatched, as needed, the fighters to bolster defenses where a break was imminent, the engineers to close up breaches in the wall.

The engineers were led by Scaeva, a centurion who had overseen many successful holdouts in Gaul. Scaeva forbade his men from carrying sword or shield. Instead, spare posts, hammers, and trenching tools were their weapons. These they employed with great skill, mending the palisade, often leaving it stronger than before. The only shield in the platoon was Scaeva's, which he used to protect his men, never himself, that they might work unimpeded. Though his shield bristled with arrows, and he bled from a dozen wounds, Scaeva stood fast and shouted encouragement to his men. And his men, fearful for the safety of their revered leader, worked all the swifter that he might retire from danger. These platoons did much to foil the efforts of the attackers.

Some fifty paces behind the attacking legions, standing upon the crest of the seized outer works, Labienus could see that his Syrians were meeting with some difficulty. The fort should have fallen by now. To spur on the stalled attack, he ordered up an auxiliary cohort of Cretan archers. The Cretans carried with them smoking cauldrons of pitch which they placed at even intervals upon the outer works. The archers then launched wave after wave of flaming arrows into the fort and the enemy camp beyond. Soon, tents, oil stores, and any other combustion source they happened to touch were set ablaze. Fires quickly raged out of control in the main camp.

Within the fort, however, the fiery missiles found no fuel, thanks to the foresight of Scaeva. The centurion of engineers had ordered vessels of water and dirt be placed at regular intervals to extinguish any flames before they could take root. Nevertheless, thick smoke from the burning camp quickly enveloped the fort and its towers, forcing the defenders to blindly loose their missiles into the haze. The poor visibility proved no less a hindrance to the attackers. The same hills that had hidden their advance now blocked the offshore breeze, allowing the smoke to hang and thicken such that the men lost sight of their standards, and officers lost sight of their men. All coordination between the attacking units dissolved.

Still, the Syrians had the numbers to overcome even this ill turn of events if they simply focused on getting through the wall to their front. They seemed to comprehend this to a man. Units shifted as more men climbed the slope until the fort was entirely surrounded. Now they were using their numerical advantage to full effect, hacking away at multiple points on every wall, unimpeded in most places. The tide was rapidly turning in their favor.

The grounds inside the fort bristled with feathered shafts. Most of the defenders lay dead or wounded. Minucius and his men had fought gallantly, but they were too few to stem the tide of the assault. Breaches were forming everywhere. They would be overrun in a matter of moments. The critical heights would be lost.

Then, suddenly, the blare of horns sounded in the fog. The sound did not come from Pompey's side, but from Caesar's, from the blazing camp beyond the fort. Shadows passed before the glow of the fires. The horns grew louder. The tramp of boots filled the air. The blood-spattered men on both sides paused in their savagery to look up.

The next moment, rank upon rank emerged from the haze, two legions strong, marching at the double-quick, shields raised, javelins poised. They were fresh troops pulled from the adjacent lines. The blood of Minucius's men had bought them time to assemble into battle order. And now they advanced to the relief of the beleaguered fort.

A battle cry, an arcing swarm of javelins, an onrush of jabbing gladii, and it was all over. The exhausted Syrians could withstand no more. Their flanks disintegrated. The breaches were abandoned.

The crestfallen Labienus made no attempt to stop the endless stream of dazed and wounded stumbling past him to the rear. With a quarter of his men dead or writhing on the field, he had no choice but to order his broken legions to withdraw. They retired under the echoing taunts of the triumphant defenders.

Blood soaked the field. Two thousand men lay dead, and yet the lines were reestablished precisely where they had been before the carnage started. Pompey's grand plan had failed.

The defeat might have turned into a colossal disaster had the defenders pursued. It was not through any lack of desire that Caesar's legates did not exploit the victory. Emphatically, they pleaded with Publius Sylla to launch an immediate counterattack. But Sylla would not allow it.

"It would be inappropriate to commit the army to a general action in Caesar's absence," Sylla explained. "Such glory and honors rightly belong to him. We shall be content with our little victory and let Caesar deliver the killing blow when he returns."

That explanation was, at least, partly true. Sylla always played the dutiful lieutenant, always placed Caesar's glory before his own. But, inwardly, his reluctance to counterattack had personal motives. No news had come from the isthmus. The outcome of the battle there was uncertain. Sylla did not know if Caesar was alive or dead. If dead, then there was a good chance most of the legions Sylla now commanded would declare allegiance to Pompey. If by chance, tomorrow found Sylla kneeling in surrender at the foot of Pompey, this show of restraint on his part might touch some merciful chord in the great general's soul.

But, alas, Sylla's precautions proved unnecessary. Word soon arrived that Caesar was alive. Once again, the consul had defied the odds. He and his cohorts had withdrawn from the isthmus in good order, using the narrow confines to negate the enemy's numerical advantage. Sword against sword, Caesar's veterans were always superior.

Pompey had suffered heavy losses. The day was decidedly Caesar's. But the battle was far from over.

XXXI

Cimon scurried up the street under the hot midday sun. He was out of breath. His heart pounded in his chest from the steep incline. But he had to hurry. Something was terribly wrong.

The slanted column of black smoke rose above the town and floated inland on the offshore breeze. It appeared to be coming from the house.

Was it on fire?

What could those house slaves have botched in the short time he had been gone? That old hag of a cook neglecting the ovens again, most likely.

Cimon had left the house only a few hours ago to make his daily rounds. He had stopped by the brothels, the wharf, the gate, the prison, the merchant's square, the brothels again, listening to rumors and gathering intelligence that he would report to Valens, as he did every day.

Last night, the senator had not returned from his business aboard the yacht in the harbor. Nor had he returned by the time Cimon had left on his rounds. Likely, the meeting had gone late, and Valens had chosen to spend the night aboard ship.

Cimon wondered if the senator's delay had anything to do with the commotion going on down at the wharf. The waterfront was alive with activity. Barges full of heavily armed soldiers traveled between the camp and the city. There were more soldiers than usual at the city gate – thousands more. And when the wind shifted, Cimon could hear the din of raised voices intermixed with the clash of steel, like a great battle was being fought somewhere on the other side of the wall.

Something was going on out there, but he did not care about that at the moment. He now cared only about the smoke emanating from the house and determining which slaves he must flog for it. They would indeed feel the lash if they ruined *this* day for him.

The day had been going so well, precisely as he had intended. Baseirta had returned in the dark hours of the morning and had reported her task completed. She had found Domitius, had lain with him, had administered the poison, and had seen him breathe his last breath before leaving him. More than pleased with her work, Cimon had allowed the exhausted woman to retire to the slave quarters for some well-earned sleep.

Domitius was dead, and Baseirta was tainted. All that remained was to deliver both pieces of news to Valens in the affable manner Cimon had rehearsed.

When Valens returned, Cimon would give a full accounting of the assassination, including how it had been necessary for Baseirta to lie with Domitius to ensure the job was done. Valens would be angry at first, but Cimon knew his master well. Ultimately, the senator would concede that the death of Domitius was well worth the tainting of his favorite concubine. With the silver mine firmly in his possession, Valens could buy a thousand unsullied Baseirtas. He would not want her anymore.

As Cimon approached the smoking *domus*, his anger was somewhat tempered by the thought that, by this time tomorrow, Baseirta would be his to do with as he pleased.

Entering the servants' door, he dashed across the courtyard to the kitchen, expecting to find the ovens raging and the morning bread burnt to a crisp. He did not discover the source of the smoke, but what he did find shocked him even more. Around the servants' table, men sat slumped over with half-eaten breakfasts before them. Others lay on the floor with faces frozen in agony, hands clasped around their own throats, wide eyes staring into space. They were the gardeners, the liveryman, the valets, and the other male house slaves.

They were all dead.

Cimon immediately concluded the smoke had not been the cause. The thin haze in the kitchen was still quite breathable. If it contained the vapors from some poisonous herb, then surely, he himself would have felt the effects by now.

Bewildered, Cimon scurried back across the cloudy courtyard calling out for the female slaves. Tracing the smoke to its source, he discovered it came from the stairwell leading down to the sanctum. At the same time, one of the female slaves rushed out of the fog, almost bumping into him. It was the cook.

"Oh, Cimon!" The old woman was frantic, her eyes wild with fear. "It is terrible, so terrible! Tragedy has struck this house! The gods frown upon us. It's horrible, terrible, so terrible!"

"Stop gibbering, hag! Talk sense!"

"The men are dead."

"I know that! What happened? Tell me this instant, or I'll have your back laid bare!"

"It was the girl," the woman said, almost in a daze. "She did it shortly after you left this morning."

"Baseirta?"

"She put something in the drink. The men died horribly, as if choking on flames."

Damn the bitch! She used my own poison on them. Doubtless, she saved some after killing the soldier. I should not have made such a large portion! She will pay for this. Oh, by Zeus, how she will pay!

"She went to the master's armory," the old woman continued. "Spent some time in there. The other women and I thought maybe she had used one of the master's weapons to take her own life, but then she came out armed with a dagger and threatened us with it. Told us to go to our quarters and not come out. We did as she said, but when we smelled the smoke, we feared the house would burn down around us, so we came out and found that she had set fire to the shrine."

Cimon nodded, somewhat relieved. There was little down in the sanctum that would burn. The entire chamber was made of brick and mortar. Even the marble statue of Mars would receive no more than a blackened blemish. It could be easily cleaned.

What had she burned then, and to what purpose other than to be a nuisance? Had she set fire to sticks and rags?

Then, suddenly, it dawned on him.

The scrolls! The master's sacred scrolls! That whore has burned up the damned scrolls!

Cimon reached out and wrenched the arm of the old woman so firmly that she gasped with pain.

"Where is she now? Where is she, damn you!"

"I-I don't know," the old woman winced. "Run off, I suppose. She was gone when we came out."

She would not get far, Cimon concluded. While she had succeeded in killing the very men he would have employed in finding her, he had other contacts in Dyrrachium. He had dirt on all the brothel owners. They would lend him their personal guards to help hunt her down. He would have to move fast. He needed to find Baseirta before...

"At least the master has returned," the old woman offered as if it were good news.

Cimon's heart skipped a beat. "The master is *here*?"

She nodded. "He arrived moments before you did. He is down in the sanctum with his litter-bearers, putting out the fire. He wishes you to come to him at once."

Releasing his hold on the woman, Cimon turned on his heel, not toward the stairwell but toward the door. The girl had run. So would he. He would run away and escape the master's wrath. He would get lost in the bustle of this city under siege, perhaps make his way aboard one of the galleys in the harbor, possibly go over to Caesar's army. Whatever he did, he would survive, and he would find that *bitch*!

"Cimon," the old woman said after him. "Did you not hear? The master desires to see you."

Cimon made no reply but marched steadily through the fog toward the exit. Ten paces away from freedom, a colossal shape suddenly stepped into his path, blocking the way. It was one of the Arabians, a giant axe laying across both muscled arms. Valens clearly did not want anyone to leave.

Deducing that the front entrance was likely guarded similarly, Cimon took in a deep breath and tried to act calm as he changed directions and casually walked toward the stairwell. The Arabian and the woman followed. With each step, Cimon's mind worked to contrive a means with which to escape this quandary.

The master would be angry, for sure. He would demand

an explanation. Cimon would reason that this was not his fault. That Parthian slut was responsible, not him! She must be hunted down. She could not have gone far. Give him the bargemen and the Arabians, and he would find her. He would personally deliver her up for punishment. That was it! He would deflect Valens's anger onto the girl, where it belonged.

Besides, even with all that had happened, he was sure the fact that Domitius was dead would be enough to save his own skin...Unless, of course, the girl had lied. Had she lied? Had she used *any* of the poison on Domitius?

Reaching the bottom of the stairs, Cimon stepped into the dark, cloudy chamber. The only light came from the aperture in the high ceiling. Valens was at the altar near the foot of the blackened statue, sifting through ashy chards of curled papyrus. His visage was dark and grim. Two Arabians stood stiffly in the shadows, axes in hand, bleached skulls dangling from their waists.

Beads of perspiration formed on the chief servant's forehead.

"Ah, Cimon! There you are!" Valens said, his tone deceptively polite.

Cimon bowed reverently. "I must apologize for this, sire. I only just returned from my morning errands. I will see that it is all returned to as it was before."

"Really?" Valens said scornfully. "Do you intend to resurrect Numa and demand he pen a new set of books? Do you intend to produce a dozen slaves worth two thousand *sesterces* each? You simple-minded fool!"

Taking up a handful of the ash, Valens threw it in Cimon's direction. As the black bits of papyrus fluttered across the shaft of sunlight, many of them landing on the chief servant, Valens seemed to get control of his rage.

"I understand this is the work of the girl?"

"Yes, sire." Cimon nodded. Evidently, Valens had already questioned the cook.

"You told me she would never discover her father's fate?" Valens said accusingly.

"I do not know that she has, sire?"

"Then why else would she have done this...this spiteful act?"

Perhaps she tires of being your whore, Cimon thought, before replying, "She is selfish by nature, sire. Perhaps she no longer cares if her father lives or dies. Whatever her motivation, she must pay for her actions. Let me hunt her down and bring her to you, sire."

A long pause ensued, during which Cimon realized Valens was studying him, seeing through his deception.

"First things first," Valens said finally. "What of Lucius Domitius?"

"He has been taken care of, just as you commanded, sire."

"He is dead, then?"

Cimon paused, feeling as though he was being led into a trap, but it was a trap he could not avoid.

"Indeed, he is, sire."

"How did he die?"

Again, Cimon paused. The truth – or, at least, one version of it – was his only chance.

"I sent the girl to Domitius with a poison. She put it in his drink, and –"

"The same poison that killed all my house slaves, perhaps?" Valens snapped hotly.

"Possibly, sire. I am just as surprised as you are that she betrayed us."

"Us?" Valens said with a raised eyebrow. "Oh, she has not betrayed you. She would not betray her partner in this crime."

"Sire, what are you saying? I had no part in this. You must believe me!"

"You, there!" Valens pointed past Cimon to the cook. "Come forward."

The old woman stepped into the light, frightened and uncertain.

"Tell me again, what you told me before," Valens commanded her. "What did the girl say before she left?"

Wringing her hands together, the cook glanced at Cimon with anxious eyes. Clearly, she was remembering how his lash had felt on her back so many times in the past.

"As I told you before, sire, it was a message meant for Cimon alone," the old woman said. "I only told you, sire, because you bad me tell you." It seemed this last was added for the chief servant's benefit.

"That's right," Valens affirmed. "And now, I want you to repeat it. What message did she give you for Cimon?"

"She said to tell Cimon she had been to see the soldier Domitius last night —"

"Yes, yes, I know!" Cimon interrupted, trying to head off any further revelation. "She reported to me when she got back this morning, sire. I sent her to kill Domitius last night, and she did precisely that. Your enemy is dead, sire. That, at least, is one thing in which we can rejoice —"

"What else?" Valens said sternly, his question directed at the cook.

"She said she had seen to the soldier's every need, just as Cimon had ordered." With quivering lips, the old woman shot another glance at Cimon. "And that she had left the soldier alive and well and much more content than before, also as Cimon had ordered."

"That's a lie!" Cimon blurted out. "The witch lies, sire! She is…"

"It is clear to me now why the attempt in the prison

failed," Valens said absently, watching his own fingers trace lines in the ash upon the altar. "I misjudged your desire for the girl. You would keep young Domitius alive to ruin me, that you might have her for yourself one day."

"N-No, sire! I do not want her. I-I mean I would never…" Cimon searched for the right words, a plausible explanation to wriggle his way out of this corner, but his throat was dry as parchment, and his mind was blank. He felt suddenly dizzy. How could he have so underestimated the girl? She had set him up! She had planned this whole scene with her carefully planted message. Perhaps the old hag was in on it, too.

His eyes darted to the stairwell, still blocked by the guard. There was nowhere to run.

Sighing, Valens made a small gesture with one hand. It was a signal Cimon had seen him use on only a few occasions, but Cimon knew well its meaning. A cold chill flooded over him.

"Sire, please!" he pleaded. "I can explain!"

Answering the summons of their master, the Arabian axemen stepped out of the shadows.

XXXII

The sun was setting on the bay when Valens stepped from his barge onto the shore. He had just crossed over from Dyrrachium to the army camp, and now marched briskly up the slope, weaving his way through the crowded lanes as his Arabians cleared a path for him.

The day's fighting was over. Physicians and camp boys tended to the rows of wounded and dying. The dead lay in much tighter rows, waiting to be thrown into the great funeral pyres now raging on the beach.

Valens glanced disapprovingly at the results of the failed attack.

Pompey was a fool! He had lost, and no wonder. He had sent inexperienced legions to execute a ridiculously complex battle plan requiring a level of coordination quite beyond their abilities. The attack had accomplished nothing and had reduced the effective size of his army by thousands.

Still, Valens was surprised at Pompey's brashness. He

had not thought the old fool still had it in him. More surprising was the enthusiastic mood that still prevailed throughout the camp, despite the loss. The army had suffered a stinging defeat, and yet, the soldiers were anything but somber. Excitement filled the air. Units were on the move. Even now, several thousand fresh legionaries marched in orderly columns down the beach, heading toward the southern end of the lines.

Nearby, upwards of a thousand horses fed on piles of barley freshly deposited on the shore by a fleet of galleys only hours before. Roman, Greek, and Eastern horsemen sharpened lances and cinched up breastplates as if preparing for action.

Was Pompey planning another attack so soon?

Whatever Pompey was up to, Valens had more important concerns right now. The loss of the scrolls was problematic, but nothing a good forger and a few thousand *sesterces* could not solve. The girl's betrayal and disappearance were also unfortunate, but she, too, could be replaced. And, of course, there was the problem of young Domitius who was not only alive but, according to one report, had escaped from the prisoner stockade. But none of these problems were Valens's chief concern at the moment.

He had spent all night aboard the packet in conference with his agent. The news from Rome was troubling, to say the least. It seemed the fragile coalition of senators he had spent the last several months nurturing with bribes and promises was dangerously close to falling apart. The fools were getting cold feet, allowing radical legislation through, bungling things far worse than he had initially thought. And now, Valens's own hand was needed to set things back on their proper course. He must go to Rome and pay a surprise visit to one or two of the more troublesome senators. Even now, his chests were packed and being taken aboard the yacht. He would sail on the evening tide. There was no time to waste.

Still, he must keep up appearances and pay his respects to Pompey before he left. He must inform the illustrious general that urgent business necessitated his immediate departure, lest he be accused of abandoning the *Optimates* cause at a time of need. He did not anticipate opposition from Pompey, who was likely still too flummoxed by today's loss to even care.

Upon reaching Pompey's pavilion, Valens found that the commander of the army was not there. An adjutant directed him to a nearby hilltop crowded with mounted officers and fluttering banners. Valens quickly picked out Pompey, conspicuous atop his horse in plumed helmet and armor, both of which were ridiculously ill-fitted to his pudgy frame. Several dozen soldiers were formed up on the hillside in ranks facing Pompey. By the time Valens reached the hilltop, Pompey was just finishing his oration.

"You no longer serve Caesar," Pompey said mechanically to the attentive soldiers as if reciting the lines for the twentieth time. "You have sworn an oath to serve me unto death. You will be held to that oath. The crimes you committed under Caesar are forgotten. Serve me well, and live. Betray me, and you will die as your former comrades did."

Valens deduced that these were the prisoners who had agreed to join Pompey. He scanned the assembled ranks in the hopes of recognizing Domitius among them, but to no avail.

"Hail, Pompey!" the former prisoners responded in a lackluster, disharmonious salute. Clearly, they were uncertain whether their prospects had changed for the better.

Then, a grim, gray-haired officer in a plain leather cuirass stepped forward as if to salvage the oration. Valens recognized him as the resolute Cato the Younger, a powerful and influential senator-in-exile. Valens had not invited Cato to join the brotherhood. The stubborn, unwashed fool would never turn his back on the Republic, and Valens still counted him an enemy for voting in favor of his exile.

"We fight against that tyrant Caesar!" Cato said with hands gesticulating, the inflection in his voice much more stirring than Pompey's drone. "We fight for the liberty hard-won by our forefathers! Do not dishonor your good names! Bear yourselves up like men! Laugh at death! Smile at our assured victory! The gods are with us! The gods are with Pompey the Great! Hail, Pompey!"

"Hail, Pompey!" the soldiers answered together with much more enthusiasm this time.

The instant the troops were dismissed, Pompey was beset by a bevy of legates and tribunes, all with pressing business. The loitering Valens pursed his lips in frustration. He did not have time to wait while these lesser men went ahead of him. Indeed, the tide would not wait. Valens was half-considering ordering the Arabians to clear a path for him when a familiar voice greeted him.

"My lord."

Valens turned to see Labienus standing there, a tired smile on his face. Vastly different from the confident, enthusiastic man who had visited him only two days ago, Labienus looked haggard and crestfallen. His hair and armor were coated in dust. Gone was the characteristic swagger. Still, he managed a small, reverential bow.

"Good evening, General," Valens said formally as if to remind him they were to act as equals in public.

"You have heard the news of the battle, I suppose?"

Labienus asked bleakly.

Valens nodded.

"Nearly two thousand dead." Labienus gestured to the field hospitals in the camp below. "And many more that will die in the coming days. It is a disgraceful defeat. My defeat."

"I'm sure you did everything you could."

"Six standards were lost to the enemy."

Labienus was clearly frustrated and, no doubt, somewhat embarrassed by the loss. But Valens had no interest in hearing any more about the imprudent attack.

"I am here to see the commander of the army," Valens said curtly.

"I believe he wishes to see you, as well," Labienus replied, evidently detecting the impatience in Valens's tone. He glanced over at Pompey, who was in the middle of a heated discussion with two legates. "He appears to be busy at the moment. The legates seem to need their hands held to do anything. They certainly do not know how to properly handle a legion in combat."

"That is because Pompey does not let them think for themselves," Valens said disapprovingly in a low tone.

Labienus's eyes were suddenly captivated by the Arabian bodyguard standing just behind Valens. He pointed a finger and asked hesitantly, "My lord, was that not your chief servant?"

The finger was not pointing at the Arabian but at the giant's belt, where hung a collection of bleached skulls, along with the grisly object in question. It was the freshly severed head of Cimon, the most recent addition to the macabre trophies, still dripping onto the guard's sandaled feet.

"General Labienus," Valens said sharply as if he had not even heard the question. He did not have the time nor the desire to discuss the well-deserved fate of his miserable chief servant. "I must see Pompey now! I will not stand here and wait while those fools bother him with minutiae. You are his deputy. Intercede on my behalf!"

For an instant, Labienus's tired eyes narrowed as if he had taken offense to Valens's demanding tone. But the sentiment passed as he apparently remembered to whom he owed his true allegiance. He gave a silent nod and a courteous gesture of the hand. Then, using little tact, he broke in on the discussion between Pompey and the legates, directing the latter to wait some distance away. The general of the army appeared somewhat grateful for the interruption.

"Ah, Valens! I am glad you have come!" Pompey said, clasping his hand warmly. "I apologize for not yet taking you up on your gracious dinner invitation. I've been unable to get over to Dyrrachium these past few days, but I assure you I shall when all this is over. That is, if the invitation still stands."

"Think nothing of it, Great Pompey," Valens smiled. "You are always welcome. I look forward to that day when Caesar is vanquished, and we can sup at our leisure."

"As do I, my friend. As do I," Pompey said reflectively, his thoughts clearly distracted by a thousand other things. He then smiled and pointed at the recently dismissed troops milling about waiting to receive their new unit assignments. "What do you think of these recruits? Did you ever see a more rugged lot? I wish I had ten thousand more like them. Had I ten thousand like these today, I would have carried the day."

"Are these all the prisoners taken from Caesar?"

"No, not all. Just the ones who have agreed to join us." Pompey shot a prodding smile at his deputy. "Labienus thinks me a fool for trusting them. He thinks I should let his Germans carve them up, but I believe that to be a waste of good fighters – and I need good fighters."

"I have heard there was an escape last night," Valens said.

Pompey seemed caught off guard by the statement. When he spoke again, his tone was guarded. "Yes. I believe I did hear that."

"One centurion by the name of Lucius Domitius," Valens added. "Do you know if he's been found?"

Pompey eyed him suspiciously. "And how come you to know that name, Senator? Is he an acquaintance of yours?"

Surprised at Pompey's reaction, Valens made every effort to sound impartial, as though he were making small talk. "I overheard one of the young officers mention his name. I was merely concerned that such a man might be lurking somewhere within the camp, planning mischief."

"I wouldn't concern myself with him," Pompey said dismissively. "We have more serious things to worry about than one escaped prisoner."

"One must not underestimate the havoc one man can cause." Valens could not help but press the subject. "A good fighter, as you called these others."

"I said you mustn't concern yourself with it, Senator!" Pompey snapped. "Leave it be!"

Valens bridled at the severe retort. He bit back his desire to put this flea in his place, this low-born man who was not fit to clean his boots. But he got control of his anger and cursed himself for a fool. His obsession with the son of his old rival was getting the better of him. Young Domitius was not his reason for being here.

"My apologies, General," Valens finally said with forced humility.

At this, Pompey seemed to regret his outburst. He calmed visibly and smiled. "It is I who must apologize, dear

Valens. The burden of command weighs heavily on me, and this day has been a most trying one. What is it you wished to discuss? Surely, not escaped prisoners."

"Indeed not, my lord. I have come to take my leave of you. I am afraid I have pressing business in Spain." He lied, for he could never tell Pompey he was going to Rome.

"Spain?"

"I know the tyrant claims to have subdued that land, but I still own mines in the vicinity of Gades. I've received word that some of my slaves there are stirring up trouble, threatening production. It is most necessary that I sail at once."

"That is most distressing news, my friend. Most distressing indeed. I wish I could let you go. But I need you here. The answer is no."

"The answer?" Valens almost swallowed his tongue at the impudence, but he tried his best to remain outwardly calm. "I don't think you understand, Lord Pompey. I came to tell you only as a courtesy. I sail for Spain tonight."

Pompey looked at Valens disbelievingly for a moment. Then, he began to snigger, holding a curled finger to his mouth as if to contain his amusement. "Oh, Senator," Pompey said after somewhat regaining his composure. "I had forgotten what a dry wit you have. Thank you. I needed a good laugh. Did Labienus put you up to it?"

"No," Valens simmered. "I tell you, plainly, I must leave."

"All jesting aside, Senator," Pompey said flippantly, still chuckling and clearly oblivious to the anger brewing within Valens. "Let us talk of the reason I wanted to see you. You know Vibullius Rufus, of course?"

Valens stood open-mouthed. Pompey did not wait for a response.

"Rufus has fallen ill with the camp fever," he continued.

"Very ill, I'm afraid. I am told he is too weak to rise from his bed. As you know, he commands the Fourth Legion. The Fourth was not engaged today, but I will need it tomorrow. And I need it led by a general who knows what he's doing."

Valens broke out of his ruminations long enough to realize where this was going. "You wish me to take his place?"

Pompey nodded, placing a hand on his shoulder. "You are skilled in the arts of war, my friend. I remember how well you served me in Spain all those years ago when I put down the rebellion of Sertorius. If we deal with Caesar tomorrow as handily as we dealt with that other traitor, the Republic will be saved."

Pompey spoke of the campaign of two decades ago like it was a mere country outing. But that was not the way Valens remembered it. The mad genius Sertorius had defeated Pompey twice in battle and had nearly captured him.

When Pompey spoke again, it was in a hushed tone. "I tell you, Valens, these young officers do not know the first thing about warfare. Our esteemed senators in Thessalonica have sent me too many of their preening sons to wet-nurse. I need professionals, not amateurs." Pompey then raised his voice loud enough for the nearby legates and tribunes to hear. "So, what say you, Senator? Will you assume command of the Fourth and allow us all to breathe a little easier?"

Valens seethed inside. Pompey had backed him into a corner. A refusal followed by his immediate departure would be perceived as dereliction of duty, or even cowardice. He could not refuse in front of the same legates he would soon be demanding allegiance from – as their king.

"You honor me, Great Pompey." Valens smiled with forced amicability. "Of course, I accept."

"You do not know how much that pleases me, Senator…" Pompey smiled. "Or, should I say, *General*."

"I assume another attack is planned for tomorrow?" Valens asked, feigning outward pride at his new title.

Pompey nodded, then knelt heavily and gestured for Valens to join him. "I have already gone over the plans with the other legates. And you and I shall go over it in greater detail, I assure you. But, for now…" Producing a dagger from his belt, Pompey used it to draw lines in the dirt depicting the opposing armies. "Today, we struck hard at Caesar's right. Tonight, he will be licking his wounds, shifting his defenses to cover the damage done there. As he strengthens his right, we will shift to his weakened left. At dawn tomorrow, we will strike him there with six legions. I plan to hold the Fourth in reserve, but I think you will likely see action, my friend. Labienus will stop by to give you the particulars later this evening. For now, take charge of the Fourth and see that they are ready."

XXXIII

A few paces away, standing with the soldiers who had just sworn allegiance to Pompey, Strabo could not help but eavesdrop on the conversing generals. His ears had prickled upon hearing the name *Valens*. And Strabo had quickly deduced that the tanned, gray-haired senator speaking with Pompey was the very man Lucius had spoken of – the man who had murdered his family.

How the gods delighted in meddling in the affairs of men, Strabo mused as he gazed at the dark waves curling on the shoreline below.

He thought of his grandfather, who had marched under Scipio against Carthage. That had been a simpler time. The enemy had been distinctly foreign. Now, nothing seemed to make sense. All lines were blurred.

Strabo did not regret his decision to join Pompey, nor his decision to report Lucius's escape. He was a centurion of Rome, after all. It had been his duty to report it, despite the fact that he had given Lucius and the druid a decided head start. Even so, Strabo could not help but wonder which side his grandfather would have chosen.

The executions had left a sour feeling in his stomach. Those hungover men with whom he had shared the stockade, those who had chosen not to join Pompey, had been put to death not an hour hence. He and the other defectors had been forced to watch while a contingent of grinning Germans had carried out the killings. They had done it with more jollity than Strabo would have preferred. The place of execution, a hilltop that stood within clear sight of both lines, had been selected by General Labienus. Romans on both sides had looked on while other Romans had been butchered by barbarians. Labienus, still smarting from the morning's defeat, had seemed to relish the slaughter.

What would old Rufius Strabo have said about that?

"It is Centurion Strabo, isn't it?" a snarling voice broke Strabo out of his daydream.

He turned and was startled to see the grim visage of General Labienus glaring at him with a furrowed brow. Strabo came to attention and saluted.

"You are one of the new converts, are you not?" Labienus said poisonously, clearly already knowing the answer and clearly disgusted by it.

"Yes, sir."

The general waved a finger at the nearby legionaries who had just been sworn in with Strabo. "It is bad enough for these common soldiers to betray Rome, but for a centurion to do it is unthinkable! It is despicable!"

"Yes, sir." Strabo could say nothing else.

"I think Pompey is making a mistake trusting you. Once a traitor, always a traitor."

"I am loyal to Rome, sir."

"Are you, now? We'll see about that. I have decided that

you, and all these, including those barbarian idiots who brought you in, shall go with one of the Forlorn Hopes in the morning. And you, my fickle friend, shall lead them. Mars save you."

Not far away, the Allobroges were milling about. They had been made to swear allegiance to Pompey as well. Roucill had been assigned as an officer in one of the auxiliary cavalry cohorts. Egu and the *oathsworn* had not been as lucky. With Pompey's cavalry short of well-nourished mounts, the Gauls' horses had been confiscated. Egu and the others had been assigned to the infantry. And they appeared none too happy about it.

Strabo wanted to laugh at the looks on their faces, but he kept his composure before Labienus. "I am honored, General."

"I expect you should be." A wolfish grin formed on the general's face. "We shall have a good test of your loyalty tomorrow, won't we, when you go up against your former comrades?"

"Yes, sir."

Labienus scrutinized him with a finger. "And I'll be watching you, Centurion Strabo. Lead well, and you shall be given a century of your own before the day is out. Betray us, turn coward, or hesitate in any way, and I'll have the archers shoot you down like the dog that you are. Is that understood?"

"Yes, sir."

The gods did indeed find amusement in the fates of men, Strabo considered after Labienus had moved on. On the morrow, he would be fighting alongside men whom he loathed against men who had once been his brothers, perhaps even the men of his own legion – perhaps even Lucius. When the lines clashed, when blood ran like streams in the trenches, would he find himself face-to-face with Lucius? Would he kill his comrade and friend?

Strabo knew he could not.

Come dawn, he would lead the Forlorn Hope. He would fight valiantly, and perhaps die valiantly. He was prepared, as he had been many times before. He did not fear death, only capture. Were he to be captured, his old comrades would show no mercy. His death would be brutal, the ignominious end of a traitor.

He swore to himself he would not let that happen. The grandson of Rufius Strabo would not die in dishonor. He would be triumphant, or he would die with his sword in his hand.

The Forlorn Hope must succeed.

XXXIV

"I have something to tell you, Lucius. Something to give you, and something to ask of you."

The Forlorn Hope had failed.

The Seventh and Tenth Legions had held their ground. The shattered enemy had given up and fled for their own lines, leaving behind many dead and wounded. Many more had been taken prisoner. They begged their fellow Romans for mercy but received none. They had the misfortune of having attacked the lines commanded by Marc Antony.

Upon learning many of the captives were defectors, Antony had ordered them all put to death. This went against the consul's standing orders, and every man knew it, but, after witnessing the brutal executions carried out by Labienus's Germans the day before, few garnered any sympathy for the condemned.

Lucius knelt in quiet contemplation beside the decapitated corpse. He scowled away the two slaves who had come to take up the remains and throw them onto the burning pyres with the others.

Blood dripped from Lucius's gladius. He had carried out the execution in one clean stroke, expertly delivered, quick and painless. The killing would have impressed even the chief headsman of Gades, yet Lucius could not bring himself to stand up, nor could he get over the gnawing feeling in his stomach.

He stabbed the sword into the ground in frustration, reached over to tilt the head toward him, and stared thoughtfully into the face of Strabo. Though the eyes were dull and frozen, the expression was oddly peaceful. This man whom he had slain, who had so briefly been his comrade in arms, might have been his brother under different circumstances.

Remorse was not the word for what simmered within Lucius. He had lost too many comrades over the years for that. Perhaps, it was regret. Not regret at having ended Strabo's suffering, for he had been mortally wounded, and Lucius had done no more than mercifully speed along the inevitable. But regret that he had failed to convince Strabo to escape with him that night – regret that he had been unable to embolden the spirits of his disillusioned comrade. Lucius wanted to lash out at Antony, Caesar, Pompey, and all others who had played a part, directly or indirectly, in the destruction of a faithful Roman and good man.

"The *primus pilum* wants that one put with the others, Centurion," a voice said.

It was one of the slaves. They had returned for the body.

Lucius looked up at them with eyes that could slay.

"You tell Regimus this was Proculus Strabo, centurion of the Ninth Legion!" Lucius growled. "Grandson of Rufius Strabo, hero of Zama. He died with honor, with his sword in his hand. He will be buried with his own!"

The slaves nodded fearfully and ran off, presumably to

tell Regimus that he was being obstinate. And Lucius would continue to be obstinate. Because Strabo, in the end, had proven to be a loyal comrade.

"I have something to tell you, Lucius. Something to give you, and something to ask of you."

The *something to tell* had been a dizzying revelation that Lucius was still trying to process.

"The man you told me about...he is here, Lucius," Strabo had said, struggling with every breath. *"The scoundrel who murdered your family... He now commands Pompey's Fourth Legion."*

The news had fallen on Lucius like a brick column. He was still trying to come to grips with the knowledge that Valens was close by, somewhere on the other side of the enemy lines. And now it was clear who had been behind the attempt in the jail. Valens was still the same blackguard, the same snake, lurking in the shadows while others did his dirty work for him.

Painful memories and long sequestered emotions stirred within Lucius. The faces of his dead family materialized before him, faces he hardly recognized. They were not distinct images, no conspicuous features, just impressions, feelings really, drawn from the anecdotal memories of a distracted teenage boy. His mother's warmth and infallible affection. His father's unwavering honesty in praise or admonition. His sister's encouragement and devoted friendship. These were all that remained of the family he once knew, trace elements buried deep beneath the hardened exterior of the soldier, the warrior, the killer he had become.

And now, his mind roiled with ideas of slipping back into the enemy camp to find and kill that snake. Every breath Valens drew in comfort was a blot upon Lucius's honor, a black stain of guilt. He had carried that stain for more than a decade. Now, he had a chance to remove it, once and for all. And he would. Precisely how and when, he did not know yet. But he would find a way to put his sword through the snake's neck. He swore by Juno that he would.

But that problem would have to wait for now. There was other, more immediate business to attend to – other scores to settle. For Strabo's revelations had not stopped with Valens…

"…*something to give you…*"

The *something to give* was much closer.

Twenty paces away, a group of prisoners sat on the ground in a tight circle under guard. There were several dozen of them, all grimy and covered in filth. They were not captured legionaries awaiting execution, but slaves and peasants pressed into Pompey's service to serve as diggers and ladder bearers. Unlike the legionaries, they would be spared. Slaves were useful.

Strabo's *something to give* was skulking within that group of slaves, and Lucius intended to collect his gift soon enough.

And then there was the *something to ask…* the most devastating of them all.

Strabo had asked to die at Lucius's hand. He had wanted a swift cut from one whom he knew could deliver it. Lucius had been taken aback, not only by the request, but by his own reaction to it. It had disturbed him deeply as if he had been asked to fall on his own sword, and that surprised him. But, reluctantly, he had agreed. What else could he do?

Before the *primus pilum* or anyone else could intervene, Lucius had helped Strabo onto his knees. Teetering there, Strabo had looked up at him, smiled weakly, then bowed his head.

And Lucius had done as Strabo had requested.

Now, as Lucius knelt there looking into the face of his

dead comrade, he swore an oath.

"*Aeneus* welcome you to the plain of Elysium, comrade. I will avenge you one day. Antony will pay. Upon this sword, you have my vow."

He placed a handful of dirt on the corpse and folded the cloak around the remains.

"Jupiter's hairy arse! You are being difficult, Centurion Domitius!" It was Centurion Regimus, the *primus pilum*. He stood over Lucius, looking down with weary annoyance.

"You should be thanking me," Lucius said with a smile as he got to his feet.

"For what, holding up my burial detail?"

"No." Lucius yanked his sword from the ground, wiped it clean, and sheathed it. "For seeing to him for you."

"Well, yes," Regimus's tone softened as he cast a solemn glance at the corpse. "A pity these men have to die. The order came from the Master of Horse, you understand? I am merely following orders."

"So am I."

The *primus pilum* looked at him with mild amusement. He looked as if he were about to say something humorous, but then a great roar floating on the wind drew his attention away. The sound of a thousand voices emanated from beyond the hills to the west. Smoke and dust obscured the landscape. A battle was raging over there, on the extreme end of the lines.

A cluster of mounted officers passed by on horseback engaged in a heated discussion. It was the legate of the Seventh and his adjutants. Their frowns and mannerisms did not portend fair news.

"Those idiots don't know what's going on any more than anyone else," Regimus confided to Lucius. "Rumor has it, the attack on our lines here was just a feint. They're saying the main attack is over there, on the left. They're saying Pompey's legions have broken through."

Lucius was only half paying attention. His eyes were focused on the captive slaves – one slave, in particular. The slave noticed Lucius, too, and subtly attempted to nudge his way into the middle of the circle to get lost among the others. But he could not escape Lucius's gaze.

"They'll be calling for reinforcements soon," Regimus said, still fixated on the distant commotion. "You'd best get back to your legion, Domitius."

"Might I make one request first, sir?"

"Request?"

"I need another trencher to replace one I lost in that last attack. It seems you have all the captives here. How about giving me one of those slaves?"

"You're welcome to as many as you like," Regimus said. "I'd rather not waste my spears watching them. I'd put the whole lot to work if they could be trusted not to run off."

"One will do, sir."

"Are you sure you don't want more?"

"No, sir. Just one."

"Alright. Which one?"

"That tall, awkward one with the stupid look on his face."

"Suit yourself." Regimus shrugged. He barked several orders, and the protesting slave was forcibly pulled out of the group and turned over to Lucius.

Grinning broadly at the terrified expression on the slave's face, Lucius nudged him with the point of his gladius, and the two headed down the line toward the trenches of the Tenth. Lucius forced his gangly captive to step lively over the scattered bodies. At every prick of the sword, the slave uttered curses in the Gallic language, and Lucius delightedly understood every one of them.

The slave was, of course, not a slave at all. He was Egu –

Strabo's parting gift to Lucius.

"See that those Gallic bastards answer for the stripes they gave us, Lucius," Strabo had muttered.

"I will," Lucius had ensured his dying comrade. "I will find them. You have my oath."

Strabo had smiled weakly. *"You won't have to look far for one of them. That blackguard Egu was in the Forlorn Hope, too. When it was clear we were beaten, and many of us would be captured, I caught sight of the bastard shedding his armor and badges to pass himself off as a laborer."* Strabo's eyes had cut to the assembled prisoners. *"You'll know where to find him, Lucius."*

And now Egu was at Lucius's mercy. The same man who had taken such sinister pleasure in torturing them in the swamp, now flinched nervously at each prod of the gladius.

"Please, Centurion!" Egu begged. "We bore you no ill will. We thought you had betrayed us. We thought you had our money."

"You mean the money you were going to steal from your men?" Lucius said dryly.

"Please!" Egu cried out, raising his bound hands in supplication. "Spare me! I will be your servant forever!"

"Just keep walking."

After walking parallel to the lines for a good distance, Lucius suddenly directed Egu to make an abrupt turn to the right and head farther into the rear.

"W-where are you taking me?" Egu asked desperately.

"Shut up!"

Smoke hung over the field, reducing visibility to no more than a few hundred yards. Lucius prodded his captive onward into the haze. They passed the lines of heavy artillery recoiling on their mounts as glowing orbs of flaming pitch were hurled toward the enemy lines and swallowed up by the mist. They passed the vehicle park, where row upon row of wagons and carts sat empty, seemingly abandoned. They passed through rows of tents standing eerily silent.

"You intend to murder me, don't you?" Egu asked desperately.

"No. I'm not going to kill you," Lucius said reassuringly. "Though that's what you deserve."

"T-Then where are we going? This is not the way to the trenches."

"Slaves dig in the trenches. Proper princes, like you, are kept as prisoners of war. Those are Caesar's standing orders. Don't you remember?"

A wooden stockade materialized out of the haze. Lucius directed Egu toward it. The stockade was guarded by a squad of yawning legionaries who came to attention upon seeing Lucius's centurion plume. The hundred or so prisoners within the palisade milled about, dark shapes within the haze.

Egu looked at Lucius with cautious elation. "Then, I am to be spared? I am to be a prisoner?"

"That's right." Lucius nodded, sheathing his sword and returning the salute of the guards. "Open up. I've got a new prisoner for you."

"We'll take him from here, Centurion," one of the guards replied.

The guards leveled their spears and took custody of Egu. The gate was opened, and the Gallic prince was admitted. But before crossing the threshold, a visibly relieved Egu turned back and grinned broadly at Lucius, his face lop-sided and stupid as ever.

"I will not forget this, Centurion!" he shouted gleefully. "I am forever in your debt! Yes, always!"

Lucius smiled back, waved, and then turned and headed back to the lines. A grin formed on his face as he heard the gate close behind him, a grin that slowly transformed into a mild chuckle. Lucius had not gone a hundred steps before a tumult resounded behind him. The ruckus was coming from within the stockade, many voices raised in anger. Soon, it sounded like a riot.

Lucius kept walking.

There was something else, too, amid the shouting – a distinct voice, feeble and pitiful in its cries for mercy. These soon gave way to screams of terror and pain. It sounded as if a man was being torn limb from limb. When the screaming finally stopped, celebratory cheers erupted from the stockade.

Egu was dead.

And that was because the unwitting Allobroges prince had failed to notice that this particular stockade held non-Roman prisoners – specifically, the surviving Allobroges horsemen rounded up after the massacre before the city walls. It had not taken the Gauls long to realize their new fellow inmate was their own treacherous prince. And they had exacted justice in their own way – the Allobroges way.

Now, Lucius would seek his own justice. The souls of his father, mother, and sister demanded it.

XXXV

"You see, General?" Pompey said smugly. "Prisoners do have their uses. My way is much more effective than yours."

Labienus did not reply. Pompey was annoying enough when he was not boasting. Now, he was almost unbearable.

Both generals sat astride their horses upon a hill just behind the works. Their vantage point afforded them a view of the enemy lines where the Forlorn Hopes had just been beaten back. The ground was littered with dead. Trails of smoke rose where hot embers still burned, the remnants of pitch balls thrown by the enemy artillery. Across the field, the victorious defenders taunted the retreating survivors with vulgar curses, exposed hindquarters, and other obscene gestures.

The Forlorn Hopes had failed. The exhausted remnants limped back to their own lines expecting to find safety there. Instead, they found grim centurions with red swords waiting to slay them outright as they tumbled over the works.

Though Labienus disagreed with Pompey on many things, he approved of this. The defectors had served their purpose. They had mounted the suicidal attacks on Caesar's center, attacks that no one had expected to succeed, and now they were no longer needed.

Still, the defectors had fought well. Most must have understood the odds were against them. The smart ones would have realized their purpose when no supporting cohorts formed up behind them to exploit the breaches. Even with that understanding, they had enthusiastically carried out their orders, assailing the lines of their former comrades with much vigor. As expected, the enemy had pulled units from the adjacent works, reinforced the center, and overwhelmed the Hopes with superior numbers.

And now, as the returning survivors were butchered one by one, Pompey seemed indifferent to their fates. They had played their role in his grand battle plan, and he no longer cared what happened to them.

Despite Labienus's opinion of Pompey, he found himself marveling at his commander's ability to play Caesar like a lute. Thus far, the lute had produced every note demanded of it. Caesar had weakened his wings to strengthen the center.

Now, it was time for the master stroke.

An attendant stood nearby holding a long pole with a bright red pennant.

"Give the signal," Pompey said. "Main body forward."

The attendant swept the pole from side to side to convey the order to the southern extremity of the lines, some three miles to the south, where another pennant acknowledged the signal character by character. Soon after, a cloud of dust rose among the hills. Then, a mass of infantry appeared, a seemingly endless river of twinkling helmets and spear points moving south at the double-quick.

They were sixty cohorts in all, six legions, twenty-six thousand men. As they approached their own lines from the rear, false walls were removed at several places along the works, opening wide passages for the surging hordes. Upon passing through, they flocked to their standard-bearers. Barking centurions could be heard in the distance berating the stragglers. Slowly, the jumbled mob transformed into a checkered pattern of orderly rectangles formed up on the neutral ground between the opposing lines. Within a matter of minutes, the main assault force was assembled and ready. Five hundred yards directly to their front lay the extreme left of the enemy line, Caesar's unfinished circumvallation, still yet a quarter of a mile from the beach.

Pompey had been waiting weeks for this moment, when the direction of the enemy construction turned west, leaving their left flank exposed to the sea. And Pompey controlled the sea.

Following standard Roman siege practices, Caesar's men had erected a redoubt just behind their lines to protect against an attack on the flank. Pompey had guessed the whereabouts of this fortification from the lay of the land, and the Allobroges princes had confirmed it. Over the past days, he had watched closely as the enemy trenchers had extended the line to the west, farther away from the protection of that redoubt. The end of the enemy line was now several hundred yards from the redoubt, and vulnerable, but it would not be for long. Soon, a new redoubt would be thrown up closer to the construction. And that was why it was essential to strike now.

Today – perhaps only for a few more hours – Caesar was at his weakest. His legions were stretched thin. His flank was exposed. Such an opportunity would not come again.

Pompey smiled with confidence as the horns sounded, thousands of voices let out a battle cry, and the distant cohorts stepped off as one. Caesar was about to learn a most embarrassing lesson. Indeed, Pompey's own legates would learn a lesson, as well. They would all learn that he was not the senile old fool they believed him to be. Now, they would see the conqueror of Asia perform his masterwork before their very eyes.

Yesterday's attack had been a wild gamble, a hastily crafted scheme to kill or capture Caesar with pinpoint strikes. Today's attack would be a methodical, calculated game of numbers, a carefully construed plan that pitted strengths against weaknesses. Pompey had pulled every other cohort from the northern lines, along with his two reserve legions. They were all fresh. None had participated in yesterday's debacle. Others might think it inconceivable that 26,000 men could be repositioned in a matter of hours without the enemy being alerted to it. His generals had said it could not be done, but Pompey had shown them otherwise. He had made good use of his high ground advantage, moving his troops along the seaward side of the hills during the night. This redeployment was something he had visualized weeks ago when he had selected this ground for his defensive perimeter. He had anticipated all of Caesar's moves, just as he had anticipated this moment.

Labienus and the other amateurs were too short-sighted to have foreseen it, but Pompey had. It was simply another example of his brilliance, another masterpiece to add to his repertoire. He was to warfare what Socrates was to wisdom – blessed by the gods.

And now, the final element of Pompey's plan came into view. Out on the bay, a fleet of one hundred light galleys emerged from behind a rocky outcropping. The galleys glided at a swift pace, their oars raking the placid waters in time with an unseen drum. They were loaded to capacity with men in leather armor carrying bow staves and bundles of light javelins. Italian *velites*, Greek archers, Illyrian slingers – some four thousand light skirmishers. They were Pompey's finishing touch.

Like prowling crocodiles, the galleys moved down the coast, passing well south of Caesar's line. Then, upon some unheard signal, they collectively turned their bows toward the shore, shipped their oars, and ran onto the sand like so many beached whales. The skirmishers flooded over the bulwarks, stringing bowstaves and shouldering javelins. They climbed the sandy slope and fell into loose ranks on the flatlands west of Caesar's dangling line. The slingers took the lead, and the whole body advanced.

The main force came from the north, the skirmishers from the west, both units moving toward the enemy flank.

The extreme left end of Caesar's line – the target of the converging formations – was manned by the Ninth Legion. Awed by the countless numbers bearing down on them, the soldiers of the Ninth dropped their trenching tools and scrambled for their weapons. They were still unprepared when the advancing skirmishers unleashed the first volleys. Waves of missiles flew into the lines. The north-facing palisade offered no protection. Stones clattered off helmets. Arrows feathered earth, mail, and flesh. The unrelenting storm harried the defenders' every movement, such that they were forced to crouch behind their shields rather than prepare for the infantry coming from the north. Many would have run had it not been for the resonating voice of the First Centurion, steady and clear above the turmoil.

At his command, the unfinished segment of the works was vacated, and the line was refused to the left. The enemy skirmishers now faced a broad wall of shields instead of a dangling flank. The legionary eagle of the Ninth was placed at the pivot point as if to proclaim to attackers and defenders alike that there would be no further retreat.

To the north, Pompey's heavy infantry advanced on the works in ten columns of cohorts, a glimmering, mile-wide carpet of polished helmets and freshly painted shields. Two hundred yards out, the formation separated. Five columns advanced on the abandoned section of the line, while the other five marched straight at the occupied works. Upon reaching the ditch before the ramparts, the front ranks drew up and unleashed a volley of pila. Each javelin had been modified to prevent it from being thrown back at them. One of the two iron nails that fastened the shank to the shaft had been replaced with a wooden nail. The wooden nail would snap upon impact, allowing the shank and shaft to pivot freely on the remaining nail, thus rendering the weapon useless.

The defenders on the ramparts were already suffering from a shortage of javelins. They chose to reserve the few available for the imminent melee. Moreover, their own skirmisher auxiliaries were absent, having been redeployed to the center to help stave off the earlier attacks of the Forlorn Hopes. And so, the men of the Ninth had little with which to harry the advancing enemy but stones thrown by hand.

The attacking infantry filled in the ditches and placed ladders against the far embankment with little disruption. They were careful not to make the same mistakes of yesterday's assault. While the front ranks worked to establish multiple escalades, those in the rear held back, keeping good order and spacing. Once the ladders were in place, the front ranks made no move to climb them. Instead, they waited and continued to launch wave after wave of javelins over the wall as fresh missiles were passed up from the rear.

Initially confused by this pause, the defenders soon understood the reason for it. To their left, the five other enemy columns were surging over the abandoned lines to link up with the skirmisher force. The columns waiting in front of the works were only there to keep the defenders in place, giving time for the flanking columns to wheel and draw up into battle order, backed up by the skirmishers.

Now, with skirmishers and heavy infantry joined, the whole flanking force advanced on the single refused cohort of the Ninth. Shields came together with a clamorous crash. Javelins arced over the ranks. A thousand gleaming swords jabbed between the battle lines.

The melee lasted but a brief moment before the defenders were overwhelmed. There was no way they could withstand the vast numbers arrayed against them. The cohort shattered. Those few who could ran.

With their flank now unprotected, the defenders on the ramparts were caught in a rapidly closing vice. As if of one mind, they fled, abandoning the works for the protection of the redoubt, some five hundred yards to the rear.

Pompey's men were euphoric at their success. Many were in a state of disbelief at how easily they had managed to push back Caesar's immortal veterans. In their elation, they stopped to celebrate and pilfer the dead. The paused frontal assault force, not wishing to be deprived of their share of the spoils, dashed for the ladders and swarmed over the forsaken works to join the looting on the other side. The entire attack force suffered a momentary loss of control.

Red-faced officers cursed and threatened their men back into line. Precious time was wasted bringing order to the chaos. It took less than a quarter of an hour to get the men back into formation, but the delay proved crucial. It gave the men of the Ninth time to rally.

Somehow, amid the pandemonium of the withdrawal, the legionary *aquila* of the Ninth had been preserved and removed to safety. The twinkling bronze eagle now stood atop one of the towers in the redoubt for all to see. It acted like a beacon to the rattled legionaries. Taking heart, they established defensive lines on either side of the redoubt, facing west, three thousand men to stop ten times that number.

The entire attacking force was now behind Caesar's works, facing east. Again, the horns blared. The drums thumped. Ten infantry columns moved forward with skirmishers on the wings, an overpowering carpet of men and arms. Their numbers alone were enough to overwhelm the Ninth Legion and make short work of the redoubt. They fully expected to sweep the defenders aside, and then move along Caesar's lines, devouring one strung out legion after another. There would have been nothing to stop them, had their legates not made one fatal blunder.

In the confusion of the initial success, every one of the attacking cohorts had crossed over to the south side of the works. When their legates finally restored order, they had not bothered to send any units back to the north side. Now, as the attacking columns approached the meager line of defenders, a sudden cry of alarm was raised by the units on the left wing. Something had been sighted on the other side of the line. The next moment, the tips of a dozen standards could be seen peeking above the works. Word quickly circulated through the attacking ranks that thousands of infantry had been sighted marching beneath those banners. The attack force was about to be flanked from the north by no less than twelve cohorts of infantry.

These cohorts were led by Marc Antony. He had pulled them from farther up the line, assembled them into battle line on the neutral ground north of the works, and marched them at the double-quick toward the fighting. He had arrived just in time, and now threatened not only to flank the attacking columns but to cut them off from their own lines.

From his perch on the hill, Pompey had seen the whole battle play out in the distance. He had seen Antony's troops forming up, sent gallopers to warn his field commanders of the danger, and watched helplessly as the message was ignored. But now the generals could obviously see the threat for themselves. Wisely, though belatedly, they brought the attacking columns to a halt. Yet, even from this distance, the confusion was evident. Perplexed cohorts were redirected to face the new menace. Some were sent to the abandoned works. Some remained in formation. Poorly led, they did not know whether to attack or defend. The impetus that had been sustained by their confidence was gone.

Angered by this ill turn of fortune, Pompey decided the risks posed by pressing the attack were too significant. The battle could no longer proceed precisely as he had envisioned, and he did not like to deal with unknowns. Reluctantly, he sent another message to all commanders.

Fall back and form defensive lines.

The legates complied smartly this time. The columns reverse marched. They rapidly withdrew to the end of Caesar's original line, shifted to the north, and formed a perpendicular line of defense running north-to-south across the neutral ground. This new line was anchored on the left by their own works.

Antony's advance was thwarted by this repositioning. He abandoned the flanking move and sent his cohorts to reinforce the Ninth Legion around the redoubt. The battlefield fell silent, and the circling carrion descended on the field of corpses between the two armies.

"There shall be no further attacks this day," Pompey announced as both sides settled into defensive postures.

"Lucretia's arse!" Labienus raged beside him. "Such cowardice! Such incompetence! They should all be flogged and stripped of their rank!"

Pompey said nothing. Despite the setback, despite the annoyance of Labienus's relentless cursing, some of which was obviously directed at him, he was quite pleased with the day's results. He had a great victory. His line had been extended a thousand yards to the south. He had turned Caesar's left and pushed him back some five hundred yards. But, most significantly, the line of circumvallation was blocked. Caesar could not hope to extend it all the way to the sea now.

Pompey would have preferred that it all ended today in one climactic battle, but this end would achieve the same results. Caesar would have no choice but to withdraw. He would retreat with his starving army into the interior. Pompey would pursue and finish him off. The war would be over.

Then, Pompey could go back into retirement. He could leave the backstabbing and scheming to the senators and return to his quiet gardens. He would be reunited with his fair Cornelia whom he had not seen in months. And, perhaps, under her gentle caresses and the soothing melodies of her lyre, the horrible dreams that had been troubling him of late would finally go away.

XXXVI

General Marcus Valens, the commander of Pompey's Fourth Legion, displayed an expression of perpetual disapproval. He watched as the four thousand soldiers under his command threw up a line of defensive works on the ground just wrested from the enemy. They all avoided his gaze. In the short time since he had taken command, even the centurions had come to fear the scrutiny of that hawkish, intelligent face.

Transformed from the dress of a statesman, Valens was attired for battle. He wore a glimmering bronze cuirass, anatomically shaped to resemble a perfect muscular physique. His helmet spouted a tall purple and black crest made of fine horsehair. A flowing purple cape draped down to the ornate greaves covering his legs from knee to ankle. Beside him stood his Arabian bodyguards, along with a handful of legionaries guarding the Fourth's eagle standard. Nearby, an assemblage of adjutants he had inherited from the previous legate whispered amongst themselves.

He had already concluded the staff officers were useless.

Aside from a few older centurions, the field officers were not much better. His ailing predecessor, Vibullius Rufus, had left the Fourth in a deplorable state. So much so, that Valens had made a mental note to remove Rufus from any position of consequence when he became king.

Today's chaos had attested to the legion's lack of discipline. The men had taken an inordinate amount of time forming into column, some of them strolling, some using their javelins as walking sticks, some even dragging their weapons in the dirt. It had annoyed Valens to the point of ordering his Arabians to randomly pull twenty legionaries from the ranks and behead them on the spot.

That had gotten their attention well enough.

Thereafter, the soldiers of the Fourth had answered his every command with swiftness and precision. Too bad he had not been given a chance to employ them against the enemy. Pompey had kept the reserve legions out of the fight.

Grisly smoke drifted across the field, the emission of a raging bonfire where several hundred stacked corpses were consumed like kindling. The sight utterly disgusted Valens, more so for the squandered opportunity than the loss of life.

Had the army only been led properly, Caesar might have been destroyed today.

Valens had observed the engagement from the rear, where the Fourth had been held in reserve. He had seen a great victory taking shape, the line breached, the enemy on the verge of a rout. For a few fleeting moments, he had actually considered the possibility that Pompey might be the gifted tactician people thought he was. Victory had been within his reach.

Anticipating the order to move his legion forward, Valens had summoned his centurions and had given them implicit instructions. Captured soldiers were to be slain without quarter. Captured officers, tribune and above, were to be presented to Valens that he might personally spare them from execution. When the war was over, they would remember his mercy. When he assumed the throne, they would throw their support behind him, if not out of admiration, then as remuneration. Valens had intended to round up hundreds of officers from Caesar's fleeing army and bind them to him in such a fashion. But the order to join the attack had never come.

One bold charge, one strike with the whole force, and the enemy would have crumbled. Instead, like a fool and his *denarii*, Pompey had kissed it all away. The attacking columns had been withdrawn, and Valens had received orders to move the Fourth up to assist in constructing a new defensive line.

Now, as the men of his legion worked quickly to erect earthworks, Valens bridled that they could have been, at this very moment, chasing Caesar's shattered army halfway across Epirus.

"Ah, Valens, there you are!" a voice behind startled him.

He turned to see Pompey ambling toward him across the uneven terrain. The army commander was helmetless and out of breath. Behind him, a tribune followed holding the reins of two horses.

"My lord." Valens greeted Pompey with a respectful salute.

"Now, do you see, my friend?" Pompey said between huffs. "Why I so desperately need skilled generals like you. If those fools who led the attack today had only followed orders, the war would now be over."

Or if you had committed your bloody reserve, you damn fool! Valens thought while outwardly smiling and nodding in agreement.

"It is indeed a shame, Great Pompey."

Pompey shrugged. "But I suppose it does not matter. Caesar is beaten. He can't complete the circumvallation now. He simply does not have the men. They're stretched too thin over there as it is."

Valens cleared his throat. "That being the case, my lord, why not order another attack without delay? An attack, now, might catch Caesar off guard."

It seemed so obvious. A green recruit could surely see it. On this end of the line, Pompey still outnumbered Caesar, perhaps by as much as five-to-one. But such an advantage would not last long. Even now, a cloud of dust stirred beyond the hills to the northeast. Undoubtedly, Caesar was shifting more troops over this way.

Making no acknowledgment of the suggestion, Pompey gave a wide grin and gestured to the nearby construction. "Your men are hard workers, General. I don't remember Rufus ever rousing such enthusiasm out of them."

"My lord Pompey is too kind," Valens replied cordially, though silently he smarted from the snub.

"We will extend our works to encompass the ground captured today," Pompey said. "A redoubt will be necessary, down there at the bottom of the creek, to anchor our lines."

Pompey gestured to a gully a hundred paces south where a creek had once emptied into the sea. The waterway was just a muddy depression now, its course having been diverted far upstream by Caesar's army.

"I give this task to you, General. Build it well."

"Yes, my lord," Valens replied evenly.

"It is only a precaution, you understand. I don't expect any further mischief from the tyrant. It would not surprise me if he sent an emissary within the hour seeking terms."

"You expect Caesar to surrender?"

Pompey nodded. "Our friend over there is faced with few choices now. He will seek terms, or he will withdraw. I'll wager the former. It is the only sensible thing to do. Withdrawal would only postpone the inevitable. He must know that. Caesar is not stupid."

"And if he does not?" Valens ventured.

Pompey glanced over his shoulder to the north. Valens followed his gaze to a broad defile between the hills where three thousand saddled horses waited, their festooned heads jerking amid swirls of dust. They were the fittest and most nourished mounts of Pompey's cavalry. Dismounted riders struggled to restrain the anxious beasts, an assortment of brightly colored vestments amid the mass of chestnuts and grays. Pennants fluttered from the tips of their upturned lances. Like the horses, the riders had been hand-picked for this task, the warlords of a dozen different nations, skilled in mounted combat.

They were the hammer that would break Caesar's back should he choose not to surrender. The course of the new lines effectively cut Caesar off from the sea and left a large gap along the shore. Through this opening, Pompey could unleash his cavalry on the countryside beyond to ride down Caesar's foragers and raid his unprotected camps from the rear.

"I know what you're thinking, General," Pompey said with a supercilious glance. "Why not send in the horse now? Am I right? But, then, I don't have to tell you, Valens, that cavalry is like an arrow. Once shot, it can seldom be recovered." There was an overtone of tutelage in Pompey's statement, and a twinkle in his eye, as if Valens was privileged to get a glimpse of his tactical genius.

"Fascinating, my lord," Valens said, then could not help but add, "But that all depends on the skill of the archer, doesn't it? An arrow that hits the target is never hard to retrieve."

Pompey shot Valens a quizzical look, then pursed his lips together, evidently realizing he was being ridiculed. When he spoke again, his voice was absent of all affection. "You will place the eastern face of the redoubt even with the lines, General Valens. Make good employment of the enemy's previous excavations. Work quickly. I want it finished by sunset."

"Yes, my lord." Valens saluted, angry with himself for letting Pompey draw raw emotion from him. The day was coming when he would put Pompey in his proper place and expose him for the fool he was. But, for now, Valens needed to maintain the façade. He must play the part of the loyal legate.

As Pompey turned and moved on to the next legion down the line, Valens considered that this day might still work to his advantage.

Unlike Pompey, he did not believe Caesar was through – not by any means. While Caesar was little more than an overblown braggart, Valens recognized in him an ambition that rivaled his own. He knew that Caesar would never accept capitulation and humiliation under the savoring eyes of the *Optimates*. Nothing less than total victory would do, even if it meant sacrificing every last soldier in his army.

No, Caesar would not surrender, nor would he run. Instead, he would do the only thing he could do. He would attack. And the attack would probably come within the next few hours, just as soon as he had shifted enough troops to this end of the line.

Valens smiled. If that happened – *when* that happened – he would have a few surprises waiting for Caesar. He would hand Caesar an utter defeat, and he would do so without Pompey's interference. Pompey would witness true tactical genius. The Fourth Legion would have a glorious victory.

And General Marcus Aemilius Valens, not Pompey, would be lauded as the hero who saved Rome – a most fitting epithet for a future king.

XXXVII

"**O**bserve the fortification yonder, gentlemen." General Quintinus, commander of the Tenth Legion, pointed across the neutral ground, to a spot where the enemy had spent most of the afternoon constructing a new redoubt. "That is our objective. Once that redoubt is taken, the enemy's line to the south will be cut off. He will be forced to withdraw to his original lines or lose several thousand men."

Quintinus conveyed the plan of attack to a score of bare-headed men standing atop the works with him. Each man held his plumed helmet tucked away so as not to attract the attention of the enemy lookouts. They were the officers of the Seventh and Tenth Legions – the ones who would lead the assault. Their faces displayed mixed emotions as they gazed at the distant enemy works, where many of them would die before the day was out.

The enemy still toiled over there. With each passing hour, the earthen barrier grew more formidable. It was an extension of the enemy's east-west line. This new segment turned perpendicular and ran south for nearly a mile to encompass the recently captured ground. The redoubt to which Quintinus referred stood in the direct center of this southerly segment, at the base of a dry stream. The fortification had been erected with remarkable speed, within a matter of hours, and was now essentially complete.

"There will be two columns of attack," Quintinus continued, his tone absent of the very confidence he was attempting to inspire in his audience. "We will comprise the left column with nineteen cohorts, while fourteen cohorts of the Eighth and Ninth will make up the right. Both columns will advance together, straight across, maintaining a separation of no less than five hundred yards. Upon reaching the works, each column will force breaches…"

Standing among the centurions, Lucius heard only every other word as he stared at the distant fortification. The half-mile of open ground that would have to be crossed might as well have been an archery range for its dearth of cover. That, and many other shortcomings of the attack plan, should have been at the forefront of his thoughts. But they were not.

His eyes fixated on the banner flapping over the enemy fortification – the standard of Pompey's Fourth Legion. If Strabo's dying words had been true, then Marcus Valens was there. Perhaps he was one of the many indistinguishable figures peering back from the ramparts.

Instinctively, Lucius squeezed the hilt of his sword in its sheath. The gods had finally answered the pleas from the grave. And Lucius intended to see the villain die on his sword, even if it meant his own death. He would break through that wall and kill Valens. And before Valens breathed his last, he would know who had taken his life and why.

Quintinus droned on, mechanically repeating the plan of

attack just as it had been conveyed to him. It was the same as a hundred plans before it, and likely just as useless. Once the cohorts crossed that ground and discovered what they were truly up against, only then would they know what to do. That was when the veterans like Lucius would be crucial, not by bringing order to the chaos, but by accepting it, embracing it, reading it as a sailor does the ocean winds, and using it to their advantage.

No plan could make up for the fact they were outnumbered by at least two-to-one. Would the advantage of surprise be enough to surmount such odds? Would Fortuna favor Caesar today as she had so often in the past?

The devastating attack of the morning had come as a surprise. No one had believed Old Pompey's legions were skilled enough to coordinate such complex maneuvers. No one had thought they could attack with so many troops in one place at one time. During those uncertain hours, rumors had abounded along the sixteen-mile line.

The left was turned! The enemy had gotten into the rear! The line was being rolled up like a scroll!

A wave of panic had coursed through the entire army. But then, Caesar had appeared at just the right moment, as he always did, riding along the lines conspicuous in his red cloak. He rode with his staff in tow, casually conversing with officers and soldiers.

And the men had taken heart.

How could things possibly be so dire if the consul himself was so calm and collected?

Caesar rode past each legion, stopping momentarily to issue quiet orders to the legates. Selective units were pulled from the line and ordered to march behind the consul. Like an ever-increasing flock of peasants on a pilgrimage to the Sibyl of Cumae, the column continued to grow until some thirty cohorts followed Caesar. In a matter of hours, he had shifted this large force to the shattered left, not to bolster the line, as most had expected, but to prepare for an immediate counterattack.

Now, auxiliary troops worked along the left of the line, constructing new works, doing their best to display a defensive posture, while Caesar planned quite the opposite. Out of sight behind the ramparts, ten thousand legionaries distributed pila and cinched up armor in preparation for the assault.

Quintinus offered a few more words of encouragement that fell flat coming from the bookkeeper general that he was. Finally, the officers were dismissed and dispersed to their waiting units.

As Lucius turned to make his way back to his century, a maliciously cheerful voice called to him.

"Still alive, Domitius? *Minerva* be praised yet again."

Lucius turned back to see that Marc Antony had just joined Quintinus on the battlement.

"Never mind, Centurion Domitius. Carry on, like a good fellow," Quintinus said, tugging at Antony's arm to regain his attention. "And so, Antony, you can tell Caesar I intend to put the Seventh in the lead with my own legion in reserve, just as you have requested…"

But Antony did not seem to be listening. Instead, he stared at Lucius with a wide grin that carried no warmth, only venom. And while Lucius could not bring himself to smile back at the lying scoundrel, his eyes returned every dagger.

"I've changed my mind, Quintinus," Antony finally said, still looking at Lucius. "The Tenth will lead the attack with the Seventh in reserve."

"I…but…," Quintinus stammered before finally nodding his flustered consent. "As you say, my lord."

"To which cohort does Centurion Domitius belong?"

Antony asked. The question was directed at Quintinus, but Lucius responded before the legate could get a word out.

"The eighth cohort, sir," he said brazenly, staring back at Antony with defiant eyes. Lucius knew what Antony was about to do, and, for the first time, he was thankful for the bastard's predictable wickedness.

"Then the eighth cohort of the Tenth Legion shall be placed at the head of the column," Antony said.

Quintinus stuttered. "B-But, my lord, the eighth is one of my best. Domitius, here, is one of my best fighters. I cannot afford to lose...Well, what I mean is...Would it not be wisest to preserve our elite troops in the event something unforeseen – ?"

"Let's have no more of your tiresome lectures, Quintinus," Antony said curtly. "Just do as you are ordered."

"Er...uh...yes, my lord."

With no choice in the matter, Quintinus acquiesced. The generals moved on, but not before Antony shot a triumphant smile at Lucius. And, this time, Lucius smiled back. Antony had inadvertently given him precisely what he wanted. For Lucius wanted to be the first inside that redoubt, the first to punch through the enemy, the first to find Valens. Antony had intended it as a death sentence, and perhaps it was. But Lucius did not care. Should the gods allow him to survive long enough to get hold of Valens, he would be content.

And he *would* find Valens. Let the blackguard beg for mercy. He would receive none, just as the ravaging mob had ignored the cries of Lucius's mother and sister. Lucius would put his sword through Valens's lying gullet and watch with satisfaction as life left those wicked eyes.

Before Juno, *he swore it.*

XXXVIII

Valens watched from the ramparts of the newly constructed fortification as a mass of infantry spilled over the distant enemy works and began forming into two distinct columns on the neutral ground. To his left and right, all along the wall, his own men stared open-mouthed at the battle formations that seemed to have materialized out of thin air. One moment, the enemy lines had been quiet. The next, they were bursting forth with fully armed legionaries. Valens judged each column to contain about five thousand men. While his soldiers were amazed at the enemy's audacity, he was not. He had expected this of Caesar.

"Should I dispatch a rider to Pompey, sir?" a tribune at Valens's side asked anxiously.

The young officer was sincere, but Valens found the suggestion bordering on insulting. But before Valens could rebuke the young officer, a centurion brandishing a toothy grin spoke up from farther down the parapet.

"It'll be a frozen day in Numidia when General Valens here needs help winning a battle, tribune."

The centurion wore the plume of a *primus pilum*. He was an older soldier, gray-haired, red-faced, with thick jowls and a potbelly. Clearly, he had come out of retirement to fight in this war. The centurion stepped forward and came to attention.

"Centurion Lars Nepo, at your service, General Valens," the man said in a throaty voice that was better suited to drill orders than conversation. "I served under you in Spain, sir, in the Sertorian War. I was just a ranker then, just another ditch digger, but we all would have followed you to the underworld and back. Yes, sir! A fine bit of soldiering that was, sir!"

"Yes, well, I thought you looked familiar," Valens lied with a smile, doing his best not to show how he truly felt about this irrelevant distraction. "I am pleased you are with me again."

"Pleased!" The gray centurion was clearly ecstatic. "The pleasure is all mine, sir! Serving you, again...I haven't the words, sir."

"Well," Valens nodded politely. "Carry on then."

"Yes, sir! And don't you worry about that rug-headed band of prick lickers out there, sir. They can't take this fort, not if they had twice their number. We'll show them! You can count on old Lars Nepo, sir!"

Valens wished to be out of the conversation but realized the younger soldiers were observing the exchange with a sense of trepidation. Clearly, they were still unnerved by the earlier executions and were uncertain how their general would respond to such familiarity. They were afraid of him. Now, he must work on endearing them to him for the day when he became their king. Someday, they would take pride in the fact that they had fought under their king when he won his great victory at Dyrrachium.

Placing a hand on the centurion's shoulder, Valens feigned sincerity. "I have no doubt of that, Nepo. I shall take comfort knowing you are on the wall. Defend it well."

The centurion was thrilled and enjoined the men to cheer Valens as he moved along the battlement. After leaving the enthusiastic soldiers behind, Valens once again looked out at the approaching columns.

"Have the Thessalonians arrived yet?" he asked the tribune at his side.

"Yes, my lord. They landed at the beach not half an hour ago. They should be here any moment now."

"Signal them to come on at the double-quick and post them as I told you before."

The tribune saluted and scampered away.

Caesar's columns were marching now, advancing on the fort. Shouted commands resonated across the field. Centuries transformed into testudos, a scaly mass of upturned shields, their iron bosses reflecting like the scales of a serpent.

Valens smiled.

My thanks, dear Caesar, for your rashness. The victory you hand me today will secure my position on the throne.

He would have preferred to pulverize those formations down there with ballistas and scorpions, but the artillery was still being brought forward, and the towers had not yet been built. But it did not matter. He was quite ready for Caesar, with or without the engines.

The men of the Fourth waited on the ramparts with bundles of darts and javelins. Centurions stood with swords in hands, waiting for his signal. Now, they understood why he had been so harsh with them, why he had pushed them to work faster, why he had encouraged liberal use of the whip.

They had cursed him before. They would be hailing him as imperator before the day was out. Poets would tell of the day when their king and his single legion delivered the killing blow to the enemy of Rome.

Then, as the first enemy testudos crept into range, the stentorian voices of the centurions echoed all along the ramparts.

"Let fly!"

XXXIX

Caesar's columns marched steadily under the blare of horns, each presenting a front of three centuries abreast. They maintained good order as the first waves of javelins clattered upon the leading testudos. Gaps were closed where men fell to the deadly missiles. The units pressed on. But there was an element of confusion among Caesar's field commanders regarding the precise location of their objective.

It was standard practice for a Roman army to locate redoubts two or three hundred yards behind the main line. But that practice had not been observed here. The fort Caesar's troops now advanced toward had been built as an integral part of the line. Consequently, from their perspective, it was difficult to discern where the fort walls ended and the adjacent lines began.

Only the fort mattered. Only the fort would give the attacking legions a defendable position against counterattacks. Victory hinged on its capture. Thus, it was vital for them to expend their efforts breaching the fort, and not waste them assaulting the lines.

Faced with this problem while under the torment of the constant barrage, Caesar's commanders made the most expedient choice. They steered their columns toward the nearest sections of the enemy line, hoping for the best. They struck the works at two different spots simultaneously.

The left column encountered a ditch ten feet deep running along the base of a twenty-foot-high embankment topped by a wooden palisade. Trenching tools were passed up, and the front centuries set about the back-breaking task of filling in the ditch. At the same time, a continuous storm of deadly javelins and skull-shattering stones felled men by the dozen and opened gaps in the stalled formation.

Some five hundred yards away, the right column approached the wall in a similar fashion but was met with only a scant fire from the ramparts. Surprisingly, the ditch here was only half as deep, the earthen wall only half as high. The men in the leading testudos rejoiced at this discovery. They were even more ecstatic upon finding a broad gap in the wall that had been previously hidden by a high berm. Assuming the opening had been left by the overconfident enemy to support future attacks, Caesar's troops recklessly surged forth to exploit it.

A handful of enemy helmets appeared above the parapet, but a single volley of javelins from the attackers sent them running. One after another, the testudos broke formation and flooded through the gap, a river of helmets and shields. A supporting contingent of cavalry, that had been holding back with the rear cohorts, now surged forward, filing among the infantry, eager to pursue and ride down the fleeing enemy.

Expecting to find the large open square of the fort's

interior on the other side, they instead found themselves contained within a small triangular space. Just ahead and to their left, a formidable set of earthworks stood at an angle, fronted by a ditch and palisade, where no less than a thousand helmets peered down at them. This was the true boundary of the fort, its north wall. To their right front, and abutted to the fort, ran the adjacent enemy line, also heavily fortified.

The attacking troops suddenly realized the gap in the false wall had been intentionally placed to lure them onto this confined killing field. As the horrifying comprehension sank in, some officers had the sense to order an immediate withdrawal. But the horn signals were drowned out by the battle cries of those behind, obliviously pushing through the gap. The surge was indivertible, a throng of men and beasts unwittingly rushing to their own slaughter.

More troops piled into the overcrowded space. Upon seeing no way out, they panicked. Horses wheeled in confusion, stomping their way through the packed infantry. Then, panic devolved into utter chaos as the first waves of javelins, arrows, and stones began to fall.

Centurions boomed out to reform testudos, but the units were too jumbled to regain order. Men dropped by the score, transfixed by missiles or crushed by stomping hooves. As the deadly fusillade rained down, it became clear that the arrows were exceptionally accurate and deadly. And that was because, unbeknownst to the panicking troops, one stretch of the wall was manned by an entire cohort of archers, the Thessalonians brought over from Dyrrachium – the same bowmen who had employed their weapons with such devastating effect against the Allobroges horsemen. They did not blindly loose their arrows at the masses below, but instead took careful aim. At such close range, they found the gaps between the shields, peeking eyes, exposed flesh. Any soldier attempting to cross the ditch and scale the walls was instantly riddled with feathered shafts.

But the horses were the choicest targets. Even the hardiest battle steed could not remain calm when so confined and pierced by a dozen arrows. The crazed mounts bucked off their riders, bounded in all directions, trampled the massed soldiers like stalks of wheat.

The infantry quickly devolved into a frenzied mob scrambling to escape the killing ground, a press of men and beasts shoving through the narrow gap. Those who fell were crushed by an endless stream of hob-nailed boots and tramping hooves. The carpet of bloody corpses grew until it blocked the opening. The keener ones avoided the deadly carnage by climbing over the false wall on either side, but most mindlessly followed the crowd, climbing on hands and knees to get over the writhing layers of the dying.

Several hundred men, either too wounded or too terrified to run, remained trapped within the walls and became easy targets for the archers who could reach any square inch of that confined space. The survivors eventually managed to organize themselves into a circular formation of raised shields, which finally rendered the storm of missiles largely ineffective. In response to this, the enemy went on the attack. Ladders were dropped from the battlements. A thousand legionaries descended to the killing ground and surrounded the circle of survivors. At the blast of a horn, they advanced, converging on the entrapped troops from all sides. A wanton slaughter ensued, a bloody feast of sword and spear, in which no quarter was given.

In the sky above, black carrion circled by the hundred, awaiting their own inevitable feast. Caesar's right column had been shattered.

XL

From the north wall, Valens watched the butchery, pleased with the results of his own military genius.

He had directed his engineers to construct the fort along dimensions that deviated from the traditional layout. The east wall, facing Caesar's lines, had been shortened to half the standard length, while the north and south walls had been built at angles such that the fort was more trapezoidal than rectangular. The adjacent lines were then connected to the rear corners of the fort. To mask this peculiar construction from the enemy, false outer walls had been constructed bordering the east wall. These had been hastily excavated and sparsely manned to lure the enemy into thinking they were unfinished. Finally, large openings had been left in the false walls to further entice the enemy into taking the bait.

And the design had worked perfectly.

Caesar's first column had rushed blindly through the opening and had found themselves trapped within a triangle of death. The Thessalonian archers had shot them down by the score. Valens had felt entitled to borrow the Thessalonians as he wished. They were, in fact, his own personal contribution to Pompey's army, mercenaries he had paid for himself. Whatever objections Pompey might have to this usage of the Thessalonians would matter little now. Caesar was beaten!

Valens found himself amused by the thought of Pompey, sunken into his cot for a late afternoon repose, suddenly bolting upright upon learning of the attack. The large man would be knocking over his furnishings to gird on his armor, shouting at his attendants to make haste. But Pompey's tent was some five miles away. It would take the incapable fool some time to get here. And Valens intended for the battle to be quite decided by then.

This would be *his* victory, not Pompey's.

"Send over the reserve to mop up that rabble," Valens said to one of his adjutants.

The young tribune stepped forward from Valens's entourage that was comprised of his staff, the Arabian bodyguards, and the soldiers bearing the legionary standards.

"Down there, sir?" the officer asked with surprise, pointing at the massacre in the yard below them.

"Yes, damn you! I want this group dealt with quickly, so the entire legion can advance together when the other enemy column routs."

"Yes, my lord."

Orders were issued, and the reserve cohorts that had been drawn up within the fort now proceeded over the north wall to assist in annihilating the remnants of the first enemy column.

All that remained now was to deal with the second column, and that would not take long. From where Valens stood, he could see that his troops packing the ramparts along the east wall were still hotly engaged, hurling javelins and stones down on the attackers. Whether by luck or intention, the second enemy column had not been enticed by the false wall. It had come against the true wall of the fort, where it now struggled to surmount the extensive defenses while being subjected to a murderous barrage. The attack would surely falter. Valens expected it to dissolve at any moment. Then, he would go on the attack. He would advance with his entire legion and pursue the fleeing enemy beyond their own lines before Pompey could arrive to take credit for it.

Valens looked at the position of the late afternoon sun. A good three hours of daylight remained for chasing down the shattered enemy. Still, the heat of the day was oppressive, and his throat was quite parched. He would need all his strength for the coming chase.

"Send me word when the enemy routs," Valens commanded one of his adjutants. "I will retire to my pavilion."

"Yes, my lord."

After a final look at the carnage outside the walls, Valens descended to the fort's interior and headed to his headquarters pavilion, accompanied by his entourage.

XLI

In the vanguard of the attacking column, Lucius crouched with the men of his century awaiting their turn at the enemy defenses. Their *testudo* inched forward at each sound of the whistle. It seemed no progress was being made on the breaches. Each successive century took its turn at the hazardous work of filling in the ditch and tearing away at the embankment. Toiling under a murderous fire from above, they suffered appalling losses yet made little headway. The front century would retire at the whistle, dragging their wounded with them and leaving their dead behind. Then, the next century in line would step up to take their place.

The defenders kept the waiting *testudos* pinned down by a constant barrage of stones and javelins. At Lucius's feet, one of the newer recruits, a boy who had joined the legion during last year's campaign in Spain, lay on the ground, his face frozen in horror, a bent iron shank buried a hand's breadth into his left eye socket. Perhaps at some point,

Lucius would feel some sense of loss, some grief for the lad. But, now, he could only think of what it meant for the century. Yet another name to be crossed from the ledger. One less soldier to feed, armor, clothe, and pay. More digging and trenching for the others. And there would be many more to scratch from the list before the day was over.

Indeed, Lucius had been a centurion for far too long.

"Close up there, Betto!" Lucius snarled. He kicked the boy's body to the side with little reverence to allow the ranks behind to close the gap.

"It's hot as Juno's crotch under here, *Vitus*!" Betto said as he plugged the opening in the canopy with his own shield. The *testudo* was intact once again.

"Shut up and look to those gaps, you mule's arse!" Lucius said, receiving a grin from Betto in reply.

Despite the protection of the giant curved shields, some projectiles still passed through. One soldier took a glancing stone on the ankle, very likely shattering the bone and forcing him to hobble along in immense pain. Another took a javelin shank straight through the calf, the weapon breaking on impact and tearing away a good deal of the flesh on his lower leg. The soldier fell out of line, grunting on the ground among the shuffling boots. Lucius could not spare a single shield to attend him.

Again, the unseen whistle sounded. Again, the *testudo* crept forward several paces and stopped. Between the gaps in the shields, Lucius could see little but the mailed backs of soldiers in the next century ahead.

To be within the confines of a *testudo* under fire was quite nearly the closest thing to Pluto's Realm in this life. It was an unreal world of tightly compacted helmets and armor, of muscled arms bracing the giant shields. The shields themselves were punctured by a dozen or more iron points, each one adding more agonizing weight. Some points pierced the arms beneath, raining blood upon sweat-streaked faces already distorted from the enormous exertion. The air was a putrid mixture of unwashed tunics, foul armpits and crotches, exhausted bowels, and swirling dust. The shaded ground was littered with broken javelins, arrows, stones of every size, discarded shields, and the writhing fallen. The *testudo* was, in fact, such a miserable experience that legionaries were eager to leave it upon reaching the enemy, preferring to take their chances amid the jabbing blades rather than remain in that wretched formation. But in this particular situation, where one could hardly survive two heartbeats outside the shields, the men seemed content to stay where they were.

"There's a pole for you to eat, my pretty," a mocking, throaty voice rose above the din. "That'll fill your belly better than that *chara*, and rip it out, too!"

The voice came from the ramparts above. Through a crack in the shields, Lucius saw many faces looking down from the parapet. Distinct among them was a cherry-cheeked centurion armed with a long pike. The centurion was older than most, with gray locks spilling out from beneath a helmet of a dated design. He laughed heartily with each thrust of his enormous weapon, taunting his victims as their severed necks and arteries spewed blood upon the wall.

"Who wants the next taste of Lars Nepo's giant prick?" the centurion jeered. "Open wide! Here you go, lad! Take that!"

The weapon was thrust downward, striking something hidden from Lucius's sight. But from the fit of laughter that overtook the centurion, it was evident the weapon had struck home, likely dispatching yet another victim in an exceptionally gruesome manner.

"Come now, my pretties, who's next? Will it be you?"

The centurion did not let up in his ridicule.

"What I wouldn't give to cut the balls off that singing canary!" Betto muttered what every man in the *testudo* was thinking.

Many had tried to bring down the hated centurion. No less than a dozen javelins spiked the palisade just beneath him, all having fallen short of their target.

It was difficult to discern just how many centuries still stood in line ahead of Lucius's, but it was evident by the intensity of the barrage and the size of the falling stones that they were drawing closer to the wall.

A stone, the size of a man's head, crashed through the testudo immediately to the right, mutilating three men all at once. This opened a brief gap in the formation, allowing Lucius to see the progress of the other column five hundred yards further down the wall.

What he saw shook him to the core.

It appeared that the other column had discovered a breach in the wall. But instead of rushing into that breach, soldiers were streaming from it. These were not merely the stragglers, but the entire column. Thousands of frantic legionaries, many bloody and without weapons or shields, ran from that opening as if it were the gaping maw of a dragon. Utterly routed, they fled back to their own lines without any trace of order.

"They're running!" a soldier exclaimed after catching a glimpse of the disastrous fate of the other column. "The bloody bastards are running!"

Several other men cursed.

"Never you mind them, lads!" Lucius scolded. "Eyes front! Keep those shields tight now!"

Though they chastised the fleeing men as cowards, Lucius knew that it was only a matter of time before his men, and those of the other centuries, were infected by the same panic. The cohesiveness of a well-disciplined cohort was a double-edged sword in battle. Men trained to move and fight as one could do amazing things, their collective confidence often motivating them to overcome the most unfavorable odds. But, when faced with the impossible, when the overwhelming sense of defeat prompted a few to break ranks, the others often followed.

At that moment, a cheer resounded somewhere in the rear. Lucius glanced over his shoulder and, catching a glimpse between the files, saw Quintinus crouching within one of the rear testudos. The Tenth's commander was easily identifiable in his gathered cape and ornamented helmet. Two tribunes were on either side of him, holding shields to protect him. More accustomed to commanding from the rear than the front, Quintinus looked uncomfortable amongst the gritty soldiers, as if his presence were more compelled than voluntary. Clearly, he would have given anything to be back in his tent reviewing his ledgers and sipping wine.

While it was truly remarkable that the general was placing himself at such hazards alongside his men, Lucius could not imagine the cheers were for him. To the rank and file, Quintinus had always been more of an amusement than an inspiration.

Then, Lucius saw something else.

Giant warriors in trousers and long mail shirts moved between the files – Caesar's Germans. And Lucius suddenly realized why the men were cheering. If Caesar's bodyguard was nearby, then, somewhere back there in one of the rear testudos, the consul himself must be crouching amongst the soldiers, spurring them onward. Caesar had an uncanny knack of being able to read his legions. He knew when the men needed the added impetus of his presence, and this was one of those times.

It was evident now why Quintinus had decided to come along. The Tenth's commander would have difficulty explaining why he had remained in the rear while the consul personally led the assault.

But despite Caesar's presence, Lucius sensed the cohorts were on the verge of breaking. The wall was proving difficult for the tired legionaries who had earlier executed a forced march from the other end of the lines. Though some progress had been made, they were beginning to waver under the interminable hail of missiles. A foreboding of defeat was in the air.

Saturn's balls! This could not be it!

Valens was on the other side of that wall – so close, Lucius could taste his revenge. But he would never realize it if the attack faltered. The tribunes and legates urged the men forward, demanded they work harder and faster, but they might as well have been blowing kisses for all the good it was doing. Lucius knew it would take much more than words to light a fire under the stalled troops.

"There's something to fill your belly, my pretty!"

The red-faced centurion droned on, driving his pike downward to the hoots and howls of his comrades on the wall with him. The pike was withdrawn, and its gore-covered point raised high for those in the rear ranks to see. This was effective, if not in frightening the men, then enraging them such that they were distracted from closing the gaps in the canopy. The sinister centurion was perhaps doing more to dishearten the attackers than were the flying javelins. For the men knew, as they drew closer to the wall, they would eventually come under the reach of that merciless pike.

"Ha ha!" the centurion's voice boomed above the clatter of the missiles. "That one took Old Nepo's prick in the mouth! Did you see the teeth bust out of that one, lads?

That's the way we deal with these traitors!"

Again, the centurion called Nepo laughed derisively, spurring the same from his comrades on the ramparts. And it was at that moment that Lucius saw an opportunity.

In every war, every battle, every skirmish, there is a pivot point that sets the course, gives one side a decided advantage over the other. It could be the quality of the arms and armor, superior organization, advantageous ground, or the oration of an inspiring leader. To some extent, all these factors contributed the eventual outcome, but, more often, one reigned supreme over the others.

Call it a sense. Call it an instinct from a hundred past fights. But, at that moment, in the combat before the wall, Lucius knew the mouthy Centurion Nepo was the key. Just as the attackers feared his pike, the defenders were emboldened by his brazenness. He was the veteran, the old uncle that gave them all strength, their leader – and their Achille's Heel. Remove him, and they would waver. Remove him, and the tide would turn.

And, so, the brash Centurion Nepo would have to die.

It was easier said than done. The old centurion was in a high position and mostly hidden behind the parapet. It would be nigh on impossible to hit him with a hastily thrown javelin. Lucius found himself wishing their own auxiliaries had not been left behind. One century of archers or slingers might have made the difference at this moment.

If Lucius had ample room to put his body into a throw, he could manage it. It was not beyond his skill. But no one could last more than a few moments outside the protective shields. He would be cut down before the javelin ever left his hand.

Up ahead, the whistle blew again. Another group of centuries relieved those in the ditch and began their turn at the sapping. Like the gears of a machine, the queued testudos moved forward as those retiring moved back. Lucius's century crept forward, moving into the spot previously occupied by the century ahead of them. They were closer to the wall but still at least two intervals away from assuming the digging.

And, suddenly, Lucius had an idea.

"Listen carefully!" he shouted to his men beneath the raised shields. He maneuvered within the crowded space and assumed a position between the fourth and fifth ranks. "First four ranks, on the next whistle, when it is our turn to move up, you will go forward. But I want you to march at the oblique and encroach on the century to our right. Do it sloppily. Your aim is to cause a commotion."

Bewildered faces looked back at him. Marching into the gap between the centuries was forbidden, since it would block the path of withdrawal for the retiring troops. But Lucius's men nodded in turn. They well knew he would abide no argument.

"The rear ranks will not move forward," he continued. "Stay with me, no matter what orders you hear from the other officers. Understood?"

The glistening faces nodded behind him. They clearly did not understand the reason, nor did he have time to explain it to them. Lucius snatched the javelin from the hands of the nearest soldier. Then took the leather *amentum* looped on his belt.

Again, the whistle blew. The column moved up. The withdrawing troops reformed testudos in the gaps between the advancing centuries and began creeping toward the rear. When it was time for Lucius's century to advance, the front ranks hesitated. They clearly realized the diagonal movement Lucius had ordered would take them headlong into one of the retreating testudos.

"Go, damn you!" Lucius shouted. "Oblique march,

now!"

Spurred by their centurion's fury, they complied. The first four ranks stepped out with their shields before them. Then, each man turned to the right and advanced at a forty-five-degree angle. This took them into the open space between the centuries, where they promptly collided with the retiring troops in a jumble of crashing shields and toppling soldiers.

Cursing officers demanded to know what the fools were doing. But Lucius's men ignored them. Instead, they stood their ground firmly, even throwing fists at troops of the other century trying to dislodge them.

Good lads. Lucius smiled.

The enemy peering over the wall were amused by the tangle below. Centurion Nepo was beside himself with mirth.

"Caesar's veterans?" he derided. "More like a gaggle of players!" He let out a deep belly laugh and pointed down at two legionaries who had run into each other, their helmets colliding and toppling both into the mud. "Look at those two, lads! They don't know their arses from – "

Nepo stopped suddenly, not of his own accord, but because his open mouth had been caught mid-sentence by the iron shank of a javelin. The javelin had emerged from the crowd below with incredible speed and had buried itself in his brain, killing him instantly. Without another utterance, Nepo fell against the parapet. His head was drawn forward by the weapon's weight such that his outstretched neck lodged between two palisade posts. And there he remained, like a stuffed trophy, his lifeless face staring out at the attackers below with the drooping javelin hanging from his open mouth, dark blood curling down the shaft.

At the sudden absence of that loud voice of ridicule, a

brief silence fell over the battlefield. Defenders and attackers alike gaped at the macabre face of the dead centurion. Those upon the wall stared with disbelief and terror, those below with sanguinity and exultation.

Lars Nepo was dead because he had allowed himself to be distracted by the turmoil of the colliding centuries. In that moment of carelessness, Lucius had acted. He had lost his favorite *amentum* to the Allobroges, but he kept spares in his kit. It was not something he typically used in the battle line, especially not in *testudo*. It required a considerable amount of open space.

There were two ways to use the *amentum*. One was to loop the strap around the butt end of the javelin as if the weapon were the stone in a slingshot. This method achieved the best range. The other way, which Lucius had chosen on this occasion, was the most accurate. It required winding half of the strap around the shaft such that the force of the throw unwound it, giving the javelin spin.

Either method required a good nine steps to execute a proper throw. The oblique march of the front ranks had given Lucius that space. He had taken eight bounding steps, released on the ninth, and promptly tripped over a body on the tenth. He had not seen the results of his throw until regaining his feet, but he had not needed to. He had known his aim was true the moment the weapon left his hand.

Men were now cheering all around him. One soldier in the ditch had taken up Lars Nepo's discarded pike and was using its massive length to jab at those on the wall. Others picked up stones and hurled them at any heads peeking over the palisade. The centuries seemed to be moving forward of their own accord now, anxious to tear through the wall. Units ignored the whistle and remained at the digging instead of moving to the rear.

The tide of the battle had turned.

XLII

"**S**omething is happening at the wall, my lord!" The adjutant was fidgeting.

"Obviously," Valens replied irritably.

He rose from the field table where he had been enjoying a cup of wine, sitting under a large, open-sided canvas shade. The pavilion stood upon a mound near the center of the fort, some two hundred yards behind the east wall – the same wall where a general tumult now ensued. It was difficult to discern precisely what was going on, but it was clear that troops were being pulled from the other ramparts to reinforce two or three locations.

"Where is the cohort commander?" Valens demanded. "Why hasn't he sent me an update?"

"I don't know, my lord," the adjutant replied.

"Then find out, damn you!"

"Yes, my lord," the young officer scampered off, his sheathed gladius clanking against his armor as he went.

Valens looked after him with mild disgust. In his clumsy

haste, the young fool nearly tripped three times crossing the yard – an exceptional feat, since the open ground contained few if any obstacles.

Being merely a strong point in the larger defensive line, the traditional rows of tents, street grid, gutters, and all other features of the standard fort were absent here. The interior was bare, save for a scattering of woodpiles and other building materials reserved for the impending construction of the artillery towers. Thus, Valens had an unobstructed view of all four walls of the fort from his elevated pavilion.

Caesar is beaten, Valens told himself, dismissing the commotion at the wall, as well as the whispering of his staff officers. *The enemy is fleeing, and the men are merely excited by the prospect of victory. Surely, that is it.*

The enemy would be repulsed. The four cohorts manning the defenses would see to that.

But after returning to his seat and taking two more sips of wine, the uproar at the wall had only intensified. At three distinct segments, men were leaping from the ramparts in panic. Then, as Valens watched, at those same three places, the rigid outline of the palisade seemed to melt away. The earthen bank beneath collapsed to half its height, leaving three glaring breaches. A cheer erupted from the other side, immediately followed by a deafening battle cry. The next instant, hordes of snarling, sword-brandishing legionaries were storming through the gaps. The defenders drew their swords to meet them. The two sides met with a great clash of steel.

"What in Juno's name is happening?" Valens exclaimed, unable to hide the sudden desperation in his voice. "Where is that cursed tribune? Where is the damned *primus pilum*?"

A tribune emerged from the growing mass of men in the yard and approached the pavilion at a run. It was not the dispatched adjutant, but the commander of the defending cohorts.

"I regret to report the enemy is inside the walls, my lord!" the officer said between breaths. "Recommend sending up the reserves."

"There are no reserves, you idiot!" Valens retorted.

There were none because Valens had sent them over the north wall to join in the massacre there. They could not possibly be recalled in time to head off this disaster.

"Return to your cohorts!" Valens ordered. "And bring some order to that mess you've made!"

"Yes, my lord," the tribune replied with a skeptical salute, then ran off.

Valens shot a glance at his clustered staff, standing there in their splendid armor, doing nothing.

"Go and assist that idiot, you fools! Kill any man who retreats!"

The young officers nervously donned helmets, awkwardly drew out seldom used swords, then ran off as a disjointed band in the direction of the embattled breaches.

Only the eagle and standard-bearers and the four Arabian bodyguards remained with Valens. The melee in the yard expanded and intensified before his eyes. Steel flashed and glimmered across the field as a thousand swords hacked and jabbed. Enemy troops continued to storm through the gaps, mingling with the defenders in close combat. Soon, it was impossible to tell one side from the other. It seemed the only distinguishing trait between the two sides was the defenders' inclination to throw down their shields and run. And they ran in droves for the rear, careful to give Valens's pavilion, and his scornful stare, a wide berth.

The melee was a contest of sword skill and fierceness, and, thus, there was no contest. The inexperienced men of the Fourth were being cut down by the wild-eyed veterans of the Gallic Wars. After enduring such punishment before the wall, the crazed attackers were bent on revenge. Yet, as bleak as things appeared, Valens was hesitant to send for reinforcements. Pompey would certainly hold it over him at every opportunity.

"My lord!" the soldier holding the eagle standard cried out in alarm, interrupting Valens's thoughts. "Look!"

The melee was spreading out, inching closer. The ground was littered with corpses and thrashing wounded. Valens's untried legionaries were losing decidedly, but that was not what had gotten the eagle bearer's attention. He was pointing at a band of soldiers that had emerged from the skirmish.

There were five of them, led by an exceptionally large centurion wearing a dented helmet. They belonged to Caesar's army. Their swords were red and dripping, their faces grim and determined, their eyes locked on the eagle. Clearly, they had cut a path through the crowd with the intent of capturing the sacred emblem. And now, with the eagle so close, they audaciously rushed the pavilion.

"Defend the eagle!" Valens commanded.

Capturing a legionary eagle was the surest way to promotion and reward. Losing one meant equally assured disgrace.

Instantly, the four Arabians hefted their giant axes and stepped forward to form a rough line of defense between the approaching soldiers and the standards. Valens did not draw his sword but confidently remained beneath the shade to watch.

The soldiers drew up at the sight of the Arabians, but it was clear they would not be turned from their purpose. Their eyes were fixed on the glimmering eagle like it was the Golden Fleece.

It was during that pause that Valens noticed the tall centurion was not focused on the eagle, like the others. Instead, the centurion was looking directly back at him, with an expression of absolute hatred. It was the face of an enraged lion, of an animal ready to pounce, filled with a primal desire to kill – no, not just kill – murder, slaughter, rip its prey into a thousand pieces.

Then, one cut of the warrior's eyes stirred a memory within Valens. The face was stained with filth and blood. It was virtually unrecognizable. Still, those eyes – those piercing eyes – Valens could have picked them out of a crowded market at a hundred paces. They bore an unsettling resemblance to those of his old rival, the man who had nearly supplanted his prominence in Spain so long ago – the man Valens had been forced to destroy.

The son had inherited those eyes, and now they sent a chill up Valens's spine just as they had back then. Judging by the sword that was slickened red from point to hilt, the son had also inherited his father's ferocity in battle.

Valens marveled at the change in the boy he once knew. The last time he had seen the son of Domitius, the lad had been nothing more than a confused, purposeless orphan. At that time, young Domitius had been naïve enough to believe the murder of his family had been the random act of riotous slaves. Indeed, the boy had even been stupid enough to lean on Valens for guidance. Valens had arranged for the lad to be recruited into one of the legions marching off to Gaul. Now, ironically, the boy whom Valens had sent away – whom he had expected to die conveniently on campaign – had returned a hardened warrior, fully capable of, and clearly intent on, killing *him*.

There was a comprehension in those eyes, as plain as the fervid hatred they conveyed. Domitius knew the truth. He knew who was responsible for his family's murder.

After the initial shock wore off, Valens quickly composed himself. He met the young man's baleful gaze with a smug smile. In his rush for vengeance, the troublesome Domitius had quite overestimated his own abilities. Now, he would pay the price for his arrogance. He and his companions were decidedly outmatched by the four axemen. The Arabians were elite warriors. Their giant, long-handled axes made the pathetically short gladii of their opponents look like toothpicks in comparison.

Valens was suddenly amused by the disparity between the two groups. And now he was glad that Cimon had failed to kill Domitius earlier. This would be much more satisfying.

With calm and poise, Valens poured himself another cup, then raised it to the glaring Domitius. After spilling a little wine onto the ground as an offering to the gods, Valens smiled and took a long drink. Returning to his seat, he settled in like a spectator at a gladiatorial game, ready to watch the son of Domitius die.

XLIII

Through the interminable slog across the ferocious melee, Lucius had been of one mind. He had not engaged any but those who blocked his path, and these he had dispatched with ruthless efficiency.

Once beyond the breach, he had not concerned himself with the direction of his century. All unit cohesion throughout the legions had dissolved. The maddened attackers and stunned defenders had amalgamated into a sprawling close-quarters struggle in which friend and foe were hardly distinguishable.

Beyond the mass of helmets, Lucius had picked out the pavilion erected on the knoll, saw the legionary standards, and concluded that Valens must be there. Hacking his way through the field of crashing shields and jabbing swords had not been easy. It had been a nightmarish morass of confusion, death, and gore. Beside him, a man spasmed uncontrollably with the shank of a pilum driven deep into his abdomen. Severed hands and fingers fell into the mud like fruit shaken from a tree. Here, the stump of an arm spewed dark blood high into the air. There, one man straddled the back of another, twisting the helmeted head of his screaming victim until the neck snapped. Two men held the arms of another between them, lifting the mail shirt while a third thrust the point of a sword into the man's groin. A howling, blood-covered slave held a shield in both hands, repeatedly smashing it down into the ruined face of a prostrate soldier.

Every turn had presented another gruesome spectacle, but none of it had diverted Lucius from his purpose.

After finally emerging from the crowd and seeing Valens there under the pavilion, Lucius found himself facing four of the largest men he had ever encountered. They had the dark skin of easterners, broad shoulders, burly arms. The polished double blades of their two-handed axes twinkled as if eager to cleave flesh. Beyond these, the object of his hate, the villain of villains, the enemy of his soul, smiled back at him with smug contempt, clearly believing himself beyond danger.

Seeing Valens there – the man whose every breath was an affront to the souls of the dead – still in a lofty station after all these years, commander of a legion, perhaps a member of the Senate-in-exile, and wealthy as he had ever been, stirred Lucius's rage to a new height. He swore by *Ultio* that it would end today.

Valens must die! Nothing else mattered.

But, first, Lucius would have to deal with the giants in his path.

Lucius was exhausted. He was without a shield. He bled from a dozen nicks and slashes. There were four legionaries with him, each armed with only a gladius, having lost their own shields and javelins to get this far. Two of the four were from Lucius's century. He did not know the other two, but the fact that they had dared to go after the enemy's eagle said something about them. They were likely better than most.

The slight advantage in numbers – five against four – was negated by the disparity in weapons. The two-foot-long gladius could not contend with the reach of those axes, whose long, iron-ringed handles equaled the height of a man. Lucius would have given a year's pay for one shield at that moment. He could have dispatched a man to find one, but the longer he waited to give the order to attack, the longer the fidgeting legionaries had time to ponder the odds.

"Septimus! Betto! Move around to the right. Get ready to take them on the flank!" Lucius addressed the two men from his century, then turned to the other two. "You both are with me. Wait for my word."

Lucius had hoped the easterners would not understand Latin, but they either understood every word, or deduced what Lucius had said, because two of the four immediately dropped back, transforming their line abreast into a defensive square – a formation without a flank.

So much for that strategy.

There was only one way, now. Lucius favored skill and maneuver over brute strength, but there were times when nothing else would do. If the men with him wanted that eagle, they would have to buy it with their own blood, just as he was willing to spill his own to reach Valens.

This was no gladiatorial arena, with flourishes and dramatic pauses as an applauding crowd urged one champion to deliver the fatal blow to another. Here, the opponents had been trained to kill, and kill quickly. Both sides knew what was coming.

What happened next happened rapidly, in the time one might take to count to five.

Lucius and Septimus moved first, both dashing at the axeman at the front right of the square. But the easterner was amazingly light on his feet and moved faster than they. He brought his colossal axe around in a broad sweep quicker than the eye could follow. Lucius and Septimus paused only just in time. They felt the gust of the heavy steel as it passed within a finger's length of their faces. When at the terminus of his swing, Lucius and Septimus attempted to rush inside the sweep of their opponent's arm. But the easterner proved too agile, dancing backward in small diagonal leaps to avoid the jabbing gladii.

This maneuver drew Lucius and Septimus closer to the rear pair of axemen. The closest of the two stepped forward and chopped down with his weapon, forcing Lucius to drop and roll to the right to avert being split down the middle. Septimus, for his part, persisted in his attack on the first easterner, jabbing and swiping at the giant's torso. These all met with empty air, except one propitious hack that caught the Arabian's exposed fingers gripped around the hilt of the axe. Three large severed digits thudded to the ground. The mangled hand lost its grip on the axe. Still, the warrior did not cry out in pain. Nor did he hesitate to choke up on the hilt with his other hand and immediately counter with a mighty back-handed sweep that caught Septimus before he could duck out of the way. The curved blade struck the side of Septimus's helmet, shattering the cheekpiece, crumpling the bronze shell, and smashing the head inside like a ripe watermelon.

Septimus dropped to the ground, dead.

No sooner had he fallen than Betto was there thrusting at the off-balance axeman. With a growl of rage, he drove his gladius into the easterner's mid-section, puncturing the leather brace and the abdomen behind it. The tip of the blade penetrated by no more than the length of a forefinger, but it was enough. A profusion of blood poured down the giant's baggy trousers. He dropped the axe and stood there like a teetering statue, clawing at the wound with meaty fingers and bloody stubs.

The easterner on the left front of the square reacted too slowly to save his comrade, but not too slow to catch Betto while he was outstretched in that fatal lunge. The axe came down in a full-bodied swing that cut into Betto's shoulder like a cord of wood, severing both the head and the extended arm. Betto fell dead in two pieces.

But the lightning-fast tit-for-tat was not finished. The other two legionaries dashed forward, delivering two well-aimed jabs into the ribs of the over-extended axeman, penetrating lungs and heart simultaneously. Before the Romans withdrew their blades, the last axeman was there, spearing the spiked points of his double-headed weapon into the neck of one legionary. Then, yanking the blade to the side, he tore out the man's gullet. Before the initial jet of dark blood spewed from his first victim, the Arabian had swung his blade around on the second legionary. With his sword still stuck between the ribs of his own victim, the legionary raised one unprotected arm in a feeble defense. The limb was instantly cut through to the bone by the axe, provoking a cry of pain and rage. The next humming swing of the axe silenced the soldier when it sheared off the top of his helmet and skull like the lid of a kettle.

This all happened in the time it had taken Lucius to scramble back onto his feet. Warriors with honed instincts had acted on those instincts. They had slain each other with brutal efficiency in a terrible exchange of skill and savagery.

One of the giants had been slain. Another shuddered on the ground, bleeding out from the wound in his abdomen. The two remaining axemen were virtually unscathed. All of Lucius's men were dead.

He stood alone.

In the pause, Lucius grabbed up Betto's dropped weapon and faced both giants with a sword in each hand.

A haughty laugh issued from the pavilion. Lucius could not spare a look at the crowing Valens as the Arabians took up positions on either side of him.

One of the easterners lunged, forcing Lucius to turn toward him to deflect the coming blow. But the axeman did not follow through and suddenly drew back. Realizing he had been duped, Lucius ducked no less than a heartbeat before the axe behind him sliced the air where his neck would have been. No sooner had he got to his feet than the other axe was reaching for him, a low swing that forced him to jump to avoid losing both legs below the knees.

Though they said nothing, the two axemen coordinated their attacks as if they were of the same mind, each successive series of swings coming at shorter intervals from the last. Lucius dodged this way and that, stepping over corpses. He managed to deflect some of the blows with his diminutive swords, but it was clear the heavy axes would win in the end. It was only a matter of time before a misstep sent him off balance.

Only one option remained – the unexpected. Go on the attack.

After dodging the next swing, Lucius launched himself at the slower of the two giants but found that the easterner was not slow enough. The axeman adroitly jumped to the side, brought the handle of his weapon up to meet Lucius's advance, and delivered a violent blow to Lucius's jaw with one of the iron rings on the shaft. As if struck by a blacksmith's hammer, the jolting pain coursed through Lucius's teeth, his neck, his skull, his knees.

The next thing he knew, he was on his back in the mud, senseless, head spinning, the world around shrouded in silence. Above him, both axemen loomed, their faces bathed in the golden sunlight of the setting sun. They held their weapons casually with one hand, clearly no longer considering him a threat. In his disorientation, Lucius reached out, clawed at the cold mud, desperately grasped for a sword, a spear, a dagger, anything his fingers might find, but there was nothing.

A muffled order was given. The axemen reached down with their free hands and pulled Lucius onto his knees. He was too dazed to resist. Then, forcefully, they bent his arms up behind him and turned him to face Valens, who had risen from the stool. The senator's eyes sparkled with delight.

This was the end, Lucius concluded. He had failed. The murderer would live on, and the spirits would never rest. And he would go to join his family as yet another of Valens's victims.

XLIV

Valens felt triumphant as he approached Domitius. He stopped two steps away, his form casting a shadow over the kneeling captive as he gestured for the Arabians to remove the centurion's helmet.

"You have grown taller since I last saw you, Young Domitius. Taller than your father, I suspect. But then you do have the blood of that Spanish whore in you, don't you?"

The blood-streaked face looking up at Valens was defiant, but there was no reply. And that was unfortunate, because, even now, with the fight in the courtyard still raging and undecided, Valens wanted to savor this moment. The older Domitius had been one of the few to ever dare challenge him, and now the final consequence of that insubordination all those years ago was about to be fulfilled. Valens wanted to remember it. He wanted to be the one to deliver the killing blow.

But not like this. Not staring into those steady, defiant

eyes that reminded him so much of the father's. Instead, Valens wanted young Domitius to die raging at the fates that had consigned him to his subservient station. The servant can never become the master. A man must know his place. Domitius would die knowing his.

"I expected you to last longer, boy," Valens chided. "Your father would have lasted longer. Indeed, I was told it took him some time to die after the lash and the flame were applied."

"He died as he lived," Domitius finally answered. "With truth and honor. Even your cutthroats couldn't deprive him of that."

"Your father was nothing, boy!" Valens snapped. "He was a failed farmer, a Gracchian acolyte who allowed himself to be misled by unfounded beliefs. After today, there will be nothing left of him. I will see that every trace of his existence is erased. Your family's tomb will be destroyed. Their bones will be given to the wolves."

Domitius twisted under the hold of the Arabians. His face was red, his eyes emblazoned with hatred. He looked as if he would strangle Valens with his bare hands were he to break free.

Now, it was time.

Valens drew his gladius from its sheath. It was a splendid weapon, crafted by the famous Nicodemo of Gades. The hilt was made of ivory, the guard gilded with gold and rare gems. A unique blend of metals gave the blade incredible strength and allowed for an edge that would draw blood at the slightest pressure. Few could afford such a precious object.

It suddenly occurred to Valens, as he delighted at the familiar feel of the weapon, that he could not remember the last time he had drawn it. With his bodyguard protecting him, he seldom wore the sword. There was rarely a need to arm himself before going anywhere. Both the sword and his armor had been tucked away in the armory within his *domus*, only taken out recently when Pompey had recalled him to military service.

The task of slicing Domitius's throat was perhaps more suited to the dagger than the sword, but the smaller sheath on Valens's opposite hip hung empty. His gem-encrusted *pugio* had been stolen by Baseirta when she had gone on her infernal rampage through the house. No doubt, the dagger would be retrieved when the girl was found. But, for now, he would have to use the sword.

Curse that Parthian whore! I'll make her dance on that dagger when they bring her in.

Valens stepped forward and reversed the blade in his hand in preparation for driving it down through the neck of Domitius's mail shirt. But, as he was rotating the pommel in his hand, a sharp sting prickled his right palm. Pausing, Valens put the hand to his face to inspect it and found a small cut beneath his index finger. It was hardly a scratch, barely drawing blood, yet, for some reason, it tingled like the sting of a scorpion. A moment later, his hand began to throb and burn like it was locked inside a raging furnace. Icicle-like sensations started shooting up his arm. They quickly spread to his chest. His breathing became short and labored. It seemed his lungs would hold no air.

What is happening?

The Arabians looked back at him, clearly just as confused. Then, in a moment of cognizance, he deduced what had happened. Bringing the hilt close to his blurring eyes, he examined it to confirm his suspicions.

Sure enough, it was there. Lodged in a small crack in the ivory was a tiny metallic sliver. It could not have gotten there by accident.

He was poisoned!

Damn the Parthian slut! Damn her to Pluto's Realm!

And now he knew why the woman had rummaged through the armory. It was not to steal the dagger but to affix this invisible barb, a barb that had doubtless been dipped in the same poison that had killed the male slaves. And now, it was also clear why she had killed the slaves. It was to keep them from discovering the poisoned sliver when they oiled and polished his weapons and armor, as they routinely did. She had killed them to ensure no one touched it but Valens.

Baseirta had planned the whole thing. It was an elaborate plot in the true fashion of a Parthian court, a woman's vengeance, and Valens had stumbled right into her snare.

His eyes began to glaze over. He dropped his sword as his body went into violent convulsions. Yet, strangely, he had the wherewithal to notice how Domitius's face looked even more like his father's through blurry eyes.

They even had the same smile.

XLV

The strong hands had released Lucius shortly before he was struck on the head by an axe handle, knocking him face down in the dirt. Both Arabians were some distance away when he came to, moving quickly toward the fort's rear gate, carrying Valens between them. The senator was spasming uncontrollably, his hands clutching his throat, his face a deep shade of purple. Too dazed to pursue, Lucius cursed in frustration. He was perplexed by the malady that had suddenly overcome the old bastard, but seeing him wracked with such pain at least gave Lucius a small measure of satisfaction.

The next moment, dozens of men were rushing past Lucius, blocking his view of the retreating trio. Steel clashed close by. He turned to see the Fourth Legion's standard-bearers, abandoned by their general, now surrounded by a dozen legionaries and fighting a hopeless battle. They were quickly overcome and savaged by the stabbing gladii. The exuberant victors raised the seized standard and eagle to the cheers of all those around.

The melee in the yard had been decided. The enemy was on the run, scampering for the rear gate.

"After them!" a familiar voice called out above the din.

A scarlet cloak and plumed helmet moved among the pursuing troops. It was Caesar. He was surrounded by his Germans brandishing notched swords. Some bled from wounds, and still more had gashes in their clothing and armor, suggesting they had endured great exertions protecting the consul.

Lucius picked up his sword, rose to his feet, and took one step before a bout of dizziness stopped him. He wanted to join in the pursuit, to find Valens among the fleeing enemy, but the blows had left him in a fog. His eyes were swollen. A large welt throbbed on the side of his head.

Around him lay Betto, Septimus, and the others. They had died trying to capture the enemy's eagle, but Lucius felt a wave of guilt over the truth of it. They had died because of him, because of his thirst for vengeance. They had died in vain.

Throughout the yard, shouting officers were attempting to reform the muddled troops into cohorts. It seemed the fort had been captured. Caesar had actually done it.

"Ah, Centurion Domitius!"

Lucius turned to see Quintinus approaching. The commander of the Tenth inelegantly navigated the carpet of corpses. His staff officers followed close behind, weapons drawn but not tarnished. No swordsman, the ungainly Quintinus had wisely waited for the action in the yard to be decided before entering the fort.

"Have you seen the *primus pilum*?" Quintinus asked perfunctorily. Then, he appeared to suddenly grasp Lucius's condition, and his expression changed to one of genuine concern. "Are you alright, Centurion Domitius?"

"I'm fine, sir."

"Yes, well, you should see to your century." After glancing around, Quintinus raised one quizzical eyebrow. "And where precisely *is* your century?"

"They'll be along, sir," Lucius answered succinctly, not taking his eyes off the enemy troops crowded around the rear gate. It was a confused mass of helmets and mud-spattered mail, but Lucius still hoped to catch a glimpse of Valens somewhere in that mob.

"Caesar desires the cohorts to reform and push the enemy out that gate yonder," Quintinus said. "But, it seems to me they need no encouragement. They're all running like…" The general's voice trailed off as he gazed across the yard.

Something had changed, and Lucius saw it, too. The enemy's mad retreat had stopped. They were no longer pushing out the distant gate. As if under a spell, the fleeing troops had suddenly wheeled around and were now forming ranks. Something had induced them to rally, and it did not take Lucius long to discern what that impetus was.

On the high ground beyond the rear wall, a mass of infantry and cavalry swarmed over the hills. There were thousands of them. They were headed toward the fort to reinforce their beleaguered comrades.

On an adjacent summit, flowing capes and standards fluttered in the wind where a group of mounted officers gazed down upon the battle. There could be no doubt who the heavyset general was. Pompey the Great had arrived, and he had brought thousands of fresh reserves. The mere sight of the legendary general on that hill sent a surge of vivacity through the enemy troops and a wave of despair through Caesar's.

Those who had fought so hard to capture the fort were now faced with overwhelming numbers they could not possibly withstand. Some were already running for the breaches, defying the remonstrations of their officers.

"Stop! Mars curse you!" the familiar voice shouted.

Lucius turned to see Caesar, red-faced with anger, marching crossways to the ranks, chastising the quavering troops. But the formations continued to melt away. The consul was without his bodyguard, probably sent off to help stop the mass retreat.

Then, Caesar noticed the two of them standing there.

"General Quintinus! Those are your men running, are they not?" he said accusingly.

Quintinus looked somewhat befuddled before answering. "Er...probably men of the Seventh, my lord. But I'll have them rounded up directly."

Without another glance at Lucius, Quintinus headed off toward the breaches, his adjutants following, perhaps a bit too eagerly, as if they welcomed any excuse to go to the rear. It instilled little confidence that they would ever return.

At the gate held by the enemy, a troop of enemy archers had just entered and were taking up positions on the parapet. Soon, they would be raining arrows upon the men in the courtyard. Most of Caesar's men had no shields. The few shields among them had been battered and holed almost to the point of uselessness. Beyond the wall sounded the thunder of hooves. Soon, the cavalry, too, would be swarming into the fort, lances poised to skewer those remaining in the threadbare ranks.

Lucius knew that a rout was inevitable. A massacre was more likely. Often the soldiers had a better gauge than the generals. Those who were already heading back to the breaches were the smart ones. He hoped his own men were among them.

"Stop, damn you!" Caesar shouted again.

Lucius turned to see the consul, now a dozen paces away, wrestling with a legionary for the captured eagle standard. The soldier was apparently attempting to take the coveted prize with him as he fled the field, and Caesar was trying to stop him.

Was the consul so delusional that he still believed the battle could be won? Or perhaps he had resolved to die here rather than run under the eyes of Pompey.

The fifty-two-year-old Caesar was substantially weaker than the young legionary. The soldier jerked the standard back and forth to wrench it free of the consul's grip. Just a few months ago, such defiance toward the deity-like Caesar would have been unthinkable. But, the continual deficiencies, the scarcity of rations, and, most significantly, the lack of pay had left the rank and file bitter and resentful. Soldiers who, at one time, would have fallen on their own swords had Caesar wished it, were now reckoning their famous general nothing more than a smooth-talking charlatan who had trodden over their backs to reach the zenith of Roman power.

After what Lucius had experienced over the past few days, he had a mind to look the other way and join those retreating. For even his own legate had already disappeared through the breaches. But then, as Lucius watched, the grappling soldier released the pole with one hand and struck Caesar across the face, knocking the consul to the ground.

Quite involuntarily, the dutiful centurion awoke within Lucius. Dashing over to the scuffle, he blindsided Caesar's assailant, striking the hilt of his gladius across the man's helmet. The soldier staggered, yet kept a firm hold of the shaft. He angrily wheeled to face Lucius, but his vigor noticeably diminished upon realizing Lucius was a centurion – and a large one, at that – covered in blood and holding an equally bloody sword.

"Release it!" Lucius scowled, putting his sword to the soldier's throat.

The man's resolve melted into shame. He paused, then handed the eagle to Lucius.

"Now, go take your place in line with the others," Lucius commanded.

"Just a moment, Centurion," Caesar said, stiffly rising to his feet while dabbing at a bleeding lip.

Lucius came to attention and gestured for the soldier to do the same. "Won't happen again, sir. The lad just got frightened, is all. He's ready to return to the ranks."

The consul gave Lucius a tiresome look, then reached out and took the sword from his hand. Without a moment's hesitation, Caesar thrust the tip into the soldier's abdomen. Placing one hand on the man's shoulder for leverage, he continued to push with all his might, driving the sword through the mail, until a hand's breath of the cold steel had sunk into the belly underneath. The shocked soldier clutched at Caesar, clutched feebly at his own pierced abdomen, his eyes bulging with pain and disbelief. Then, Caesar rotated the blade through half a turn and ripped it free. A profusion of dark blood poured out onto the ground like the contents of a punctured wineskin. The dying soldier had hardly dropped to his knees before Caesar handed the weapon back to Lucius and turned his attention to the forming enemy ranks.

"Our position is untenable here," Caesar said as the writhing soldier gurgled up blood in the mud, not two steps away. Caesar's voice was calm as if he had just vented all his own aggravations and could now think clearly.

"It looks that way, my lord," Lucius replied evenly, unsure if the consul was speaking to him or to himself.

"Pass the word to all units, Centurion," Caesar said

finally. "We will withdraw."

XLVI

Caesar did retreat. His withdrawing legions were subjected to a harrowing flight by Pompey's fresh infantry and horse before they could regain the safety of their own lines. Many veterans who had survived the long campaigns in Gaul and Spain were left stretched on the field. With the works sparsely defended and the army in disarray, it seemed nothing could stop Pompey's cohorts from overrunning Caesar's lines. But that did not happen.

Incredibly, the horns sounded, and the pursuit stopped. Pompey's troops were recalled. By the time the light of the western sky dimmed to gray, the victors had returned to their own lines. As night fell, both sides licked their wounds. The moans of the wounded drowned out the howls of the wolves.

On the shore within Pompey's camp, a group of slaves and soldiers carried a litter under torchlight toward a waiting launch. Two giants bearing axes walked on both sides. Upon the litter, a white-haired man shivered beneath a silken cloak.

The procession passed a huddle of officers conversing in the darkness.

"Is that Valens being carried by?" one of the officers said, stepping away from the huddle.

A tribune in the procession raised one hand, and the litter stopped as the heavyset officer approached.

Pompey stepped into the torchlight to look down on the prostrate Valens. He could not have prepared himself for what he saw. The senator, the commander of the Fourth Legion, a man who had seemed in the blossom of health, was in a most pitiful state. Valens's skin was beet red and dripping with perspiration. There was not a finger's width that was not marked with raised blisters or dark streaks. His whole body trembled as if the slightest movement was excruciating. Shallow, whistling breaths escaped between cracked lips drawn tight across grinding teeth.

"Dear Valens," Pompey said, taking the wretch's hand. "Brave Valens. It grieved me to hear of your sickness."

There was no reply from the convalescent aside from a cut of his jittery eyes.

"Forgive me, Lord Pompey," the tribune mediated. "General Valens is unable to speak. However, we believe he can hear us."

Pompey nodded, then returned his gaze to Valens.

"You fought well, my friend, like Ajax. Do not worry. I assure you now, just as I assured the Senate in my report, I will recover your eagle. Have no fear of that. And I will restore the honor your legion so appropriately deserves. You have my vow."

Valens's teeth seemed to clench tighter. Veins swelled on his forehead as if he struggled to speak, but no sound escaped him save a long, guttural groan.

"Do not try to speak, my friend. There is no need to

thank me. I must thank you for holding the line until I could gather enough forces to come to your rescue. I have also included those details in my letter to the Senate. They will know how you so valiantly held the field until your malady struck you down, and how your legion would have been overrun had I not arrived when I did."

Again Valens grunted loudly, his eyes bulging. His hand gripped Pompey's like a vice. Pompey concluded the illness must have robbed the wretch of muscular control to result in these periodic, involuntary outbursts. No doubt, this was one of those terrible afflictions that often struck a man down in his older years without notice.

"Rest, my friend," Pompey said, awkwardly detaching himself from the clenched hand and placing it back on the litter. "I shall sacrifice to Aesculapius for you." Pompey smiled at Valens then nodded to the tribune. "See that he is well cared for."

"Yes, Lord Pompey."

The tribune saluted, and the party proceeded toward the boat.

As Pompey looked after it, Labienus appeared beside him in the darkness.

"There goes a poor, poor man," Pompey said. "I am sad for him. I doubt he will ever walk again."

Labienus nodded impatiently. "Indeed, my lord. But might I bring us back to the matter at hand?"

"Yes, yes, General," Pompey said tiredly. "But we have more important concerns at present. There are many hundreds of fallen to collect from the field."

"Surely, the enemy has thousands to collect of their own."

"I know what you would advise, General," Pompey said. "But we will not attack tonight."

Labienus was beside himself with aggravation. "The

enemy is breaking camp, Pompey! We can hear them from our own lines, for Juno's sake! If we attack now – "

"As I said before, it is likely a ruse. Let us not turn a victory into a defeat. If Caesar is leaving, as you believe, then all the better. We can destroy him on the march more easily than when he is behind his works."

"And what if he makes it to the mountains? We have the advantage today, my lord. Tomorrow, we might – "

"See that my physician is sent to Valens," Pompey interrupted. He was still watching the litter, which was now being hoisted over the bulwark of the boat.

"I'm sure that can be easily arranged, my lord," Labienus said through gritted teeth, clearly frustrated that Pompey had once again deviated to trivial matters.

"Arrange it now, if you please," Pompey said curtly.

"I?" Labienus retorted. "But I must see to the lines, my lord. Surely, a tribune would be better –"

"I want you to do it, General? I know you are a friend of Valens. Go to Dyrrachium and see that he is made comfortable. See that my physician tends to him. While there, you can inspect the city's defenses."

"The city's defenses?" Labienus exclaimed incredulously, but he managed to hold his tongue and say nothing else. The next thing out of his mouth might have led to his own cashiering. Then, quietly enraged, he saluted and marched off to obey his orders.

Upon dismissing the other generals and attendants, Pompey made his way to his pavilion. The long day had taxed him. He was exhausted and needed a rest. Moreover, he needed time to think clearly. And that was why he had sent Labienus away to tend to Valens. His nagging deputy would be out of his hair for at least a few hours.

The servants took Pompey's armor and helmet. He dismissed them and entered the bedchamber where towels and a basin of fresh water had been prepared for him. He was in the midst of washing the day's dirt from his arms and hands when he suddenly noticed a robed figure standing in a dark corner.

Pompey was startled, at first, then smiled as he casually patted his arms dry.

"I was wondering when you would turn up again?" Pompey said. "I was beginning to think you had abandoned us and headed back to Gaul." Pompey sat down on the chair and let out a deep breath. "Well, your plan to capture Caesar did not succeed. What have you to say for yourself?"

"It is you who did not succeed, my lord Pompey." The druid hissed, stepping into the lamplight. "The spirits placed the accursed tyrant in your hands before the town. Your men failed to slay him."

Pompey yawned and put his feet up. He poured a mixture of water and wine into a cup.

"I don't suppose you would like a drink?" Pompey offered.

"I do not partake in the grape of the foreigner."

Pompey laughed. "Ah, but you used to."

"Bah!" the druid hissed again.

"Then what brings you here tonight, Catugna, my old friend?"

The druid's lips turned up in a small smile. "I come at the bidding of Prince Roucill. He inquires about his cousin Egu and if there is any news of the Forlorn Hope."

Pompey looked as though he had not been listening, then responded. "One of the many dead heroes of the day, no doubt. Tell your prince that if he wishes to honor his brother's sacrifice, and repay those who slew him, then he should continue to serve me loyally. Lord Roucill shall ride with my auxiliary cavalry as we pursue the enemy into the interior."

"He will not like that answer."

"If he wishes to be king of the Allobroges when all this is over, then he will accept that answer."

The druid gave an uncaring shrug. "I will tell him, my lord."

"And have you any new dire prophecies for me?" Pompey changed the subject. "Any more portents of doom?"

"None. The spirits are often silent at the end of a moon."

"And what does your druid lore say about persistent dreams?"

Catugna's eyes looked back at him from the shadows of the hood. "The dreams again?"

"Nightmares, more like." Pompey nodded. "And our Latin priests are at a loss. They give me libations, perform rituals, tell me to eat less and sleep more, yet the visions continue. If anything, they have been more vivid in recent days. They stick in my mind, even now."

"The white-haired man?"

Pompey nodded. "It is the same as I've told you before. The same every time, without fail." He stared into the dancing flames of a nearby urn as if seeing the vision in his mind. "The white-bearded man – a holy man of sorts in a white frock – lies on a stone stair dripping with blood. He shakes his fist at me, lambasts me, curses me. He is shouting at the top of his lungs, but I cannot hear what he is saying. I try to move closer, find my legs are too heavy to move. Then, I am suddenly underwater, unable to breathe, unable to swim. Just as I begin to lose consciousness, a hand reaches out and draws me up into a boat. I cough and heave. It is not water streaming from my mouth but blood. Then I look up and see my rescuer is the same man. We are the only two in the boat, and again he is cursing me, and again I cannot hear him. I hear only the voices of my wife and son in the distance, crying out in anguish. Then a wave upends the boat. It is cast upon the shore and bursts to splinters. When I come to, the sun is setting on the sea. Further down the beach, a pyre burns vigorously. The old man is close by, raising his hands to the heavens in praise. I move closer to the fire,... and closer,... I try to identify who is the dead one being consumed...then I wake." Pompey looked at Catugna. "I always wake at that moment. And my heart is always pulsing out of my chest, my clothes drenched as though I had actually been in the water."

The druid stared back at him for an extended interval as if profoundly pondering something, as if he had an idea as to the significance of the images. But, finally, the head shook within the cowl. "I am sorry, my lord. It is a mystery to me."

Pompey sighed. "I assumed as much." He yawned, downed the rest of the cup, and rose. "I must dismiss you now, my friend. My cot is beckoning for me. Come back tomorrow. I may have more work for you."

XLVII

Catugna moved through the camp dragging the skirt of his black robes behind him. He was a shadow in the night. He went unnoticed as he walked between the rows of tents, past campfires where soldiers joked and feasted, past the armorers hammering away.

It was not precisely a yearning within him, perhaps more of a comfort, to hear the familiar sounds, to smell the leather and steel. He despised the Latins to his very core, but he was drawn to the distinctive order of a Roman legion. And there were times, though seldom, when echoes of his former life awoke within him.

As he watched the cajoling soldiers from the darkness, Catugna found himself swept away to other places, other times – the forests of Gaul, the mountains of Armenia, the deserts of Judea. He was a druid now, a creature of the forest, a conduit for the spirit world. But there once was a time when he had been a mere man, when he had stood among the Romans, when *he* had been one of *them*.

The Latins were an accursed race, and Caesar the chief devil among them. Caesar had slaughtered the people of the northern lands. His conquests had produced more suffering than the worst wars or plagues in the memories of the old ones. He had set the tribes against one another, seducing the weakest and vainest chieftains with promises of silver and land. Men, women, and children had been massacred, entire settlements put to the torch and removed from existence.

These crimes were reason enough to despise Caesar. Still, Catugna had a personal reason for hating the tyrant, a grudge that could only be resolved with blood.

Caesar had killed his mother.

In truth, Catugna's mother had died by his own hand. He had cut her down by accident in a moment of confusion. But Caesar was to blame. Still, it was very likely the tyrant was ignorant of the whole affair. The killing had been no more than a minor incident, one of the thousand discounted tragedies that result from a conquering army moving through a subjugated land.

But Catugna would never forget. Nor would he forgive.

His mother had been a creature, too, the chief priestess of The Three, a sorceress of wood and water. The tribes had looked to her for the wisdom of the spirits. Now, they looked to him. Her power dwelt within him.

When Catugna had lived as a Latin, he had thought like a Latin. He had been too consumed with their vain ways to hear the voices of the ancient ones. It was only after casting off all ties to his former life that he had even begun to listen. For years, he lived naked upon the land, wandering deep in the wood, surviving like a beast of the field, alone with the guilt of his crime. He had nearly gone mad. The tanned, burly form of a soldier had withered to the malnourished, boney frame he now inhabited.

Then, one day, in the heat of summer, under a dark, brooding boil of cloud, the great spark from the sky had struck him down, and he had slept. He did not know how long. His soul had journeyed through the unseen world where the dead endure for all time.

When he finally woke, he was no longer a man. He was a creature, like her. The spirits spoke to him as clear as the caw of the raven, the hoot of the owl, the cry of the wolf. The soul of his mother spoke, too. She was among them, dwelling in water and wood, from which she imparted her sacred power to him.

When he emerged from the forest and made himself known to the Gallic tribes, they came to revere his word as they had hers. What the oracle at Delphi was to the Greeks, Catugna of the forest was to the Gauls. In time, even the other druids sought his insight on matters surpassing their own skills and understanding.

Over the years, he had guided his people, not with a sword at the head of an army, but with divination and wisdom. His was the whisper in the ear of the chieftain, the fortuitous prophecy that stirred reluctant warriors to battle, the sacrificial dagger that sealed pacts in blood.

The rise of Vercingetorix, the would-be savior of Gaul, had been one of his orchestrations. The charismatic young king had been acting under Catugna's advisement when he had united the tribes in rebellion against Caesar. Unfortunately, after some initial successes, that campaign had ended in disaster. The failure had probably been due to a disingenuous sacrifice by one of the coastal tribes – the ignorant fools often recklessly substituted a bull or ram for the required human offering. Now, Vercingetorix was a captive in Rome. The Gauls were subdued and afraid. And Caesar was still alive.

And so, Catugna had tried different means. Borrowing

one of Caesar's own tactics, he had pretended to be a friend to the Romans, a willing accomplice in their subjugation of his people. He had established an open relationship with Caesar. The tyrant had been more than eager to have an ally among the druids. At the same time, Catugna had fostered a secret relationship with Pompey and the Senate, who desired firsthand accounts of Caesar's atrocities in Gaul for use in their own political schemes.

Romans fighting Romans, just as Gauls had fought Gauls. That was what Catugna had sought. And that was what had eventually happened, just as the spirits had foretold.

Catugna had accompanied Roucill and Egu and their troop to Greece, where he had served as an agent for Pompey within Caesar's army. He had often passed unseen between the camps. That was how he had arranged for the defection of Roucill and Egu, without their prior knowledge. That was how he had helped Pompey stage the ambush on the isthmus.

He could never go back to Caesar now. Last time, he had used the unwitting Centurion Domitius as his passport through the lines. But there was nothing now that would save him from being crucified should he ever venture into Caesar's camp again.

No, he would remain with Pompey's army, and he would continue to serve that buffoon Roucill who, even now, was still oblivious to his shadow dealings. Pompey would use Catugna, and Catugna would use Pompey.

Catugna had only recently revealed to Pompey the truth of his former life, that he had once been a soldier of Rome and had marched under Pompey in Asia. Surprisingly, the revelation had been well received. Pompey had not seemed to care that one of his former soldiers was now a druid. And they had spent many hours recounting days gone by, like old comrades.

It was an unholy alliance. Catugna despised Pompey as he did all Latins. But, for the time being, Pompey was a necessary evil. They shared a common purpose in the destruction of Caesar. And that purpose would need to be carried out without delay – before Pompey met with the dreadful fate that awaited him.

For his dream had foretold of an impending doom.

Catugna had indeed understood it. He knew who the white-frocked old man was, just as he knew whose corpse burned on the pyre. Like the arrogant Roman he was, Pompey could recount every one of his battles in intimate detail. Yet he had forgotten about the people he had crushed, the walls pulled down, the towns burned, the sacred places defiled.

But Catugna remembered. He remembered in Jerusalem, after the great battle there, a white-haired priest in a white frock had stood on the stone stairs of the Jews' temple, blocking Pompey's path. At Pompey's order, the priest had been run through. With his blood cascading down the steps, the dying priest had rebuked Pompey with a curse like no other Catugna had ever heard before. Pompey had simply stepped over the priest and moved on, but Catugna had been shaken to his foundation. He had never quite gotten over it, even after all this time. It was one of the few incidents from his former life he could recall vividly.

If the curse held true, then Pompey's end was near, and there was no time to waste. Caesar must be dealt with before that happened.

As Catugna continued to watch the soldiers around the fire, he overheard them talking of the day's fighting and how many enemy corpses had been counted. He found himself pondering the fate of Lucius Domitius.

Many times, on that dark trek between the lines, he had

come close to telling Lucius who he was – who he had been. Years ago, they had been comrades in Caesar's army.

If their paths ever crossed again, would he embrace his old comrade, or would the spirits demand yet another sacrifice? Would they demand he plunge his poisoned dagger into Lucius's heart?

The Fatal Sisters laughed as they twisted the threads of life.

Again, Catugna heard the voices, not those of the spirits, but those of the men he had marched with long ago, Lucius's among them. And they called him by another name, a name he had tried so hard to forget.

Vitalis…Vitalis…Vitalis…

XLVIII

The following day, the light of the dawn revealed that the tumult heard by the watchmen in the night had indeed been the departure of Caesar's army. The besiegers had struck, leaving behind an assortment of wrecked vehicles, abandoned works, and smoking funeral pyres. Cheers rolled across Pompey's lines as news traveled from one legion to the next. Work parties were sent forth to unblock the streams, and thousands of men and horses finally drank to their hearts' content.

Again, Labienus intreated Pompey to pursue, but Pompey refused, instead choosing to dispatch only his cavalry to follow and harass the fleeing enemy. There was no need for haste, after all. He would give his army a few days to reprovision and prepare for the coming campaign, which would surely be the final campaign of the war.

With the siege lifted, Dyrrachium was once again open for trade. Wagons and travelers appeared on the *Via Egnatia*. Merchant galleys hitherto held for army use were released, and many weighed anchor that very day. Some were loaded down with goods long overdue in distant lands. Others rode high in the water, returning empty from whence they had come.

Aboard one of the vessels bound for eastern waters, a raven-haired, olive-skinned woman wrapped in a modest cloak stood at the bulwark gazing back at Dyrrachium. Her lush lips uttered a prayer of sorrow and of yearning, drowned out by the steady drumbeat and the creak of the dipping oars.

Baseirta was not sure why she prayed. The gods had ignored her pleas for so long. Every night, she had prayed that she and her father might someday return to their native land and gain back the holdings so unjustly taken from them. But, now, she was journeying back to Armenia alone. And the bones of her noble father lay in some pit of refuse among those of common criminals.

Her fingers ran across the amulet around her neck, felt the familiar engraving.

Mithra, preserve me! Give me strength to think clearly, to do what must be done.

She had escaped with little difficulty. The only thing that had ever kept her bound to the bed of her tormentor was the promise of her father's safety. Her father's death had freed her of that bond. Suddenly, she had been free to use the skills she had suppressed for so long, the skills she had learned as the daughter of a governor. The noblewomen of Parthia were alluring, elegant, and charming. But they also had a sinister side, a lurking, brooding malevolence that never forgot and seldom forgave.

From an early age, Baseirta had learned the subtle means by which one navigated the intrigues of the royal court. Her father's spymaster had taught her the assassin's ways in the interest of avoiding their snares. A poisoned needle could be easily hidden in a gift, a bouquet of flowers, the palm of a hand – or the hilt of a cherished weapon. And so, she had concealed the barb on Valens's sword, coating the tip with the last trace of the poison she could scrape from the vile, hoping it would be enough. She had inadvertently used too much in the cups of the male servants.

She felt no guilt over the servants' deaths. Like Cimon, they had often watched her repeated ravagings with lustful, amused eyes. None had ever lifted a hand to help her or console her in any way. They had died painfully but quickly – certainly better than they deserved. By *Mithra's* good fortune, the poison would be just as effective in Valens's blood as it had been in the stomachs of the slaves.

May his sinful hand find the fatal spur. May the foul potion despoil him as he despoiled me.

Upon leaving the house that day, she had assumed the guise of a common harlot and made her way to the market. There, she had been largely ignored. Everyone had been too obsessed with the battle over on the mainland to pay her any mind. Valens's fine dagger had fetched hardly a fifth of its worth. Still, it had been enough for her to gain incognito passage on a galley heading for Asia.

She vowed never to return to this accursed land. Her heart was set on Gugark, and the castle where she had once lived happily with her father. She would be mistress of that house again. Slaves and servants would bend to her every need as they had before. By *Mithra*, she *swore* it would be so!

But, for those aspirations to be realized, she would have to be cunning as the fox. She would have to use every skill in her repertoire, including those of irresistible beauty and carnal seduction. She would be the fox among the sheep, quietly devouring one while the others mindlessly grazed nearby. And there would be many sheep to eat, chief among them the Parthian king himself, Orodes, the one who had betrayed her father.

With the bit of money she had, she could just make it to Armenia. There, she would go straight to Prince Phraates, the son of Orodes. She would go to him in tattered garments – deliberately rent in all the right places – and beg him to take her in as a refugee. She would offer her body to him, and he would be unable to resist her. The stuttering, clumsy prince had always gazed upon her with a drooling desire. She would be outwardly submissive to him, all the while placing him under her spell. Then, playing the soft nymph in his bed and the adder in his ear, she would slowly turn the dimwitted Phraates against his father. She would convince him to usurp the throne from Orodes. And the betrayer would finally learn what it meant to be betrayed. The villain would know, in his final moments, who had caused his overthrow. She would make sure of that. And she would force Orodes to say her father's name before he died.

The noblewomen of Parthia did not make idle vows. As sure as she was Baseirta, daughter of Varaz Vizur, *Marzban* of Gugark, she would see it done.

XLIX

"The deed is done, Lucius," Jovinus said in a low tone. "Saturn's balls! I hope no one saw me."

"Those bastards are napping like the sons of Somnus," Lucius assured him. "Not a one so much as stirred."

Lucius and Jovinus stood beside the entrance to a stone bridge where a column of weary infantry filed along in full kit. The bridge spanned a chasm fifty feet deep with sharp cliffs on either side. On the road before the bridge, carts and wagons were backed up for nearly a mile, waiting for the infantry to cross.

"Saturn's crotch!" Jovinus said apprehensively. "I'll be lucky if I'm not scourged for this! Tell me again why you couldn't have one of your own men do it?"

"They're good lads," Lucius replied. "But I don't trust them as I do you – and none of them know the workings of vehicles."

"In any event, you owe me for this, Lucius!"

"Really? Remember the whore in Belgica, the one you

were so enamored with, the one I helped you sneak out of the legate's tent?"

Jovinus looked at him incredulously. "That was over four bloody years ago!"

Lucius grinned. "Now, we are even."

Jovinus managed a laugh.

Three days had passed since the army had struck camp in the middle of the night. They had hurriedly packed anything that could be carried, and burned the rest, including upwards of two thousand of their own dead. Surprisingly, Pompey's legions had not interfered. By sunup the next day, Caesar's army had placed a full eight miles between the tail of the column and the ruins of the siege lines. The forced march had continued through the heat of the day, every step an exertion, a test of mettle. They had trudged onward until well after sundown, up into the foothills and the mountains beyond.

All through that day, Caesar had ridden up and down the column, calling out those who had distinguished themselves in the siege, often awarding decorations on the spot. Scaeva and Minuscius, the centurions who had successfully fought off the enemy attack on the first day of the battle, were among the scores who were decorated. So many awards were issued that day that no soldier, no matter where he marched in the ten-mile-long column, went without witnessing at least one of these presentations. It was said the consul had given out so many awards, that he had been forced to borrow medallions from the breasts of his own adjutants.

Now, the army was on the move again. Caesar was pressing them to gain another march on the enemy. The farther they ventured into the rugged elevations, the more hindrances they encountered. In many places, the road was blocked by rockslides or eroded away by past floods.

Moreover, the column's progress had been slowed considerably by a handful of deep chasms spanned by deficient bridges, such as the one where Lucius and Jovinus now conversed.

A large section of the bridge had crumbled in the recent past, likely from an earthquake, opening a significant gap over the bridge cavity. The army's engineers had spanned the missing section with the few materials at hand. Still, the rickety span threatened to collapse under the weight of a marching column. Thus, the master of engineers had decreed that no more than two wagons, twelve horses and riders, or two single-files of infantry could cross at any given time. To enforce this regulation, two cohorts of the Tenth had been detached, Lucius's among them. This opportune posting had allowed Lucius to yank Jovinus out of the ranks when the Seventh Legion had marched by more than an hour ago.

Lucius had coaxed his reluctant comrade into performing the aforementioned special task. And now, with that task done, Lucius and Jovinus stood by the bridge entrance, casually observing the stalled train of *impedimenta*. They were watching one wagon, in particular – the ninth in line. Two heavily armed Illyrian mercenaries lounged atop chests piled high on the wagon's bed. The Illyrians were supposed to be guarding the cargo but were instead using the chests as their personal daybeds. Both men lay on their backs, apparently asleep, with cloths draped over their faces to shield them from the sun. Meanwhile, the pair of mules hitched to the wagon were being kept calm by the dismounted driver.

"I'll bet Antony is going to wish he never hired those worthless buggers." Jovinus smirked.

"You'd better get going," Lucius said. "The *primus pilum* is probably looking for you by now. Regimus probably thinks you've deserted."

"Aye," Jovinus sighed. "He's going to be mad. Just as sure as Scaevola learned to jerk himself with his left hand. I'll be lucky to escape the lash."

"I'm sure you'll manage it."

Jovinus frowned. "I don't know why I let you talk me into these things, Lucius." Hefting his kit onto his shoulder, he smiled. "Let me know how it goes."

Lucius nodded and the two shook hands.

Jovinus joined the files of soldiers marching across the bridge, disappearing amid the throng. A short time later, he emerged on the high ground on the other side, then broke into a run to catch up with his legion.

A raucous braying drew Lucius's attention back to his own side of the bridge. Twenty paces away, an angry mule was tied to a rotted pine, one of the few trees spared by the engineers in their scrounge for material. The mule was protesting its captivity most vociferously.

The animal had a reputation for being particularly skittish near high precipices, and this cliff was no exception. Today, the mule had already bucked off three packs and had kicked a slave in the head, knocking the man senseless. The master teamster had ordered the ill-tempered animal unburdened and pulled out of the line to let it cool off, but the mule was still testy. It jerked and yanked at the rope restraining it, while three of Lucius's men tried to subdue it. Their efforts only seemed to further excite the beast, much to the amusement of the passing infantry who slowed their step to have a longer look at the commotion.

"Damn it, Domitius!" General Quintinus reined in his horse nearby. "Can you not keep those men in line? That is General Mamurra, the master of engineers, on yonder hill with Caesar. I can tell by the look on his face, he is most displeased by the disorder here. I can only imagine what he's saying to the consul this very moment!"

"If the master of engineers thinks he can handle that mule any better, sir," Lucius said callously. "Then I invite him to come down here and try."

Quintinus looked flustered. "To Hades with the mule! Just throw the bloody beast over the side!"

"That would go against the orders of the master teamster, sir, who said no more beasts were to be put down without his approval, sir, seeing as how we're so short of them. Maybe if the master teamster and the master of engineers got together, sir –"

"Just deal with it, Domitius," Quintinus said with a tired sigh, unable to summon the vigor to rebuke the surly centurion.

"Yes, sir!" Lucius threw up a sharp salute, then turned to his own men who, in all honesty, could have been doing more to stop the gaggle of spectators. Swatting his vine branch against a nearby stand of shields, Lucius made a loud clatter that got their attention. "Get those men moving, Numerius, Calvus, and you others! Keep them moving! Two-yard intervals between them. Step to it, lads!"

As his men attempted to restore order to the column, Lucius looked past files of men and through the swirls of dust to see the hill where the senior officers observed the crossing. The generals looked like the rest of the army, haggard and strained by the rapid pace they must maintain to escape the enemy pursuit that was sure to come. Caesar sat his horse apart from the others, not watching the procession at all, but writing in a book as he was wont to do on the march. Antony was there, too, bareheaded, wiping the sweat from his brow, hardly paying attention to the gesticulating master of engineers beside him.

Lucius saw Antony cast an anxious glance at the wagon with the sleeping mercenaries, just as Lucius had seen him do many times since the army had left Dyrrachium. A few casual questions to the quartermasters had confirmed Lucius's suspicions. The wagon carried Antony's own personal items – the trappings, carpet, and furnishings that would adorn his tent when the army finally made camp again. It was indeed odd to have such things guarded, since they were essentially useless to the ordinary soldiers.

"That's it, *Vitus*," a legionary reported to Lucius. "The last cohort of the Sixth is crossing now."

"Get the wagons moving, then," Lucius commanded.

"Yes, *Vitus*."

As orders were being relayed down the line, Lucius turned to the soldiers tending the ill-tempered mule. "You men let that beast alone and help the others direct the wagons. Only two vehicles are to cross at a time. Get to it!"

Gratefully, the soldiers left the wild mule tied to the tree and hurried off.

The road where the train of *impedimenta* was stopped was slightly higher than the bridge by several feet. This higher ground hugged the canyon wall and only descended to the bridge level after a sharp bend in the road a hundred yards before the bridge. The decline was not severe, but it was steep enough to necessitate braking, lest the weight of a vehicle drive it toward the bridge and the cliffs beyond at an uncontrollable speed. Thus, as each vehicle reached the turn preceding the downward slope, the driver would halt his team momentarily to install drag shoes on the rear wheels.

When the wagon carrying Antony's goods stopped to perform this procedure, then continued down the slope, it became apparent almost immediately that the driver was having difficulty controlling his team. The mules seemed at odds with the reins. Peculiar noises emanated from the undercarriage, inducing even the two guards riding on the back to sit up with concerned faces.

"Look out!" a voice cried out in alarm. "That bloody beast is loose!"

All heads turned to see the wild mule was no longer tied to the tree. Somehow it had slipped its bonds and was now kicking and spinning amid the line of vehicles. This stirred a reaction in the hitched animals who were themselves already skittish about the slope. Carts and wagons veered as the panicking drivers struggled to regain control of their vehicles. Some ran off the road. Some narrowly avoided collision. Two flipped over, spilling their drivers and cargoes.

But Antony's wagon fared worst of all. The violent movements of the frightened team jerked the vehicle's tongue with such force that the beam detached altogether. No longer encumbered, the two frightened mules turned together and ran back up the road dragging the detached shaft and the driver behind them. After plowing through the dirt for some distance, the driver finally let go of the reins. He had hardly skidded to a halt before popping up and setting off at a sprint after the driverless wagon, which had somehow broken free of its drag shoes. The wagon was barreling down the slope completely unimpeded. Straining wheels rattled over stones and divots as the wagon rapidly picked up speed. Men dashed left and right to avoid being run over. The vehicle's swerving course was carrying it toward the precipice, a realization the horrified guards came to at the last possible instant. Both leaped clear a heartbeat before the vehicle careened off the cliff.

Moments later, a loud crash echoed off the canyon walls. Men rushed to the edge to stare with morbid curiosity at the destruction below. When the dust finally cleared, a heap of splintered wood and broken chests were all that remained. The wagon had been pulverized on the rocks. All was silent, save the rattle of a single wheel that had somehow survived the fall and was now rolling along the canyon floor.

The next moment, Antony was there in a flurry of dust, leaping from his horse, angrily brushing off any who got in his way. He reached the edge to gaze down at the shattered remains just as the surviving wheel wobbled over onto its side. His jaw hung open in disbelief.

"M-My sincerest apologies, my lord!" the driver said in near hysteria as he fell to his knees beside Antony. "I do not know what happened, my lord. I – "

A boot to the face knocked the driver to the ground. He wisely said no more, choosing instead to scurry away holding his shattered nose. No one else dared go near Antony until Quintinus arrived. He dismounted and warily approached Antony at the precipice.

"I'm terribly sorry, Antony," Quintinus said consolingly. "Terribly sorry. All your apparatus! It's just dreadful!"

Antony said nothing. He simply gazed despondently at the wreckage below.

Lucius, who had been hanging back, stepped forward suddenly and spoke out in a strident tone. "Not to worry, sir! I'll send my lads down there to fetch everything that can be salvaged."

Antony seemed to go rigid at the recognition of the voice, then slowly turned to face him.

With excessive enthusiasm, Lucius continued. "It'll take at least a couple dozen men to bring it all up, sir. But have no fear. I've got the lads to spare. I'll make sure they collect everything of value, sir. You can count on that."

"Yes, yes!" Quintinus said cheerily, utterly oblivious to the tension between the two men. "That's an excellent idea, Centurion Domitius. See to it, please. Don't worry, Antony. We will have it all back up here in no time."

"Still alive, eh, Domitius?" Antony said icily, ignoring Quintinus. This time there was no trace of a smile. "*Minerva* be praised."

Lucius could read the thoughts brewing in Antony's mind as clearly as if Antony had spoken them. He was deducing that Lucius's presence here, at this moment, was too much of a coincidence and that he must somehow be connected to the mishap. And that deduction was correct.

Lucius was indeed behind it. At Lucius's bidding, Jovinus had loosened the tongue from the wagon's front axle, as well as the chains for securing its drag shoes. Jovinus had done this while the guards had been snoozing and the driver had been preoccupied with calming his team. For his part, Lucius had set the skittish mule loose while everyone else had been busy directing the line of vehicles.

Now, a suppressed indignation rose within Antony, and Lucius knew why. It was not because his furniture now lay in splinters across the ravine floor. It was because the wagon had also been carrying the thirty thousand silver *denarii* Antony had stolen – the money that had been intended for the Allobroges horsemen.

Once the army had packed up for the march, it had not taken long for Lucius to determine where the fortune was. The excessive guard around the wagon had raised his suspicions. Antony's obsession not to let the wagon out of his sight had confirmed them. Lucius had then waited for the opportune time and place to act.

He had hoped the errant wagon would topple before going over the cliff. It would have been much more satisfying for Antony's ill-gotten gains to spill out onto the ground in front of all these men and the generals up on the hill. Lucius would have enjoyed watching the bastard try to weasel his way out of that one.

But this outcome would certainly do.

"What are you waiting for, Domitius?" Quintinus said, clearly perplexed by Lucius's delay. "Send your men down there, at once, to fetch General Antony's gear. We haven't got all day!"

Lucius did not reply, nor did he move. Instead, he kept his eyes on Antony.

"Damn it, Domitius!" Quintinus said impatiently. "Did you hear what I said? Get your men moving!"

"That will be unnecessary, Quintinus," Antony finally interjected, just as Lucius knew he would. "Leave it."

"Are you sure?" Quintinus looked perplexed. "Certainly, something can be salvaged –"

"Leave it!" Antony said firmly. "The enemy will have better use for it than I."

Antony's adjutants appeared, having followed him from the hilltop. One had collected his horse. Antony took the reins and vaulted into the saddle. A flash of utter disdain crossed his face as he looked down at Lucius.

Had this been any other occasion, Antony surely would have ordered Lucius arrested and punished, simply for being in charge at the bridge when the mishap occurred. But these were not normal circumstances. This was a beaten army, unpaid for months, on the verge of mutiny, and deep within hostile territory. Caesar was lucky to still have an army at all, and he well knew it. In the past, he had used the threat of decimation to bring the contentious troops into line. But that would likely meet with disastrous results now. With that understanding, the consul had ordered all his generals to overlook all frivolous infractions. The men were to be dealt with leniently. Any officer who dared defy the order risked incurring Caesar's displeasure.

And so, Antony was powerless to harm Lucius – at least for the time being.

At that moment, Caesar rode up, flanked by a pair of

tribunes.

"What is amiss, Quintinus?" he asked with annoyance. "Why has the column stopped?"

"Er, it is nothing, my lord," Quintinus stammered. "Just a minor accident. No one harmed. I was just about to order Centurion Domitius here to get things moving again."

"Domitius?" Caesar said, as if trying to place the name, then repeated it. "Domitius…"

"My lord!" A rider was hailing Caesar from the rear of the column. The rider was fast approaching, driving his mount up the road at full gallop. Clopping to a halt ten paces from the consul and dragging along a choking white cloud of dust, the rider saluted Caesar with one arm across a powdered breastplate. "My lord. General Sylla sends his respects. Enemy horse has been sighted on the road behind us. At least two cohorts."

"A reconnaissance, no doubt," Caesar said, looking back down the road as if he could see the tail of the column, which was some five miles away and hidden by several bends in the canyon. "Ride back. Tell Sylla to deploy the auxiliary cavalry to our rear. Keep them at bay. I'll be along directly."

"Yes, my lord." The rider saluted and galloped off.

"Domitius…Domitius…," Caesar said again. Clearly, his mind had returned to contemplating the name, as if the sighting of the enemy cavalry were trivial in comparison. "Domitius, of course!" he finally blurted out. "He's that brave soldier who stood with me when the battle turned against us. I owe my life to that young man." Then, grinning at Lucius, he said, "Good to see you again, Centurion. We had quite a time the other day. Nearly had hoof prints on our backs, didn't we?"

"Yes, sir," Lucius replied.

"The enemy cavalry damn near rode us down. We were

fortunate to make it back to our lines. Showed them how fast a consul and a centurion can run, didn't we?"

"That we did, sir."

"You have my thanks, again."

"Just doing my duty, sir."

Caesar studied Lucius for a few moments in silence, while, behind him, Antony looked as if he was trying not to vomit.

"As I was saying before, Antony," Caesar said, turning to his Master of Horse. "We must be better about rewarding our soldiers. Wouldn't you agree?"

"Mmm?" Antony mumbled. "I'm sorry, Caesar. I was lost in thought for a moment."

"Especially the valiant ones, like Domitius here," Caesar continued. "Gives the rest something to aspire to, eh? Keeps them motivated for the march. You would be well-served to take note of this for the day you command your own armies."

"You are an Aristotle to us all, Caesar," Antony replied mechanically. But when Caesar turned away, the Master of Horse rolled his eyes at Quintinus, who instantly appeared discomfited by the hidden communication.

"See that he receives a decoration, Antony," Caesar said. "A gold *phalera* will do, I think."

"A decoration...for Domitius?" Antony asked in disbelief.

But Caesar had already turned his attention back down the road. "Do the honors for me, won't you, Antony?" he said distantly, looking after the rider that had just disappeared around the first bend. "I must go see what our friends are up to."

"The last gold *phalera* was given out yesterday, my lord," the tribune behind Caesar reported after rifling through the contents of a small chest strapped to his saddle.

Caesar's brow crinkled, but his face suddenly lit up again when his eyes lighted on the decorations dangling from Antony's cuirass. "You have a *phalera*, Antony. Give him yours. That will suffice until a proper medallion can be attained."

"Mine?" The thunderstruck Master of Horse fingered the medallion on his chest. He cleared his throat and seemed to have difficulty forcing out the next words. "It shall be as you command, Caesar."

The consul and his attendants then galloped away, leaving Antony facing Quintinus and Lucius. With a look of revulsion, the Master of Horse slowly dismounted.

As if taking the cue, Quintinus sang out uncomfortably, "Attention to orders while Centurion Lucius Domitius receives the gold *phalera* for valor!"

Every soldier and officer within earshot stopped what they were doing and came to attention, facing Lucius. Antony stepped forward, unhooking the decoration from his own armor with twitching fingers. He dropped it on the ground twice, as if by accident, very likely to make sure Lucius did not get an unsoiled medallion.

And Lucius did not care. His face remained stoic as he stuck out his chest to receive the award. But inside, he was laughing.

And Lucius knew that somewhere in Elysium, lounging under the shade of a tree, Strabo was laughing, too.

Printed in Great Britain
by Amazon